Speakeasy

A novel by
Jimm Chanson

Speakeasy

LIBRARY OF CONGRESS CATALOGING-IN-PUBLICATION DATA

Chanson, Jimm., 1962-

Speakeasy / Jimm Chanson

   p.   cm.

ISBN 979-8-218-96798-7

First printing, January 2024.

10 9 8 7 6 5 4 3 2

FOR
My Family

Speakeasy

I knew some of the people in this story. No one, I'm sure, knew all of them. As I'll explain later, I've accumulated sources for almost everything described, whether through interviews (done by me and those I hired) or various kinds of documents, including items in the paper that are not necessarily to be trusted. The rest is based on speculation and filling in gaps, large and small.

I figured I should tell this story because no one else has ever sorted out what happened. Not all of it, anyway. No one ever did learn who killed Suthrin, not even the people who put to death that poor wretch they pretended had done it—much less the countless folks who assumed it had all been wrapped up, because why else would somebody have been put to death for it?

So I'm telling this story to a man who will write it down for me and make it a book—the kind of book someone might read, which I wouldn't know how to do. He's a novelist and I'm just somebody with a story to tell.

When he's describing conversations and moment-to-moment events—let alone what people were thinking, which I have insisted be limited to only one person per chapter—my ghostwriter will be obliged to take liberties. But this isn't a work of history, where you aren't supposed to do that sort of thing. Suthrin's death isn't important enough for historians. It was important to me, though, and I'm the only one who can tell the story. But now I'm already repeating myself, which shows you why I had to hire somebody to corral all my notes and tapes and put them in the proper form.

I haven't decided yet whether I will read this book when it's done. I don't want to inadvertently discover anything I'd prefer not to know.

PART ONE

December 25, 1931 (a.m.)

1.

T HE BACK DOOR WAS AJAR only enough to be salient against the otherwise flat wall aligning the alley. There was no light within or without, except the very high full moon invisible behind the flurries. Jud pulled the door far enough to peer inside with his torch. Seeing nothing in the middleground or deep in the room, but neglecting to shine the beam at his feet where no danger was likely, he stepped inside and with the second halting step his heel slipped over all the blood, and the toe of his boot shot forward and caught under Suthrin's sprawled body and Jud fell backwards into the blood. The flashlight cracked against the ground and went out. Jud couldn't hear anything but the wind. He was confident no one else was about. He handled the body while still on the floor, kneeling, with a cigarette lighter, then got up and checked the door from the room to the rest of the building, expecting correctly it would be locked. Then he went back outside. Even with his torch he hadn't been able to see more than a few feet in the foglike cloud of swirling snow. Hastily making his way around the building in the deep drifts, after a couple of yards he trampled on some disturbed snow where, at arm's length, more blood could be seen dimly under the overcast Christmas midnight.

He couldn't call it in. There was no straw box for half a mile. In any case the family had to be roused, too, so he continued around through the yard and the street to the front door and threw his body against the door until the alarm went off. He knew all the alarms in the area, at least the ones meant for the police. This time of night the family never answered nor perhaps even heard the doorbell, rung only by drunks. Jud was big and his force finally splintered the frame enough for him to push the heavy door open against the latches. Now he could holler inside and be heard over the alarm. At the same time he took off his gloves and put them in a pocket.

"Police. Come to the door. Police. Boys, it Jud Minor. Officer Minor. Wake on up now yall. Mother, come on down here."

They knew his name and more important his voice. Even so the first responding boy, one of the middle ones and still in his underwear, was holding a baseball bat when he let Jud in. The lunch counter stools had been removed from the penny restaurant but the chairs and tables were there. Without willing it Jud stomped the snow off his boots and rubbed his hands. The alarm was unpleasant but much louder outside than in.

"Somebody broke in?" the boy said. "Where they gone? They out there?"

"No. Wait till yall get down here. I ain't repeatin it ten times for yall."

"Cripes, they broke the frame. Lemme get on my shoes and I can catch em."

"Set still. I broke the door in to commence yalls alarm."

"What you go and do that for?"

In the dark Jud imagined the dumb look on the boy's face.

"Just stand there, son."

Jud wanted the other boys to see him in the company of the first, the two of them at peace and no commotion. They might not have heard Jud announce himself. There was at least one gun in the house and he wasn't eager to see it raised. The room was dark and even in his uniform the first thing they would see for sure was a colored man beneath a ringing alarm at midnight. It would take less time to pull the trigger than it would to make out his features. Maybe a quarter-second less. More than enough. He knew that the boys, any boys, would enjoy nothing more than to level a gun at a man intruding and squeeze the trigger in self-defense. When you were allowed to. The only time you were allowed to.

He waited for the two oldest boys to appear but after a minute only four of the six stood there, circled around him in their nightclothes and babbling questions, the smallest two jumping up and down as if Jud would take better notice of them that way.

"Where the oldest boys at?" he said.

"They're out."

Of the four, only the boy with the bat had a man's voice. Jud wouldn't want a kid's voice calling it in.

"You put that bat down and get on your telephone to the station. Just ask the operator. Say third district. Tell em I'm here and there a man down, and to meet me round back by the door to your speak."

"You want me to turn off the alarm? I know how to turn off the alarm."

"After you done talked to the station and got some clothes on. Go on now."

The boy hastened with an air of importance into the next room, ignoring the payphone. Jud looked down at the other three. He had been inside the front of the house, the penny restaurant, for not much more than a minute. He knew what he had to say.

"Okay yall, quiet down. That enough. Listen here. When I'm out the door, and I will be in a minute, don't yall cut back through the house to get into the other place. Y'hear? You stay out of there. And go get them lights on. Make yourselves useful for once."

They nodded. But then Mother came downstairs in a nightgown that no longer fit, her white hair down like a witch wig, and the boys went to her, forgetting the lights. Jud was surprised to see the little colored girl, at first invisible back of Mother's girth, creeping in behind on the stairs. He'd expected she would stay in bed.

"Mother, tell them boys to shut their mouth and switch on some lights."

She did and then said, "This ain't no false alarm. We ain't never had no false alarm."

The three younger boys had stayed quiet for as long as it took her to say this but then they all began squawking again.

"Shut them boys up and get them lights."

The colored girl stood apart in a corner, maybe afraid of the dark. She did not try to find comfort by clinging to any of the others. When the lights came on she did not blink. Folks called her Spook but not around Jud. Even the youngest of Mother's boys knew better than that. These were northerners. They called her Charlotte around Jud if they paid her any mind at all.

Under the lights Mother took the measure of Jud without much affection. "So what you got. I heard you say man down. What, in the alley? That ain't this alarm."

The older boy came back and said the phone was broke. The blizzard, he reckoned.

Jud thought about this and then addressed all the boys.

"I gots to wait here till the men come inquirin on account of the alarm. We got to leave it ring to get them down here. Then they ain't gonna know but what a robber in here. I got to be up here in front to relieve them of that. So yall gots to do somethin for me. Yall throw on some shoes and coats and get round back. You ain't in no danger. Ain't nobody out there gonna bother the four of yall. They long gone. And listen here. Stand back in the alley, on the paved part, a good piece from the door. Don't go nowheres near the door. We got evidence there and we don't need yall messin with it. Stand still and just make sure no drunk walk into the speak or nothin like that. Keep people out if they around. And do not get into your fool head that you wanna go inside. Just wait your turn, and you can see what-all's there after we done with it. If you go inside I'm gonna make it my bidness to see yall can't sit down till New Year."

Mother parted her jowls at the last phrase and showed her teeth. "Don't you be talkin to my boys thataway. You may think you're some high and mighty cop but your kind ain't got no business bein all uppity to my boys."

Jud ignored the insult. He'd heard something like it every day, sometimes every hour. He studied her blackened teeth while she was talking and then said evenly: "Well, you tell em then. This is police bidness. They gots to be told what to do and what they can't."

"You still ain't said what's goin on. I got a right to go back and take a look inside my own place of business."

"You gonna stay right there, Mother. It ain't been three minutes I done troubled yall. You can wait four. And I thought yalls place of bidness was this room, not that other one." He looked at her with his mouth down. "Now send them boys out."

The boys had fetched boots and coats and were putting them on. Mother relented and said: "Get. And stay away from that goddam door or you'll know what."

Excited and now fully awake the boys obeyed her and chased each other out the door. The native cold wouldn't bother them for a while. Jud grabbed the oldest one as he followed.

"Wait. Just remembered. The lights in the speak … they switch on from the hall, right? Go on back there and switch em on. Door locked from that side. Leave it that way and use another door to get on outside."

The boy nodded, on an important mission, and headed the other way and out the room.

Jud leaned out the front door and called to the other three: "The middle of the alley. Just the middle. Nowheres else."

Mother regarded him with less affection than before, which was less than none. She was outraged she even had to speak to him without it being her decision to begin with. And she didn't like it one bit that he'd said wait and be patient, as if it was for him to decide when to tell her what was going on. She kept her mouth shut theatrically, like a comic old biddy in the movies, Jud thought, so as not to give him the satisfaction of her curiosity, let alone her anxiety.

"There a man down," he repeated, "like you done heard me say. I's just walkin the beat. Reached yalls alleyway. The door back there was sittin out just a mite, not open but not closed neither. Weren't but the with of my thumb what was showin of it."

Jud knew width had a "d" in it but he pronounced it "with". As a cop he could tell folks what to do, even order them around, without much more than the usual resentment, but as a colored man any time he sounded too educated it was a strike against him, no matter who was listening. He'd learned that a long time ago. He probably never hadn't learned it.

"I went in not spectin much," he continued, "and straightaway I done slipped and broke my torch. But I ain't needed to see what I done slipped on ... or done landed on, even if I didn't know who. And I got close to his face till my eyes fixed, and it was an officer down. He ain't gettin up again. It Suthrin."

Mother shook her head at the name Suthrin like she'd never heard of him. Jud frowned with annoyance and displeasure and swallowed hard and took a breath. He made sure she saw him do this.

"I know you know him cause I know he come round to your speak as often as anyone do. So don't you nod your head no, Mother. Not to me. And while we on it, from here on you best be tellin us everything you do know. This here's an officer down. One way or another, we gonna find out who put him down. And when we find him, and turns out you keepin somethin from us, and that we could of found him two minutes before we did, y'know what that is? That obstruction. You can go upstate for obstruction. And when it one of our own what's down, and you ain't playin ball with us, we ain't likely to be so inclined no more to play ball with you. You know what that mean, but I'm gonna say it still. It mean we don't look the other way no more every time we pass by your speak. Or when we know a load's comin your way in a milktruck down that dead-end driveway out back. And we stop cleanin up the winos back there when they get to be more trouble for you than they was worth before they was winos ... and then you don't get no more respectable bidness, when we do let you have any bidness at all."

Mother was trying to make some sort of sound in response to this, without losing face. "I didn't hear no shootin," she said.

"Stabbed and cut up from the look of it. Arteries. Too much blood for gunshot. Look here."

Jud swiveled briefly and she saw the rump of his coat where he'd fallen, and he parted the front to show the knees of his trousers where he'd knelt to check the body. At about the same time he took his gloves from his pocket and waved them and then put them away again. The whole demonstration didn't take two heartbeats. Jud was trying to scare her some, at least as much as she was willing to be scared. Mother glanced at the broken doorframe and Jud knew she wanted to ask about it but she was staying mum in spite.

"He was in uniform, away from his district," Jud said. "He'd unbuttoned his coat, maybe fin to take it off for a fistfight not knowin the other fella brung a knife. Fact, this might not even have nothin to do with your place. I ain't at all sure they got him inside it. I think the two of em had at it in the alley, if there was only the two of em, and Suthrin was left there to die. But then he done made his way inside your speak before he couldn't go no further."

"Don't see how," Mother said.

"Maybe he had a key."

"I ain't never given him no key." Mother was quick to amend: "Whoever he was."

"Maybe you didn't. Maybe somebody else did."

For no reason Jud looked over toward the corner where the colored girl had been but she had since moved silently to the stool behind the cash register.

Watching his eyes Mother laughed hollowly. "She ain't gonna say nothin. If she can even know what it means, what we're sayin. Hard enough for her to learn the words sweep and broom. Nine years old and don't know any more than she did the day she was born. Dumb as a dogwhistle."

Jud didn't nod or otherwise respond. He'd heard it before. It was one of Mother's favorite little stories to tell, and she told it to just about everybody, in one variation or another. All of her customers in back had heard it, and not just the regulars. She enjoyed saying it. How dumb the dumb girl was.

Finally Jud let Mother win the contest of wills by explaining the damage to the front door without her having asked. He wouldn't have time to explain once his back-up arrived, and the story had to get on the record with Mother. She was the owner.

"There ain't no straw box close enough walkin in this snow to make a difference," Jud said. "And yall don't answer your bell. Everybody know that. So I busted yalls door to commence the alarm and get yall on down here to call it in, while I went out back and looked it over again."

Mother said nothing. Stared at him. Deliberately didn't reexamine the doorframe.

Jud wrapped things up, repeating himself. "But you ain't got no telephone workin and now I'm stuck here waitin for my fellas to drive on up in front, let em know what's what, before there any more trouble. I don't suppose Suthrin goin nowhere."

He waited indifferently. Her eyes remained set.

"You'll be payin for that there doorframe, boy."

"I expect I will," Jud said.

Idly the colored girl opened the cash register. Almost before the sound of its bell reached them, Mother spun and howled. Jud jumped, startled at her sudden ferocity. The girl lived with it every day but it startled Jud enough to make him jump.

"You shut that goddam register you stupid fucking little n...."

Mother started to bellow the word but then was stifled by Jud's presence.

With no real pause and still as loud, she concluded: "…piece of shit."

To his great surprise Jud felt tears well up and he looked away, humiliated but not by the tears. He ground his teeth and swallowed. The girl shut the register and sat there without expression. Neither of the two adults spoke again before the first cop arrived, each out of spite to the other, not wanting to give the satisfaction.

2.

JUD HEARD the siren approaching.

The penny restaurant always closed well before sunset and there were no lights on the facade. Good lighting would have been a needless expense for a place that needed no advertisement. None of the closest houses had any lights on, either, and the snow-covered streetlights were widely spaced.

"Okay, Mother," he said, "cut off that alarm and go on outside and wave at the car and tell em I'm inside."

"I'll do the alarm," Mother said, "but you can do the rest. I ain't your slave."

She went to turn off the alarm and Jud said, "I need em to see you so they knows you ain't in danger."

"If I was gonna do it anyways, why ain't you out back instead of my boys?"

"If I was out back, how would I know you was gonna do it?"

"Well." She couldn't think of a follow-up so she repeated: "I ain't your slave."

"Mother, all I'm askin is you show yourself and say Jud Minor here. I don't know who all they sent and some of these fellas ain't exactly fond of me. Out in the dark, with that alarm goin off, if they want a shot they can call it mistaken identity. Fact, they would call it mistaken identity."

"They ain't gonna shoot at nobody in uniform."

"None of em gonna shoot at no white man in uniform," Jud said. "A few of em would be much oblige for the chance to shoot at me, uniform or no. By mistake. They know folks like you don't never forget no good deed."

"Bullshit," Mother said. But she was tired and wanted to be done with it, so after she turned off the alarm she went to the door and poked her head out and waved at the car. "Ain't nothin wrong," she called out. "Everybody's fine."

She stepped outside, stoic in bare feet. The cop rolled down his window. "Mother? You okay darlin?"

As the cop was parking, in the middle of the street where the snow drifts were manageable, Mother said: "Hey there, Flint. One of yours is already here. Wants you to come on in and talk. And now I'm done with it and I'm going on back to bed."

Officer Flint said: "Well, then, Merry Christmas, Mother."

Jud passed her as he and she exchanged positions, and said quietly: "I'll send your boys back in and tell em to lock up. But we gonna be back to talk with yall tomorrow."

Mother ignored him. When she reached the stairs, where the colored girl was waiting, Jud called from outside the open door: "And we'll need to talk to the two oldest boys, too. You make sure they ain't off somewheres when we get here, if you seen em again by mornin."

Mother paused and looked as if she were about to protest. But instead she grimaced like she had to spit something foul out of her mouth and gave a disrespectful and dismissive little wave of her arm downwards as though to shoo Jud away, and then she grabbed the colored girl roughly by the wrist and dragged her upstairs without another word.

3.

On the force Jud had long since learned there were three kinds.

One kind hated him before they knew him. Hated him as soon as they'd discovered he existed as a cop, and let him know it.

The second kind suspended their hatred and were mostly civil but watched Jud vigilantly. Waited for the first excuse from his behavior to hate him. Jud being a careful man, most of the second kind were still waiting. But for some the wait was over and they felt righteous.

The third kind had the same attitude toward almost everybody, Jud included. A small few of the third kind had become Jud's friends, to the extent he had any. Some of those few sometimes set Jud's teeth on edge because they were a little too proud of their tolerance and highmindedness. But he accepted it, and wouldn't think of mentioning it. It was a lot better than the alternative. Meanwhile the first kind hated, on principle, that small tolerant few of the third. And were suspicious of those who didn't.

Flint was of the second kind. Through the window he told Jud to come and sit in the car where they could talk, out of the goddam cold. But Jud said: "We got to go on back to the alley. I'll tell you why on the way."

Flint glared angrily at this and Jud knew Flint was weighing the hatability of Jud's response. Work was work, though, and Flint let it go.

"We got an officer down," Jud said. "It Suthrin. From downtown district?"

"I know him." The news didn't seem to make much of an impression on Flint. But information was power and he wasn't about to give Jud any more of that than necessary.

"Well, he be on the floor of the speak out back. They got lights inside but ain't none outside. And my torch is broke."

Jud described his mishap and the broken flashlight and displayed the blood on his uniform. Flint looked at the blood distastefully as though it were evidence of Jud's poor personal hygiene. Once a few years back Jud had gone to fetch something in the breakroom when it wasn't his break and Flint was sitting at the table with his back to the door, bullshitting with the guys, and he was saying, "Y'ever notice how they all got that smell about em? Don't matter whether they wash regular or not, it's always there." And while Flint was talking, the others started clearing their throats and rolling their eyes and so forth and Flint shut his mouth without having turned around or seen Jud, who said, "Hey, fellas," and got what he needed and left. This event had probably been an aggravation for Flint and his audience, or most of them. Jud was the first and still the only colored police officer in Wisconsin. Ten years now.

"An officer down," Flint said. "Cry-yi. Why the fuck didn't you call this in?"

"Straw box is too far away and telephones is all out. Reckoned if the alarm kept soundin it would draw yalls attention."

"Which. It. Didn't," Flint said with mocking singsong emphasis, like an adolescent. "Some knucklehead down the street phoned it in. Sheesh."

"Thought the lines was down. Mother's boy done said they was. If it one house, it the whole block and then some."

"The lines ain't down. Cripes, I already said that already. And why didn't you just turn the lights on in the speak, when you was back there?"

"This an old building. Switch ain't in the speak. It on the other side of the door to the hall, and that door locked. Had the boy go back and turn it on a few minutes ago."

Flint thought this over. He seemed annoyed that his criticism was unfounded.

"I reckoned we'd take a look outside with your torch," Jud continued, "and then you could drive on back to the station and call in a detective while I stand watch. Too late for it to be any good to hurry someone else on down here. We ain't gonna see no more now than later, and I been an actin detective enough to know what's what, so we may as well see what we can, first."

Flint said they were short-handed on detectives anyway, it being Christmas Eve and past midnight and all, and there was a case just called in at some rich folks' house out on Twelfth Street and plenty of dough to go around there, probably, so half the squad took off after it. "And we wouldn't wanna call downtown for back-up on our own case too soon, ain'a?" Flint laughed. "Yeah sure, so it's one of the downtown boys that's down. But it's our case, hey. They can wait and read about it in the papers."

Flint thought this was really funny. He hated them, downtown, where they were all so stuck-up with their private schools. He was supposed to hate them, he thought. Dutybound. Just like in high school. But Suthrin, Jud knew, hadn't come from any kind of privilege. All you had to do was meet him once to figure that out. Flint surely knew it too, but that didn't matter. Suthrin was from downtown, with their stuck-up private schools.

"Well, it gonna be a manhunt," Jud said.

"Big waste of time, I'd bet." Flint spit invisibly on the snow. "Pullin over cars and such. Don't matter if they start right now or half an hour from now."

"I'm with ya there, bud. But let's not be too long. They gonna want to get on the horn about this to every district."

"So they can pull over more cars. Round up more bums at the train stations. Bring in more repeaters and have more guys around to hit em with phone books." Flint laughed, but not with any scorn.

They had rounded the side of the sizable building and were stomping a high slow march through its yard. The swirling thick flurries of the previous hour had mostly died down and Jud could see clear to the alley, a dead-end half-block extension of Reservoir Avenue, extending like a third leg from the point where it curved past the river.

"I reckon they got into it back there and the killer done took off, leavin Suthrin to bleed out. But Suthrin, he crawled on up to the speak and done gone inside on his last breath."

Flint poked him with the flashlight. "Just occurred to me, hey. They're closed on account of it being Christmas and all. So how'd he get inside?"

Jud pulled a key from his pocket. "Found it on him when I checked the body. It in his hand. Clutched tight. Weren't on no keychain."

"Sheesh. Would you look at that."

They rounded into the small unpaved area between the diagonal alley and the house. The door was opened wide, flush against the wall, and light came from within. Mother's boys weren't there.

Jud spat. "Dang blasted kids," he said to Flint before they entered. "Two eldest ain't around. Told the rest to keep any blind drunks from stumblin in. Told em to stay in the middle of the alley and set still."

"Whoa! You left them kids to keep watch?" Flint was glad to hear this. Jud fucking up.

"Had to have a word with Mother. Couldn't get them boys outta earshot no other way."

By the light of Flint's torch from one side and the open door on the other Jud pointed out where the struggle must have taken place in the snow, including the part he'd trampled on while heading out. They saw the blood he'd stepped in and now, with the flashlight, much more of it besides. Saw the sliding track of the body from and through the blood to the door. Saw the four boys' footprints circling and crossing over all of it.

"Well, thanks to them boys and the blizzard it probably ain't so clear no more," Jud said.

They'd almost reached the open door approached by the truncated alley, slowly making their way through the high cold wind and massive drifts in the unpaved yard.

Flint scanned further around and about with his flashlight. "Don't see no other footprints out there, hey. Where'd he run to?"

Jud followed the beam. "You right. Musta gone the same way as me. Opposite way you and me and the boys went, around the house. Fact, he and Suthrin musta come that way, beforehand. Usually folks use the dead-end, but guess it don't make much difference in this snow. Hold that torch still." Jud studied the scene. "Must be, oh, two set of my prints, one of yours, one for each boy, uh, one of Suthrin's, and two of his. Two of the killer's. Reckon he got up to roundabout where your car at, then down the middle of the street. No chasin him now."

Inside the boys were gathered around the body, wide-eyed and utterly absorbed, the smallest boy standing back in fright as the others prodded Suthrin with the toes of their boots and chattered about whatever fleeting thoughts and questions the scene provoked. Snow was blowing in and melting on the floor. One or more of the boys had stepped in the blood and tracked it. Jud didn't bother to scold them. It would serve no purpose. So he just raised his voice and said, "Out. Get on outta here now, and I mean now."

With that done Jud and Flint leaned over the body. Suthrin was face down with his coat sprawled like wings on both sides of his back and thighs. His cap had fallen off and skidded across the room, apparently from the force of his header onto the hard wood floor.

Jud said, "Outside he musta been tryin to make his way to the door durin the fight, and the other fella finally sliced him across half the neck and run. But Suthrin musta held the wound closed for a coupla seconds while he unlock the door and make it inside, before passin out flat on his face."

Jud rolled the body slightly and showed Flint the single deep cut across the thigh, the knife having been sharp enough to pierce and split thick trousers.

"Reckon it started out as a fistfight and rasslin and such, and Suthrin had him in a rasslin hold, course he from down south, maybe his arm round the back of his neck and forcin his head down and his back bent, and the fella was losin and he done pulled a knife and swung it any which way and it caught Suthrin's femoral."

"That's the blood outside, ain'a?" Flint was warming to the investigation. "So ya gotta ask. Why else would he of cut into the pants. And got him in the thigh. If that ain't the only meaty place for him to get at."

"Right. You bent over and pushed down, it the only good-size target, the thigh. Wouldn't of gone for it if he ain't had to. So straight off, Suthrin in serious trouble and bleedin hard from the femoral, and rightly surprised you can bet, cause he ain't gonna have no man in a rasslin hold who he think done brung a knife, and so it like he stuck his hand on a hot stove. He jump up and let go and back off."

Jud showed him the defensive wounds on both of Suthrin's hands.

"And the fella start swingin the knife, and Suthrin hold his hands up and he back on up to the door. Ain't nowheres else to go."

He rolled the body a few inches and showed Flint the pokes and gashes on the belly.

"And then the fella start jabbin and scratchin him in the middle while Suthrin's dodgin this way and that."

And finally he showed Flint the coup de grace, three inches across the side of his neck.

"And then he just take one big swipe toward Suthrin's face, not really aimin at nothin, and slice the side of his neck, and the blood shoot out and he make a run for it, probably never seen blood squirt outta nothin like that before. Suthrin go down but then crawl over and get on his hands and knees and unlock the door and pull hisself to his feet, holdin his neck best he could but it weren't good enough, because how could it be?"

"Couldn't," Flint agreed. "Couldn't be no good at all."

4.

Neither Jud nor Flint gave much thought to the familiar room where they stood, which looked basically the same as had any saloon in the neighborhood, and most of the saloons in the state, before Prohibition shut them down. The penny restaurant had been closed that morning for the holiday. As opposed to the speakeasy, the penny restaurant was closed a lot, every chance it could be.

The adjoining walk-in closet, both men knew, held boxes of dry goods and other supplies for the restaurant. In the unlikely event of a raid due to an unforeseen shift of policy, and given enough time if the raid had been tipped, while the booze was being hidden away the barstools could be shoved in the closet and the boxes brought out and piled on the long fake-mahogany bar, and the room would then resume its fictional status as a storage area.

Still, it was not merely a sterile, functional space. It worked also, as it had to, as a meeting area and hangout and social environment. No matter how desperate people were for easy access to alcohol they also expected some of the old familiar amenities of a bar. Like all places where rendezvous occur the interior was dark even with the lights on, with three or four booths in addition to the bar and a couple of tables. The brown wood panels on the walls disguised thick sound-proofing beneath, so that no noise would escape into the alley at midnight or at three in the morning or however late Mother might decide to stay open. Mother probably would have kept it open Christmas Eve, which she did not celebrate, but she knew the ladies of the neighborhood too well for that. There were limits even to their indulgence. It would have been a strike against Mother if on Christmas Eve or Christmas Day their husbands should be at the speakeasy rather than at home. So Mother closed the bar down on those two dates, plus Thanksgiving and Easter, and not another day in the year.

Jud was about finished with all he had to say. "I figure after he fell down, the wind musta blown the door shut but not all the way, which is how I saw it stickin out a little."

Flint took a cursory stroll around the room. Behind the bar he found a girl's doll and held it up. "The decisive clue," he said, his tone imitating the radio serials.

"Huh," Jud said. "They treat that little girl like a dog. Wouldn't of thought Mother would give her no expensive toy like that."

"Expensive?" Flint said. "How the fuck would you know? You collect dollies?"

"No," Jud said, "but my wife do. Used to, any rate. Boxed em all up a coupla years ago."

Flint knew about Jud's wife. He let the subject drop. Everybody always let the subject drop.

They heard a tap tap tap on the door behind the barkeep's area. The door led to a hallway connecting to both the restaurant and the residential area of the building. Jud had told Flint that the door was locked from the other side and Suthrin's key didn't fit. There was blood on the doorknob from Jud's gloves.

Flint hollered, "Whoever's knockin, it's locked. You know you got to be the one to open it up, hey."

A little boy's voice responded. "Am I allowed to come in?"

Jud said: "No you ain't, son. Go on back to bed."

The door opened. It was the smallest of Mother's boys, maybe seven or eight years old. One of the adopted ones, their mother serving time for killing their father to stop him from beating her.

"I won't come in," he said. "I just wanna ask you somethin."

"Get on outta here, son," Jud said. "I told you once."

"Is he really dead?"

"Yes, he is. You saw him."

"He ain't gonna get up again?" he asked.

"No he ain't."

"Is he a ghost?"

Flint held out the doll to the boy, who had stayed on the other side of the door in the hallway. "No, he ain't no ghost, kid. Now here, take your dolly and go to bed."

"Where'd that come from? That ain't my doll."

"Must be Charlotte's," Jud said.

"Spook… I mean Charlotte… don't have none. Why would mama give her nothin?"

Flint put the doll in the boy's hands. "Take it anyways, kid, and get out. Santa Claus is comin tonight, so you oughta be in bed."

"Promise he ain't no ghost."

"No, he ain't. Now go to bed cause Santa's comin." Flint closed the door.

"They had Christmas three weeks ago," Jud said.

"What the hell's that mean? Tomorrow's Christmas."

"Not for them it ain't."

"Well last time I looked everybody got the same calendar except maybe in China and whatnot, and tomorrow it's Christmas on all of em."

"Not for them folks it ain't," Jud repeated. "They some kind of eastern catholic. The old man come over from Trieste, he told me once. Said his people was Bavarian, and he come over here on a boat and married Mother and she done convert to whatever he was, and then she decide to stay that way after the old man died, since the kids been raised in it."

"I don't give a fuck where he was from, Batavia or whatever the hell you said, I'm tellin you, tomorrow is Christmas. It's Christmas Day. Says 'Day' right in the name of it. Christmas Day. So would you mind tellin me how could it be some other day? Sheesh."

"All right then, Flint."

Satisfied, Flint said without implication, "What you doin out here tonight anyways, hey."

Jud frowned. "Walkin a beat. What you think?"

"You ain't sposed to be walkin a beat no more. Jeez, you been with the force longer'n me, even." Flint thought twice and added: "Though not by much."

"I's spellin young Halvorson. The rook. Nice fella with his wife and that little girl at home Christmas Eve. Reckoned he should get to play Sandy Claus."

Flint smiled knowingly. "What he give ya, hey."

Jud's brows lowered as he caught Flint's eye. "Ain't gave me nothin. Fact, never spoke to him. Called him up on the telephone but got his wife. Told her to insist upon it." Jud paused, then said: "She can't be but twenty. Already got a baby girl, too, must be three or four year old."

"Hmm," Flint said. He thought about it for a moment. "Yeah, she's a looker. Seen her at the Fourth of July picnic." Then he laughed. "Well, guess you can call it your Christmas gift to Halvorson, ain'a."

Jud thought Flint might be considering a move into Type Three.

"Better than the package he woulda got," Jud said, looking at the body.

5.

 $\mathbf{J}$ UD STOOD WATCH IN THE ALLEY outside the door as the other cops approached. Flint, now back at the station, must have described the scene well. The handful of men who arrived were careful to step left right left along the building's wall from the opposite direction and avoid messing up any footprints that had not already been obscured. Inconveniently, to preserve evidence they had parked on the continuing part of Reservoir Avenue rather than bring their squad cars into its short alley.

Jud did not know any of them well. He had interacted with various lab guys during brief periods as an acting detective. But he had rarely worked with the ten-to-seven shift after his thirtieth birthday or so. And there was one face he didn't recognize at all.

"Minor, I'm Detective Rhodes."

They shook hands. Jud had heard the name. Some kind of college boy. "Pleased to make your quaintance, sir."

"Because the officer is dead, we have requested no ambulance as yet. One will be dispatched, after I return to the station, to collect the body when the preliminary work is done. We also have no medical examiner at the moment."

"Ain't much to examine," Jud said. "Suthrin died of a bleed-out from a knife. Don't get much simpler than that."

"Suthrin," Rhodes repeated unsurely. Then he got it. "Oh. Yes. I understand the men called him Southern."

"Mm-hm. Everybody call him Suthrin. On the force or not."

Rhodes was a new hire who had moved from Madison, meaning prior to that the sticks, shortly after promotion at an unusually early age. This was probably one of his first cases. Jud wondered if that would have a better or worse effect on them getting along. They would effectively be partners on the case, Jud presumed.

Rhodes was accompanied by a vaguely familiar patrolman named Warren and the night sergeant, Borkowski, whom Jud knew slightly, plus the two lab guys. It was uncommon for a sergeant to come to a crime scene, but an officer was down. In any case, Borkowski was letting Rhodes run the show. And watching him do it.

"Can we step inside without disturbing the scene," Rhodes asked, "or must the lab work be done while we look through the door?"

"There some room to skirt around the body without touchin much, and then situate ourself in the little dance floor of the saloon ..."

"Come again?" Rhodes said. "Saloon?"

Jud heard the sergeant start to laugh but disguise it with a cough. "Didn't Flint tell you?" Jud said, pausing as they reached the doorway. "The room a saloon, sir. It a little saloon. A speakeasy."

"We left immediately after Patrolman Flint informed us that an officer was down by multiple knife wounds and that we should avoid anywhere south of the alley where the attacks apparently occurred, and make access along the drive to the building from the northeast. Oh. And he said the phone was out and you'd deliberately set off the building's alarm. He left the rest to you."

Jud opened the door and showed them the logical route inside. Once the six of them were gathered away from the body, Jud said: "You can set your things on the bar. Whoever done this never come nowheres near the bar."

Sergeant Borkowski said: "We'll let the lab crew decide that, boy."

"We've got to put it somewhere, sarge," one of the lab guys said.

Rhodes nodded to them. "The far end of the bar. I think a reasonable perimeter around the body should be sufficient."

"The only evidence much further than that," Jud said, "is where I done tracked the blood when I gone to check the door behind the bar. My torch was broke and I couldn't see nothin. Good thing the kids stay close, though they poke at him with the toe of their boots."

"Kids?" said Rhodes.

"I guess Flint didn't say that neither. I had to stay up front with the owner of the building while waitin on the response to the alarm. I sent her kids back to the middle of the alley and told em to stay there and not disturb nothin and make sure no drunk walk in thinkin the saloon was open. That woulda cause all sort of trouble. Had to keep the drunks away. But the kids come in and stand around the body for a minute."

Other than the patrolman, who showed no expression, none of the men in the room looked very happy to hear this. Jud felt obliged to add: "Sir, I ain't had no other choice."

Sergeant Borkowski looked at Jud and said: "Wonder why we never hire any more of youse."

The lab guys were putting out their powders and chalks and strings and thumbtacks and rulers and cameras. "Preliminarily," one of them said, "I'd guess there isn't enough blood in here for him to have bled out. He probably wasn't in here for more than a few seconds. Most of the blood must be out in the snow."

For the third time that evening Jud described what had happened since he'd entered the alley at midnight, but this time he inwardly cursed Flint for not insisting that the others stay at the station long enough to get all the facts.

Still looking at Jud, Sergeant Borkowski said: "Why ain't we inside the house talkin to Mother and her kids right now? What makes you so sure they wasn't involved, boy?"

"The two eldest ain't at home," Jud said. "Even if Mother or any of the little ones, the oldest bein fourteen, fifteen, but even if they coulda overpowered Suthrin, which don't seem likely, I got in there and saw em all while the body was still warm. Weren't a speck of blood on any of em. No way they done cleaned up that fast."

In the distance a siren sounded, steadily becoming louder.

"How do you know the oldest two weren't at home?" Rhodes asked.

"The kids told me. They just kids, the rest of em. One of em woulda said somethin or let it on somehow. They all sleep up on the second floor, share a toilet an so forth. You could tell ain't none of em have no idea nothin out of the ordinary goin on. Uh, y'know, beside the alarm go off."

For the benefit of anyone looking, Borkowski scowled. "Are you tellin me you didn't even search the house, boy?"

"Sarge, there wasn't no one else in there. Stake my life on it. I know these folks. If one of the two missin boys done it, they old enough to know they gots to clean themself up someplace farther away from a dead body they done just killt than a hallway and some stairs, with the man they killt still lyin there in the building where they live. Them two oldest, they ain't in there. Just ain't no doubt."

Jud had begun to sound angry, which he was, and tried to tone it down.

"Reckoned I might start tryin to track down them two boys," he said, "after I done met with yall here."

"Okay," Rhodes said, "write a report for the teletype and get it to the papers. We want to get out ahead of this and make sure our version of the story is what everyone hears first. There's going to be a lot of gossip and rumor mongering. Don't mention the phone being out, just yet. I mean, in writing. We'll tell the press when they call, but keep it from the public for the time being."

Jud had expected, routinely, to write the report, but he didn't understand why Rhodes was mentioning it now. "Write the report here, sir, before I go look for the boys? You want to review it, or ..."

"No," Rhodes said. "Patrolman Warren will drive you back to the station now so you can change clothes and write your report."

"Send your uniform to the station house laundry," Sergeant Borkowski ordered, "and then get back on Halvorson's beat."

While they were talking the siren kept getting louder, and before Jud could respond they heard the squad car pull up in the alley and outside the door.

"Aw, for pete's sake," a lab guy said. "What damn fool is ..."

The door swung open. Another unfamiliar face in uniform.

Sergeant Borkowski said dryly, "Step around the body if you would, please, Sergeant Messerschmidt."

Without humor, and quietly enraged, Detective Rhodes said, "This is a crime scene, sergeant."

"Which is why I called three more men from the first district to get up here after me."

"Called them?" Sergeant Borkowski said sharply. Everyone knew the squad car radios were one-way, receiving from the station houses but unequipped for response.

Messerschmidt circled around the body into the speakeasy and said, "On the phone. After I got called out of bed at one in the morning on Christmas Eve and was told that one of my own men is down and that the third district is taking over the case."

So he'd had a squad car at home, Jud thought. Sure he did. Called in on the phone. But had gotten a car. Couldn't just go inside the station when he picked up the car. Wherever he had been, Jud noted as the sergeant passed him by, it hadn't been bed. He smelled like someone had dumped a quart of whiskey on him.

"This is the third district's case, sergeant," Rhodes said.

"Like hell it is," Messerschmidt shouted. He pointed stiffly without looking at the corpse. "That's one of my men."

Sergeant Borkowski responded: "And your other men don't know the neighborhood."

Jud couldn't resist: "Though Suthrin knew this here spot pretty good."

Messerschmidt turned on him and thundered: "What's that supposed to mean, boy?"

Jud was innocent. He scanned the saloon and said, slowly, "Just mean I seen him in these here parts now and again, of an evening." He added: "Or an afternoon or morning."

"Patrolman," Rhodes said to Warren, "please go with Officer Minor back to the station."

Jud said what he'd been about to say before the squad car had arrived. "Detective, this should be my case. I found the body, saw the evidence fresh. I been actin detective often enough...."

"This is not the time nor the place, Officer Minor."

Another siren came into earshot.

Messerschmidt roared with artificial laughter. "Your case, boy? That's a howler all by itself. But it ain't even your district's case. I've known some dumbass monkeys, boy, but you beat em all in the dumbass monkey department, you stupid ..."

Jud barely knew Borkowski but the sergeant interrupted: "You watch how you talk to my men, you filthy beerswilling kraut ape."

Messerschmidt lunged.

Jud stood back as Warren and Rhodes and the lab guys kept their first district rival separated from their sergeant. Struggling, Messerschmidt got away and pitched forward and fell on top of Suthrin's corpse. The others grabbed him and pulled him up and the struggle continued.

"Sergeant Messerschmidt," Borkowski panted, "I demand you leave my crime scene."

The siren got louder. Rhodes clutched onto Messerschmidt along with the other three and said, as if nothing were happening, "Warren, you and Officer Minor get down the alley and keep that squad car away. I don't mean the men, you can't stop them, I mean the car. Tell the men at least to take precautions in the area of the crime scene. Then get back to the station."

Messerschmidt managed to punch Rhodes weakly in the jaw as Patrolman Warren extricated himself.

Realizing that this was indeed neither the time nor the place to discuss his assignment, Jud nodded to Warren and the two of them hurried out the door. Following the old Jansky Metal Works driveway, they departed in the opposite direction from which both had come, and walked through the snow to the conjunction of East and West Reservoir Avenue.

6.

HAVING WAITED IN THE COLD for the car from the first district and then alerted its occupants, Jud and Warren walked around the block to one of the squad cars on Hubbard Street.

To Jud's surprise, Warren said: "Don't much like how they all say boy. Blah blah this, boy. Blah blah that, boy. Except Detective Rhodes. Seems like he's got some manners."

"Not mannerly enough to let me keep my case," Jud said. "But I preciate what you said."

"My mother is a member of the NAACP."

"Don't say."

"A real do-gooder. Temperance too. Would have been a nun if we were Catholic. But then, where would I be?"

"Reckon just a twinkle in daddy's eye."

Warren laughed as they got into the car. Rather than risk getting stuck in the snow with a U-turn, he drove around the block to Brown Street, avoiding busy Walnut Street on the way back to the station. Jud figured Flint must have taken the same route.

Warren shifted into higher gear once they were out of the drifts. "Say, Minor, I was wondering. Just out of curiosity. I'm sure it doesn't come as any surprise that people talk about you at the station sometimes. So I, uh ... I heard you were decorated in the war."

Jud looked out the window without much interest. "Not by the U.S., I weren't."

"Really. I heard you were."

"Not by the U.S."

"Well, I ask because I didn't think any of your people saw combat."

"Not many of em did." They turned left onto 12th Street, a couple of blocks from the station. "Listen, can we swing around my place before we get back? Change my uniform. Won't take but a minute. Just keep straight on to Juneau."

"Surely. I'm not in any hurry to go out and scour the hotels for riffraff."

"Gots your detail in the manhunt, then."

"Yep. Christmas day."

"That it is."

"So what were you, service core?"

"Blue Helmets."

Warren said nothing. It was clear he didn't know what Jud was talking about. But then the war had ended when Warren wasn't old enough to shave, and even older Americans had generally been unaware of the colored battalions. Advertising their existence had hardly been a priority for President Wilson's propaganda team.

Jud decided to elaborate. It was only polite. Warren seemed to be Type Three. No harm making a friend.

"Ninety-third infantry. Saw action in France. And don't mean to make nothin of it, but since you done brought it up and folks talkin anyway, I'll tell you the French were the ones done pinned me. Wilson, he from Virginia. Weren't gonna let no colored infantryman get no medal if he could help it. Ain't even let us fight longside nobody but the French. Wouldn't let us fight longside no Americans. Anyway, I got a coupla fellas out of a scrape, and one of em French."

"Gee. That must have been something."

"Yeah, it was that. Somethin."

"Whereabouts in France?"

"Outside Nancy." Jud paused. "I weren't but twenty and I'd of liked bein inside Nancy a whole lot better."

The old joke, not original to Jud, got a laugh like it always did. Jud didn't tell it to white people too often, though.

"That my house up on the corner there."

At home Jud's wife was asleep. He removed his clothes in the dark of the front parlor and then went to the cold basement and put the clothes in the electric washing machine with some soap and started it up. The gloves he just threw away. He'd get docked for that but the hell with it. Almost out the door in a fresh uniform, he thought twice and returned to his gloves, shoving them deeper into the wastebasket so his wife wouldn't see them. See the blood. He was relieved he'd thought of that.

Warren had pulled toward the curb to let Jud out and now discovered he was stuck in the snow. He offered to be the one to push but Jud answered by getting out of the car. While bent over with his hands on the Pierce Arrow's bumper and his feet pushing for traction against the snow, Jud looked up and saw the curtain move at the far end of his small house. The bedroom. The red glow of the dim nightlamp. His wife must have been awakened by the washing machine. She appeared at the window, smoking a cigarette. Her arm moving mechanically, bent at the elbow. To her mouth and slowly back down. Like some kind of a small motorized billboard, advertising cigarettes. The squad car was revving it up in the quiet night and Jud was right there in the street but she didn't look toward him. She stared straight ahead. There was nothing much across the street for her to look at, in the dark. Another house, a snow-covered yard, a corner, an idle intersection.

Finally the car moved and Jud, having fallen down twice in the effort to push, hurried to the running board and got in. He looked toward his wife and now saw her in silhouette through the opened curtains. She had turned away from the front window toward the other one, its mate, facing ninety degrees away in the corner bedroom. She was staring at nothing across the street from that side of the house, too.

"Heard the scuttlebutt?" Warren asked. "About the payrolls, I mean."

Thinking about his wife and not whatever Warren was saying, Jud grunted.

"The city's out of money," Warren continued. "Well, every city's out of money, but this one's going to be the first to respond by printing its own. Not exactly. But what's happening is that sometime next year they're going to start paying us in scrip."

"Scrip," Jud said.

"It's a piece of paper that says ..."

"I know what it is."

"Well, so, now every time you buy anything, the guy selling it to you is going to be making a little loan to the city, I guess. Then he's going to have to try to pawn that loan off on somebody else who sells him something. Either that or hang onto it and maybe find out it's only worth ninety percent this week what it was worth last week."

Jud was still too distracted by thoughts of his wife to focus on what Warren was babbling about. Somehow he managed to say, "Thought you needed either an army or a company town for scrip."

"And a company store ... right. No, here I guess you'd say the company is the city and the store is everybody selling anything within its limits. You've got to redeem the scrip within a certain time at a bank or it's worthless, and then the bank sends the scrip to the city and gets a credit on its taxes. Or you can send it in and get a credit on yours, the big taxes you pay on making zero dollars."

Jud regained his focus. "Yeah. Things is gettin pretty bad. They already done cut our pay this year by near a quarter of it. If you right, now we ain't even gonna get no real money at all. This rate, we'll be payin them for our jobs. Like we don't already pay enough for bein a cop."

"You said it, brother."

Jud laughed. "They should put me on the radio."

And after he said this, having nearly pushed the thought from his mind, Jud was reminded again of Sally. *They'll put me on the radio. In the papers. In the magazines. In the pictures. Sally.*

7.

OFFICER WARREN AGREED he would give Jud a ride back out to his beat, after Jud had written and teletyped his report. The two men parted inside the station and Jud was surprised to run into Halvorson, a short man who compensated for his height with an addiction to physical culture and so, with his baby face and curly brown hair, resembled a high school wrestler more than a grown cop. Like Warren, who was about the same age, Halvorson had been affected by radio and the talkies and his speech was self-consciously regionless, featuring none of the local color that older men like Flint took as a sign of being a regular guy you could have a beer with. But whereas Warren spoke thoughtfully, seemed even to be educated, Halvorson didn't come off especially bright and talked fast like a guy you might expect to be chewing gum and jerking sodas at a nickel drug store. Despite the difference they both sounded like they had no native region other than the radio and the talkies. Maybe everyone would, one of these days. Maybe everyone already did and Jud just hadn't been around enough to know it.

"Didn't spect to see you here," Jud said.

"They cancelled my day off."

"Day off? They ain't given you no day off. You was scheduled for beat three."

"No, I mean tomorrow night ... sixteen hours from now or whatever it is," Halvorson spat out rapidly. "They called everybody and told them about Suthrin. They canceled all days off, and I had one tomorrow, meaning later today. But they gave us a choice when to come in. So I just came on down and then I'll go back home after sun-up to watch my little girl find the presents Santa left under the tree and then come back in a few hours and do a split shift and get to stay home tomorrow night. Uh, I mean tonight."

"Well, guess if it everybody got their day off cancelled, can't complain."

"Anyways, I was keeping an eye out for you, Officer Minor." Halvorson called him officer because he was a rook. "Figured you'd have to come in and file the report early, it being such a big deal and all. Wanted to talk to you."

Out of habit, as he did in every conversation at the station, Jud looked around to see if anyone was listening. His speech had to be adjusted to its audience. They were in the hallway to the assembly room, beside the desk sergeant's so-called office where Jud and Warren had just signed in. A detective and a patrolman conversed while leaning against the rail of the low wood partition next to the swinging slatted panel that represented the door to the otherwise unbounded open-air office. Above the unstaffed desk, next to a page-a-day calendar that still displayed the number 24, MANHUNT was written neatly in big letters on a chalkboard with unreadable scribbles below. A man in once-sharp but now shabby civilian dress, and wearing a center-blocked tan homburg also past its prime, spoke on the payphone affixed to the wall behind the two cops, glancing repeatedly at the big clock above as though the minutes might pass more quickly than he expected. A lawyer, maybe. Probably. Uniformed men in various stages of fatigue, boredom, irritation walked in and out of the assembly hall, where at this unexpected mid-shift hour of the morning they would be receiving their spontaneous and unwelcome instructions for the impending manhunt. No doubt the first district station was buzzing with excitement over the thrill of losing a man, but here at the grubby run-down third, with its low ceiling, bad wiring, lousy heating, it was business as usual but with an extra dose of gripe. Down the hall the door to the lieutenant's office was closed but through the copper-trimmed window in the door Jud could see the lights were on, revealing the gun cabinet against the wall but not whomever might have been inside the room. Jud and Halvorson were standing next to one of the three or four spittoons immediately within sight, beneath the portrait of Chief Laubenheimer, a stern and somewhat haggard germanic face with circles under the eyes and well-defined creases and no flab. This ubiquitous photograph always reminded Jud of one of those guys who played Dracula and Frankenstein at the pictures, how they might look without the ghoulish makeup. A Lon Chaney type.

Seeing Jud's eyes dart briefly about the building, Halvorson lowered his voice. "So, a couple of days ago Suthrin came into the station." Halvorson waited for a response. Got none. "I guess he looked at the duty roster because he found me and said he knew I was gonna be on beat three, Christmas Eve. I didn't even know the guy so I said, what's it to you. And he asked me to steer clear of that alley. The one where he died." Halvorson raised his brows. "He said he was on some kind of a stakeout and he didn't want the guy, the suspect or whatever, to get spooked by seeing a cop in the area."

Jud didn't know what to make of this. "What he doin here, talkin to you? Why he on a stakeout in the third?"

"That's the thing. No one knows. First district didn't know anything about it. He was in uniform but he wasn't even on duty."

"So he bullshit? Then why he tell you to stay clear?"

"Who knows. Maybe he was working a case on his own, you know, moonlighting, in his spare time, to get brownie points for a promotion if he made a surprise collar. Or P.I. work, off the books, make some extra cash." Jud didn't offer a thing. "Who knows," Halvorson repeated. "But when my wife said you'd called, and thanks again by the way, it means a lot, we had a real swell night, but she gave me a big kiss because she was happy about the news, that I would be home Christmas Eve, and, well, she kisses me and I tend to forget things. It slipped my mind to get Suthrin's message to you. Good thing, too, I suppose, or who knows when somebody would've found him. One of Mother's little kids, maybe, bringing some dry goods out." Halvorson tried to sound savvy and knowing and experienced by including the detail about Mother's business practices. "That would've been ugly," he added.

"Already was ugly. But I get ya. Even uglier." Jud took off his cap and scratched his head. "So, either he stakin someone out, and that be the likely killer, or he bullshittin and had some other kinda bidness back there."

Again the savvy pretension: "Some whore, maybe, from what I hear."

Jud leaned in and narrowed his eyes. "What you hear?"

The rook didn't register Jud's stare. "Oh, I don't mean anything in particular. It's just that he liked paying for it, they say. So that's a good possibility, at least, for whatever he might've been up to." Jud didn't respond and Halvorsen, unsure of the conversation's drift, added: "No offense if the guy was a friend of yours."

"He weren't no friend of mine," Jud said, looking away again. After a moment he said: "If it was some ho, he sure ain't spectin her to bring no knife. Fact, maybe that make more sense than if it some crook he after."

"How's that?"

"Look to me like they was in close combat, so to speak. Hand to hand."

"Whores get that way sometimes. Combative. Not that I would know." Halvorson blushed and Jud stifled a laugh. "Anyway, just wanted to let you know, and thank you again for the ..."

"Say, rook, I seen you typin once. You awful fast at it."

Halvorson saw the shoe dropping. "Yeah?"

"Well, after I write out my report, I gotta teletype it. And I type like granny's drawers. So I reckon you'll have a break later in the mornin and maybe ..."

Halvorson laughed. "Yeah, yeah. Okay. If I'm still in the building."

He was. When Jud finished, he dropped off the handwritten report with Halvorson and found Warren in the breakroom paging through a crime magazine.

"Ain't got enough of that every day you gots to read about it too, huh."

"You ready to get on back?" He put down the magazine on its spine, as though he would return to the same page later.

"Ready as I'll ever be."

Warren dropped Jud off in Bronzeville. Jud got out of the car but then turned around and tapped on the passenger window. Warren rolled it down and looked at Jud expectantly while leaning across the seat.

"Occurred to me to mention. Just wanna be square with you. I weren't ever outside nor inside Nancy. I just like that joke. But, France. Hell yeah."

Jud turned around and headed deeper into Bronzeville.

8.

On this picture postcard Christmas morning the sixth ward looked, if anything, worse in contrast to the clean white blanket of snow that would ornament it until the snow turned black during the course of the day. Inevitably trash had piled up in December outside the shabbiest of the tenements. Reduced access and much slower vehicle mobility led to rationing of city services, meaning exclusive concentration of them in the better areas. The cycle would feed on itself when tons of dumped sand and then snowplows, similarly rationed, would make other streets passable but not these. If Santa Claus had come to any of the houses and apartments earlier that evening, he would certainly have rationed his deliveries, too. And his list would include only the very good children, that half of all of them whose exceptional goodness was demonstrated by the fact that their father or mother could find a job.

Jud had gotten a working torch and so was free to view the army of rats in bright definition, rather than as three-foot shadows noticed only when demonic ravening snouts and grotesque hairless pink tails scurried startlingly past at arm's length. The worst parts of Bronzeville, all but a few square blocks of it, were lately very bad indeed, as bad as anything Jud had seen down south. And for most there was no escape. Even Jud as a cop had been unable to buy a house more than half a mile away, barely outside the five-block-wide corridor reserved for almost all the city's colored folks, less than a square mile, Third through Eighth Streets stretching from Juneau to the broader commercial strip on Walnut and then on northward to however far someone might extend the blight, lately Brown Street. One of these days the northern limit would be fixed by speculators designing secretly covenanted neighborhoods, and none of the Jim Crow residents would even know they'd been altogether enclosed till one of them went up to explore the suburban development and was unquietly asked to leave, perhaps by one of Jud's "Type One" co-workers, moonlighting for money not scrip. But that day was distant in an era when no one ever built any new houses anywhere at all on planet earth.

Jud passed by one of the many juke joints and jazz clubs the papers touted as the jewels of Bronzeville, with its slaphappy nightlife and randy energetic young men and women. The locals were probably about as randy as anybody else but usually, by evening, a lot less energetic. Bronzeville was indeed a popular exotic weekend destination for the more adventurous college kids, boys and girls, arriving in groups with one boy or another protected by daddy's pistol, tucked negligently into his belt beside the flask in his pocket. Every year or two Jud or whoever traveled the beat would have to rescue one in drunken terror after a couple of his toes had been blown off and his pecker burned black. But otherwise they were all right, the white kids. They spent their money and didn't cause any trouble except when occasionally the drunkest and stupidest got rolled by a hooker. And, so long as they were in a group and showed up only on Friday or Saturday, they were permitted by the communitarian street entrepreneurs, hiding around corners and in the alleys, to conclude their safaris and depart with their wallets still of any immediate use in their inner coat pockets.

A lot of people said the south side's third ward was just as bad, packed with Italians a decade or two from Ellis Island. Jud hadn't been to the third much so he wouldn't know. But he doubted it was worse. The Depression for Milwaukee's colored people began in '27 and '28, when local manufacturers started expanding to other cities and states. Plant after plant in town, now one of many towns in an expanding rustbelt, would reduce its workforce by firing all the colored folks first. And that was before any talk of a crisis. Meanwhile, after the crash, it took a couple of years for the more general Depression to reach the rest of Milwaukee, which until recent months was cited as an economic oasis. But the nation's papers and magazines weren't making that claim much any more, and lately not at all.

Walking by a couple of so-called Polish Flats, with their older wooden four-room bodies raised up and set on newer but not at all new concrete and brick rental basements, Jud pointed the torch in the narrow gap between them and inadvertently awakened Willie the ragman, lying atop discarded clothes on the snow in a cocoon of broken cardboard boxes and newspapers and more clothes.

Jud shined the light briefly on himself for identification, and Willie said, "Hey, Button." He called Jud Button because Jud was an okay cop and the big white buttons on his uniform were more relevant than the dangerous badge. "I can look at your coat and don't have to see no badge," Willie had said after a few encounters. It was also, however, wordplay: "but-in," which even the okay cops always ended up doing if you saw them often enough.

"Yeah, it me again, Willie."

A few years ago Jud knew the names of most of the street people in the ward because there weren't all that many. Now nobody could keep track of them, even with the most conscientious effort. Not that he knew any of them by their real names. These people all lost their real names somewhere along the way. Along with everything else.

Jud removed his silver dollar sized police-issue earmuffs. "Couldn't find no one to take you in tonight, huh."

"Or maybe they couldn't find me." Willie sat up and felt around to make sure his cart was still nearby. Under a filthy trenchcoat too tight to fasten he had at least four sweaters on. Some of the holes in the first two layers overlapped and you could see the third.

Jud took a couple of quarters from his pocket. "Could be that, maybe," he replied.

"Thanks, Button. Ain't seen you around here much no more. Now your boss just send me ofays. Them boys don't treat a workin man with no respec."

"Well, I'd say just mention my name to them, but that probably do more harm than good."

Willie didn't laugh at the little joke. "Think so?" he said.

"I's just playin with you."

"Oh. Okay, then."

"But you right. They don't make me walk the beat so much no more, in my old age."

"Don't suspect you'll find much goin on round here in all this." Willie gestured at the snow. "They know all you gots to do is follow the tracks."

"Matter of fact, a whole lot goin on tonight. But only amongst the buttons."

"Well, they make tracks, too."

"That they do. You gonna see a lot of em in the next coupla days. One of the boys from the first district, downtown, got hisself stab to death over yonder. By Mothers. On Hubbard?"

"I ain't never down that far, cept to go fishin in the river or maybe all the way down to the lake, of a sunny mornin."

"Boy named Suthrin. Know him?"

Willy knew the name. He nodded. "Don't personally. Hear the twists talkin about him now and again. You know how they like to get to talkin when they stand round together and ain't nothin much else happenin."

Jud had just been jawboning. The last thing he expected was for Willie to answer him yes. He crouched down to converse more respectfully, his forearm across his knee. "Oh yeah? What them girls say?"

"Oh, say he no good, he don't give em nothin but grief, wish he go find some other place to make trouble, that sorta thing. Say he mean to em. Beat em sometime. And say he pay sometime and sometime it just a handful of gimme, mouthful of much oblige, as the man say. What they gonna do? He stay away from the ones got someone reliable runnin em. Thing is. Thing is, he come round often enough, what I hear, you gotta figure it ain't just because they don't have enough twist walkin down by his. Somethin bout these girls he like specially. Girls who just happen live hereabouts." Willy almost laughed. "Can't imagine what that could be, can you. Southern boy."

"You happen to remember what any these girls called?"

"Well, like I said, he go with the ones ain't got no one reliable runnin em. So that mostly the older ones, on their last legs. Thirty, forty. So that where to find em. I ain't always so good with names."

"See if you can try."

"Well, I ain't fin to call the law down on any of em."

"I ain't the law." Jud almost smiled. "I's Button."

This time Willie did laugh. "Okay, but you ain't heard it from me."

"Nothin happenin to none of them old girls," Jud reassured him. "From me or no one else."

"Well," Willie said at length, "I reckon there's Dolores, and Carlotta, and one go by Peaches, and, and, and Lizzie, and Becky, and, oh, let's see."

Not at all in a good mood, Jud had to keep from laughing anyway. "Y'know, Willie, I think that'll do."

"Oh. Okay, then."

Jud dug out a couple of dimes. "Now I done give you enough all told for three day's groceries and then some. They don't let you get in the grocer, tell em who done give you the money and they think twice. Just go in and do your shoppin and don't be mumblin to yourself or nothin like that. Get yourself a few things you can keep good in the snow, and some can goods and such."

"But I ain't got no can opener," Willie said.

Jud started to respond to this. But then saw that Willie was just playing with him.

9.

WHEN THE SKY STARTED BRIGHTENING Jud headed toward the nearest straw box, and was relieved to find the bulb atop it unlit. He would be spared overtime. The beat cops, in theory, checked one straw box light every hour if not otherwise engaged, but no one really expected you to do that, especially on a snowed-in morning like this. Instead the boxes were checked irregularly, depending on whether one was nearby. A light meant the station had received a call but either couldn't or didn't find it necessary to dispatch a car. The beat cop saw the light, then got into the small snug booth and called the station and found out where to go. Often, in warmer months, the relayed news was already known and dealt with, due to the chain of information extending through people on the street, usually in the more dramatic cases involving an assault or big street fight or alarm-triggering burglary. Of course, alarms in white neighborhoods, like Mother's, always resulted in a vehicle response. Not so in the slums, where the station regarded break-ins as routine commerce, or at best the cost of doing business.

Jud had been signaled by a box only once that morning. A domestic disturbance on Third Street, in an anomalous old-money corridor. A daughter who hated her mother-in-law. It was the holidays. Lots of yelling, car windows being broken in the drive-way, bottles smashed against the walls outside. The drunken aristocrats were probably more alarmed by the arrival of a colored man to their home than by anything else that had happened. Other than the help, Jud was probably the first dark-skinned person ever to set foot inside the nineteenth century estate. He had to walk on eggshells or everyone there would have filed a complaint, each focusing either on something he did or something he didn't do. He spent much of his mental energy reminding himself not to absentmindedly touch anything in the house. He'd been accused of stealing often enough for one career. The daughter was put to bed in a guest house and Jud left, replacing the cap that he'd humbly removed for the duration.

Jud called his ride and stepped back out of the straw box and absently regarded it. The peculiar structure had been hailed as quite a technical innovation when first introduced a decade before by innovation-minded Chief Laubenheimer, who had also dreamt up one-way car radios a year ago as well as that unique novelty at intersections, the silent policeman, controlling traffic by green and red lights. People inevitably commented that the straw box looked like a one-man teepee. On especially cold nights the cop might spend half his shift inside a series of the teepees, making a daisy chain while ostensibly being extra-vigilant in checking as many signal lights as possible. You'd look at your pocket watch till half an hour had passed and sensation had returned to your fingers and toes, and then head out for the next. During daytime, of course, coffee and donut shops were much better alternatives. Here in the north it was sometimes more a matter of sitting a beat than walking one.

Walking not sitting this morning's beat, Jud had tried to put himself in the mind of a seasoned detective. If nothing else the mental exercise helped pass the time and get him through the black chilly morning. He thought: What sort of questions would a detective ask? A good list of questions would define the whole approach to the case, until the time when the answers started adding up and pointed in a new direction.

Jud didn't know much about Suthrin. He saw him sometimes in the speakeasy, Jud in uniform passing through and Suthrin not. But he left him alone, didn't say a word. Presumed any intrusion no matter how friendly would be resented. Presumed that Mother's was Suthrin's local, that he lived nearby, which only stood to reason given the cop's frequent presence in a saloon noteworthy only for being there, there on the northwest side of the Milwaukee River with none other in the immediate vicinity. But Jud had also considered the opposite, that Suthrin lived in the first district and simply chose a place close enough for convenience but safely distant from the domain of his coworkers and all the people he knew from his beat downtown. Suthrin hadn't been among those embarrassed in the January speakeasy raid, after all.

So that was one question. Jud had a leg up on the detectives already. If it turned out that Suthrin didn't live near Mother's, it meant he favored the location for its proximity to those vulnerable girls on the streets of Bronzeville. And only Jud knew that. For now.

But that still left the question of what Suthrin was doing at the speakeasy on one of the rare nights when the place was closed, and in a blizzard no less.

The key. The commotion with Sergeant Messerschmidt had derailed the line of Rhodes's inquiry. Rhodes never reached the question of how Suthrin got in the door and Jud, sticking to the questions asked, hadn't mentioned it. And now? Now the key was in Jud's washing machine, in a pocket of his clothes that he ordinarily never used and hadn't emptied out when he changed uniforms. But, he thought: Why not keep the information to himself? That would give him another advantage over Rhodes, until he was asked about it. And Rhodes might just accept whatever story Mother made up about the issue. Of course, either Mother had given Suthrin the key, or one of her boys had, or Suthrin had stolen one or had somehow made a copy. Jud had showed the key to Flint, so it wasn't as though he was keeping it a secret. And Messerschmidt's disturbance provided cover for Jud's failure to mention it to the others. He would sit on it for a while and think it over. Let them assume it was just another of the stupid lapses of a dumbass monkey, to quote the beerswilling kraut ape.

The supposed stakeout. That was another question, now no doubt reverberating through both district stations. Either Suthrin had been telling the truth or not. If true, it was a stakeout he was pursuing independently, for his own reasons. Or possibly it was a first district operation revealed only on a need-to-know basis, and that fact had not yet been released. But then why would Suthrin have mentioned it so casually to Halvorson, a man he'd never seen before? No, it seemed unlikely to have been a district operation. Otherwise Halvorson, told to avoid the alley, would have received the word through different channels, captain to first district lieutenant to third district lieutenant to sergeant. And without a stakeout being mentioned. In fact, with no explanation given to the rook at all. Or even given to the lieutenants and the sergeant. So Suthrin was doing it on his own or not doing it at all. If the latter, he was up to no good tonight in the alley, on business arranged at least several days earlier when he had carefully checked the duty roster at the third.

Jud was satisfied he had parsed the questions exactly as a detective would.

So that was the where, if not the why.

So, then, who.

Three possibilities. First, whomever Suthrin was staking out. Second, if there was no stakeout, it was whomever Suthrin was scheduled to meet. Or, third, it was just random.

The first two were vastly more probable. What was Suthrin involved in and who were his associates? Who were his enemies? Besides, that is, a half-dozen or dozen or however many colored streetwalkers without a pimp. It would be tricky for Jud to answer this, or even know how to approach it. If he tried to look into it, no one in the first district would show any interest in talking to him. Quite the opposite. The best he could do was to follow the gossip at the third.

Jud's ride showed up at the straw box about twenty minutes or so before sunrise. At the station he scribbled some notes about the rich girl's tantrum, which he would later write out in an exaggeratedly neat hand as required. Then he went to the almost snowfree parking lot and got into his old Model T and left. For the time being he kept to himself the names Dolores Carlotta Peaches Lizzie and Becky.

10.

As Jud had feared, Sally was sitting on the bed and still staring out one of the bedroom windows. He knew she had been up almost all the night doing that, since the time he'd started the wash. He walked in the room without knocking or otherwise announcing himself. He knew she must have heard his car pull up, and anyway she didn't startle easily these days. To say the least. A startle reflex would have been a welcome symptom. So he just walked in the bedroom and said, "Morning, Missus."

"Oh, Jud, I hadn't expected you back so soon."

He had been gone almost eleven hours.

"Did they let you off early, dear?"

The sun was up. The room was bright.

"No, Missus, I worked a full shift."

"Are you hungry? I could make you a hamburger."

When she was like this, she always offered to make him a hamburger. Always a hamburger. Even if there was no beef in the refrigerator. She was unaware of the repetition.

"I'll just make a snack and go to bed. It's been a long night."

"Yes it has been. There still isn't anything on the radio but static."

Jud blinked. "The radio is off, Sally."

"I checked it before, though. When it was still dark out. I checked it over and over again. I thought Eddie Cantor might be on."

"Eddie Cantor is only on after suppertime, once a week. On Sundays."

"I thought he might have something special to say."

When she was like this, Sally believed that the people on the radio were communicating with her.

"Now, Missus, you know he doesn't have something special to say. He tells a few jokes and then the Russian man plays the violin and then there are some vaudeville routines and then he says goodnight. It's the same thing every week. So. There is no. There isn't a. There is never any kind of. Of special message."

"Amos and Andy were on. I think they're in some kind of trouble."

"I know. I was here and we listened to it together."

When she was like this, she thought Amos and Andy were two colored men named Amos and Andy. That she was hearing their actual lives, broadcast in daily fifteen-minute increments. Never mind the absurd stereotypes of their characters, types never encountered by Sally or Jud or anyone else, and denounced by colored groups for contributing to prejudice, and also denounced by police associations because the show dared comically to suggest, whenever Amos and Andy got in trouble, that the third degree actually existed and was used.

But because the show was on every day and you couldn't miss it, heard it almost anywhere you might go, and even movies in the theaters were interrupted to play it on loudspeakers for the audience, and even prisons in states where they didn't have daylight saving time rioted when daylight saving time ended elsewhere and the show was on too late for the prisoners to be permitted to hear it, even in the third district stationhouse and every other stationhouse in the country, because the show was on everywhere every day at six o'clock central time Amos and Andy could sometimes serve as a gauge for Jud of where Sally was in her madness. If over the course of a few weeks she gradually started talking about the show as if it featured two real colored men, that meant the bad times were coming on. Like a recurring fever from an infection that seems to heal only to flare up again. When the reverse occurred, and she moved toward understanding that two white actors were reading a script and sitting in a studio and making sound effects and so on, the spell was lifting.

But even at her best, for years now Sally had not been altogether present. Even when rational she was vacant and disconnected from the world. She was kind and good to Jud and loved him, and was able to cook things besides hamburgers, and could hold simple conversations, and had a sex drive, and even sometimes left the house on her own. But it was as though she were in a dream, or going through the pantomime motions of a hypnotist's subject, earnestly relating to an environment that wasn't really there. As the years passed Jud's optimism faded, his belief and later his wish and finally his fantasy that one day Sally, in the cyclical upward arc of her recovered rationality, would push on through beyond the usual apex and become a full person again.

Her folks were coming up after New Year's and would see her this way. But they wouldn't hold it against Jud. He, they thought, had been their victim. At some point he had realized, long after the fact, that they would never have permitted him to marry Sally if she had been well, even though he had learned to speak properly around them and imitate their manners. He had met and courted Sally during one of her lucid periods, which in her youth were free from the disconnection, the affectless void. It had lasted well into their marriage, perhaps prolonged somehow by her love for Jud and her happiness. At the time Jud had no reason to suspect what was in store for him, and her parents didn't volunteer the information. They had surely despaired at her prospects. Her condition was well known in their little world, and suitable beaux never came around to visit anymore.

Although they'd lived in Atlanta during most of Sally's life, her family came from what Jud later learned were called the three-B's: Boston's black brahmins. Her father was a lawyer who had won a number of highly lucrative liability cases for an all-colored clientele and had then been recruited by a burgeoning colored firm in Atlanta. Sally's parents had always made it clear that Jud was beneath them, his skin many shades darker than theirs, his Southern Baptist background uncivilized compared to their northern Episcopalian, his lack of higher education not compensated by the French war medal.

Jud had met Sally in Atlanta straight out of the army, still wearing his uniform all the time because it was the only decent thing he owned. Sally lived at home, had dropped out of college after a year but claimed she was merely taking a break. She had ventured out to a music club with three cousins who were visiting and Jud, handsome and neat and well-built in his uniform, asked her to dance.

Men always said this about their wives, but in Jud's case it was true: She was the most beautiful woman he had ever seen. At thirty-four she still was. Nothing in his life, before or since, had astonished him as much as her willingness, eagerness even, to be courted by him. It seemed impossible. But she loved him, for his integrity and honesty, his dry sense of humor, his decency. She also liked, very much, how he looked. Could barely keep her hands off him at first. And later too, sometimes. Besides being beautiful she was also quick, bright, read books and told Jud about them. And she was sweet to him and Jud thought that somehow, for once, heaven had smiled on him. Well, it had, because he never regretted marrying her even after she started to disappear. But heaven also demanded a price. Her parents had sent her to the best alienists, who were of no use at all. Schizophrenia, they said. Jud did not know what that meant because nobody knew what it meant.

"Are you sure you don't want a hamburger?"

"Yes, I'm sure." Jud smiled at her a little. "Thank you for asking, though."

She smiled back prettily. "Well let me know if you get hungry."

"I will, Missus."

"I like it when you call me Missus."

"I know you do. That's why I do it."

"I bet the photoplay magazines will say that you call me that."

When she was like this, Sally read a lot of fan magazines. She liked reading them for their own sake but she also wanted to see whether any of them mentioned her. She believed that Eddie Cantor was interested in having her on his show and then taking her to Hollywood where she would be in the pictures. The gossip writers were bound to mention it, eventually.

"Those magazines like little details like that," Jud said.

"I wonder if Hedda Hopper will come to the house when Mama and Daddy are here. I'll have to buy a new dress."

"Hedda Hopper isn't going to come to the house, Sally. You don't have to prepare for that at all."

"But she'll want to interview Mama and Daddy, too. That way she won't have to go all the way down to Atlanta."

Jud did not know how to answer this. He said, "I have to go take care of the wash."

"She follows me around with a camera whenever I go out. I always have to be so careful to look my best."

"You always look beautiful, Missus."

She smiled again. Jud leaned over and gave her a kiss then headed for the basement. He heard her start humming to herself: I'm Just Wild About Harry.

Jud got his uniform out of the cold water wash and removed the key and put it in his pocket. The blood probably hadn't all come out but it was no longer visible on the black fabric.

Sally's parents had bought them the electric washing machine two years ago, just before the crash. It must have cost more than a hundred dollars. A Maytag. The Archer Kent radio Sally depended upon surely ran them at least another eighty. Impossible sums. Far more than Jud's yearly payments on his four-year-old Model T. Her father's money was all in U.S. bonds and in cash in the biggest Georgia bank. His only other investments were his house and his law firm. The crash hadn't hurt him at all. Since most of his work was done on contingency, he hadn't lost much business, either. One of his partners had speculated and gone bankrupt, though, so the firm lost capital and had to move to a suite of smaller offices on the outskirts of the outskirts downtown, the outskirts of where a colored business was permitted to operate.

Sally's mother had a little seamstress shop to give her something to do. And perhaps to help her not think about Sally too much. She looked down on Jud but was nice enough to him and Jud liked her. In the early days when Sally was at her best Jud could see what a positive influence her mother had been on her. How she'd given her confidence and dignity and a good ethical sense. But no parent could do anything to prevent or ameliorate a brain disease no one on earth understood. As for her father, he was decent enough but basically a bastard to Jud. Never in almost fifteen years had a kind word for him. Barely even a respectful word, and that with only the greatest effort under the eye of his more generous and diplomatic wife. Jud didn't look forward to seeing them. Never did. But he hoped it would be good for Sally to be around them all day, responding to their attempts at conversation, listening to radio shows together, going out to shops and restaurants and the pictures and maybe to hear some music at the city's only colored key club, if her father had kept his expensive membership at that upscale private speakeasy. If they did go there, Jud was certain, it would be on a night Jud had to work late. And he wouldn't be invited to catch up with them.

Jud hung his uniform up to dry. To take off his boots, their soles cleaned of blood by miles walked in the snow, he sat down on the ratty old couch next to the washing machine. The couch had been in their parlor until Sally's parents bought them a new one. Although her parents never gave them any money, refused even to co-sign the loan on the house, they bought Sally all sorts of things, and not just furniture and appliances. Her photoplay magazine subscriptions. Her jewelry and makeup. Every month or so they sent a couple of care packages with non-perishable food, some fiction books Sally might read when she was well, dozens of packs of the tailormades Sally smoked.

Jud gazed down at his boots. What an awful night. He'd had a dead man's blood on him. He'd had the unpleasant and unwanted encounter with Mother at the penny kitchen. He'd been insulted by two sergeants. He'd been taken off a case that should have been his. He'd eaten humble pie at a millionaire's home where he wasn't welcome because he was colored and they let him know it. And he'd come home to Sally, sitting on the bed and staring out the window and wondering if Eddie Cantor would come on the radio in the middle of the night to give her a message.

"Are you sure you don't want a hamburger?" Sally called from upstairs.

"Yes darlin, I'm fine, thank you."

"Well, you'd better hurry up then. You'll be late for work."

Jud stared at his boots. He sat still. His brow was knitted and his mouth was slightly open and the muscles in his face were tense but he didn't know it. He was breathing deeply through his mouth but didn't know it. There was absolutely nothing in his mind. Nothing but his boots and the area around them, and that only because it was where he was looking. He sat still and he stared at his boots with his mouth open and then he put his head in his hands and he sat there on the couch like that for a long time with his mouth closed and his eyes closed and then he sat there on the couch like that for a long time and cried.

Milwaukee Tribune

FRIDAY, DECEMBER 25, 1931.

OFFICER SLAIN BY MYSTERY MAN

Stabbed Dozens Of Times, Crawls From Pitch-Black Alley To His Death In Storage Room

Christmas Eve Butchery Shocks Northwest Side

An unknown assailant attacked and killed a Milwaukee police officer last evening in a snow-bound alley near the corner of N. Hubbard and W. Reservoir sts. in the city's 6th ward. So far police have revealed no clews as to the killer's identity.

Patrolman Landis Lee "Southern" Humphreys, 1492 W. Clybourn st., a five-year veteran of the 1st district, was found just before midnight lying in a copious pool of his own blood inside a storage room in the rear of the large building that holds both Mother's Hubbard Penny Restaurant, 1866 N. Hubbard st., as well as the residence of the family that runs the restaurant. Humphreys was twenty-six years of age.

Death Struggle In Dark Alley.

Based on the initial report of Patrolman and acting detective Judson W. Minor, Jr., negro, who was walking "beat three" in Brewers Hill when he came across the grisly scene, Humphreys was attacked and stabbed dozens of times in the alley before seeking refuge in the building.

It is believed Humphreys, backed up against the wall just beyond the half-block E. Reservoir st. alley behind the building, tried the door to the storage room at hazard in the last desperate moments of his life. Contacted by this newspaper, Mrs. Lothar C. (Herta) Odenwald, widowed proprietress of Mother's Hubbard Penny Restaurant, stated that her youngest boy must have left the door near the alley unlocked after playing in the alley's snow on Christmas Eve. No damage or theft was reported.

Blood "Everywhere".

Del Odenwald, 15, third of six Odenwald sons, described the bone-chilling, nightmarish aftermath of

(Turn To Page 2, Column 1)

(Continued From Page 1, Column 1)
the massacre.

The obviously shaken boy reported:

"There was blood everywhere. It covered the floor inside and was just about everywhere outside, all over the snow. I have never seen anything like it. Officer Humphreys was face-down on the floor and cut to pieces. I could plainly see where he and the killer had fought outside in the snow. It must have been a mighty struggle. All I can say is, I hope the knife-wielding maniac has gone a great distance from here and will never again approach our home."

Killed In Line Of Duty.

Humphreys was found in uniform, although his death occurred almost two miles from the downtown station he served. It is not unusual, however, for officers to pursue their cases beyond the geographical bounds of their districts.

Questioned about this aspect of the murder, Patrolman Minor replied:

"This is an ongoing investigation and it would be imprudent to speculate about it at this time. Furthermore, it might possibly hinder our attempts to apprehend the perpetrator if we were to release any further details. We are prepared to say, however, that Officer Humphreys was killed in the line of duty."

Chief Laubenheimer stated:

"The Milwaukee Police Department, and especially the brave men of the first district, have suffered the tragic loss of a beloved 'brother in blue.' We extend our sincerest thoughts and prayers and deepest sympathies to Officer Humphreys' family and loved ones."

—by Walter R. Meinecke (with assistance from John Carson)

Milwaukee Tribune

SPECIAL AFTERNOON EDITION

FRIDAY, DECEMBER 25, 1931.

PORTRAIT OF A HERO

Beloved "Southern" Always Lent Helping Hand

Landis Lee "Southern" Humphreys, the Milwaukee patrolman slain in the line of duty on Christmas Eve, was known to all as the soul of generosity and kindliness.

"He never had an enemy in his life," said his grief-stricken grandmother, Mrs. Ernest B. Clayton, who resides at the farm she and her husband own in an unincorporated area north of Grafton.

"When he was a youngster, you never saw a more popular boy at school," added Humphreys' grandfather.

His colleagues in the downtown 1st district were unanimous in their agreement. "At every opportunity, whenever he had a moment to spare, 'Southern' would try to find some way to lighten the load of anyone who happened to be there," recalled one fellow patrolman. A detective added: "He was always assisting on cases that weren't his own, researching crimes that weren't his responsibility. He had his nose in everything."

Family Moved No. In '23 Recess'n

Born in 1905, Humphreys grew up in Mississippi, where he was raised by his maternal grandparents. After the family were nearly wiped out in the farming depression a decade ago, they pulled up roots and moved north to farmland they inherited shortly after young Landis finished high school.

Fulfilling a lifelong dream to be of service to his community, Humphreys applied and was accepted to the Milwaukee Police Department in 1926, where he quickly gained his affectionate nick-name.

Capt. Floyd McGuire, supervisor of the police training school where even veterans must attend weekly classes, said that at the age of 21, Humphreys was mature beyond his years. Capt. McGuire recalled first seeing Humphreys as a trainee:

"I said, 'You're telling me that man's only 21? That is not possible.' I was amazed. I had known fellows twice that age with only half his maturity. Of course, those fellows get weeded out sooner or later, never advancing past beat 'cop'. That's why it's doubly tragic. This southern gentleman was a 'keeper'. I expected him to be around until the day I retired."

"He wasn't the type to do a lot of gabbing and gladhanding," said Sergt. Ernst Messerschmidt, Humphreys' immediate supervisor. "He always just kept his head down and concentrated on the job before him, and then would go home and tinker with his motorcycles. That guy sure loved his 'bikes'. He must have put every spare dime into that hobby. But then, back at the station house he put everything else out of mind. You couldn't find a more dedicated public servant."

(Turn To Page 12, Column 7)

(Continued From Page 2, Column 4)

According to Lieut. Thomas O'Donnell, head of the 1st district squad, Humphreys sometimes did service as an acting detective and was planning to enroll for detective training, and from there to seek placement with Det. Sergt. Arthur Schiffelbein's newly reorganized Morals Squad. "He would have been first in line for promotion with the new squad," Lieut. O'Donnell said. "I am told he assisted in the March raid at Morgenroth's Plankinton sporting parlor." Prior to the repeal of the Severson Act, Humphreys had his highest hopes set on joining the state's Office of the Prohibition Commissioner, now defunct.

Humphreys was unmarried. No date has yet been scheduled for his memorial service.

—by Walter R. Meinecke (with assistance from John Carson)

PART TWO

December 25, 1931 (p.m.)

11.

"**G**OD HOW I HATED that redneck prick."

"I'm sorry, sir, what?"

Meinecke laid the afternoon proofs on his desk and picked up the folded white towel. He slouched in his chair, put his feet up, and placed the damp towel over his eyes.

"Nothing," he said.

"Well, sir," said the other one, the wiseguy not the lickspittle. "As a would-be reporter I must learn to be hyperperceptive and to describe accurately what I observe. And I observe that you had one hell of a swell Christmas Eve."

"What?" said the lickspittle.

"Ah," Meinecke said. "The hungover newshound. That, old sport, would be a cliché. Excellent. You must learn to use them as often as possible."

"But our professor said …"

"He's putting us on," the wiseguy interrupted.

"I most certainly am not. I don't joke. How could I? The situation is far too serious for that. Life is shit. The country is broke. Within five years we'll be either red or fascist. The world has gone to hell."

"The hungover, cynical newshound," the wiseguy said.

"You're two for two. If you had added hardboiled, I would have given you bonus points." Meinecke adjusted the towel. "It's Rickheimer, right? I shall call you Weisenheimer."

"I'm Carson. He's Rickheimer."

"Please don't call me Weisenheimer, sir. It wouldn't look good to the others. I intend to work with these men, come thirty-three."

"Why would I call you Weisenheimer?"

"I don't know why but please don't. I worked very hard to secure this internship."

The two kids sitting earnestly in front of Meinecke's desk probably had, in fact, worked hard. Dumbshits. A couple of ambitious seniors from Marquette. Journalism majors. What the fuck was that? But he had to put up with them during their whole winter break. Six weeks. Of which this was week one.

Meinecke really did believe that life is shit. And fully expected a red or fascist takeover. Once half the country was out of work, something that was surely on the horizon, what else could possibly be the result? Hell, Milwaukee was already socialist, and that was halfway toward either.

Meanwhile the coloreds down south were trying to get rid of the poll tax and vote themselves all the money. Incipient communism. And shotgun-toting noose-tying crackers were killing them for it. Nascent fascism. The latter was more likely to prevail. There were a lot more whites than blacks.

On the other hand, in the northeast and California there were almost as many immigrants and Jews and intellectuals as Americans. Well, it could break either way. Meinecke would keep his eyes open and do whatever he was told to do by whomever ended up with the most guns. Once the money had finally run out and, as in Germany, there was none left no matter who you were, there would still remain, this being America, plenty of guns.

He wondered which extreme would prove more attractive to his acquaintances with the tommy guns, on both sides of the law. Sometimes simultaneously. Everyone assumed fascism. But Mussolini hadn't exactly been a good friend to the Black Hand, and who needs the cops when you have the army and no justice system. So maybe the two groups, the two sides of the law, complementary and sometimes intersecting, would end up going the other way.

"But it's actually avenue," Rickheimer was saying.

"What?" said Meinecke. "Oh, sorry. Must have dozed off. What was that?"

"I said, in the afternoon proofs you wrote Reservoir Street. But it's actually Reservoir Avenue."

"Avenue."

"Yes, sir. And the part in front is West Reservoir Avenue, but the part in back, where the murder occurred, is East. It divides at the deadend alley. So the story should say East."

"Well, then, don't delay. What are you waiting for, son. Stop the presses."

Rickheimer ignored this. Tried to kiss up. "I suppose with your grueling schedule, you are obliged to avail yourself of frequent catnaps."

"If you must know, today I got out of bed at two. In the morning. So it's not a hangover. It's been a long day. I enjoyed trips to the third district station and the first district station in the freezing fucking cold weather before the sun came up. Later in the morning I had to go, actually had to fucking go, to Reservoir Avenue, which looked like a street to me but how can you tell with all the snow, and was privileged to speak with the lovely and glamorous proprietress herself because, of all the houses in that block, they are the only ones whose fucking phone doesn't work."

Rickheimer was quick. "I don't remember seeing that detail in the proofs, sir. About the phone, I mean. It could be a ..."

Meinecke interrupted. "It could be a clue. A vital clue. Excellent, young John Carson."

"He's Rickheimer," the other said. "I'm Carson."

Meinecke finished what he had been saying. "Which is why the police, guardians of the truth, gently but emphatically requested I not mention it."

Thrilled, Rickheimer said: "The killer took out their phone."

"I didn't say that. Neither did the police."

Rickheimer was eager. "But it only stands to reason. We should start looking into it at once."

"Forthwith," Carson said. "By applying ourselves diligently to the facts, the three of us could very well solve this mystery. And crack this case. Becoming heroes in the process, like valiant Officer Humphreys."

Carson having anticipated and stepped on his line, Meinecke refrained from further abuse of Rickheimer. The words came slowly. "Well, kid, we can't publish the facts about the phone until the police say so. But you've got the right idea."

Meinecke took the towel from his eyes and sat up, prepared to dispense wisdom. He regarded the boys before him. The chubby one with oily black hair matted flat on the top of his head. A virgin. The athletic one with the smirk. Scoring regularly.

"You are," he said, "quite right to concentrate on the initial details. That is the basic principle you have got to follow when chasing down a story. One thing leads to another and the first thing leads to the rest. This is the inexorable law of the universe, as theorized by the great Aristotle and demonstrated by Mr. Newton." Meinecke had no idea where he was going with this. "You know, they just proved a few years ago that the Milky Way is not the only galaxy. There are thousands of them. Maybe millions. And we can see, with the naked eye, many of the other galaxies. They look like any other star. But that star is a whole Milky Way. The Magellan nebula. Funny looking star they've been studying in their telescopes for years. The best minds in the world, for centuries, didn't have any idea what they were looking at. Which should tell you something about your own lying eyes. Because it's not a star. It's a galaxy. But then, Kant already figured that out a long time ago."

"Kant," said Carson. "Is he one of those German fellows working with Einstein?"

Meinecke wasn't sure whether the boy was kidding. "Yes. His college professor. Advised young Albert to never, ever resort to clichés."

"That's all very interesting, sir," said Rickheimer, "but shouldn't we correct the name of the street to East Reservoir Avenue before going to press?"

"I have a question," Carson said. "You wrote that the body was found just before midnight. But the report simply says midnight. How can you know whether it was just before or just after?"

Meinecke nodded with somber appreciation. "You can't. But that way we get to say the murder was on Christmas Eve and the manhunt was on Christmas Day. See? We get two holidays into the story instead of just one."

"If they don't know," Rickheimer said, "shouldn't you say so?"

Meinecke shrugged, too tired to be annoyed. "It happened somewhere around then. Minor told me it was about midnight but he couldn't be more specific than that. Y'know, speaking of which. That Judson Minor. He's a bad actor. Probably set a record for the most complaints ever filed against one cop. Nearly quit after his first year. But Hoan had pulled strings and wasn't about to let him go, not without causing a lot of aggravation. But ... but then, maybe Minor's not so bad. I don't know. Could just as well be that people are ten times more likely to file a complaint against a colored cop. So Hoan did learn something from it, I would wager. White people won't tolerate being policed by darkies. The cops haven't hired any more of them, that's for sure. And it's been ten years. Could be another ten. We'll see."

Milwaukee Tribune

SPECIAL AFTERNOON EDITION

FRIDAY, DECEMBER 25, 1931.

CITY'S 1ST NEGRO OFFICER FOUND BODY

Gained Job With Mayor's Assistance

Patrolman Judson W. Minor, Jr., 1202 W. Juneau av., who discovered the body last night of Patrolman Landis Humphreys, is perhaps best known to some as the first Negro officer hired by the Milwaukee Police Department.

Minor, 34, a native of Lee County, Georgia, arrived in the city after serving in the War, in which he was decorated for helping to save the life of Milwaukee native Pvt. Terrence Nelson. In correspondence begun several years after the War, Nelson learned that Minor hoped one day to become a police officer, but despaired at his chances to enter such an esteemed profession. What "Jud" Minor didn't know, however, was that Pvt. Nelson's father, a professor of economics at Howard University, was a confidant of J. Harvey Kerns, then president of the Milwaukee Urban League. Kerns arranged a meeting between the elder Nelson and

(Turn To Page 12, Column 7)

(Continued From Page 2, Column 2)

a certain Daniel Webster Hoan. Owing his son's life to the Negro, Nelson described the boy's plight to Hoan shortly after the Socialist Mayor won re-election to his second term in 1920. Mayor Hoan's enthusiastic response prompted Nelson to encourage Minor to move to Milwaukee and pursue his dream in our tolerant city.

Hoan to Laubenheimer: "Hire This Boy!".

During his busy years in office, Hoan's numerous well-known acts overshadowed a small detail: He also arranged for Judson Minor to be accepted for service by the Milwaukee Police Department in 1921. Although famous for his hatred of nepotism and disdain for patronage, Hoan importuned Chief Laubenheimer personally to "ask the 3d district to hire this boy." The Lieutenant in charge of the district obeyed. Minor was the city's first Negro ever so honored.

"It was important to begin the process of allowing the Negroes of Milwaukee, concentrated so heavily in the 6th ward, to police their own," a spokesman for the Mayor recalled after hearing of Minor's role in last night's tragic events.

After ten years as a beat cop in the 3d district, home of the 6th ward, Minor has paid his dues and has been assigned primarily to office work and frequent one- or two-month stints as an acting detective; however, he still walks a beat on occasion. He plans to seek promotion to detective as soon as he can find the time to prepare for the rigorous training and examinations required.

Minor is married without children.

—by Walter R. Meinecke (with assistance from George Rickheimer)

<h1 style="text-align:center">12.</h1>

Meinecke leaned back again and positioned the damp towel. Folded his hands over his paunch.

"On another subject, sir." Rickheimer was pale with confusion. "And I don't mean to look a gift horse in the mouth. But you gave credit in the bylines for assistance."

Beneath his towel, Meinecke waited long enough to be sure the boy wasn't going to say anything else but not so long to suggest he had again dozed off. "Yes," he said.

"But we didn't assist you. In fact, because it's Christmas, we didn't even get here till half an hour ago."

"Of course you assisted me. You did the research and legwork and I put it together and wrote the stories."

"I don't understand. You know very well we did not."

"You two did the interviews. Got all the quotes."

"You said yourself you had gone this morning to the two district stations and to Hubbard Street."

"Well. Yes. I did go to Hubbard. Couldn't avoid that."

"So you phoned the stations. But what difference does ..."

"You remember," Meinecke interrupted, "those raids last January?"

"Of the speakeasies on Wells Street," Carson said. "Yes. We read your articles about them as part of the research for the ..."

"Ycleped," Meinecke laughed. "I used the word 'ycleped.'"

"Shakespeare," said Carson.

"Right. Which is the only place anyone ever sees that word ... except when someone is trying to look fancy by pretending it's the sort of word he writes all the time, even though he's never seen it anywhere but Shakespeare, either, and then had to look it up. I wrote that the stoolpigeon was quote 'ycleped Bradley for the nonce' unquote. I was typing and there it was, like Athena from the head of Zeus. Ycleped Bradley for the nonce. The nonce. Couldn't stop laughing. Had to take a little break."

Carson said: "Bradley was the fake name used by the fed pretending to be a safety match salesman."

"Ha!" Meinecke said. "What a joke. As though they needed to infiltrate those places to confirm they were speakeasies. You've got twenty-five saloons in a three square block area downtown. An area known to everybody as Liquor Lane, Gin Alley, Speakeasy Square. There's a blanket store without any blankets. A cigar store without any cigars. Hookers are going in and out of unmarked so-called storefront offices at two in the morning. So, the hard thing." Beneath the towel, Meinecke paused for breath. "The hard thing would be not to know. Not to know they were there. You'd need to have the safety match salesman go undercover at a hospital for the deaf, dumb and blind. Actually that would be a good story. Fed experiment confirms. Colon. Possible to be unaware of two dozen speakeasies in three square blocks downtown. Italics. Secret is to employ deaf dumb and blind agent."

"But as I recall, sir," Rickheimer said, "there were a few places raided outside those blocks, too. Way out on Blue Mound Road, and also Sailor Ann's place on the south side."

"Who cares. Think about it. For six months they've got a guy on the federal tit throwing around money, getting hammered every night, gambling, screwing whores. Then the story is all about him, about this Brad Bradley. Don't you get it? It was just public relations. The guy wasn't infiltrating anything. He just made the story better. More colorful. Another interesting detail for people to talk about. Made it look like Father Cunningham was earning his paycheck in the eastern prohibition enforcement district. Do you know how many saloons there are in Milwaukee? Five hundred. At least. What else would you expect in a free-thinking-German brewery town with more than half a million people who endure five months of winter every year. And do you remember the grand total of arrests in that raid?"

"Thirty or so."

"Thirty-eight. And in the four years Cunningham has been in office, that was the single biggest raid. And it took seventy-five agents from four states to do it."

"But the bylines," Rickheimer said. "We didn't assist you on any of the ..."

"And do you remember what the story's other big detail was? Besides Brad Bradley, good time charlie and safety match entrepreneur. The other memorable hook. What was it?"

"Nobody got tipped off," Carson said.

"Nobody got tipped off. The grapevine was neutralized. Father Cunningham and agent Charles Brown a-k-a Brad Bradley and their seventy-five agents from four states had masterminded such a brilliant, foolproof sting that they eviscerated the notorious system of tip-offs that had proved the bane of law enforcement in three downtown square blocks with two dozen speakeasies, so difficult to discover and raid. The secret being, of course, to follow a long-term and very expensive undercover infiltration with, brilliantly, deployment of two-man teams all at once in a bunch of places, rather than seventy-five guys in one joint." Meinecke laughed despite wanting, as comedian, to maintain a straight face. "Who would have thought of doing all the raids at the same time. A masterstroke. So, no tip-offs. That was the other big hook in all the stories I wrote. But in only one story, and only in the last few paragraphs, on a continuing page, at the back of the paper, did I happen to mention a certain detail. They successfully raided twenty-six joints. But they targeted thirty-one. So what happened to the other five?"

"Two days before the ..." Carson began.

"Two days before the raid," Meinecke said, "by coincidence, the other five all shut down, leaving no evidence behind. Yes, I actually wrote the word coincidence, with no nod and nary a wink in the connotation-less context. Shamelessly." He paused and waited for a response, but got none. "But tell me. Why should I be the one with any shame. Father Cunningham, with his thirty-eight arrests and seventy-five agents, wanted the story's hooks to be Brad Bradley and no tip-offs. So I did my job."

Rickheimer said, "Perhaps it is your duty to persuade the ..."

"Not," Meinecke continued, "that the raids were random. The Wells Street complex was a center for pimping, dice games, roulette, poker, lotteries, slot machines, pinball machines, the numbers racket, you name it. Are you starting to get the point?"

The boys did not attempt to guess Meinecke's point, so he spelled it out:

"Whatever it may have been to begin with, prohibition is now simply the cover for a federal vice squad. Something that once would have been inconceivable. Traditional police powers of the states and all that. Right? And, believe me, they don't give a fuck about speakeasies. The only thing of interest in Wisconsin is the rum-running route from Canada to Chicago, and their only interest in that is the lucrative rewards received for ignoring it. Meanwhile the Wisconsin police all but declared, years ago, that they would no longer waste their time arresting people for buying or selling a drink. Okay, so they go after some of the stills occasionally. But that's a public health issue ... and not inspired by the Ladies' Morality and Dictatorship League, chaired by Miss Buttinsky of Damsinners, Maine. Otherwise the Milwaukee cops ignore the issue. Which," Meinecke concluded, "is one reason why it's the cleanest big-city force in the country."

"That's true," Carson said. "Both the Wickersham report and *Time* magazine have said that the Milwaukee Police Department, and Mayor Hoan's administration generally, are the least corrupt in America. Sewer socialism would appear to work."

Meinecke didn't interrupt, involving himself instead in sitting up and focusing his eyes. "But I haven't even gotten to the point yet. Those stories I wrote were peppered with authentic quotes, from authentic types. All unnamed, but the very sort of people our less worldly readers might imagine would commingle with, as I put it, the liquorati."

"That was good," Carson said. "Liquorati."

"I stole it. But about the quotes. I think I can actually recite some of them, so plangently do those authentic voices ring in memory even now. One fellow says to a newly incarcerated violator of the Volstead Act, 'Chump, this is a fed charge. You ain't springin your own mother if you got a million for bail.' How colorful. Just like the real people in Hollywood gangster pictures talk. And upon inquiry as to the fate of a barkeep, another replies, 'He's up at the safety building wonderin what they're gonna give him for breakfast.' To which his shadowy companion quips, 'With that new sheriff up there, he'll maybe get a bale of hay.' Better than Hollywood. Now let me ask you two. Have you ever heard anybody talk like that? Colorful comments and clever retorts, and by men facing years of detention and economic ruin. Do you really believe that such men would banter playfully? And note, too, that they all say 'gonna' not 'going to,' and they all drop their g's. But a lot of people do. Do we routinely transcribe our quotes phonetically? No. Never. Unless we quote one of these colorful Hollywood characters."

Rickheimer said: "So you ... you made the quotes up?"

"You're free to visit those unnamed gentlemen living at the state's expense and ask them yourself, I suppose. Strangely, no one ever does."

Carson got the point. "So we got credit in your byline for assisting you by not collecting quotes that no one actually said."

Rickheimer was shocked. "You mean the quotes in today's stories are things which ..."

"Not every word," Meinecke clarified. "Only nine out of ten. Several years ago a detective said something to me about Humphreys that is quite similar to what my fictional detective says today. And I did speak this morning with the woman at the penny kitchen. She told me what her son had told her and I improved his style. He'll be thrilled to be quoted. And the mayor's quote is based on what he said to me on the phone today."

"The mayor isn't quoted. It's his spokesman."

"Right. As I said, I spoke to the mayor."

Rickheimer, appalled, said: "But the slain officer's grandparents?"

"If you are outraged that I didn't drive up past Grafton for two sentences of copy, you can leave right now. It's a goddam farm. They haven't got a phone."

"But they will surely read the ..."

"They've never read a paper in their lives. Yes, they will cut out the story and paste it in a scrapbook to be produced for every guest. Maybe one day they will read it themselves, if they learn how to read. Finally they will both remember the day the reporter came to the farm and wrote down word for word their fond recollections."

"What about Minor?" Rickheimer said anxiously. "And, for heaven's sake, the police chief?"

"If the subject ever came up, which it won't, they will both thank me. Neither of them, nor the chief's press officer, now needs to waste any time composing boilerplate. I've done it for them. Through a connection, I got a copy of Minor's police report on the teletype. Minor's shift, since he was on a midnight beat, ended at seven A.M. A bit early for this reporter."

"A bit early," Carson repeated. "So your main point. The gist of all of this. What you're getting at. Is that it is in fact a hangover."

Meinecke got a flask from his desk. "Here's to the almighty cliché, the newspaperman's best friend." He unscrewed the flask and took a drink. "Well, second best, anyway."

13.

Meinecke went downstairs to the lobby to buy a pack of Juicy Fruit, hoping it would help him in the transition from chain-smoked tailormades to the occasional cigar. The interns were gone, sent home for Christmas by their mentor after he concluded that they had learned more about newspapers from his half-hour monologue than they would in four years as journalism majors, whatever the fuck that was.

When he got back to his desk the girl had left a note saying the mayor called. He tried calling the mayor but couldn't get him on the line. He looked out the window at the depressing late afternoon darkness. Imagined the cold and snow. Cursed. He regarded every moment outside in Milwaukee's winter as a personal assault inflicted upon him by the gods. From the moment he left a car or building or taxi or streetcar until he'd reached the next oasis he uttered oaths under his breath, which he could see, and vowed to find work somewhere a reasonable person might live. Daydreamed about a desk at the Los Angeles *Times*, or even at a podunk paper like the San Jose *Mercury*. But in the middle of the worst depression in history you didn't seriously consider changing jobs.

Besides his curiosity about Hoan's call he also wanted to talk to the mayor about something that had occurred to him. The interns' ignorance had given him an idea. After they left, he had called the third district station and spoken to Detective Rhodes and learned that Judson Minor was off the case.

So, a true martyr, he now wrapped himself in the absurd ensemble of gloves and scarf and sweater and vest and coat and overcoat and earmuffs and socks on top of his socks and boots and woolen cap under his straw hat, lately coming back in style two decades after he'd bought it, and told the girl he'd be back in an hour and headed into the arctic, cursing. Immediately in frostbitten pain. He had a good parking space he didn't want to lose and he also didn't want to waste money on a cab, and it would be ridiculous to take a zigzag streetcar route with two transfers to go half a mile. So he walked. Almost at once he realized he could use the exercise. The act of hauling his corpulent body put him out of breath a block from the newspaper's office on Fourth and State, an address visitors were always reminded was a funny coincidental pun on fourth estate.

Meinecke crossed the Milwaukee River on the Kilbourn Bridge, named for one of the city's trio of founders and sometimes violent rivals when east west and south sides were still too proud and stupid and greedy to combine. As he passed from what used to be called Kilbourntown into what used to be called Juneautown, he looked to his left at Pere Marquette Park, where a small army of bums and hobos was setting up shop for the night. Two years and two months ago they'd probably all owned shares of

Telephone, of Radio, of Steel, of Electric. Of Russian-doll trusts that combined little pieces of dozens of other trusts made up in turn of little pieces of funds that pooled little pieces of holding companies whose assets were little pieces of other Russian-doll trusts, leveraged.

Meinecke had lost a big not little piece of his little not big nest egg and was now damned to crank out lies and propaganda and covert racial and ethnic slurs and the corporate line until he was seventy, if he lived that long. Maybe seventy-five. Around the time Amos 'n' Andy celebrated its twenty-fifth year as the number one serial on the radio, if Stalin and Il Duce and Adolf still permitted it to air. Fortunately Meinecke had other sources of income. But when Prohibition was finally declared dead most of this income would dry up, like all the alcohol was supposed to have done by now thanks to Mr. Volstead and Miss Nation and Frank Cunningham and no doubt the father and the son and the holy ghost, too.

Down Water Street, in dense crowds, he passed the old Pabst Theater. Its namesake, once the second biggest brewery in the country next to Schlitz, whose beer had made Milwaukee famous, now produced malt syrup, candy, cheese, chewing gum, ice cream. And, of course, prescription medicines for the hundreds of thousands of people who had suddenly developed convenient illnesses with alcohol-based cures, coming down with their maladies as soon as the loophole was drafted and codified in the Volstead Act. More Americans contracted Volsteaditis in the latter half of 1919 than had caught the Spanish flu in the two years previous.

As for the theater, it advertised a comedy with Milwaukee native Alfred Lunt and his wife Lynn Fontaine, who lived way out in the Wisconsin boondocks past Waukesha, even further away than Al Capone's country estate in Brookfield. They were interrupting their Broadway run for a special homecoming appearance. Also, there was some highbrow New York show about the Civil War with the indecipherable title *Mourning Becomes Electra*, the first word being perhaps a typographical error. There was also something with one Mary Wigman, "creator of the modern dance." Ugh. Meinecke would much rather see any of the pictures in the neighborhood, *Monkey Business* with the Marx Brothers, a western with Warner Baxter called *The Cisco Kid*, a new sound version of *The Big Parade*. He could skip the Helen Hayes melodrama. And like everyone in the country he'd already seen *Frankenstein*.

Alternatively, the RKO Vaudeville had a funny ventriloquist from Chicago everyone was talking about, Edgar Bergman or Berwyn or something like that. Ultimately the poor kid was probably doomed by his choice of act, a routine with little upside in the age of radio.

14.

AFTER HIS EXHAUSTING TWENTY-MINUTE TREK Meinecke at last reached City Hall, the trapezoidal Old World tower fitting snugly on its gore of land at the thirty-three-degree intersection of Water Street and archaic diagonal Market Street. During its forty-year history no one ever thought it necessary to ask why the building was shaped that way, like the huge spire of a gothic church but without the church. They simply accepted that it was designed to fit its little triangle. But that just begged the question, why build it there in the first place. Meinecke presumed it had been nothing more than the experimental perversity of Gilded Age Germans, obliging their architects to solve a problem arbitrarily inflicted upon themselves, for show.

He stopped in the lobby to divest himself of his winter armor. Also to catch his breath before heading up the stairs to the second floor, which like all those above was an office-lined causeway circling around the trapezoid with a clear view in the empty middle to all the other floors and the ornate ceiling, atop which the flag flew at half-staff in honor of that bastard Humphreys.

Henry Hellerman, the mayor's longtime secretary, opened the door after Meinecke knocked. Looked at him without pleasure. Said: "Meinecke."

"Hellerman."

They did not shake hands. Hellerman disliked Meinecke on principle as a lapdog for the capitalist press. And Meinecke couldn't stand idealists, Hellerman having been known to march in any picket line he could find when not needed on city business.

"He is not expecting you."

"The phones were engaged. I couldn't return his call."

"You came over to the city hall after dark on Christmas to return a phone call." Hellerman knew something else was on the newspaperman's mind. But he wouldn't be able to learn what it was till after the mayor sussed it out. And that greatly annoyed him. Which Meinecke loved.

"I thought I might enjoy the crisp December air."

"Sure you did. Enjoy seeing it, every time you breathe. Well, go on in. He's on the phone but it's nothing he wouldn't want you, and everybody else in the country, to hear."

Hellerman sounded a bit weary. Hoan had recently returned from a wide-ranging tour of cities, spreading the Socialist gospel. Meinecke entered his office and Hoan waved him over to a chair. He was using a telephone he'd jerryrigged to hold in one hand, the speaker hooked onto the mouthpiece, both parts coordinated to fit against his mouth and ear. Clever, Meinecke thought. Then wondered why phones weren't designed like that, all in one piece. Maybe because then you couldn't hang them up.

His ear on the speaker as Meinecke grew impatient, Mayor Hoan finally said: "That's excellent. I like the thing about Capone being nothing compared to the racketeering and grand larceny of big capital. Though now it might seem a bit dated, what with the good Alphonse enjoying the hospitality of Cook County Jail. Maybe you should name a different gangster."

When not made hoarse by the long, entertaining, rabble-rousing speeches he gave in the neverending campaign necessary to sustain support for his policies, Mayor Hoan's voice was high and rendered folksy by a midwestern twang. Not unlike, perhaps, that of his ostentatiously proclaimed idol, Abraham Lincoln. Lest anyone imagine his office to be a clandestine church of Marx and Lenin, he had a photograph of Lincoln on the wall. A head to toe statuette of Lincoln on the bureau. A pair of Lincoln-profile bookends enclosing some volumes on the shelf. And a big bust of Lincoln on his desk, now next to the feet he swung around and placed there, his long legs knocking a pen set onto the blotter beside it.

Along with his voice Hoan's tall skinny frame resembled that of his hero, though the shaggy mop of brown hair, graying now that he was fifty, was unfortunately arranged in the manner of Hitler's, swept heavily over one eye. He might want to change that, Meinecke reflected. But it had always been that way, like a trademark, as had the thick dark burgher's mustache, perhaps dyed of late.

Hoan again listened for a long while, his free hand holding one of those long yellow notepads favored by lawyers. He had once spent eight years in the practice, first as private counsel for the State Federation of Labor, with whom he had managed to craft and pass the nation's first workmen's compensation law, then as city attorney, carried into office in the Socialist landslide of 1910. And from there, six years later, the mayor's office, winning every election since. And absolutely, without question, bound to win the next. So Meinecke, surrounded less by Lincoln than by Hoan's past and future career, bided his time and kept his expression blank.

15.

"**W**ELL, I'VE ONLY GOT SOME NOTES," Hoan said at last into the phone's jerryrigged mouthpiece. He looked at the yellow pad. "I'll read you the best parts. Okay: 'Twenty-five years ago,'" Hoan started reading but broke off with a laugh. "I resisted the temptation to say one score and five years ago. Neither did I condemn the reactionary base-ten numeral system, so unfair to exploited workers who have lost a finger or two in unregulated industrial accidents. Okay: 'Twenty-five years ago Milwaukee reeked with graft and corruption. Over two hundred indictments of officials were returned by the grand jury for bribery, extortion, crooked contracts, and thievery of public money.' Et cetera et cetera. 'Now our people receive a dollar's worth of services for every dollar paid in taxes. We have cleaned out the dens of vice and iniquity. Less than three decades ago a house full of painted ladies was maintained near the city hall for the benefit of city officials.' Blah blah blah. 'The Police Department was overhauled by the Socialist officials' something something, 'and the merit system was introduced.' And then after more of the same, I say, 'Not an intelligent idea has come out of Washington since the Great Engineer has been president.' And what a stupid idea it was 'to lower taxes on the rich when so much money was needed for public works.' And I finish with something about, 'We believe Socialism can do for the nation what it has been doing for Milwaukee for twenty-odd years.'"

During his first-draft rehearsal he laid the pad in his lap and experimented with mock-slamming the table at various points, trying to find the most effective punctuation. He also wagged his finger. Wrinkled his brow. Hunched and unhunched his shoulders. Thus an actor prepares, thought Meinecke. Hoan's oratorical skills were a great part of his personal appeal. Halls filled everywhere he spoke, with the possible exception of Delaware, the nation's capital of corporations, where recently the local government officials refused to appear in public with him or any other godless Socialist. He had also failed to capture the heart of that great populist William Randolph Hearst, in whose Milwaukee paper this very afternoon Meinecke, looking as usual at all the papers, had learned that the mayor of the nation's twelfth largest city was a communist who openly demanded the destruction of the family, the home, and the Christian religion.

Finally the call was done and Hoan disassembled the phone in order to hang up.

"Mr. Meinecke," he began, removing his feet from the desk. Hoan was probably the only man in town who called him Mister. To everyone else he was just Meinecke, or, when not actually in the room, That

Goddam Meinecke. "I didn't expect to see you. I called only to express my displeasure at having been misquoted by you in the afternoon edition."

"Misquoted? I'm not sure what you're ..."

"You had me use the phrase, 'allow the Negroes to police their own.' I would never say 'police their own.'"

"You said 'police their own.'"

"Yes I did. But I would never say that. I would say 'look after their community.' And by the way, if the word 'police' were necessary, as a noun rather than a verb, I would say 'peace officer' instead."

"Peace officer," Meinecke repeated with a straight face.

"Yes. Has a nice friendly ring to it, don't you think?"

Meinecke thought Peace Officer was one of the stupidest euphemisms he had ever heard, one that was more likely to elicit howls of derisive laughter than a nice friendly feeling. But he didn't say so. "I apologize, your honor. There was a great deal of work to do very quickly on the afternoon edition. I'm sure its subject is one of the reasons you and Mr. Hellerman are here so late on Christmas."

"Actually, I spent the whole afternoon trying to make a deal with certain members of the common council, whom I pray will soon be spared the frigid discomfort of our fair city and find themselves instead in a subterranean region of eternal warmth. But I struggle to be patient with my prayers, believing fervently that good things come to those who wait. They're holding up my appointment to the sewerage commission, on the sensible ground that he is a man who actually knows something about sewerage. They are also holding up my appointment to the harbor commission, a man unqualified because he is familiar with harbors. If I didn't know better I would think they were trying to put the screws on me, because they are also holding up my appointment to the park board."

"Well, your honor, there's word that when the national elections in thirty-two sweep Democrats into office from coast to coast," Meinecke laid it on thick, "two of your opponents on the council will agree to begin voting with the Socialists."

"Oh, is there? I hadn't heard. That is why I rely on hardworking members of the press like yourself to tell me what's what."

Meinecke laughed fraternally. "So after sixteen years, you'll at long last have a Socialist majority, de facto if not de jure."

"Yes. And at long last, to borrow your expression, I'll be allowed to buy the city's electrical system, as so many Stalwart Republican and Progressive Republican municipalities have already long since done, in their staunch allegiance to capitalism. But because it's me asking for it, well, it must be another step toward serfdom. I have been trying to buy that utility since I got here. It will be a dream come true. Anyway, wrangling over the appointments all day kept me from preparing my address for tonight's tree-lighting ceremony."

"At Saint James Episcopal."

"Yes, a somber occasion delayed by last night's blizzard." The mayor pinched and rubbed his eyes. "Pity, too. I could have had five thousand people last night. Tonight all of them will be at the roadhouses and hotels and clubs and theaters and cinemas and restaurants and all the other sophisticated entertainments our sparkling metropolis has to offer."

Meinecke picked up on the s-p in sparkling. "Sparkling speakeasies and sporting parlors, too? What was that in your speech just now about dens of iniquity? In twenty-four, Mr. Rose must have picked up ten thousand votes against you just by pledging to, quote, 'make Milwaukee fun again.' You Socialists don't want to be thought of as wet blankets."

"Well, the ladies like to hear me say those things. About the dens of iniquity and so forth. Poignantly, I defeated Rose with the help of the nineteenth amendment. They know it means getting rid of the gangster element and keeping vice out of the suburbs, not just shutting everything down and making you eat your porridge or no dessert. And it was, quote, 'bring a little more life to Milwaukee,' not quote 'make Milwaukee fun again,' though your mistake is justified as being equally meaningless. And by vice and iniquity I don't mean the speakeasies. Actually, next month I am appearing before a women's group that favors repeal, and I plan to come out, for the first time, in favor of it. Not of repeal but amendment."

"Beck-Linthicum." Meinecke named the bill now making the rounds in congress.

"Yes. A resolution to amend the amendment." For a moment Hoan pretended to consider the matter. "Not even sure that's constitutional. Think you need a whole nother amendment."

"So you avoid the word repeal. Smart. You come off sounding like a moderate. Needless to say, it is repeal, no matter what it's called. Giving the states the right to opt out of prohibition is precisely the equivalent of what we had before 1919, when states already had the right to be dry. Opt out of permitting, or opt out of forbidding. A distinction without a difference."

Hoan frowned. "I trust your paper will not give away the game. In any case, the best thing that ever happened here was the repeal of the state prohibition law a while back." He quoted himself: "'Prohibition has taken liquor out of the realm of legitimate business and put it into the hands of the worst element.'"

"The federal government." Meinecke laughed at the old joke.

"Such wit, Mr. Meinecke. But I'll add that the Volstead Act costs Milwaukee two million dollars annually in real estate taxes and income taxes and license fees."

Meinecke wanted to get to what he'd planned to say, but thought it best not to rush. "Was that your tree-lighting speech I heard, and saw, you trying out for size on the phone?"

"Lord, no. We're putting together a Socialist event sometime next year, centered around Norman Thomas and the usual gang. That just now was a fellow who will be speaking, as will I, and we were comparing notes to avoid stepping on each other's lines. As for the tree lighting, let me read you what I've got. Pending further inspiration, it's all of one sentence."

Hoan flipped through the yellow pad and read aloud. "'This alleged Christian nation must be called to answer the piteous cry of eight million Americans who in this land of boasted riches plead with outstretched arm, Oh, brother, give us work, that we may fulfill the command to earn our bread by the sweat of our brows.'"

Oh brother is right, thought Meinecke.

16.

Hellerman stepped in to tell Mayor Hoan that a council member, one of the opposition, had unexpectedly arrived to discuss the park board. Meinecke knew his afternoon had just gotten longer.

"Don't mind him," Hoan said to the alderman with a nod at Meinecke. "He's safe. No one who reads his paper cares about the board. He would lose readers if he wrote about it."

For fifteen minutes Meinecke feigned interest in the conversation, if you could call it that. The alderman, bespectacled, curly-haired, Jewish, said prudence and fiscal responsibility were his goals, which in translation meant he would oppose the mayor's park board appointment. And the mayor recited his litany, familiar to all. Milwaukee had the lowest crime record among large cities in the nation, and therefore the lowest burglary insurance rates. The lower rates were thus a de facto tax rebate to business, large and small. This, he claimed, was due to the city's unusual abundance of parks and playgrounds and its fine educational system. The alderman said that forty percent of the budget already went to education, parks, and playgrounds, twice as much proportionally as in New York City. Hoan responded that New York had to spend eight times as much of its budget on courts, three-sevenths more on police, and twice as much on interest on its debt, which was $380 per capita compared to $76 in Milwaukee, a city with the second lowest per capita debt and second lowest tax burden per taxpayer in the country, under a Socialist mayor. Yet it was also a city able to devote twice as much of its budget as New York to public health. And the comparison with New York was fair because the two cities were tied for first, per capita, in the number of first- and second-generation immigrants.

Meinecke wondered what on earth was actually being communicated between two rivals who each knew the other's lines by heart and could in fact have served as understudy for the other's role. But as the alderman pretended to listen at great length without interruption, Meinecke got the point, which had nothing to do with the park board. By coming to the city hall unannounced late in the afternoon in the freezing cold on Christmas and on a Friday no less and allowing the Mayor to bore him for a quarter-hour after only a perfunctory opening sally, the alderman was signaling his willingness not to vote for the Mayor's small potatoes appointment but rather, following the inevitable 1932 Democratic landslide, to vote with the Mayor's coalition in 1933. He was, in short, paying obeisance. No fly on the wall, or had it been a telephone conversation no ultramodern wiretap, could have produced evidence of this, because the alderman said nothing at all. And therefore everything.

Finally the charade was over, the alderman speaking for the third and last time, reiterating his refusal to vote for the Mayor's park board appointment, and then leaving without a glance in Meinecke's direction. Had he even wished to, the reporter could not have reported anything at all about the meeting. Nothing, apparently, had happened. However, he did now have a lead on the 1933 coalition story. A story of no interest to his readers in 1931. Or, probably, in 1933.

"A bit of a soft pedal on his part, wouldn't you say." Hoan used the fashionable new motoring slang.

"Well, he slammed on the brakes at your appointment."

There was a pause. The subject was changed.

"So, Mr. Meinecke." Hoan sat back and waited to hear why the reporter was so inconveniently returning a one-minute phone call.

Meinecke said, "I spoke to the third district station this afternoon. Having been first on the scene, Judson Minor would have been a logical choice as acting detective on the Humphreys case. But they've taken him off it and assigned a new fellow named Rhodes, to whom no such favor is owed."

Hoan studied the bust of Lincoln on his desk. Shifted it a few degrees. Perhaps the direction of the Great Emancipator's gaze was a private code. Or a mnemonic device.

"An hour ago I read your piece on Minor. Hard to believe it's been ten years since he joined the force. Of course the negroes, or at least the followers of Mr. Josey, tend to vote Republican except when one of their own ... uh, I mean a member of their community ... runs and loses in a common council primary."

"Yes," Meinecke nodded. "Ten years. Hard to believe." Now he was the one whose eyes were on Lincoln.

"Needless to say," Hoan said, "the department would never stand for a negro being promoted. But. But acting detective. In a case that will sell a great many papers every time it is mentioned, from now until the killer is convicted."

Meinecke nodded again. "We have to do something with all that typesetting space, mercifully free of the phrase 'park board appointment.'"

"Your readers do prefer a good narrative to dry exposition. Long before Mr. Hearst had even heard my name, much less cursed it, as a young man I gobbled up the stories that he inspired your previously not at all yellow-tinted paper to start placing on the front page, day after day. I wonder, did they ever find even a stitch of that poor woman's clothing?"

"When she was found strangled in the river," Meinecke added to the Mayor's invention.

"Clutching a string of the world's most precious pearls."

"After her heart was broken by the millionaire gambler who had stolen them for her."

Hoan laughed. "I have been remiss in not following up, not adding to Minor's numbers in the people's force."

"Adding to his numbers," echoed Meinecke. "One plus one. But one plus zero can seem like a lot more than two, if put in the papers every day, or five times a day. Not to mention the radio."

"The principle of advertising. Repetition. And also, repetition, too." Hoan paused but it was clear he had not finished his thought. "You know, I am a great believer in the new science of public relations. That is why I travel so widely and often and see to it that papers all over the country, even the world, mention my name and with it, our esteemed city."

Meinecke got to the best part. "And a lot of people will be unaware of the distinction. In rank, I mean. They'll think acting detective and detective are the same thing. No promotion necessary. No further hires."

Hoan smoothed his mustache and looked thoughtfully at the ceiling. "Those poor boys in Scottsboro. A town whose name will never again be free from that taint, at least among the civilized half of the nation."

Meinecke leaned forward. "Yet Milwaukee, every day, could advertise its negro detective, a negro man not condemned by the state but acting on its behalf, in the most public way possible, assigned to solve the city's first cop-killing in six years."

"And a particularly lurid killing at that." Hoan put his feet back up. Continued to stare at the ceiling. "But. Let me tell you something. This is on the record. My father's best friend was one of the men unjustly accused and convicted, railroaded, in the Haymarket Square bombing in eighty-six. Funny, no one remembers the Bay View massacre in Milwaukee, the same week, in the very neighborhood where I now reside, when the governor ordered the state militia to shoot to kill any strikers who dared do anything made a capital offense by the governor's decree. And the extremely well-regulated militia did as instructed, killing and wounding among others innocent children. Innocent children."

Hoan rubbed his eyes, then kept them closed for a while. Meinecke knew better than to interrupt.

"Uncle Albert, I called him. Still in short pants. I was ... what is the word that is so au courant, thanks to the alienists? Oh yes. I was traumatized. Au courant or not, I really was, genuinely. A terrible experience. A loved one not just gone, not just dead, not just murdered, but murdered by the state itself, with the greatest premeditation." He got to the point. "I do not want this uneducated southern negro's incompetence to bring before the public a scapegoat, and your paper's advertisement of the suspect's identity to result in public damnation, never to be fully withdrawn and in the worst case leading unstoppably to a capital conviction in the court of public opinion, which the real courts, the ones with the nooses and electric chairs, may feel pressured to sustain."

Meinecke nodded and said: "Laubenheimer can tell Rhodes to investigate quietly. Pretend he's not on the case. Send Minor on wild goose chases to keep him out of the way. Even out of the state. All that matters is that he do something, anything, every day. And submit his reports with as much irrelevant detail as possible. Then it will be up to me to make his reports literature, to liven them up. All he has to do is give me the notes and I will supply the melody, harmony, rhythm, and lyrics."

"With the readers as your chorus. Well, Mr. Meinecke, I'll see what I can do. Although the chief is appointed for life and under the law I have no power over him, I am, after all, the most prominent member of the Policemen's Pension Board."

For the last time in Hoan's office that evening, Meinecke nodded.

17.

CHIEF OF POLICE JACOB G. LAUBENHEIMER, JR. was sitting in the back of an unmarked car on the way to the safety building when the call came over WPDK, the squad car radio station. In code. The mayor wanted the chief to give him a lift to St. James Episcopal. Hoan presumably had a car, since he daily commuted all the way from his cheap little frame house in the cheap little seventeenth ward. He must have wanted privacy. Privacy without the chief being seen at the city hall or the mayor at the safety building.

Laubenheimer was in a good mood, having received complaints all day from the federal dry agents whose cars he'd had ticketed the day before when, as they always and most aggravatingly did, the dozens of agents and attorneys and assistants had taken up every available parking space in the streets around the busy post office in the building that also housed their headquarters. Accustomed to immunity in inconveniencing an entire neighborhood, the feds had been quite surprised by the chief's long-contemplated Christmas gift, and demanded, one after the other, to have their tickets fixed. They had called the day before but were instructed to call back the next. On Christmas. Just to stick it to them a little more. Not wishing to waste an officer's time fielding calls, Laubenheimer assigned a civilian stenographer to man the phone and pretend, without saying so, that he was a member of the force. The stenographer wrote down every word of the complaints, which the chief read with pleasure on and off throughout the tiring day, spent tokenly conducting a huge manhunt that would lead nowhere.

Laubenheimer, the son of the former assistant chief of police, had himself begun his career as a stenographer, joining the force in 1893. He enjoyed a good working relationship with the mayor, who had appointed him a decade earlier after the resignation of his predecessor, in poor health following thirty-three years on the job. Given his own long service and, literally, pedigree, Laubenheimer was Hoan's only possible choice, but he never took advantage of the fact and Hoan appreciated it. And now, at fifty-eight, he was chief for life, earning an impressive $6500 a year and able to retire at any time on a full pension, his twenty-two years having been up even before the war. Given the pay cuts already incurred, the additional cuts inevitable in 1932, the proposed mandatory annual month off without pay, and the imminent scrip financing of the department's payroll, he estimated that within a year or two he would be making only fifty cents a day more while employed than he would on his pension, which was vested and thus not hostage to the depression. But if he retired he would no longer be able to do so many things he enjoyed, such as giving parking tickets to federal dry agents on Christmas Eve.

The driver made a dramatic U-turn and skidded back toward the river, narrowly missing a snowplow hauled by one of the many plow-horses cluttering up and shitting on Wisconsin Avenue. The car, its radio receiving calls to every patrol, eventually pulled up at the city hall beneath Hoan's second-floor office. The driver reached out to place the siren on the roof and then sounded it twice to bring the mayor to his window. Passersby, and there were a great many of them here in the heart of downtown, were unable to see the well-known Laubenheimer through the car's tinted windows.

"When he gets in, just drive around," Laubenheimer ordered. "Somewhere near Saint James."

"Ninth and Wisconsin it is," the driver said. He saw Hoan approach and got out and opened the rear door.

"Hello, Danny."

"Evening, Jake. Thanks for the lift at such short notice. Wouldn't want to keep the huddled masses, tired and poor, waiting to light up that big tree."

"An Episcopalian tree. Shouldn't you be at mass, guzzling consecrated wine like the good wet Catholic you are?"

"My wife attends mass at least one hundred and four times a year. Insofar as man and woman are one flesh, by church doctrine between the two of us we average weekly reverence."

The chief laughed and Hoan added: "Well you seem to be in a good mood. So different from your usual, uh, what is the word the press favors today. Ah. Your usual implacable self. Make that grimly implacable. Not to mention inscrutably determined."

The chief quoted the evening paper: "I'm like Sitting Bull."

"No fix-em, no fix-em," Hoan laughed, also quoting the parking ticket story, with its funny Indian jokes. "Nice little Christmas gift you gave our friends from the eastern prohibition district."

"I thought they had it coming. After they raided the saloon near the old soldiers' home on National Avenue. A street *named* National because the home is there, for chrissake. Lonely old men who fought for this country and now just want to gather at their local and have a shot and a beer together. Disgraceful. Granted, the West Milwaukee chief, without any help from the damn feds, was right to get rid of the gamblers over there, the bastards. Using a fixed roulette wheel to steal the money of those impaired old codgers. But the saloon. Pennyante poker games, at best. I suppose I can understand the feds making a show out of Wells Street. After all, a federal vice squad's got to have something to do. But why the veterans?"

"A hot tip, no doubt. Rather like the one you got about the master builders convention, or should I say masturbators."

This time the chief did not laugh. He was sick of the mayor's teasing over an admittedly imbecilic raid but one that was almost five years ago. A stag party with three strippers, a film projector, and half a dozen dirty reels. The city's convention bureau never let him forget it, either. A Sunday School city, they said, will lose business. And for a while it did. But an ambitious captain had gotten a false lead that gangsters were present, representing Chicago concrete interests, and Laubenheimer duly authorized the fishing expedition.

"And now," Hoan further teased, "I see you are being sued for sixty-five grand by the fellow with, allegedly, the stink bombs."

"Thug," the chief said. "Three times he's ruined the evenings of hundreds of people who spent their hard earned fifty cents to go to the pictures only to be chased out by stink bombs."

"Couldn't possibly be some kid, playing pranks. So you just had to raid that union office, based on a hunch. Take all their papers. Which are sure to contain a detailed ledger of stink bomb appropriations. A map with theaters circled."

"We know it was him. Union thug."

"Well, I suppose it is your business to know. But in this case, it is my business to doubt."

"Agree to disagree then."

"I suspected you were not a true comrade when you went to Madison recently to argue against the eight-hour day. Funny, I was just thinking about Haymarket Square. Almost fifty years ago and that's what all those protests were about, too. Only for them it was six not five eight-hour days a week. Eventually they won Saturdays. Those were the very first May Day parades, you know, back in eighty-six. All over the country. The biggest was led by my honorary uncle, Albert Parsons, in Chicago."

Laubenheimer knew the mayor was exaggerating with the uncle reference, made with tiresome frequency. Hoan's father had been the sole subscriber north of Chicago to something called *The Alarm*, a socialist rag published by one Albert Parsons, but otherwise the two men had been strangers. When Parsons decided to go on the lammister, he showed up unannounced at the elder Hoan's doorstep in Wisconsin and hid out with the family for six weeks before calmly walking into the notorious Haymarket trial during opening motions. He was hanged for conspiracy to commit murder, a charge even an implacable chief of police knew was absurd. None of the executed men had anything to do with the bombing but, because they had dared free speech, they were part of the bombing conspiracy. To speak in favor of the forty-eight hour week was to encourage the real conspirators, still unknown.

"I oppose the eight-hour day," the chief recited with no irony, "because our men are on salary, which is already inflated to assume occasional overtime. If we have to pay time and a half whenever they go beyond eight hours, they'll all find reasons to start harassing people just to keep the clock ticking."

"Yes. You were impressively frank on that point when testifying before the committee."

"I tried to think of something other than the truth to say, but I couldn't."

"Socrates could not have put that better. But the committee members' jaws must have dropped in a very satisfactory way. Imagine police harassing people merely to pad their own pockets."

"I think the Wickersham report has proven that if our force's only potential corruption is avoidable by not adopting the eight-hour day, we're doing pretty well."

"Of course you are, and I wouldn't think of suggesting otherwise. But there is always the occasional bad apple." Hoan tapped the chief on the knee. "And contrary to that figure of speech, sometimes it is useful to leave it in the barrel after it's found."

Hoan nodded toward the driver, whose ears were uncovered beneath his cap. And the chief said quietly, "Just avoid specifics."

Hoan lowered his voice in turn. "When someone else removes the bad apple, though, it means you are no longer the only one who knew it was in the barrel, and why it remained there."

"Which makes the investigation even more important."

"No. You're never going to discover who removed it. And looking for them may lead others to discover you had left it there, deliberately. And wonder why."

Hoan did not use the word "wiretaps." But Laubenheimer got the point. Wiretaps were, possibly, illegal. No one was really sure, except in the sense that you couldn't admissibly refer to them in court. But you wouldn't want to anyway, because then the public at large would know that you had granted yourself the right to spy on anyone for any reason you deemed valid. It was no different from sneaking into someone's house and photographing all their papers, going through their laundry, reading their kid's diary. Even the feds had been obliged to stage that big song and dance for the Wells Street raids, planting an undercover agent in all the saloons so they could pretend he was the source of their information.

Dropping the apple-barrel imagery, Laubenheimer said quietly: "Well, now he won't give us any more leads, not that we'd managed to get any yet, anyway. Too bad, too. He was getting reckless."

"Reckless. Apparently someone else thought so, as well." Hoan paused. Then changed the subject, probably so he could circle back to it without being so obvious. Odds were the driver wasn't paying attention. And the bursts of speech on the radio were loud and distracting. But it was best to be prudent.

"Speaking of your tribe," Hoan said at normal volume, "who so admire the implacable and inscrutable Sitting Bull. I phoned the morning paper today. Pulled some strings."

Laubenheimer didn't know what Hoan was getting at. "Oh, did you. Personally I never have to. Got em in my pocket. Every chance I get, in an interview or official release or appearance before a public committee, I name the press as our most important ally in the private sector. A truly faithful ally, always spreading the word to the public to be good and to despise those who aren't. And helping us out with their crackerjack investigations."

"Yes, the newspapermen do appreciate Sitting Bull's talent for public relations. Public relations are essential."

Hoan coughed and Laubenheimer waited.

"Well," the mayor continued, casually, "that boy. Minor. It's been ten years and you haven't hired another. And he'll never be promoted." Hoan coughed again. And then said: "But today I got an idea. I persuaded Meinecke to follow Minor's every move."

Laubenheimer remained baffled. "Every move doing what?"

"Every move as acting detective on the case. Meinecke didn't like me pressuring him, but eventually he agreed. Funny, he'd had the mistaken impression that a kid named Rhodes had been assigned to it. But, obviously, as you and I know, it's Minor's case."

For the first time, the chief sensed the driver might be listening. Anything about the colored cop got people's attention.

"It's Minor's case," the chief repeated tonelessly. "Because after a decade on the force he has acquired the skill to uncover every detail about Suthrin's murder."

"And as a southern negro with a high school diploma, and as a man always privy to the most sensitive operations, he is surely both intelligent enough and well enough informed to ..."

Hoan trailed off.

The chief said, "I wonder why Meinecke thought it was Rhodes. Clearly we shouldn't have anyone else at all on the case."

"I agree. And every resource should be provided Minor to follow his capacious brain wherever it might lead him. Even out of town for extended periods, if necessary. Meanwhile Mr. Meinecke will ... uh, report. He will write and arrange and highlight and dramatize every exciting detail of Minor's quixotic quest."

Laubenheimer smiled. Hoan knew that the driver would not understand the word "quixotic."

"Well, Dan, we both hope his quest will be exactly that."

"Chief, I've no doubt it will be. With Mr. Meinecke as his Cervantes. Minus the satire and parody."

Laubenheimer smiled again, but did not say what both of them were thinking. Often, Meinecke's articles were nothing but satire and parody, a fact lost on most of his readers. The puff piece on Suthrin had made the chief laugh out loud. "Well," he said, "I'll call the third and make sure they tell Minor to put as much detail as possible into his reports. I'm sure they are already planning, as you put it, to provide him with every resource."

"Of course they are," Hoan said. "They do that for every acting ..." Again Hoan trailed off.

"Detective," Laubenheimer finished.

18.

25 CENTS ADULTS ONLY CONTINUOUS ALL DAY BODY BEAUTIFUL LIVING MODELS 25 CENTS the marquee read above the entrance to the Gayety Theater on Third Street below Wells. Tickets had been seventy-five cents before the depression. But back then the place had been of higher quality and attracted even well-off men and their wives, or so its owners claimed whenever anybody asked. For the thousandth time, Meinecke contemplated with awe the fact that Mae West, as yet unknown, had appeared regularly at the joint when she was still in her teens. Now she was rumored to be the moll of Owney Madden, crime lord of Broadway and owner of the Cotton Club, when she wasn't balling Madden's former bagman, George Raft. Obviously, Meinecke had chosen the wrong profession.

The theater was next to a Thom McAn shoe store, its windows advertising a display of three-dollar shoes. But shoes were less relevant to some who frequented the Gayety than the fact that the McAn chain, named after a Scottish golfer once in vogue, had been an especially popular target for stick-up men all over the country ever since the small stores first appeared in Manhattan a decade earlier. Odd, Meinecke thought, that its Milwaukee owners should choose such a disreputable location, as if inviting theft. Maybe there was a connection he didn't know about. Money laundering?

Above the two businesses was a branch of the Lincoln Printing company, its windows advertising 20 XMAS CARDS $1 but not the French postcards Meinecke assumed the company made on the sly. Lincoln Printing was currently the plaintiff in a suit against Samuel Insull's empire of utility holding companies. Lincoln held all of eight-thousand-dollars' worth of notes from Insull, whose indebtedness amounted to three billion. The empire was going into receivership, setting a record for the largest bankruptcy in the history of American business. Its companies included Wisconsin Power and Light, which Mayor Hoan, plotting America's ruin, no doubt wanted the state to purchase. The empire's holdings, spread into the grids of thirty states, were often subsidiaries of subsidiaries of subsidiaries of subsidiaries, the sort of arrangement no one ever questioned before 1929, presuming it to be the product of higher business intelligence available only to the likes of Samuel Insull. Some 600,000 people, mostly employees, had lost their lives' savings when the company went under. So what else was new.

Intriguingly, Samuel's brother, a former president of the holding company, held a large block of Lincoln Printing shares and so in a sense was now suing himself. Meanwhile, Samuel had fled to Europe to avoid the wrath of one Harold L. Ickes, lawyer, an Illinois Republican who wanted to press charges. This was quite a great fall. During the twenties Insull had been powerful enough and rich enough and foolish enough to stage an opera in which his wife, who'd had no theatrical experience other than months of singing lessons, was cast to play the leading role. In an event well-known to Meinecke's circle, a newspaperman named Herman Mankiewicz had written a subtly devastating review of her performance, thus ending her career several years before the market's unsubtle review ended her husband's. At the time Meinecke had presumed Mankiewicz's career was over, too. But the reviewer went to Hollywood.

Meinecke wondered, not for the first time, why the scrolling lightbulb banner atop the marquee spelled burlesque with a k. Above the ticket booth, as if the fact weren't already stated well enough, an interior marquee said UNIQUE LIVE SEX SHOW. The booth had photographic cutouts of the heads of two women pasted on its lower half, in keeping with a dozen other headshots pasted around the entire entrance area, two of them forming the floppy ears on a board shaped like a bunny and itself covered with much smaller pictures of the girls in their outfits. On the other side of the entrance a conventional pasteboard featured similar full-body pictures of even more girls. So, one might conclude, there were lots and lots of underdressed girls behind the door. For twenty-five cents.

The theater's former owner, Charlie Fox, was currently serving a year and a day in Leavenworth for conspiracy to embezzle from a Wisconsin bank. He had been acquainted with a teller. Now the Gayety was run by Charlie's old partner, Joe Kraus.

Charlie Fox had once been celebrated in the press for having drag, meaning influence, with police and various judges on grand juries, regarding whom he was described as a friend and associate. The police usually left the Gayety alone, thanks in part to Charlie's friendship with so many cops, who as in all big cities tended to have a curious affinity for the managers of strip clubs. A few years back Charlie had gotten out of a bad liability case for crashing into the car of a married couple. At the scene a motorcycle cop ignored the couple. Instead, he concentrated exclusively on Charlie's report, creating the only evidence available should the case go to court. With the cops already sympathetic, Charlie hired, on the spot, Brainy Louis Saichek, one of a team of so-called ambulance chasers, affiliated lawyers or quasi-lawyers who kept close tabs on the small number of ambulances in town. When Charlie arrived at the police station Brainy Lou drew up an agreement, which the cop instructed the wife to sign. Obediently she didn't read it. She was later surprised to discover it stated, falsely, that her hospitalized husband had been drunk while behind the wheel. This was not the sort of event available for review by the Wickersham commission. Charlie ended up with only a $100 settlement against him. Recently Brainy Louis Saichek had been subpoenaed on criminal counts by a grand jury whose judges no longer included Charlie's friends and associates.

Charlie Fox had somehow also dodged a much bigger bullet. In the mid-twenties an ambitious alderman named John L. Bohn responded to the concerns of a number of church organizations who had sent their outraged spies to the Gayety and then complained. Meinecke still enjoyed what he'd written about the campaign's leading clergyman. "The Reverend accuses actresses at the Gayety Theater of an excess of indecency; we are glad to see he is a cleric who believes in all things in moderation." Somehow the complaints disappeared but John L. Bohn had managed to put himself on the map, and now was one of the mayor's staunchest opponents, rumored to have his eye on Hoan's office. But he was also known to have alienated the very alderman whom Meinecke had seen earlier that night at the city hall, Hoan's new ally, Samuel Soref of the sixth ward. As Meinecke now realized, Bohn's mayoral ambitions would most likely have to be put on hold even longer than the five years everyone presumed.

As for Charlie Fox, besides being in Leavenworth he had lately gone bankrupt. He claimed $140,000 in assets but owed $180,000, which included $6200 to the Franklin State Bank of Wisconsin. In an unrelated incident, the Franklin Bank's president, after learning he'd been called before a banking commission, told a friend he was sitting on a keg of dynamite. This cryptic statement was clarified when he was later found guilty of continuing to take deposits even after the bank was insolvent. The bank's depositors lost everything, as usual.

19.

MEINECKE PAID HIS QUARTER, and also slid forward a black button with a green piece of string tied through one of its holes. The kid in the booth pretended he didn't notice the button when he dropped it in the cash register. Meinecke went in to find a seat toward the back and to wait, for however long it took the button to make its way to the proper authorities and for one of their representatives to appear. Sometimes it was minutes, sometimes an hour or more. But no one else knew he was in the theater. The girl at the office would think he was still at the city hall, while anyone who'd seen him there would assume he'd gone home or back to work.

Inside there were several bars which sold soft drinks for exorbitant prices. Customers were encouraged to buy plenty of soft drinks for the girls. No one ever said why. The federal vice squad thus had no business there, which must have been frustrating for the dry agents, their onward march obstructed, the cross of Jesus unempowered by the sadly alcohol-centric Volstead Act.

When Meinecke sat down it was between shows. In the aisles a kid was hawking bags of candy kisses, small wrapped pieces of taffy, claiming that some bags contained a valuable prize. As usual the first person who bought a bag, a ringer in the front rows, found a swell watch inside. And then no one else found any other prizes.

Soon there appeared against a painted street scene two typical vaudeville comedians in the Mutt and Jeff style, both Yiddish, doing some ancient routine which the rubes tolerated while waiting for the girls to come back onstage. The audience of young ethnic working men laughed occasionally, in spite of themselves, but otherwise sat passive and expressionless. After a few minutes of schtick one of the crowd began to clap his hands rhythmically and soon was joined by the rest, quietly at first but then increasing in volume. When the clapping became too loud for the comics to be heard, the two did a final pratfall and left the stage as a parade of almost naked girls took the runway and the clapping stopped.

These were not the skinny flat-chested girls of Ziegfeld but robust farmers' daughters from around the state, in rude health as they inched beyond the age of consent. Most of them no longer bobbed their hair, or never had, a fact of interest to the reporter's eye but undoubtedly not noted by the crowd.

Eventually the featured performer took center stage and with exotic musical accompaniment began a cooch dance, because of which she wore brown foundation on her face and was advertised and supposedly dressed as Babylonian. The more agile of the girls surrounding her were able to imitate if not mirror her belly's undulations, while the rest, some not even smiling, just stood around to capture any wandering eye. When the cooch dancer's last veil lay on the floor and she showed her breasts and G-string, she stood still in keeping with the state regulation that bare breasts onstage must not be disturbed by any movement, as though to acknowledge that paintings of them in art museums were acceptable to polite society but one must go no further. This being Christmas, however, she eventually gave a few shimmies, knowing that on the holidays the law was more indulgent, or so Meinecke presumed. Nevertheless the men remained impassive, staring with hunger, until the girls left the stage and the rhythmic clapping resumed.

An illustrated curtain fell over the comics' street-corner backdrop and replaced it. Meinecke knew from the two-dimensional urns and columns and Egyptian statues that he was about to see, yet again, the Anthony and Cleopatra sketch, revived every couple of years with new jokes. One of the comics, the tall one, reappeared in a toga and knelt before the cooch dancer, who'd taken up her place on a divan. She now wore a slinky short dress whose expansive decolletage reached below her navel, allowing her torso to be fully exposed every time she leaned forward. The other girls drifted across the stage in twos and threes in whatever skimpy period costumes were at hand. Diminuitive Julius Caesar wore a tin helmet and smoked a cigar when he appeared on a bicycle from stage left and smacked Anthony across the ass with his sword. After a few comedic routines, during which the cooch dancer broke character by laughing and mugging at the crowd, a chorus of Egyptian slave girls assembled around the trio. The small jazz band in the pit, having previously announced Caesar's entrance with fanfare, struck up a brief overture and the cast broke into a call and response minstrel song, allowing the slave girls to wiggle with raised hands. At the end of the song, Cleopatra requested the asp, which she called a wassup. Receiving a gold box with a serpent painted on its side, she removed a foot-long dildo shaped like a rigid snake. Then she went much further in being bitten by the asp than Meinecke had ever seen before. This was, indeed, the depression. It astounded Meinecke to observe the cooch girl perform an act so ribald in a public theater, apparently without fear of a raid the next day. The authorities, it seemed, just didn't care anymore. Not when, say, 600,000 people, more than the entire population of Milwaukee, had lost everything thanks to one fully clothed and formerly celebrated crook named Insull. Not when those 600,000 people had much bigger things to worry about than whether a woman masturbated on stage in front of two hundred first-generation laborers, a third of them without work. And more relevant, not when half the men in the crowd might any day go fascist and the other half red. Best to let them watch Cleopatra shove an asp indecently, and hope they dispersed without any police presence to ruin their evening and inflame their anger.

20.

JOE KRAUS WALKED UP THE AISLE FROM THE STAGE and scratched his nose when he reached the row in front of Meinecke. Both men pretended not to see the other. Joe turned and headed through the uncrowded row as though looking for something on the floor. Then he walked back down the next aisle toward the stage and disappeared through an employees-only door.

Meinecke waited a minute or two, watching the juggler who had replaced Anthony and Cleopatra, then left the theater.

As always, the kid in the ticket booth let him pass by and walk a few steps.

"Excuse me, buddy, just a minute."

Meinecke turned around and went to the booth.

"Someone brought this in to the lost and found."

The kid returned the black button, its green string replaced by a red one which in turn was tethered to a key, numbered 8. Under the button there was a twenty dollar bill, a bit less than what Meinecke made in two days as a reporter, after taxes. A down payment, the rest contingent on whatever followed.

The red string meant red light, as in district. Meinecke strolled casually through the cold, heading four blocks north on Third Street to Charles Crupi's chicken shack. Charles had returned in 1930 from a six-month stint in the house of correction for bootlegging, but soon adapted and set up shop as a pimp.

One of Meinecke's many services had been the elevation of Charles Crupi's brother, Vince, to the status of Milwaukee's Vice Lord. The smallest of small-time players, Vince Crupi had owned the Green Light, a low-rent five-woman brothel on the east bank of the river just south of downtown.

The place had suffered a routine raid of the kind that usually led to the payment of some fines and then business as usual. Everyone accepted such things as an alternative form of property tax. But acting as a middleman in order to ingratiate himself with Joey Vallone, corn syrup wholesaler, unlucky Vince had just received a substantial amount of heroin. He was supposed to hide the stuff for an hour or two and wait for the pick-up. But almost immediately after the package arrived, an event unknown to the cops, the routine raid occurred and poor Vince was standing there, literally holding the bag. Meinecke's role in the situation was not conceived until several days later.

Both the cops and the press always ignored Joey Vallone, corn syrup wholesaler. People had to get their booze from somewhere, after all, and the large number of one-off stills was not enough to satisfy the demand nor reliable in terms of efficient distribution. So Vallone's name had never once appeared in any of the city's papers. The Milwaukee Boss answered to Chicago, which in turn answered to New York, even before the recent reorganization of the national commission into five families. Vallone kept his men in line and there were very few Chicago-style gangland killings in Milwaukee, nor much armed robbery except in retribution or, an inspired Meinecke now imagined, as a form of money laundering facilitated by the likes of Thom McAn.

Boss Vallone's protection racket controlled the third ward and certain zones elsewhere, such as downtown Wells Street, but that was just an aspect of modern business practices and of no concern to anyone other than those involved. The corn syrup wholesaler ran a lot of gambling and prostitution but stayed away from the drug traffic. In arranging the Green Light pick-up, like Vince Crupi he had been acting just as a middleman for the heroin in question, in this case as a favor to Al Capone, then still very much at large and occasionally enjoying the country life in Brookfield, Wisconsin, where he kept tabs on Vallone and collected his cut.

The feds appreciated Milwaukee's protection racket. It made their jobs easier. Vallone's organization kept track of every still in the county, and most of those in the state. When an alky fell too far behind in his payments to the so-called tippler rings, and other means of persuasion were exhausted, the protection now being withheld took the form of giving the feds a surefire tip. Cooperatively, the agents went in and destroyed all of the alky's expensive capital, and fined and jailed him to boot. The destruction of stills made frontpage news for the feds and no one's legs had to be broken.

But with so many exciting gangster stories coming out of Chicago, it was bad public relations for the Milwaukee police to avoid all judicial interaction with local organized crime, which everyone knew existed because how could it not. So in exchange for forgetting about the heroin, punishable by a very long sentence, the cops offered Vince Crupi a deal and requested Meinecke's assistance. Vince would be touted in the papers, absurdly, as the Vice Lord of Milwaukee, and then go to prison for a couple of years before being deported. In the meantime, he would continue to make news via Meinecke by seeking gubernatorial pardons or trotting out his weeping wife or describing prison parties and the bribery of unnamed prison guards or saying he feared for his life if he were to be deported to Il Duce's Italy, where he was acquainted with no one, absolutely no one. And again and again he would be described as the former Vice Lord, with no further information to substantiate the fictitious title now accepted as fact. The police would appear to have gone to the very top of the organization, to the Lord himself, and so would be off the hook for a couple of years while continuing to leave alone the discreet and often helpful corn syrup wholesaler, who in 1930 had gone so far as to finance the campaign of one of his underlings, Angelo Guardalabene, for third ward alderman, though as it turned out even Joey couldn't buy enough votes for that. But Angelo was related to two of Vallone's predecessors as Boss, the late Vito and Pete Guardalabene, so the money, as goodwill, was well spent.

With notorious, infamous Vice Lord Vincent Crupi put away, the occasional gang killings that did occur could be attributed to so-called beer wars, in which one supposedly wildcat brewer would be done in by another whose smallfry territory was, again supposedly, being encroached. In August, for example, a gangster from Milwaukee was shotgunned through the window of a shuttered restaurant in Racine where he and his companions were fashioning a bomb out of three sticks of dynamite, intending to beat their rivals to the punch. As usual the press called him a wildcatter, there being no organization he could possibly belong to because the papers never mentioned any. A while later, somebody was blasted while parked in a car owned by the landlord of the very same Racine restaurant, a place that had been slated to become a beer depot. This time neither the shooter nor the bloody victim was found, the latter having fled the scene after telling eyewitnesses to scram if they knew what was good for them.

The car's owner, landlord Dominick Zizo, at the time sitting home with his wife, soon got out of the beer depot business, which as far as the papers were concerned he'd never been involved with in the first place. It was just a coincidence that he owned the shutdown restaurant three blocks away, where the other guy had been killed, and clearly someone had borrowed his car without telling him and had then been the victim of a random shooting.

Meinecke's stories said so.

Similarly, Tony Kuzmanovich, a first-generation Serbian known as TK, had been beheaded in his car by a sawed-off shotgun just past the viaduct into Wauwatosa on Wisconsin Avenue, conveniently bothering the Sheriff's Department with the investigation and giving the Milwaukee police a break. TK once owned the Paradise Gardens resort, which cost thirty grand to build. After it was closed due to TK's eight-month visit to a state penitentiary, he set up the Idlewild, another posh resort frequented only by lawabiding citizens, and he also opened four downtown Milwaukee speakeasies and a restaurant. TK was worth more than a hundred grand, maybe twice that. The day before his death he'd made a quick sightseeing trip up to Canada, or so his wife claimed. He was actually seeking out a cheaper rum-running connection than the one offered by Capone. Within hours of returning from the daytrip he discovered he was being stalked by four men in a touring car with Illinois plates. They were bold enough to dine in TK's swanky restaurant, the Tee-Kay, in downtown Milwaukee. TK made desperate phone calls to not one but two district captains, but was ignored. His killers were never found. It had been a robbery gone wrong, though none of the eight hundred dollars TK carried was taken, not even the nine significantly clutched in his hand and used to wipe up some of his brains, nine dollars being the Canadian discount per unit.

Meinecke did his part by later writing an article about how very little money bootleggers actually made, using TK as the prime example. After all, Meinecke reported, people like TK didn't leave great fortunes in probate. That their money might be in large bundles of unprobated high-denomination bills was a possibility which Meinecke, in his innocence of such things, hadn't dreamt of suggesting. He and his readers knew that crime didn't pay.

As for the third ward, the Italian ghetto, gang killings were almost impossible to solve there or even understand as such, due to the code of silence. One of the few killers who was caught, a fellow known as Crossed Eyed Jack, had pleaded self-defense for openly shooting another model citizen, colorfully named Dago Pete. Crossed Eyed Jack said he'd driven away from a pool room argument but then his path had been blocked by a passing train and so he was obliged to turn around and drive back, only to see Dago Pete waving a gun in the road. A dozen eyewitnesses, including Mike Vitucci, known as the King of the Third Ward, backed up the gunman's story, all of them having seen the train. But the local station master insisted no train had been anywhere near the area at the time. Actually, Dago Pete had been working for a rival would-be operator who was unwisely trying to establish his own tippler ring racket, demanding $300 each from various local brewers for not turning them in to the feds, and the ranks had closed around Crossed Eyed Jack at the insistence of the King of the Third Ward, Mike Vitucci, vassal to the emperor who'd ordered the murder in the first place, Joey Vallone, corn syrup wholesaler. Despite the best efforts of Vitucci's circle, Crossed Eyed Jack got twenty years, in payment of an otherwise unpayable debt.

Meinecke's article characterized the event as a drunken pool room argument that had ended in a random tragedy. He was duly rewarded.

21.

CHARLES CRUPI WASN'T AT THE FRONT DESK of his hourly motel, so Meinecke had to wonder who'd been assigned as his contact. Rather than talk to the underling in front, he went directly to room eight, removing his winter gear on the way and pocketing it or draping it over his arm. He knocked.

An unrecognizable voice behind the door answered. "If you got the key, use it."

Meinecke unlocked the door and saw a pair of legs in well-tailored pants and expensive shoes stretched out across the cot. The inner latch prevented him from looking in any further. He didn't want to announce himself. Whoever the guy was, he must have known it was Meinecke at the door, since both of them had just been sent there.

The legs slung off the cot and the guy stood up, still blocked from view. His hand appeared and undid the latch, briefly closing the door and opening it again. Meinecke stepped inside but before he could turn fully to his left to see around the door he got popped, hard, in the mouth, and then immediately got popped again by the other fist and he fell, spraining his right wrist against the floor. The door slammed and the guy kicked him in the ribs, hard enough to make a point but definitely not with full strength. Meinecke's straw hat fell off and an open newspaper came down over his head. It was the whole newspaper so it didn't tear. The force behind the paper smashed Meinecke's face into the ground, where he was left with the newspaper still spread out on top of his head like a nun's habit. He did not dare look up.

"You think that was funny, what you wrote?" the guy yelled. "That bit about, He always had his nose in everybody's business? That your kind of a funny joke?"

Meinecke was kicked again as the guy screamed: "And you quoted his fuckin grandparents?"

He recognized the voice. Alby Tusa, fight promoter. The burlesque joint put on fights twice a week and Alby's crew handled both the substantial wagering as well as the occasional fixed fights, lucratively mixed in with the rest. Which meant that Alby Tusa was also a blackmailer, specializing in successful boxers who were due to take a fall whether they wanted to or not. Among other things, his crew also managed the policy racket in the colored neighborhoods, where ten-cent insurance policies were sold every day as a very slightly more legal or less illegal variety of the numbers game. And like everybody in the racket, his crew did a lot of loansharking across all territories.

Alby paraphrased very loud another quote from the Suthrin article: "And you say, He was always helpin out on cases that ain't his. He was always doin research on crimes that ain't his. That some kinda keystone cops shit for you? You writin for the fuckin Marx Brothers now?"

Alby gave him another kick, about as rough as the others. A former boxer himself, Alby would perhaps have been recognizable simply by the fact that he conducted this assault so skillfully. Meinecke wasn't hurt much, but he was scared. He remained on his hands and knees wearing his afternoon-edition habit. His winter clothes were still bundled down his left arm.

"And then you got, You're tellin me that guy was only twenty-one when he joined. And, That ain't possible, how could he'd of only been twenty-one, he seemed so much older. Whoa, I am laughin so hard I feel like rippin your fuckin head off. So that is just fuckin hilarious to you? So goddam fuckin funny that you couldn't fuckin bring yourself to just leave it the fuck out of your dumbshit comedy-routine newspaper story?"

Alby smacked him against the head, through the top of the newspaper. That one really stung and Meinecke felt dizzy.

Meinecke heard Alby plop back down on the cot. Apparently the beating was over.

Not even breathing hard, Alby lowered his voice. "Okay. You can talk. What you got to say for yourself."

Meinecke was no fool. In the universe of utterances only one was permissible.

"I'm sorry, Alby. Very sorry. Really. It was a fucking stupid thing to do."

"You bet your fuckin ass it was a stupid thing to do. Your goddam little pissant wink wink, wink fuckin wink. You think we can't read? Huh? You think we're just a bunch of dumbshit dagos just got off the boat and we don't know how to read your funny vaudeville stories in the biggest fuckin paper in town? And, listen, you kraut scumbag. Do you really think that nobody but the guys in our thing noticed it?"

Alby had begun to yell again but he quieted down and finished.

"You fuckin moron. If you and him ain't of managed the Wells Street tip-off you'd be dead right now, too."

Meinecke was confident he would not have been killed for his three-paragraph joke in the Suthrin story, no matter what. If that option had been discussed, even though decided against, Alby's beating would not have been so gentle. In fact, Meinecke was gratified to hear that Joey Vallone's gang still appreciated the Wells Street tip. That bit of intelligence had allowed them to demand, without explanation, a large premium added to the protection prices the week before the raid. Just for fun, they'd made the premium optional, quote unquote based on the ability to pay, and only five joints had been smart enough to get the joke and come through.

Those five were the ones that shut down just before the raid, thanks to police gossip about places to avoid frequenting that week. And thus to Suthrin's information relayed through Meinecke. The day after the raid, the extra premium in the protection fees was made permanent for every full-service speakeasy in the city, like those formerly on Wells Street and the new joints that would replace them. From then on, everybody had ability to pay.

Meinecke repeated: "I'm sorry, Alby. I really am."

"You can get up."

Meinecke looked below the edge of the newspaper at Alby Tusa, aging Alby the Vallone capo with his squashed nose and his black toupee and his expensive suit, reclining on the whorehouse cot, his hands now folded behind his head and his legs crossed at the ankles. Alby nodded toward the only other piece of furniture in the hourly room. Meinecke removed the paper habit and got up and grabbed his hat and took the chair, relieved he didn't have to stand. He set his things on the floor beside him but put his hat back on so he wouldn't look like too much of a beggar. The gangsters weren't big on pathos.

"Okay," Alby said. "So now we are square. You made a dumb little mistake and you paid for it with a dumb little beating. Piddu is a big believer in proportionality."

Piddu was the family's name for Vallone. Anyone else who ever used it ended up regretting having done so. Regular people called him Joey because that was his name and that was how things were done, and only a dope would call him Mister. If they wanted to show affection or suggest intimacy, they called him Padrone, because he was the highest of the padroni.

Meinecke avoided rubbing his fat lip or massaging his ribs. "Well, I have good news for our friend."

"So spit it out. Along with that tooth I have loosened."

"They were going to assign this genius new kid from Madison to be the ..."

"Yeah, Rhodes. We already got some stuff on him."

"Well, that would've been a bad thing, for him to get the case. So I talked to the mayor and ..."

"You fuckin what?" Alby took his hands from behind his head in preparation, but did not sit forward.

Meinecke flinched a little.

"No, no. It was good. Nothing to worry about. Completely out of left field. I didn't say anything about Suthrin. I pitched the mayor on the idea of putting that colored boy Minor in charge, instead. Rhodes is off the case. As far as the mayor is concerned, what I said to him had nothing to do with Suthrin at all. Could have been any dead cop, or any big murder story whether or not it was a cop. I said it would help with the sixth ward vote if there was lots of press about a colored detective."

Now Alby did sit forward.

"Why. The fuck. Would we want. Lots. Of press."

Meinecke gulped in spite of himself, and tried not to wipe the sweat from his face as his bowels contracted.

"That's the whole point. Nothing will come of it but false leads. We're talking a southern colored boy who barely finished high school. He doesn't know a damn thing about anything, except how to walk a beat in Bronzeville and bust muggers and pimps. But these stories will make it look like, I mean, I will make it look like the greatest investigation in history is taking place, with no stone unturned. And so that will be the end of it. A dead end. When it's over, not one new thing will be known about Suthrin. Or about, um. About whoever did it."

Alby smiled, but not nicely. "Oh, so you think you know who did it." Alby squinted his eyes. "Is that what you're tellin me."

"No, no, I ... I didn't mean to imply ..."

"Because you know what. I think you was the one that did it."

Meinecke stared with terrified incomprehension.

But fortunately Alby Tusa wasn't serious: "I think you and Suthrin had a little lover's quarrel, cause you wanna cut down from givin him four blow jobs a day to just three."

Meinecke tried to laugh at Alby's wit but his throat was too dry. He had never been assaulted by the gangsters before, much less ambushed. In fact, he had never before had a capo as his contact on this sort of venture. This was an even bigger deal than he'd realized. Good thing he'd gotten in touch with them on day one.

Alby laughed at his own joke and leaned back again. "Anyways, that's two guys we lost on the inside this week. Benjy the fink just got taken down for bribery."

Meinecke knew that Benjamin G. Finke, incredibly his actual name, was a corrupt agent in the eastern prohibition district, but that was about it.

"Really. That's news to me."

"They're still grillin him. Haven't pressed charges yet, so word's not out. But we didn't put nearly as much work into him as Suthrin. The feds are one thing, but it's fuckin impossible to get a guy inside Laubenheimer's squeaky clean machine. That's why Piddu always considered Suthrin one of his most brilliant projects. Dates back to when he was still just Vito Guardalabene's underboss."

Of course Meinecke remembered this all too well, and hoped his own contribution was in turn vividly remembered. But he didn't want to let the conversation stray, because he didn't know where it might lead. And he didn't want it to lead to him getting slugged again. So he said, "Well okay, Alby, that's all I've got."

He waited to be given his leave. But Alby was busy cutting the end off a cigar. The image was not a welcome one. Meinecke's head pounded as Alby lighted the cigar at leisure. Then the capo sat there without looking at him and smoked long enough to get an ash, which he tapped onto the cot.

Still staring straight ahead, as if talking to himself, Alby nodded and said: "I like the part about the mayor. Cops will think it was his idea, or the chief's. Or maybe a dumbass captain or lieutenant. Anybody but us, I figure. Okay. Go see the kid up front. Tell him I said to give you number three."

Meinecke immediately gathered his things and left the room and hurried down the hall, relieved by every step closer to the street outside. He didn't stop to put on his overcoat.

The kid at the desk was unfamiliar. He let his gun show under his coat and smirked at Meinecke's fat lip.

Meinecke wanted to limit conversation and get out as fast as possible, but he was struck by a thought that worried him. Referring to Alby's very loud volubility in room eight, he said: "Don't you think somebody else probably heard that?"

"We cleared the place out while you was ooglin the titties."

Meinecke got it. Of the half-dozen contact locations, each signified by a different color of string on the black button, the chicken shack was the best place to scream at Meinecke and beat him up. It was a simple matter to roust all the fifteen-minute and thirty-minute johns.

"Oh, right. Well, I'm supposed to tell you, uh, number three."

The kid nodded and took five twenties from the cash register. "Add this to the twenty from before and put it all on the bum, the next time the yid is slated for the third card."

The bum could have been anybody, but the yid was a middleweight named Hiram Snyder, undefeated after twenty or thirty bouts. He fought a lot but he might not be scheduled for an evening's third bout, specifically, till next month or six months from now. Or maybe never, if Alby was playing a joke in retaliation for those in the Suthrin article.

"Wait till an hour or so before the fight and use a bookie from the commission."

By commission, the kid didn't mean the national crime commission, recently formed after a truce was called in the Castellammarese wars. He meant the grocery produce commission on lower Broadway in the third ward, where Joey's wholesale business was located among dozens of other fruit and vegetable vendors.

The kid explained: "By that late in the betting we will have it up to twelve to one. Lock that in. Don't get greedy. Not a dime more than a hundred twenty. And don't get any other ideas. Keep it to yourself."

So if it wasn't a joke, Alby must have been very pleased indeed with the promotion of Judson Minor to acting detective in the Suthrin investigation. Twelve to one meant a $1440 payday. More than Meinecke made on the newspaper in five months.

"Too bad about Suthrin," the kid said.

Meinecke grunted. He wanted to leave.

"But," the kid added, "they say prohibition's ending in a coupla years. So, say la vee, I guess."

Meinecke turned around and headed for the door. When his hand reached the knob the kid barked: "Hey, buddy. You wait just one fuckin minute."

Meinecke froze. Then craned his neck to see what the fuck else was in store.

"Merry Christmas," the kid said. Which gave him a good laugh.

Part Three

December 26, 1931

<h1 style="text-align:center">22.</h1>

PATROLMAN VIC HORSTMANN TOOK A SEAT in the collapsible bleachers and studied the dance floor, a tiled linoleum rectangle the size of an Olympic swimming pool covering most of the former warehouse of Midwest Novelty Golf Supply, now defunct after several years of manufacturing humorous decorations and other equipment for the incredible number of Tom Thumb golf courses that had sprouted in the late twenties and then died in the early thirties.

The big flip cards on the wall read 179 and 92, tallying respectively the dance marathon's total hours and the number of couples still on their feet. Horstmann didn't want to make a scene so he let the competition continue until the break, due in twelve minutes. Also, he wanted to get off his own feet for a little while, having spent most of the past six hours canvassing every all-night drinking establishment and dive and pool hall he could find as well as, eventually, all the early morning taxi stands and streetcars and a couple of churches plus two Catholic boarding schools that made the kids get up at five in the morning for breakfast at five-fifteen, even on the Saturday after Christmas.

Horstmann was carrying photographs of Jacob and Ernst Odenwald, the two eldest of the boys who lived and usually worked at Mother's Hubbard Penny Kitchen. He was one of a handful of guys on night patrol assigned specifically to find the two boys, or rather men, both of them several years out of high school.

He had finally gotten a lead while on the route thirty-five trolley, which he'd ridden from Vliet Street to Park Hill Avenue in the part of town known as Pigsville, showing the kids' pictures to everyone who boarded. Empty except for people headed for work on a Saturday, at one stop the trolley picked up a dozen typical fares trailed by a haggard couple who sat down and, leaning against each other, literally fell asleep before Horstmann finished with the other new passengers, surveying them while waving the Odenwalds' photos. Hoping he wouldn't have to make a bust for public intoxication, he awakened the attractive pair, who possessed what Horstmann knew was called movie star good looks, and they immediately recognized Ernst, who had buck teeth and a crew cut and wore big hornrimmed glasses with thick black frames.

Horstmann was gratified, and relieved, on two counts.

First, the couple wasn't drunk, so there would be no arrest and no extra paperwork. They were worn out from one hundred and seventy-eight hours of a dance marathon whose judge had just eliminated them following their last-place finish in a relay race. They said they traveled around the midwest to just about every dance marathon, and claimed to make a living at it but today had temporarily reached their limit.

Second, they said Ernst was one of the marathon's remaining competitors. Horstmann did the very simple math and realized Ernst could not possibly have been Suthrin's murderer, someone who had escaped less than a day and a half ago. It was an unbeatable alibi.

In other words, Horstmann had gotten lucky. He had found his man, or at least one of them, meaning he would be given credit for a job well done. Even better, there was no need to rush back to the station, because Ernst was neither the guilty party nor likely to know anything about what had occurred in the alley behind Mother's.

Good thing he'd caught that trolley.

So now the patrolman sat cooling his heels in the bleachers with two hundred other spectators, who had evidently been there all night, and watched Ernst drag his homely young partner around the floor. Thanks to the couple on the trolley he'd learned that the marathon took a fifteen-minute break at three-quarters past the hour, every hour, right after a five-minute relay race that heightened the sport's gratifying sadism and sometimes, if desirable, served as an elimination round.

Once the race began, Horstmann was impressed by Ernst's stamina. The kid was in first place the whole way, making up for the exhaustion of his partner and ensuring they would finish in at least the middle of the pack and so avoid possible elimination.

Horstmann had never seen a dance marathon before and was surprised both by the size of the crowd and its attentiveness. Then he took a closer look at the people in the bleachers and recognized at least ten inveterate gamblers, guys routinely nabbed in sporting parlor busts. Undoubtedly, book was made anew at the beginning of every round, offering hourly betting opportunities in a season without horse races except on the radio, and, unlike the waking-hours radio, at all hours of the day.

But there were also quite a few old ladies, lonely spinsters who, he soon learned, took a maternal interest in this or that couple and tended to them as soon as the fifteen-minute break began. In addition, a few dozen college-age girls, clutching signed photographs of contestants sold for a dime at jhe concession stand, cheered on the most handsome and well-built men, cool lotharios who seemed to know a thing or two about how to attract and sustain an audience. About three-fourths of the crowd, in fact, were women, shockingly staying out all night to keep their fifty-cent ticket. No wonder the mayor wanted to shut down the event, and was encouraged to do so by the Milwaukee Women's League.

Many of the couples wore signs indicating sponsorship by businesses both local and national. The marathon was broadcast during some of the late afternoon and evening hours, when a small orchestra played instead of a phonograph or a radio. Several stations in Wisconsin and Illinois took turns in their coverage. The sponsored couples were thus employees, hired billboards, and got paid whether they won or not. The final three couples would receive large cash prizes. The final twelve, merchandise. And according to the pair on the trolley, everybody who entered the marathon got snacks every hour as well as three meals per day, eaten at a chest-high buffet while standing up and dancing, which meant moving their feet. There were probably worse ways to make a living in the depression.

The relay race ended and the truncated hour was over. Most of the people in the stands got up to stretch their legs and several, including Horstmann, headed for the dance floor. As far as he knew, Ernst had no reason to want to avoid him. Nevertheless the kid turned around and went the other way as the uniformed officer approached. But it wasn't clear he'd seen Horstmann, since most of the contestants headed the same direction. Meanwhile, the kid's dance partner had removed her shoes and reclined on the floor while having her feet massaged by one of the old ladies, whose purse was conspicuously open.

Horstmann passed by a small kitchen and then the men's room entrance, clearly not Ernst's destination, and followed the kid into a temporary backstage area walled off by a curtain and in turn separated into an avenue of forty or so little cubicles. And there, to his surprise, he lost the trail. Irritated, he checked one partition after another, irritating in turn the occupants, packed three or four apiece on cots as if the backstage were a barracks.

Finally, after he passed the last cubicle, he saw a door beside it marked FIRE. Ignoring the possibility of an alarm he pushed the door open into the early morning daylight, reflected bright by snow. There was no alarm, so the kid must have gone out that way. Footprints in the snow led around the corner of the warehouse and Horstmann followed the trail. Next to the warehouse, three small houses trisected the yard and the footprints continued between two of them. The cop assumed that other marathon facilities were located in one of the houses so he felt no need to hurry.

But when he reached the alley he thought his eyes were playing tricks on him. Past the houses and on the other side of the street stood not one but two kids with crew cuts, buck teeth, and big black glasses. They were the same height and dressed identically.

The patrolman stopped and stared at them, trying both to make sense of the situation and also to figure out which of the two was Ernst. While passing each other the boys did a strange thing with their hands, slapping their palms together above their heads with their arms bent at the elbow and at right angles to their bodies. Then they began to head in opposite directions. And then one of them saw Horstmann. At first paralyzed by the sight of the cop across the street and down the alley, after a moment the boy turned and ran, followed at once by his twin.

Instinctively, Horstmann took off after them, but the way was narrow and icy and snowbound and full of junk. Before he'd cleared the alley his boot caught under some hidden object beneath the snow and he went flying chin-first into the side of one of the brick houses. In the attempt to break his fall he straightened his free leg and jammed it hard. The lightning bolt of pain in his knee distracted him at first from the considerable damage done to his face by the brick wall. He rolled on his back in the alley shrieking and cradling his knee in both hands. By the time he was able to stand up and lean against the wall he knew Odenwald and his twin were long gone.

23.

PATROLMAN VIC HORSTMANN LIMPED HIS WAY IN PAIN back to the marathon warehouse, finding the fire door unlocked. He was intensely angry and made no attempt to restrain his voice as he yelled, "This is the police. I am looking for the girl who was dancing with Ernst Odenwald. Anyone who attempts to hide her from me will be arrested."

A nurse in a lowcut outfit poked her head and substantial breasts out of a cubicle and said quietly, "She's down there. Stop shouting. They're trying to sleep another few minutes."

The nurse, an unusually attractive girl with bobbed black hair and bright red lipstick, and certainly not hired by the marathon for her medical expertise, led him to the cubicle where Odenwald's partner slept along with three other women.

Horstmann shook the girl roughly but she didn't awaken.

"By this stage that doesn't always work," the nurse said. "Here, let me do it." She removed a vial of smelling salts from her pocket and waved it under the girl's nose.

The girl gagged and coughed and said, "Twelve minutes already?" She focused her eyes and saw the uniform and badge. "Say, what's this all about? I ain't got nothin to say to no cop."

Horstmann put on his toughest expression, which wasn't hard to do considering how bad his knee hurt, not to mention his face. "You got plenty to say, sister. Like for starters, how come your partner's got an identical twin and they both just run for their lives when they seen me."

"They did?" she said, but then caught herself: "I mean, he did? He ran away? How am I supposed to do the next round?"

"Like I said, him and his twin both ran. And you got some explainin to do."

"I don't know nothin about no twin. I'm tellin you, I got nothin to say. I was just mindin my own business."

The nurse put her hand on Horstmann's shoulder and said confidingly, "I think you better talk to Eddy. Also, you look banged up pretty bad. I should take care of your face."

"Just get me a coupla ice packs. I don't need to talk to nobody else. I think I can get all the information I need from this dame."

The nurse smiled at him and winked. "I've done a hundred of these things, all over the country. Now that she's disqualified, that girl will be dead to the world any minute. You'd do better to let her get some sleep before you talk to her. Talk to Eddy instead. Believe me, he'll tell you everything you need to know."

In the time it took the nurse to say this, the girl, Odenwald's partner, passed out. Horstmann surrendered and said OK and sat down in a chair beside the cot, massaging his knee. Before the nurse left she handed him a damp cloth and he wiped the blood from his face. Then he realized that in his dazed and furious condition he hadn't made his way to a telephone. He limped into the warehouse past the backstage curtain and spotted a phone on the MC's stand. Without explaining himself, he grabbed the phone and called the station to give Odenwald's last known whereabouts. At the same time the nurse returned with a short stocky middle-aged guy wearing a brown felt cap and biting down on an unlit half-smoked cigar.

Horstmann hung up and the guy shook hands with him and said, "Edward Buer, Manhattan Bottling Works." He pronounced bottling with two syllables. "Call me Eddy. We should go backstage where we got some privacy. I told the MC to give the kids an extra ten minutes, so we can talk in peace." Eddy led Horstmann back behind the curtain and said, "Listen, I understand you scared off the Odenwald boys."

"Boys?" the cop asked. "I only seen one of em. The other Odenwald don't look nothin like his brother." He produced the two photos, one of which featured a kid with a full head of hair, no glasses, and proportional teeth.

Eddy affected a conspiratorial expression, trying to draw Horstmann in. "Officer, you gotta understand. This is theater. Every few days we gotta spring a big dramatic surprise on the folks to hold their interest in this bunion derby, which, frankly, between you and I, is pretty dull, and I should know since I bankrolled three hundred of em."

"Get to the point. I ain't in such a good mood, and I know the Mayor is lookin for any way he can to shut you guys down."

"And losing in court, every step of the way," Eddy laughed, changing the subject and slapping Horstmann on the back. "Ever since the so-called acting mayor gave us a permit. That fella Corcoran, y'know, while Hoan was out of town. Well, since then we've had all the most righteous citizens bellyaching and forcing us to move from one place to the next. First the downtown auditorium, then the Avalon Ballroom at the Antlers Hotel, and now this dump." He lit his cigar, which took a while. "But the state supreme court just decided two days ago that the Mayor ain't got a say in it. They said he wasn't no dictator, and gave us at least another three weeks, by which time the contest will be over." His tone changed. No more backslapping. "So I am glad to help, but spare me the threats. We got some well-compensated lawyers who ain't scared of no beat cop."

"So sue me," Horstmann said, and smacked the top of the guy's head. The cigar remained in place but now Eddy was off-balance and flinching. "I am investigatin the murder of an officer. You get it, schmo? We will fuck around with this place every way we can, if it turns out you was harborin a cop killer."

"Take it easy, buddy." Eddy rubbed his wounded ear and looked anxious. "This ain't got nothing to do with no cop killer. It's simple. The other Odenwald kid, right? Well, he just cut his hair off, put in some fake Halloween teeth, and got identical frames but with glass lenses. They dress alike and from a distance they look the same, and the shorter one, I can't remember which one it is, but he wears lifts and has thicker heels on his shoes. They take turns every six hours, one dancing while the other one sleeps in the basement of the house I'm renting."

The pretty nurse had an icepack and was dabbing Horstmann's chin with antiseptic. He let her do it, and took a chair so she could apply the ice pack to his knee. "That still don't make no sense," he said. "If you know they're cheatin, why would ..."

"Like I said, it's theater. Later in the contest, right near the end, we were gonna have a big dramatic scene where we discover, ha ha, that they been cheating and it's a big ruse and then we disqualify them, with much shame and theatrics."

"Meanin that you cheated the gamblers."

"I don't know of any gambling." Eddy took the cigar out of his mouth and frowned. "I am strictly legit. Of course, I cannot control what others may do, though."

"So why did the kids run from me?"

"How should I know? Maybe they think it's illegal to put on a little show for the folks. When they first applied, to compete like normal contestants, I got the idea of hiring em as an act. And I told em these events were partly a show and partly a competition. Maybe they don't get that we have every right to put on the show part. This ain't the fuckin World Series."

An air horn blasted much louder than necessary and Horstmann jumped, messing up the nurse's placement of gauze on his chin. She redid the gauze as the cubicles emptied and the contestants went back out to the dance floor. The ones who looked like Wisconsin rubes ignored Horstmann, but the more professional types eyed the cop with some alarm.

As he watched the rubes and the pros file out, the implication of Eddy Buer's statement sank in on him and he realized he had a new headache, in addition to the one caused by his encounter with the brick wall. "Is there anybody else stayin at the house you mentioned?"

"Me, sometimes, but the basement's got its own entrance and I ain't never gone down there except the day I hired those two."

"So there's nobody who can verify that one or the other of them's been there all week?"

"Why should there be? And anyway, why the hell you lookin for those kids? They didn't kill no cop."

"Get it straight. I ask the questions, not you. Got it?" Horstmann closed his eyes as the nurse dabbed at them. It felt good. "So, uh. So, uh, what are the hours of the kids' shifts?"

"One to seven and seven to one, twice a day."

"We're gonna have to get a look inside that basement. Do not go near it till we're through."

"Anything you say, buddy." Now seated, Eddy regained his confidence. "But let's be clear. The kids ain't had no access to the rest of the house whatsoever. You can leave that alone."

The nurse started working on his cheek and he opened his eyes again. "Oh, so you got somethin to hide."

"I know my rights. I'll let you in the basement, but you'll need a warrant for the rest of the joint. This is fucking Wisconsin, not Alabama."

Horstmann grit his teeth but didn't press the point. There would be plenty of time for that later. "Do you know which of em was on the dance floor during the hour or so before midnight on Christmas Eve?"

"Why? did somebody knock off Santa?" Eddy laughed like he had ad-libbed something hilarious.

"Answer the fuckin question."

"I don't keep track. Are you nuts? And I left em alone, so I don't know which was which. I don't even know if they stuck to the six-hour schedule. But maybe the girl would know."

The nurse moved around behind the chair and began to massage Horstmann's shoulders. He let her do it. Her perfume was nice. Horstmann hadn't smelled perfume in a while.

"Maybe she'll know," the nurse said, "but I doubt it. Once you get past the sixth or seventh day it's all a blur. When she wakes up she's gonna remember nothin except whether or not she's been paid. She won't even remember those boys' names."

The MC's voice came over the loudspeaker. "Ladies and gentlemen, how long can they last? I have been informed that we lost a marathon couple just now during the break. So those of you who favored couple number one-forty-six, that's number one-four-six, you'd better start looking for a new favorite. Stumbling, staggering, on they go. Who will be next to be carried off the floor? Ladies and gentlemen, how long can they last?"

Horstmann knew he was screwed. He had allowed not one but both of the Odenwald boys to get away, when he could have nabbed one on the dance floor and gotten his story and then just waited for the other to show up. Even worse, at least one and, in a weird way, probably both of them no longer had an alibi for Christmas Eve. The only thing that could keep him out of the doghouse would be Suthrin's blood in Eddy Buer's basement. But the kids had had plenty of time to cover their tracks if one of them was guilty and the other conspiring with him.

"Why so glum, chum?" the nurse said. "You know, I get off at noon. I love a man in uniform. Maybe you could come over to the place I'm rentin and have some, uh ... some luncheon." Still massaging him, she leaned over and pushed her breasts against the back of Horstmann's neck.

"Maybe I should leave you two alone," Eddy said with a wink.

"Why do I get the feelin you two are runnin some kinda scam on me?" Horstmann said. But then he realized it was the best possible scam he could hope for, and reminded himself that he was no fool, and he leaned back into the nurse's breasts and prepared to be dressed down not just by his boss but also, at noon, by the nurse, and he figured you're only young once, and what with the lousy pay he got he deserved some kind of decent compensation from being a cop, and he decided to make one more phone call and then take it easy and forget about it for a while and also forget about the two goddam Odenwald kids. Fuck them.

24.

ORDINARILY, A DETECTIVE LIEUTENANT with twenty-seven years on the force might stay home the Saturday morning after Christmas and maybe even take the whole day off, maybe go out to his vacation home at Glen Cove on Pewaukee Lake and do some ice fishing. But this year Adolph Kraemer had the bad luck to be the only Detective Lieutenant on the force who had spent his career at the third district station. Even the chance to sleep in an extra hour had been denied when his phone rang that morning and he was told about the wiretaps on Suthrin, previously known only to the highest officials plus the captain on the phone. He would never have learned of Suthrin's treachery if not for the captain's need to explain the bizarre order that followed.

"We want you to take Rhodes off the case and assign it to Officer Minor."

Having been promoted only in October, and at age fifty-two already scheming to one day become captain of detectives for the whole city, Adolph Kraemer groggily wondered if this was some sort of test of his leadership ability. He didn't need that. But he had to come up with a response, test or no test. Breaking protocol, he dared to object to the captain's order, insisting that Jud Minor didn't have the brains or experience to lead such an important investigation.

"That's the point, Dolph," the captain replied. "I'm sure that after you've had your morning coffee you'll figure it out."

But even as he drove the four miles to the station from his suburban home at 59th Street and Meinecke Avenue, Kraemer was furious that his first major act as Lieutenant would be viewed as moronic if not insane by everybody except a few of his superiors, who were letting him take the rap for something he'd been secretly ordered to do. He decided that today he would adopt, for the first time, the strategy he intended to deploy whenever he wanted to convey to his men, in code, that he was protesting a decision made by the higher-ups but which he had no choice other than to obey.

He would smoke his pipe, in his office.

It was strictly forbidden to smoke while on duty, and although everybody did it, no one dreamt of smoking while actually inside a stationhouse. Kraemer wanted to establish a pattern of doing so only when he was ordered to do something stupid. Eventually the men, particularly the code-conscious detectives, would make sense of the pattern, and he would have a foolproof method of committing insubordination without word of it reaching anyone above his own pay grade.

Also, the pipe-smoking would reinforce one of the great legends of Kraemer's career. As a rookie in 1904, making eighteen dollars a week for working seven lazy ambulatory twelve-hour days, the young patrolman, while traveling a midnight beat in summer, had stopped randomly by a fire escape to light his pipe. The struck match illuminated his badge and almost at once a previously hidden man fell from the fire escape and landed at the cop's feet. The yegg had been attempting to jimmy windows into a third-floor business when he saw the badge, prominently visible like chiaroscuro in the dark night, and had lost his footing. Confronting the muscular cop, made intimidating by a decade in an iron foundry beginning at age fifteen, the guy surrendered on the spot and Kraemer was spared the fistfight usually inevitable in any felony arrest in 1904, particularly those involving street gangs like the Teutonia Indians or the Bloody 64.

At the time, Kraemer was already considered something of a maverick for refusing to grow the handlebar mustache that was almost as much a part of the old uniform as a hard helmet and Prince Albert coat. In fact, on his first day he'd been publicly humiliated by a sergeant, who loudly speculated that a testosterone deficiency rendered the twenty-five-year-old unable to raise whiskers. Offended by the gratuitous insult, a number of older men appeared cleanshaven the next day, and from then on the handlebar faded from local police style as a nineteenth century relic.

As he had for several months now, Kraemer drove the route down diagonal Lisbon Avenue past Washington Park, scanning the perimeter to see whether the Lincoln Park Hooverville had begun to spill over into its spacious neighbor. As yet there was no sign of the scrapyard shanties that so plagued the poor saps traveling a beat in the fifth district, not to mention their bosses, but Kraemer was certain the third district would soon be equally burdened. Lincoln Park would fill to capacity with the desperate and unemployed and homeless, and Washington Park was too nearby and attractive to resist. Kraemer made a mental note to begin organizing an early response strategy for the day when Hooverville would expand into the third, but he'd made the same note many times before, and presumed he would forget about it once he arrived at the station.

And he did forget. He'd barely reached his office before being presented with a problem. One Gordon Chambers, his shirt torn almost in half and his face, explained the arresting cop, made black and blue not by the third degree, which of course was never administered, but by a bad fall sustained while leaping over a fence in making his getaway from a B and E. Kraemer sighed as he listened to the cop lie about Chambers's injuries, but betrayed no sympathy when the suspect said he'd been beaten by four cops during his interrogation, with his hair yanked and his face smashed onto the floor. The cop quickly interrupted and informed Kraemer that one of the suspect's three alleged collaborators had slightly wounded another cop with scattered buckshot fired from the running board of a speeding car. Kraemer knew the injury meant he must never reprimand anyone for beating Chambers, who claimed to be an innocent bystander.

Next, before Kraemer had time to summon Detective Rhodes to his office, he was introduced by another cop to a Greek immigrant who'd appeared during the futile manhunt for Suthrin's killer. The Greek was conveniently unable to speak or understand any more English than necessary to say he'd been nearby Mother's restaurant two nights before and a bloodsoaked man waving a bloody knife had robbed him of seventeen dollars. When asked to give even a single corroborating detail, the Greek lost all vocabulary beyond his rapidly babbled native tongue. Behind his back, the cop winked. Kraemer waved the man over to a chair and dismissed the cop. Then, sitting in his impressive office, clearly that of the highest ranking man in the station, Kraemer proceeded to ignore the supposed robbery victim for the next fifteen minutes while shuffling papers, sharpening pencils, filling pens with ink, cleaning his pipe, organizing his filing cabinet. It was all necessary housekeeping, so he figured he may as well do it at the beginning of the day. And he was not at all eager for the uncomfortable meeting with Rhodes.

Although invisible in the room, the Greek kept babbling the whole time, and appeared increasingly anxious at being treated as if he were a ghost. A patrolman, waiting for his fifteen-minute cue, stepped quietly into the office and stood by the door, listening. Unhappily for the immigrant, the patrolman actually knew Greek. After a minute he asked the guy exactly one question in Greek, at which point, head now in hands, the immigrant confessed, in flawless English, that he had not been robbed after all, that he'd lost the seventeen dollars gambling and had read in the papers about the murder and then made up the story to appease his wife. On the spot the cop arrested him for nuisance and making a false report and the two of them left as Kraemer, who had not spoken a word, smiled and punched the intercom, requesting an audience with Detective Rhodes.

Once Rhodes arrived and had a seat, Kraemer elaborately filled and lighted his pipe. It was probably the first time in decades that anyone had smoked within the walls of this or any other stationhouse. Rhodes duly noted the peculiar gesture. Thus the first seed of the new code was sown.

Tonelessly, Kraemer informed the detective that he was off the Suthrin case, raising his voice above its monotonous level only when, between staccato puffs on the pipe, he explained, a few words per puff, that the decision had been his and his alone and had nothing, nothing to do with any instructions from his superiors.

Having just joined the department, Rhodes accepted the information meekly, but made a point of staring hard at the pipe after Kraemer emptied it and placed it on the corner of his desk.

Soon the mystified Rhodes was out of the office. Kraemer phoned the captain, who that morning had instructed him to do so, for further instructions prior to giving Minor the news.

"Okay. Rhodes is off the case. I told him it was my decision."

"Good," the captain replied. "Someday you'll be in the race for chief of detectives, Dolph. We won't forget this."

"Well, until then, I'm the lieutenant here, at the third. The men aren't going to like this. You know, Minor isn't even allowed to drive a squad car. The cases he's done as acting detective were all confined to Bronzeville, and whenever any leads pointed outside the area we got someone else to follow them."

"Which brings us to the subject," the captain replied. "We want Minor to follow every lead no matter where it takes him. Out of state, even. Just so long as the leads have nothing to do with the area of activity I described earlier."

The wiretaps. That meant Minor could do anything he wanted, go anywhere he wanted, but would be forbidden to approach, even peripherally, the subject of gangs. In particular Joey Vallone's gang, the only one that mattered.

"I'll never hear the end of this from my men," Kraemer said.

"Look, Dolph. There's no way we're going to find Suthrin's killer, unless it was just a fluke assault and the guy gets stupid. But under the circumstances, what with Suthrin making up that cock and bull story about doing a stakeout in the alley, we've got to presume he ran afoul of the people in question. So that means two things. First, whoever did it is already well hidden, behind a wall of silence. And second, if we did find the killer, it would be a disaster, opening up a can of worms for everybody from me to the chief to the mayor. So you're just going to have to take one for the team and let your men gripe about it. After the manhunt, they probably figure there's no way it's going to be solved anyway. But at least it will never enter their minds, or anyone else's, that the case has anything to do with that unopened can of worms."

Kraemer had to admit, if only to himself, that substituting Minor for Rhodes was a good way to ensure the case would go nowhere. "But," he said, "one way or another Minor is going to ask at least a couple of obvious questions. Like, what was Suthrin doing in the alley and what's with the stakeout story and so on."

"So let him look into it and report back to you with every theory he's got. Then it's up to you to steer him firmly in the direction of the wrong theories, and see to it he wastes as much time as possible on them. Eventually the trail will go cold in every direction, and not just the wrong ones."

And so, on his first major case as Detective Lieutenant, Adolph Kraemer found himself ordered to avoid solving it. He tried to think of anything redemptive about the situation. All he could come up with was that, at least, for the one and only time in Jud Minor's career, the colored cop would imagine he might achieve the impossible and earn promotion. Though of course he would not.

25.

A FEW MINUTES LATER Jud Minor stood in Kraemer's office. He was nervous and fidgety and before Kraemer could explain the situation, Minor placed a key on his desk.

"I really is sorry, sir," Minor said. "I done told Flint about the key, but then when the two sergeants gone at it, I plumb forgot and straightaway I's ordered back to the station and told to wash my uniform. Well, the key end up in the wash, and I ain't noticed till I got dressed this mornin."

Without smiling, Kraemer tried to appear friendly, or at least non-threatening. "Have a seat. I didn't call you in on a Saturday morning to ask about a key. In fact, the proper person to receive such information, whatever it is you're referring to, has changed." Kraemer paused for dramatic effect. He rather enjoyed the moment. "That person, from now on, is you."

Minor looked exhausted. It seemed to Kraemer he wasn't quite listening, as though he were so nervous and preoccupied about the key, a subject he clearly believed would lead to reprimand, that adrenaline had plugged up his ears. Minor sat and stared at his recently promoted boss and then cleared his throat and said, "Come again, sir?"

"You are in charge of the Suthrin case. I believe your sergeant was, perhaps, conforming more to the status quo than to common sense when he took you off of it. Understandable, of course. People almost always do whatever has been done the longest."

Minor responded to the information without referring to the promotion. Instead, obliquely, he flattered the boss by following his digression.

"Like handlebars," he said, deadpan.

That was bright, Kraemer thought. He laughed, impressed that Minor had lightened the mood, steering the conversation away from the subject of race. "Oh, so you've heard the handlebars story?"

"Reckon everybody done heard it, one time or another."

Kraemer blushed. "Funny how a thing I did at the age of twenty-five will probably end up in my obituary."

"Ain't nothin funny about no obituary, sir."

This too got a laugh out of Kraemer, and he was reminded of something he'd noticed before. Minor had a certain charm, a quality rather thin on the ground in any stationhouse.

It was a shame the man was colored. Like every detective sergeant, Kraemer had kept his distance from all the patrolmen in the previous years. But he particularly avoided fraternizing with the sole colored patrolman. He had wanted, and still did as lieutenant, to avoid being thought of as soft and liberal, a deadly combination in a leader of violent men, much less a leader always seeking promotion.

But if Kraemer ever became chief of police, after reaching captain of detectives and then deputy inspector and then inspector, he planned to integrate the department a bit more. He already had his eye on a negro hire in the stack of applications, a promising boy named Sidney Loveless.

Kraemer's people had come from Pomerania and Mecklenberg, and like most Milwaukee Germans he prided himself on his open-mindedness. Ever since the war, with its anti-German propaganda, people had forgotten about the distinguished tradition of free-thinking shared by American Germans in the Midwest. Indeed, Chief Laubenheimer's great-uncle John, one of Milwaukee's first generation of non-Indian residents and a cop, a fireman, and a civil war veteran, had established the Freie Gemeinde, that local bastion of atheism and social conscience.

But 1931 was still too early, Kraemer knew, for a lieutenant in Milwaukee to appear friendly, as opposed to coldly professional, around any colored man. That was true whether or not the lieutenant was ambitious, but it was especially true for someone climbing the ladder in an institution with a long memory, where years could go by and yet he might still be passed over for promotion because of an old story about being too friendly to the coloreds. So the legacy of Pomerania and Mecklenberg would have to wait.

"Well," Kraemer said, "I reserve the right to laugh at the thought of my own obituary. Anyway, go ahead and take that key and make sure you report its existence to yourself." Kraemer smiled. Minor did not. "Seriously, though, since you were the first man on the scene, and have experience as an acting detective and know the sixth ward so well, it only makes sense that you should lead the investigation. All of your initial conclusions, in your finely written report, have been seconded by everyone else, including the lab men, though Doctor Hoyer has not yet performed the autopsy. But everyone agrees. Suthrin got in a fight in the alley and was cut on the thigh and ... Oh." Kraemer knitted his brow and, no longer acting, looked at the key. "Now I get it. That's the key to the speakeasy."

"Yes, sir. Like I said, I done showed it to Flint but then ..."

"I don't know if you've heard this. The men who spoke with the penny restaurant's owner were told by her that one of her boys had accidentally left the door unlocked."

"Well, maybe they did. But Suthrin had the key, anyways."

"She seemed pretty certain about her story, I'm told. It would be most interesting if she were emphatically lying."

"Wouldn't put it past her. I known that woman pert near the whole time I been travelin a beat. Far as she concern, honesty the worst policy. But I guess prohibition do that to folk."

Kraemer laughed again. "Refresh my memory. What did she say to you about the matter."

"Said she ain't never given Suthrin no key. Fact, pretended like she ain't even acquainted with Suthrin, which is ..." Minor stopped abruptly and caught himself.

"Bullshit," Kraemer finished for him.

Now Minor smiled, charmingly. "Yes, sir, that what it is. I seen Suthrin in the speak just about every time I gone in there."

Kraemer narrowed his eyes. Frowned. "Gone in there."

"On duty, sir. Not as no customer."

Kraemer leaned back casually and picked up a pencil, which he tapped on his desk as if in deep thought. "Before his death," he said at length, "did you ever mention to anybody else that Suthrin was always 'in there'?"

"No reason to. Weren't none of my bidness. He ain't even a cop in this district. Though even if he was, there ain't no reason to mention it then, neither."

Someone knocked on the door and entered the office. Not a cop but the day shift clerk, the guy who handled the station's phone bank and who also, nowadays, broadcast commands from the third district on WPDK and dealt with the incoming teletype. It was unusual for him to deliver news in person, leaving his station to be manned by an inexperienced substitute. "Lieutenant, we have word from Officer Horstmann. He changed what he said before." Out of respect, having barged in, the switchboard guy paused.

In only the first hour of the morning, Kraemer was annoyed at being expected to understand this message. "What," he asked sharply, "did he say 'before'?"

"Half an hour ago he gave the last known whereabouts of Ernst Odenwald. He said that Odenwald had an ironclad alibi and also probably didn't know anything about Christmas Eve. Horstmann injured himself chasing him, and the kid got away. We sent a squad car to the area with no results." Again he paused.

Kraemer rubbed his eyes with his thumb and forefinger. He realized he was tired. "Go on."

"Well, Horstmann just called back and advised that, in fact, he'd seen the kid and his brother both. Only he hadn't recognized the brother. Another witness informed him later, I guess." The clerk's voice had gotten congested and he cleared his throat. "He also said that his previous belief about an alibi was wrong."

Kraemer sighed. Analyzing the situation, he remembered that Rhodes would keep his demotion to himself. So now was as good a time as any. He started the chain of gossip and ill will by saying, "Detective Minor is the lead on the case. Give Detective Minor the details about it after we finish our meeting."

For a moment the switchboard guy looked like he thought Kraemer was joking. But Minor's gaze forced him to regain his composure. He nodded and left the office, about to broadcast something much more interesting than squad car instructions.

26.

Lieutenant Kraemer pretended that neither he nor Minor had noticed the switchboard guy's expression, with its implicit insult. "So, detective, do you have any thoughts on how to proceed?"

Minor responded quickly. "Well, it strange Mother's boys run from Horstmann. For the record, they both big enough to rassel Suthrin. They was the first ones I reckoned I oughta talk to, anyways, specially considering that Suthrin done got that key from somewheres. Oh, that remind me. I ain't told Mother I found the key. She don't know we have it, for sure, though she probly figure we do."

"Do you have any reason to suspect the boys?"

"No, but maybe there some history between them and Suthrin. He known em long enough. Which is somethin I wanna look into, not just with them boys but regardin all the regulars at the speak. I think I oughta spend some time with all of em there, at Mother's, to get a picture of Suthrin from the outside. And I wanna look into Suthrin's background. As for the fellas in the first district, you and me should discuss that more. Later. But in the sixth ward, I already done some preliminary."

Kraemer noted that all of Minor's ideas, particularly those having to do with Bronzeville, would lead away from any hint of the Vallone gang. He pretended to be impressed. "You've done some preliminary in the sixth? When?"

"On my beat Christmas Eve, or rather mornin. Yesterday. Talked to a fella. Reliable guy when he ain't drinkin, which he weren't. Well, he said Suthrin got a thing for the colored girls that walk the street in the sixth ward."

Minor filled in the rest of the details he'd gleaned about Suthrin and the hookers, and Kraemer said: "Good work. Hard to believe, though. And I'm not sure I do. You'd think we would hear some gossip about that." Which of course Kraemer had. And which again was unlikely to lead to Vallone, who did not deal in unconnected sixth ward streetwalkers.

"Seem like there is some gossip. Officer Halvorson, the rook, said he heard that Suthrin like payin for it. But he didn't mention no colored girls."

Kraemer nodded and made some notes. Then pretended to make some more. Minor waited respectfully.

"Okay," Kraemer said when he was done, "that's good. Talk to the regulars at the saloon. Talk to the Odenwald boys once we find them. And look into the streetwalker angle. Maybe we'll get lucky and he got stabbed by some whore who was tired of him smacking her around. Or maybe one of the colored girls has gotten herself a pimp your source didn't know about."

"Maybe. But if it ain't no pimp, I don't think none of them starvin girls strong enough to take on Suthrin. Y'know, unless three or four of em ganged up on him, but the tracks didn't look like no ambush. He didn't have no head injury, neither, so it ain't like he got jumped or nothin."

Kraemer nodded. Acted the sage. "Still, it's part of the central question. Maybe the only question. Who was Suthrin planning to meet that night, and why. It was important enough for him to tell Halvorson to stay away, which in a way was somewhat risky. Though perhaps not so much, since Halvorson was a rookie, and likely not to make a fuss about it." The Detective Lieutenant tried to look wise and canny. "A rookie would presume it was over his head and that he would seem stupid and inexperienced for mentioning it to anyone." Minor nodded at the wisdom and canniness. "But that's the central issue. Why was he there. You have to admit, the most logical choices are either the hookers or a pimp, or the two Odenwald boys, or the saloon's regulars, since they might've happened to have been there looking for a drink."

Kraemer got up and went to the rolltop desk beneath the corner window. Outside, the morning sun reflected harshly off the snow. The sky was cloudless and bright blue. Kraemer paused to look out the window, squinting. "Days like this must have been quite a surprise to you when you left Georgia. From inside, the sunny blue sky makes you think it's a warm comfortable day. But in Milwaukee in the winter, that's a sure sign it's freezing out, even colder than when it's overcast or snowing. But I guess you've been here long enough to ..."

Kraemer trailed off, as though a new thought had struck him. "Do you remember back in twenty-five, it was exactly a day like this when they found poor little Buddy Shoemaker." He paused, again. "You know, I was lead detective on that case. For anything outside the sheriff's jurisdiction, I mean." His tone indicated he was done speaking and a response would not be an interruption.

"I remember. Beautiful day. That a fact." Minor cleared his throat. "Course, it was summer. But looked exactly the same."

Jud was too tactful to mention that Kraemer had never solved the case. A ten-year-old Wauwatosa boy and his friends hopped a train, just for a quick joyride. They were immediately chased off by a hobo who leapt after them and caught the boy, who was found dead two weeks later with signs of sexual assault. Two morons had falsely confessed, but that was all. Kraemer had failed.

The Lieutenant bowed his head for a moment, in memory of poor little Buddy Shoemaker. It was good for the men to be reminded of his personal stake in every case.

Then, drama concluded, he sighed, waited a respectful moment to fully conclude the scene, and finally removed, with a sense of weighty significance, an ungainly scrapbook from the rolltop desk, and set it before Minor. "Recently the feds, the Bureau of Investigation, went through our files and put this together. It's the records and pictures of everyone ever arrested in Milwaukee for violent crime, except those who are dead or no longer at liberty."

Kraemer was lying. The scrapbook included almost everyone he described, but not any of the gangsters from the third ward. The captain had called in that morning and told a discreet clerk to remove the gangster files, as he'd explained to Kraemer on the phone.

One of the advantages of having Minor on the case was his previous sequestration in the sixth ward. Other than the policy racket and some of the prostitution, Vallone's gang couldn't do much business in the sixth for the simple reason that everyone there was broke. Everyone except the men whose work was unsuited for the protection racket, those few colored professionals who had clawed their way out of poverty and wanted nothing to do with criminals. If crooks rob banks because that's where the money is, Vallone avoided the sixth because of its appalling poverty. The margins just weren't good enough. The risk-to-return ratio was too high. With luck, Minor would not notice the absence of gangsters, as opposed to unconnected third ward punks, in a volume so large.

Kraemer sat down and continued: "During the manhunt we've managed to eliminate quite a few suspects, so they've been removed from the file. We will continue checking out the rest. I am authorizing you to assign your fellow patrolmen to look more intensively into anyone in the file whose alibi is uncertain, though of course it is up to you how you wish to allocate your resources. I do not, however, want anyone but you to investigate Suthrin's background. That's an order."

"I understand, sir."

"So I believe we are done here." He leaned forward again and made strong eye contact with the colored patrolman. "I hope you realize what a grave responsibility you have undertaken. What a stupendous burden has been placed on your shoulders. And what an honor it is to be called upon in this circumstance by the police department of the twelfth largest city in America."

"Yes sir, I do. Thank you, sir. It really mean a lot to me. I mean, after a decade on the force. It mean a lot to me after a decade on the force to be considered for, uh. For actin detective. Actin detective on, uh. On a big case."

Of course it meant a lot to him, thought Kraemer. Though it meant absolutely nothing to anyone else, or at least anyone who mattered. Kraemer waved the poor colored fool, carrying the useless scrapbook file, out of his office, and looked at his pipe, wishing he could smoke even when he wasn't specifically trying to convey in code his disapproval for a dumb order from his superiors. But then it occurred to him that he could smoke if no one else was in the office, and the act wouldn't be perceived by those whom the code was meant to impress. So he filled his pipe and lighted it, very pleased indeed with his recent promotion and all the perks it entailed.

27

SALLY LIKED IDA COX, a singer from Georgia whose voice reminded Jud of the Georgia girls he'd heard in church before the war. Beginning with "Wild Women Don't Have the Blues," Sally bought every record Ida Cox made, many of which bore on their labels the mysterious words Port Washington, Wisconsin. There were fewer than eight thousand colored folks in Milwaukee, so Jud couldn't imagine what a down-home blues singer had to do with an all-white harbor town twenty-five miles north of the city. Out of curiosity on a slow spring day walking his Bronzeville beat before the crash, he showed one of Sally's records to the boys at a barbershop.

That was how, today, he determined the address where he might try to get some initial leads on Suthrin's grandparents, the Claytons, whom the papers said lived on a farm north of Grafton. Mother's speakeasy wouldn't open till later that afternoon, and the sixth ward girls wouldn't be up and about till hours after that, so Jud had decided to drive up to see the Claytons. It would be the first time he had ever been permitted to drive a squad car.

But with all the station house's resources, and even after phoning the Ozaukee County Recorder, he'd been unable to get a lead on the Claytons' whereabouts. Apparently, the farm wasn't in their name. And he didn't want to call the reporter, Meinecke. Jud had not spoken with any reporter about the story, and after seeing himself quoted in the paper he didn't trust a man who simply made things up. If he called Meinecke, he might again see himself lied about in print.

Meanwhile, the only direct order Kraemer had given Jud was that he must involve no one else in exploring Suthrin's background. Jud figured politics were involved so he didn't question the strange dictate. Kraemer's order precluded him from contacting the Ozaukee County Sheriff's office, or from sending a patrolman up to Grafton to ask around. He would have to go himself. No problem, if only there were some colored folks north of Milwaukee. But there weren't. Or none but a very few.

At first Jud thought he would have to cold-canvas pedestrians and store clerks, for whom he would be about as normal a sight as the man from Mars. Such a fishing expedition would be hopeless in a town full of Germans less enlightened than their city-dwelling Milwaukee cousins and sometimes partial to Adolf Hitler. Rumor had it that some of the locals broadcast records of the Nazi politician's speeches on loudspeakers during weird rituals in the woods. Badge or not, Jud faced a chilly reception. In fact, word would probably reach the Claytons that a colored cop was asking questions about their beloved heroic grandson. If there was anything fishy about Suthrin, they'd have their phony answers ready to go for every question that might lead somewhere.

But then Jud remembered Ida Cox and what the fellas at the Bronzeville barbershop had to say. The record's label read Port Washington, the city where the business was headquartered, but in fact the recordings were done in Grafton. One of the barbers told Jud that when the first colored talent scout arrived to speak to the label's owners, children massed around and followed him through the streets, block after block. They'd never seen a colored man before. Jud figured he would get the same reception in Grafton, which was only a few miles west. It wouldn't do to be so conspicuous on a murder investigation. His presence would get around at the speed of telephone lines. Soon Meinecke would have another made-up story.

One place in Grafton, though, might offer a solution. The obscure river town held an obscure corner where colored folks were common, a sprawling industrial complex just inside the southern city limits occupied by something called the Wisconsin Chair Company. The grounds even included a private boarding house where colored folks were allowed to stay, something unheard of in the rest of the town or for that matter most of Wisconsin. The business thus saved money it would otherwise have spent in boarding these singers and musicians in the sixth ward and shuttling them back and forth on the interurban between Grafton and Milwaukee.

Jud was told that hundreds of southerners had been to the recording studio over the past decade. Somehow, the Wisconsin Chair Company had become the country's leading producer of race records, which it released on its own label, Paramount, occasional home to Ida Cox. Out-of-town musicians would have nothing to say about the Claytons, but they could introduce Jud to a few locals at the chair company, and that would be a start. And even if today nobody was in town recording, the white employees on the grounds would be comfortable, as opposed to panicked, at the sight of a colored man.

So Jud drove up Green Bay Road for twenty miles, then before anyone in Grafton had even spotted the squad car he veered off Falls Road just inside city limits to reach the industrial driveway.

Most of the rest of the drive had been through farmland, on a major truck route whose snowdrifts had already been packed down by heavy traffic. The roads were easy. But this driveway, marked by no sign and terminating at a dam on the Milwaukee River, was trouble even for the Pierce Arrow. Slowly Jud followed fresh tire tracks through the high snow to an ugly copper-colored three-floor building made of wooden planks.

He had marked this building, which housed the recording studio itself, on his hand-drawn version of a fire insurance map described to him during his second call to the County Recorder's Saturday clerk. Having found it, Jud backed down the driveway and parked the squad car on Falls Road. He put on a big overcoat he'd borrowed from Officer Warren and replaced his cap with a hat before proceeding back on foot, in search of the boarding house. He no longer looked like a cop.

A viaduct connected the driveway to an abandoned plant, a pre-depression remnant. Jud headed over to see whether the plant might now be the boarding house. When he was maybe fifty yards away he spotted a well-dressed man leaving the plant with an instrument case about the size of a fiddle.

The man doffed his hat. Up close his suit, though proper and dignified, revealed itself to be inexpensive and a bit threadbare. "Ain't no auditions today," he said as Jud approached, "and if you got money in yo pocket to wax sumpin to peddle, you ain't spendin it. We got the station booked."

Jud removed his hat and extended his hand. "Jud Minor," he said. "I ain't no musician, just thought maybe a fiddler could introduce me to the white folks around here so I could talk to em."

The fiddler shook Jud's hand. "Folks call me Lonnie." He sized Jud up without malice. "If you ain't gonna use the record station, what you wanna talk to them white folk for?" Another well-dressed colored man emerged from the plant, this one with an uncased guitar hanging down his back from a string looped over his shoulders. "This here my cousin, Walter Jacob. Walter, meet Jud." The introduction was done with humor and curiosity. Jud shook hands with Walter, then put his hat back on.

"What you play?" Walter asked. "Ain't carryin nothin, so I reckon Mr. Spirit musta brought you in on piano."

Jud smiled. "Fact, I do play some. Picked it up in church, and then a fella taught me some barrelhouse in a Paris hookshop after the war."

"I got a couple brothers usually play the piano when we tourin," Lonnie said, "but they ain't here. Record station ain't big enough to hold all of us."

"Or to pay," Walter joked without much pleasure.

"Big family, huh," Jud said, trying to be personable.

Lonnie laughed. "My daddy had sixty chillun, but he only claimed the dozen by my mama."

"Oh, you know that ain't true," Walter said. "Yo daddy always did talk big. And now yo brother Sam claim he half brother to Charlie Patton, just cuz Charlie done got hisself a few some dollars."

"Charlie Patton," Jud said, nodding. "I heard his records, one or two leastways. He pretty good."

"We go way back with Charlie, but he ain't no relation. Fact, my family was the ones introduce him to Mr. Spirit. Fore that, Charlie had about spent his money out down to nothin."

"Ida Cox the one my wife like."

"She from Georgia," Walter said. "She look down on us uncultured Mississippi folk."

"Long way from home for both," Jud said. "But that why I come up here, too. Need to talk to some folk from Grafton and figured this here the only place in town where anybody give me the time of day."

"Why you gots to talk to folk in Grafton?" Lonnie asked for the second time.

"White boy I know in Milwaukee done got hisself killt. I'm trackin down his kin." It was the truth, if not the whole truth. "Figure somebody at this here factory might point me in the right direction, and vouch for me with whoever I find there."

"Well, I reckon Mr. Klopp might know. He done lived in this cracker town his whole life. We's headed over to see him, and it cold out for a Jackson boy, so come on." Lonnie turned and started walking toward the viaduct.

"Jawbonin in this freezin air ain't gonna do my singin voice no good, neither," Walter added. The three trudged through the high snow in silence, Jud taking up the rear.

When they reached the door of the ugly wooden building, Jud said: "I heard anything yall done?"

"Stick around," Lonnie replied, "and you will." All three men stomped the snow off their boots. Inside, the ground floor was abandoned. There was nothing else on the whole floor, not even junked machinery or furniture. A common sight to Jud, who in recent years had seen many such buildings on his beat.

"I heard you fore that?" Jud said, repeating his question.

"We go by the Jackson Blue Boys," Walter said, and for some reason both of them laughed. Jud guessed they were known, if at all, by a different name. "You mighta seen us with Lonnie's whole family on some of the finer planations in Mississippi. Mr. Spirit, he go from planation to planation lookin for what he call talent."

It had been years since Jud had heard "plantation" pronounced without the first "t". "Can't be much money playin plantations," he said.

Lonnie was good-natured at Jud's somewhat rude remark. "Man pay you sixty cent a day for plowin, then invite you in his parlor and give you five dollar so all the white folk have sumpin good to dance to. And once we finish layin by the crop in June or July, we go out tourin all over, even far as Chicago lately. That one reason we up here. Playin Chicago New Year Eve. Ain't sure why Mr. Spirit tag along." He and Walter found their way to a stairwell and headed up.

"Yall sharecroppers, then," Jud asked, making conversation, "when you ain't playin."

"My daddy owned his own farm," Lonnie said while climbing the stairs. "Brung us all up musical. Man gotta get away from home, though, so I done worked some other places, too."

The recording studio, a surprisingly big room, was on the second floor, apparently the only part of the block-long building still in use. Two white men were in an adjacent booth, visible behind a large square window. Absorbed in a conversation over some electrical equipment, they ignored the musicians' arrival. The floor creaked insecurely under padding, and the walls were covered by burlap and thick red blankets. There was a dampness to the heated air, like a locker room. A microphone, buried in a half-football-shaped acoustic horn, dangled from the ceiling in front of a chair. A similar mic was propped on the floor in front of a well used honkytonk piano. Both had cords snaking back to low holes in the wall of the booth. Other than a shiny guitar Jud presumed to be expensive, nothing else suggested the big room had any function at all, much less that any commercial music could ever emerge from it.

One of the men in the booth opened the door and spotted Jud. Dressed as a Southern gentleman but with the body and face of a bulldog, he said hello to Walter and Lonnie, who were entirely at ease in his presence, and shook Jud's hand. "H.C. Speir," he said.

"Jud Minor."

"So what you play?" asked Speir, whom Jud figured was the Mr. Spirit previously mentioned.

"He play piano," Lonnie said with a straight face.

"Oh. Good." Speir nodded toward the beat-up keyboard. "If I'm going to buy this place, I want to get a level on that worthless old thing."

"But I ..." Jud began to protest.

Walter interrupted him. "Buy the place?" he asked Speir. "So that why you come up with us."

"Otto Moeser offered me a one-percent royalty and all rights to their catalog if I take this white elephant off his hands for twenty-five thousand dollars. Otto wants to get right out of the music trade. Then he can go back to his true calling, the making of chairs for school children." Other than a charming whistle on the letter "s," Speir's voice barely betrayed his obviously southern background, the latter essential for a man who made it his business to go "from planation to planation." Jud was struck by the sense of equality between Speir and the two farmers' boys in the room.

"Where you get that kinda money?" Walter asked suspiciously.

"Gonna have to sweettalk the Jackson Chamber of Commerce, I reckon. Tell those good old boys this place is worth a million. Or will be once the hard times end. Don't need this godawful huge damp room. I can move everything down home. The rights and royalties will take care of themselves." He pointed to the piano bench. "Sit down and we'll get a level," he said to Jud, then asked Walter, "You got one suited for piano?"

Walter was amused, and let the joke play out. He looked straight at Lonnie. "Well, I spose 'Gone Long Gone' don't need no fiddle."

Lonnie returned the insult. "That one no good anyhow. Put me to sleep."

"Put yo woman to sleep," Walter replied, "after I done sung it to her this mornin, when the cock crow and she wide awake." He sat down before the suspended microphone and strummed his guitar.

Lonnie took the trick by playing a rooster call on his fiddle, followed by a woman's cry. "That sound more like Mr. Spirit's woman," he said. "You sho the sun was up, Walter?"

28.

H.C. SPEIR DUCKED HIS HEAD around the door to the booth. "Arthur, we're going to get a level on the piano. It's for future reference, next time I send somebody up here."

The sound engineer stepped into the big empty room and nodded to Jud, as though he thought they might have met and he didn't want the embarrassment of introducing himself twice. He was a skinny responsible-looking man, like a banker, maybe fifty or so and of middle height with a pronounced stoop, as though he were favoring an injured back.

"That Mr. Klopp who Lonnie mention," Walter told Jud. "Been here his whole life."

Klopp began adjusting the floor mic, apparently having not anticipated use of the piano. Crouching with a wince, he accepted Jud's hand. "Arthur Klopp. Didn't expect a trio."

"No, Mr. Klopp, my name Jud Minor. I got some questions I wanna ask ..."

"You do good by us," Speir said, "we'll do good by you. Get this sound check, then Arthur will tell you everything you want to know."

Resigned, Jud sat down on the piano bench and removed his overcoat. He folded it on the bench, setting his hat beside it, and huddled over the keyboard, facing away from all but Klopp, whose view at eye level was blocked by the piano. No one noticed Jud's uniform.

"I make it easy on ya, Jud," said Walter. "We do it in C. Hit just bout any ol white key and we do fine."

Klopp finished positioning the mic. "What's it called," he asked over one stooped shoulder as he returned to the booth.

"'Gone Long Gone,'" said Walter.

"'I'll Be Gone, Long Gone,'" Speir corrected. "Looks better on the label." He closed the door behind Klopp but remained in the studio. "I presume Minor is your stage name," he said to Jud. "Given what these fellas play, Major would be more like it. Can't recall a single tune they do that ain't major, almost all of them B-flat, C, and F. They're like vampires around garlic if somebody tries to do one in A or D."

Jud was looking over the piano at Klopp in the booth. On the wall between its door and the partitioning window there was an upright rectangular box with two lights, one green and one red, just like a silent policeman at the intersections downtown.

"It go like this, only slow," Walter said to Jud, and he played eight bars of the song very quickly while humming a sketch of the tune. Jud barely had time to turn around and look before the rehearsal was done. "Just the three chords. When that green light come on, jump in."

Klopp busied himself in the booth for a while longer. Then he looked up at Jud and the light turned green.

Before he knew it, Jud was playing a minimal accompaniment to the slow three-chord blues song. Nervously, he came in early on the first verse after the brief introduction. Walter was beginning the third verse when the silent policeman turned red.

"That do for a check," Walter said.

"No, no, wait," said Speir. He opened the door to the booth. "That one was aluminum, right? Go ahead and put a wax one in."

Jud had no idea what this meant. He pushed the bench back and began unfolding his coat. During the truncated song Lonnie had come to the piano to look at Jud's hands. Now, studying the front of Jud's uniform with bemusement, he said: "Stay put. Mr. Spirit want to make it a side."

"A side?" said Jud.

"Do the whole song, not just a check." Lonnie stifled a laugh. "If that all right with you, officer, sir."

"When we almost done," Walter explained, "the light turn red, meanin we on the last verse, like it or not. They can't wax much as four minutes. Had to split up one of Charlie Patton's songs, put it out in two parts, one side each. Guess Charlie say he ain't gonna end a big ol song just anywheres."

"My brother Sam the same way," Lonnie said. "Say the man in the booth ain't no musician, how he know when the song oughta end."

The light changed from red to green and for the next three or four minutes Jud faked his way through "I'll Be Gone, Long Gone." Once again, he came in early on the first verse.

Walter had a fine reedy tenor voice, with an attractive vibrato at the end of certain lines, and sounded like a man who had earned his disdain. Intermittently he enhanced his strumming with sudden runs of single and double notes up and down the scale, bending the high strings and finding surprising punctuation from the low. Once, halfway through, he stopped singing and said "step on it." Obligingly, as Walter played a break, Jud stumbled through a modest variation more prominent in the background, picking out a riff and rolling off its keys with his thumb while his middle finger rolled off each white key two notes higher, his fingers straddling the key between them just as he had been shown in Paris. During Walter's second solo, after the last verse, Jud even managed to pick out the melody and incorporate it in the riff. It was easy but Jud knew he wasn't playing anything special. In truth, he had missed more than a few of the changes, though it hardly mattered in a three-chord song that could almost have been done as a holler.

During the second solo, the light turned red and they wrapped the song up. Jud wondered if there were verses that had been left out. On the other hand, at times he thought Walter was making the words up as he went along, or throwing in old sayings every farm boy knew: "You sho miss yo water, honey, when yo well go dry."

"Not bad," Speir said. "Where'd yall meet this fella?"

"Just over the viaduct," Walter joked. "Town called Grafton. Ain't never laid eyes on him fore that."

"Didn't know he was no cop," Lonnie said with delight. Jud swiveled around on the bench and for the first time let Walter and Speir see his uniform.

"There ain't no still on these premises," Speir said.

"Mr. Spirit, I thought we was gonna have Rita Moonshine sing backup," Lonnie said, giving Walter a laugh.

Jud stood up and went over to Speir. "City police," he said. "Been years since we cared one way or another about no still."

"He ain't no dry agent, boss," Lonnie said. "Feds don't hire no colored man."

"Cops don't usually, neither," Walter said. "Now, where Rita Moonshine at."

"You can give these fellas a drink if you like, Mr. Speir," said Jud. "I'm here to see if somebody at the chair company can help me find a coupla old white folks in Grafton. Kin of a city cop who got killt day before yesterday." Then Jud explained again that the presence of Paramount Records on company grounds would make it easier to find a local there who might cooperate with a colored policeman.

"Well," Speir said, "Arthur knows his way around, and he can probably introduce you to some other folks who do, too." Speir paused, then added: "Sorry for lying about the still. It's right behind the place where these fellas board." He went into the booth. Klopp, placing a wax disc into a cooler, was oblivious to the scene in the studio. After a moment, Speir returned with him.

"This some kinda promo gimmick, H.C.?" Klopp asked, skeptically reviewing Jud's uniform for signs of inauthenticity.

"Not a bad idea, now you mention it," Speir said. "Could market it. The bluesman in blue."

"Mr. Klopp," Jud said, removing Suthrin's photograph from his breast pocket, "this man got killt Christmas Eve. I been named actin detective on the case in Milwaukee, and I been told his granddad got a farm up north of Grafton."

Klopp glanced at the photo without reaching for it. He seemed impatient, and Jud sensed that Walter and Lonnie had arrived late for their session. "I take the Milwaukee papers," Klopp said, meaning he'd read about the murder. "I haven't ever heard of him nor his family. What are you doing here, asking me about it?"

Jud started to answer but Speir had decided to help him out. "Well, Arthur, it's one thing for our friend here to be a detective in the big city. They got a whole colored ward, just about. My talent used to be obliged to board there, at Brewers Hill."

"Still don't see ..."

Speir ignored the interruption. "And here, in the colored mecca, or should I say oasis, of Paramount Records, Detective Minor thought he might find the same sort of tolerance for a public servant of his particular race. He ain't about to just walk into the Grafton town square and start making friends. So, wisely, if I may say, he's beginning his inquiry at this celebrated recording station, which shortly, may I remind you, I could very well purchase and find myself your supervisor in these operations, should you choose to continue splitting time with your duties at the chair company."

H.C. Speir knew how to lay it on, Jud thought.

"We can talk about that when the day comes, Henry," Klopp said. He plucked the photograph from Jud's hand and looked it over while glancing impatiently at Walter and Lonnie, who were discussing a scrap of paper Jud took to be a song list.

"Can't do em all in B-flat," Jud heard Lonnie say.

"All I'm askin," Jud said, "is for the names of some folk in Grafton you think could help. If you can vouch for me, maybe phone em up, I bet before sundown they get me to this, uh, this tragic young man's family, and I can pay my respect to them poor old folks and ask em to help me solve this crime."

"Papers already talked to those people on the farm," Klopp said. "Call the editor."

"We tryin to keep things quiet. Don't want the man who done this crime to read about every step in the paper."

Again Speir tried to help. "Surely, Arthur, there's got to be someone acquainted with the farming families around here. The detective is just asking for a word of introduction."

Walter had walked over to the three of them. He still had his hat on. "Mr. Spirit," he said, "you think the label let us do one about a preacher goin to hell? I gots it in my head."

"If there's a market for it," H.C. said, "they'd let you do one about the devil going to heaven."

Lonnie laughed from across the wide room. "And drinkin home-brew with Jesus. Put that in, Walter."

"Okay," Klopp relented as he watched Walter step away, "I know what you can do. Go on up to Betty's Lunch, a diner straight up Highway 57 to Saukville, at the intersection with 53. If the roads are any good, you'll be there in fifteen minutes."

"Saukville," Jud repeated, wondering if he was being conned.

"Look," Klopp explained, picking up on Jud's tone, "every two-bit farm in the state has got a still, and from here to Green Bay they all truck their booze up and down 57 to Milwaukee on the way to Chicago. Every one of those trucks has stopped at Betty's. She and her fiancé Al own the place. If there's anybody who knows every farm around, it's them."

"They got any problem with colored folk?" Jud asked.

"They're good people," H.C. said. "Been up there once or twice myself. Had to explain to Betty what grits was. You tell them Arthur and H.C. at Paramount sent you."

"But come clean about it being a police investigation," Klopp added. "I don't want them to find out later, and then think I set the law on them. Long as they know you aren't a dry agent, I don't see why they'd mind helping out, if it means catching a cop-killer." Still holding Suthrin's picture, he reached in his pants pocket with the other hand and removed his wallet. "I'll scribble something on my business card and you can give it to Betty."

To get at his card Klopp offered the photograph back to Jud, but H.C. narrowed his eyes and grabbed it. "I know this cuss," he said with surprise.

"You spend time in downtown Milwaukee?" Jud asked.

"No," Speir said. "I know him from down home. Jackson."

"Well, he moved on up here as a boy," Jud said, not yet grasping how unlikely Speir's statement was.

"The hell he did," Speir said. "This damn fool pulled me over in Jackson every time he spotted a colored fella in my automobile. Rode a motorcycle. Back when I was first starting out, five or six years ago. Kept it up for the best part of a year and then just stopped and I ain't never seen him again, the son of a bitch."

Klopp had returned to the booth to get a pencil. Jud saw him through the window leaning over a table and writing on the back of his business card.

"Due respect, Mr. Speir, that ain't possible. Maybe it his cousin or somethin."

"What do you mean, it ain't possible. He ain't in uniform in this picture, but I never forget a face, specially not the face of a man who was nothing but trouble. Fact, a couple of times I was transporting singers, colored girls, and he'd get the girl out by the side of the road and move his hands all over her. Said he had to frisk them for weapons." Speir scratched his chin thoughtfully and looked at the ceiling. "Had a real ordinary name, Deputy Jones or Johnson or Smith, something along those lines."

Across the room Walter sang, "He calls that religion, but I know he's going to hell when he dies." Jud noted how careful he was to pronounce the final "g" in "going" and "s" in "calls," as though obeying an instruction he'd been given that went against his habits. Focusing intently on his partner, Lonnie experimented with a fiddle part. He seemed never to have heard the song before. Maybe Walter was composing it on the spot.

29.

BETTY FALKNER HAD BARELY SLEPT since Thursday. Rather than slow her down, her exhaustion made her curiously happy and lighthearted, as though she were drunk. She wanted to talk to somebody, but Al was napping. Tonight he had an all-night shift in the gentlemen's club downstairs, open only on the weekends. Because it had been closed for Christmas, they expected a bigger crowd than usual in the cardroom and speakeasy, a popular destination even for the sheriff's men, who enjoyed their weekly marathons of poker and skat alongside more than a few men who Betty had bailed out on drunk and disorderlies, not to mention farmers and truck drivers known to consort with criminals.

One such criminal combination was to blame, in part, for Betty's punchiness. She'd been up before sunrise to meet a truck driver on a whiskey run from a farm near Fredonia, where they had loaded barrels into the hold and then stacked frozen beef and pork for the Milwaukee Stockyards on top, worried not about the Sheriff, whose men were all related to moonshine distillers, but about an encounter with dry agents, those big-city Protestant bastards.

Fresh-faced Betty, twenty years old and easily taken for a farm girl with her Amelia Earhart looks and haircut, did not fit the rumrunner profile, so her innocent presence was doubly appreciated. In the nearly three years she'd worked at the diner she had helped turn it into a profitable transfer depot between Green Bay and Chicago, a factor in Al's decision to not only buy the place, including its Standard Oil service station, but also rename it after his new fiancée Betty, who could cook just about anything and had been known to turn out twenty or thirty pies a day. She was easily the best-connected girl in Ozaukee County, putting to shame the snooty socialite debutantes she'd known before dropping out of high school at sixteen.

Besides the whiskey run that morning, and on top of the usual business at the diner, she'd spent Christmas making free dinners for all the lonely old folks and unemployed men in Saukville. She and Al agreed that charity was not only good for the soul but good publicity, too. And it was paying off. With the diner, the service station, the gentlemen's club, and the depot commissions, they were thriving, if not sleeping much, during what everybody said was the worst downturn in history. Betty wouldn't know, since she'd never paid much attention in school to history or to anything but cooking before she got her first job, where her boss, an accountant, whiled away the slower days by telling her everything he knew about the mystery of leveraging land purchases as collateral to buy more land, a lucrative endeavor now that so much land was in bankruptcy and up for auction.

Betty was determined to save her money and buy land and buildings first chance she got. Guiltily, she hoped the downturn would last that long, so she could stand on the courthouse steps bidding at the seedy auctioneers. When she was rich enough, she would go into politics and astound her German Catholic father, a laborer in Port Washington, by declaring herself to be Republican, the proper party affiliation for a small businessman such as herself. But she had already decided to tithe and donate enough to redeem her immortal soul, which belonged to the Immaculate Conception Parish. She was certain the old parish was especially holy, since its first chapel had been built the very same year the Virgin Mary had appeared to the venerable Blessed Bernadette at Lourdes and identified herself as the Immaculate Conception, an event unknown at the time to those who had so presciently named the parish.

Keeping an eye on the drunk slumped over the counter, she took the order of the only other customer, a wealthy old widower so blind his glasses made his eyes wider than his face.

"Hamburger still a nickel?" he said, pretending to read the portion of the wall menu in front of him, which in fact listed custard, cherry, and rhubarb as the Pies of the Day.

"Hamburger's a nickel, egg, cheese, ham, or steak sandwich a dime, the blue plate lunch is thirty cents, and, between you and me, the slot machine against the wall hasn't paid out all week." She said the last part in case he'd blurrily mistaken the slot machine for a jukebox.

"Hamburger is fine. Well-done." He drained his water glass and then asked for more, the old tightwad. When Betty made her money, she vowed, she would never again settle for water at a restaurant. "What kind of fixings do you have?"

Betty was in the mood to play. "Fixings are an extra nickel." Of course, fixings were free, but she wanted to see how the skinflint would respond.

"Okay, then, just mustard. Yellow, not the fancy stuff."

As Betty headed for the kitchen in the back, she glanced out the front windows and saw a patrol car enter the lot. It was a Pierce Arrow, not one of the sheriff's cars. She hoped a cop she didn't know would come in and get something to eat so they could have a little chat. She hurried to remove the premade patty from the icebox and set it on the grill, then grabbed her heavy winter coat and met the patrol car as it sidled up to the third of three Standard Red Crown pumps out front. She could pump the man's gas and still get back in time to flip the burger.

Before the driver-side window had even begun to roll down, she grabbed the pump and set the handle to sale. Then she turned around and leaned over the window and had already said "Fill it up?" before realizing with mild shock, and a weird sort of embarrassment, that the cop in the car was colored. Even more surprising, he handed her a card and said, "Detective Jud Minor. Arthur Klopp and H.C. Speir at Paramount Records told me to ask for a lady called Betty."

Confused, Betty went back and removed the gas cap and started filling the tank. Then she realized the man hadn't said how many gallons he needed. She released the pump and returned to the window. "You're looking at her," she said as she squinted to read the small neat handwriting on the back of Arthur Klopp's business card. He wrote like the boys she'd known in high school who had taken mechanical drawing so they could be architects and make skyscrapers in Chicago. She hadn't thought of those boys in years, or any boys lately. Everybody had known Al was her sweetheart from just about the night they'd met, at the Firemen's Hall country dance. Then there was no doubt after he quit his job at Badger Raincoat, bought the diner where Betty worked, made her its boss, and named it Betty's Lunch. She expected to marry Al just as soon as they built up a little nest egg. She even had her eye on a twelve-dollar white lace dress.

"I be much oblige if I could ask you ..." the cop said.

"About a murder," Betty interrupted, excited at what she read on Klopp's card. It also said she didn't have to worry about booze.

"Right," Detective Minor said. "Go ahead and fill up the tank, and we can talk right here while it pumpin."

"Don't be silly," she said, thrilled to be part of a big city police investigation. "Come on in where it's warm. I've got to go back and flip a burger."

"Come in?" Minor repeated uncertainly. "But you, uh, ain't it, you know ..."

"You see what it says," Betty laughed, pointing back at the diner, "on them two ..." She corrected her English, something she'd been working on since becoming a businessman. "... those two awnings? That don't ... doesn't ... say White People's Lunch. It says Betty's Lunch."

Of course, if there'd been certain other customers in the restaurant, besides the drunk and the blind guy, she might have thought twice. On the other hand, this colored fella had a uniform on, and had pulled up in a patrol car. And it was cold out, and she'd been feeling so happy and delirious already and now here she was, helping to catch a murderer.

"That awful good of you, Miss, uh, Miss ..."

"Everybody calls me Betty. We'll take care of your tank after we talk. Come on, I'll give you a nice slice of pie." She winked. "And we've got all sorts of different beverages to wash it down with."

"Well, pie sound good," Minor said, and repeated, "I be much oblige." Betty was charmed by the way he left the final "d" off this authentic Southern expression, just like she was meeting somebody in *Tom Sawyer*, which her English class had been halfway through when she'd dropped out.

"You go ahead and leave your patrol right there. It'll scare away the troublemakers, and if the busybodies come in we can say you were just prepaying for your gas."

After a little thought the detective turned off the engine and said, "I be much oblige," then rolled up his window and got out.

At the door to the diner Betty checked the exterior thermometer affixed to the prominent Super Pyro sign, whose grinning snowman held a giant red quarter reading "25¢ QUART" for, as it said at the bottom, "The MONEY SAVING ANTI-FREEZE" which "*Lasts Longer*". She was tickled by that sign with its real thermometer, and Al sold a lot of anti-freeze. Today wasn't too bad though, thirty-four. It was often up in the low thirties a couple of days after an early winter blizzard like the one they'd had Christmas Eve. And it was only December. The really bad month was February. She remembered one February during junior high when the temperature did not go above zero for a single minute, twenty-eight straight days, and she still had to walk to and from school and mass on Sundays. But she had secretly loved being so stoic, and pretended she was with Admiral Peary at the North Pole.

When the drunk came in he had collapsed onto the first stool inside the door, and the old man unwittingly had sat only one stool over, so she put the detective down at the far left end of the counter, where he wouldn't be visible through the windows.

"Betty," the old codger said, "I believe it may be possible that we have forgotten about my water."

"Sorry, sir," she said. "Guess I got distracted by seeing the detective's patrol car." She knew he would glance at Jud Minor and make out only his uniform and cap, never realizing that Betty's Lunch was serving its first colored customer.

"This is the sort of service that deprives one of a tip."

Betty had a vision of going outside and filling his glass up with snow, then adding some water and telling him it was on crushed ice. But she never did anything like that, such as spit in rude customers' food as a busboy she'd known at Catechism had bragged of doing. Even had it not been a venial sin, seen by God, she just didn't believe in that kind of behavior. It didn't matter if somebody else was bad. It only mattered that you were good. Hers was the only behavior, she knew, that she would ever have the power to control. Though she had to admit, she did try to get Al to drink less. She didn't want him to end up at the funny farm. So, that was a principled exception to her rule. If she didn't look out for Al, who would. He was twenty-seven and not going to listen to anyone else. She didn't want to be a widow in her thirties or forties.

But when she thought about it, she also thought about Mr. Niederkorn, who owned Simplicity Manufacturing and pretended to be her business mentor whenever he stopped in for the blue plate, and she wondered if he would marry her should Al die in a decade or two. The priest had not been very sympathetic to this line of thought during her last confession. Lots of Our Fathers and Hail Marys. But she didn't have anything else to confess. It never occurred to her that there was anything sinful about the whiskey runs, which were just a way to make a living in a county where the sheriff didn't care and in fact openly despised the federal agents who would look at the matter far more critically than any priest. Besides, the parish got huge shipments of sacramental wine, every drop legal and few devoted to Holy Communion. Sometimes Betty giggled at the thought that those old German priests must have wished the cup at the Last Supper had held beer. But of course she would never share such a blasphemous joke with anyone, not even Al. And it would shock a pillar of the community like Mr. Niederkorn, though sometimes she was sure he was flirting with her.

She refilled the water glass and flipped the burger before giving the detective a slice of rhubarb pie. He had a southern accent and she made up her mind that southerners would definitely like rhubarb best. She'd heard they ate dandelions. She wondered when she would finally have enough money to visit exotic places like the south, beyond the Wisconsin borders that she had never crossed unless you counted ice fishing on Lake Michigan. She had never even been to Chicago. Her father said everybody there was a crook. Maybe the Chicago fella, whoever it might be, would have time to talk with her tonight, when he drove his truck up to fetch the barrels hidden behind the oilshed out back. The Chicago fellas weren't German, mostly, but they seemed to like Betty a lot, and, incredibly, would let her keep the change from a five dollar bill for gas and sandwiches. Al didn't know anything about these spectacular tips. One day Betty would surprise him with how much money she'd saved, gradually accumulating in the hidden compartment of the ornate Chinese Box her aunt had bought for her during that one summer at Wisconsin Dells. Al didn't know anything about Chinese Boxes, either.

30.

Whatever mental impression Jud had gotten from Klopp, he hadn't been expecting this. Betty's Lunch was just a shack. And Betty herself not much more than a girl. A sweet, naive girl who couldn't possibly know anything, much less everything, about all the moonshiners in the county. Even if Klopp's description were correct, she probably never wondered why so many trucks came up from Chicago driven by Italians. Still, that didn't mean she was unfamiliar personally with the farmers selling wholesale. And the girl sure wanted to talk.

Approaching the crossroad, Jud had worried the directions were wrong. There was a gas station with three pumps and a big sign that said STANDARD SERVICE, and he needed to get a few gallons anyway, so he'd already pulled in before seeing the much smaller sign beneath the first with only the word LUNCH and one of those old-fashioned stylized drawings of a closed hand with an extended index finger pointing to the left or right. Then he realized that the tiny building he'd taken to be merely shelter for a cash register and some shelves stocked with oil was, as the awnings said, Betty's Lunch. A snow-obscured sign on the sloping tin roof advertised homemade chili and sandwiches between two American flags, their colors repeated in three small wedges of bunting festooned over the narrow facade.

Inside, the counter could barely accommodate seven or eight stools, which weren't even fastened to the ground by silver poles as they would be in nearly any Bronzeville diner. Jud suspected there was more to the place and saw a door on the end of the wall opposite the doorless passage to the kitchen. Immediately he guessed it led to a basement, meaning a blind pig. You didn't get to know every farmer in eastern Wisconsin by selling nickel hamburgers, even at a major crossroads.

So Jud was determined to meet this guy called Al, identified as Betty's fiancé by Klopp. Al would be the bartender for the blind pig downstairs, no doubt. Probably the one who'd served the drunk currently head down and snoring on the counter.

"Milk just fine," Jud said when Betty asked what he wanted with the pie after she returned from flipping a burger. He'd have to pretend to like rhubarb, an ugly green stalk-like weed with stringy red innards only the most dirt poor rural Georgians ever bothered with. "Mmm," Jud said, taking a bite as Betty grabbed a glass from dozens stacked on the shelf beside a big refrigerator, whose expensive girth took up a lot of wall space behind the counter and sat below a sign reading MILK. "That mighty fine rhubarb. You bake this yourself, Miz Betty?"

Betty poured the milk while standing by the refrigerator's open door, then replaced the uncovered jug. "When it's busy season, I bake around the clock." She set the glass down beside Jud's pie, raising a heel behind her to kick the fridge shut.

Jud tilted his head toward the drunk at the other end of the counter. "Want me to do anything about him?"

After giving him his milk Betty leaned over and put her elbows and wrists on the counter, clutching her hands together, and said, "I've dealt with every drunk in the county. They know better than to cause me any trouble."

Jud drank some milk, which had a funny taste unlike that of the city milk bottled in industrial quantities and brought by the milkman to Sally's door twice a week. He'd heard from some of the farmboys at the station that after the crash Wisconsin's smaller dairy farms stopped letting their cows go dry over the winter before calving season, instead milking the deficient cows and giving them inferior feed stored during the long-past harvest. They couldn't afford three months without fresh production. So you had milk that tasted funny during winter, once you left the city. The thought gave Jud an idea.

"I bet you friends with the folk done milked this cow," he said, holding up the glass.

Betty laughed. "That's from Fritz and Audrey Schneider. Every delivery is like a different vintage. The dairy farmers are so desperate to sell, we gotta rotate them, try to give everybody a little business. Might have to go to a lottery system one of these days." Betty laughed at what was clearly an oft-repeated joke. "You feel guilty, buying it so cheap. Don't ... doesn't cost half as much as when I started here. Never thought that if the day came when everything cost less, everybody would be worse off." She paused and, proud of her knowledge, finished by explaining: "That's called de-flation."

She had made a point of bringing Jud in, giving him milk and pie. It wouldn't do for him to ask a few questions and then just book. And anyway, he'd all but literally sung for his supper to get only two items of information at Paramount Records. In exchange for a half-hour of idle talk and playing the piano, he'd learned that he should meet with Betty and Al, and that Suthrin had a dead-ringer, with luck an older cousin, riding a motorcycle on the highway patrol in Jackson, Mississippi.

So Jud let this flighty girl go on for a while about whatever came into her head. She probably would, in fact, be as good a source as Klopp suggested, since she apparently liked nothing more than talking up a storm with whoever came in. Jud had known young girls like this before the war. Girls who never even considered holding his hand or necking, much less what all that might lead to, but hungered for his company just to talk and talk and talk.

And Jud egged her on. Asking easy questions would prime Betty to be equally as voluble about the hard ones. He cast his eyes about the small cluttered room, at first trying to dream up some small talk about the slot machine against the wall to his left. That line of thought led nowhere, but it did prompt him to note an incongruous bookshelf set snugly in the left-hand corner behind him. Its contents faced forward, so he hadn't noticed it when he'd walked over to the stool and sat down.

"Got a sideline sellin dolls?" Jud asked, turning around toward the shelf. "My wife collect em."

"No, it's more what you call ... a 'trademark.'" Betty articulated the term with care, as though quoting a lesson she'd been taught about business practices. "Something cute that people will identify with this place. You know, give it some character beyond just your usual diner."

"You a character," Jud said, turning up the corners of his mouth just enough.

Betty accepted the warm compliment and blushed a bit, then laughed. "I suppose that's part of it. I had a doll from when I was a girl in here for good luck, right after I started, and one day when it was crazy busy, Fourth of July before the crash, a fella said he'd spent all his money on fireworks but had brought in another doll to keep mine company, said he'd found it in a box while cleaning the attic, and was just going to blow it up with an M-80. So he offered to trade it for a sandwich. I thought that was funny and the doll looked like an antique, so I just shook his hand and said Deal. Well, some folks were listening in, and the place was packed, must've been thirty people in here jockeying for sandwiches to take along to the big fireworks show at the park, and when I said Deal you'd think it was the funniest thing they ever heard. Never heard a laugh that big at the pictures. So then people just started bringing in dolls. If they're all beat up, I trade them for a free Coke, but for the nicer dolls I'll put an extra patty on their hamburger. Limit one per customer. Nobody tries it twice. Then I give them away if somebody brings their little girl in with them, so I figure I break even on the extra business." She thought for a moment and added: "Funny. Sometimes little girls like the beat-up ones the best."

At Jud's urging, Betty told a few more stories of equal length. Finally, though, after the old man had paid for his hamburger and walked through the snow down the street in the chilly late afternoon, Jud tried to move forward with the investigation: "Mr. Klopp, he say you engage."

"Oh, yeah, you bet," Betty said enthusiastically. "Al and me run this place."

"Sure you gotta get back to work. Think I could talk to Al?"

"Not unless you stick around past sunset. He's napping before he has to work all night at the, uh, I mean, up here in the diner."

"Up here," Jud said, giving her a knowing look, one conspirator to another. "I figure that door over there lead someplace downstairs maybe help you make ends meet."

Betty said nothing, but smiled and pretended to lock her lips and toss the key.

Jud laughed. "Maybe I can come back tonight when Al workin downstairs and drop in...."

"I'm sorry but, well ... I don't have any say in who gets into the, you know, the basement. I mean, not even I'm allowed down there, unless the place catches fire. It's invitation only, and, you know, those guys, well, I don't see it. Wait till he's running the service station on Monday." She straightened the shoulder ruffles on her white sleeveless blouse, an outfit which put Jud in mind of a nurse. "But I should stop gabbing and let you do your job. Fire away, detective. There's nothing Al knows that I don't."

Jud put his fork down and wiped his mouth with a napkin, having been unable to prevent Betty from bringing him another piece of rhubarb pie. "All these farms sellin you milk and such, I figure you know just about every farm around. The man that got killt has kin on some farm north of Grafton. His granddad called Ernest B. Clayton, but ain't no land ownership record round here under that name. These would be two old folks, a married couple in their sixties or seventies, maybe older."

"Clayton doesn't ring a bell," Betty said at once.

"Well, here what might help. These folks from down south. Bound to have accents you likely to remember."

"Tell you the truth," Betty said, "you're just about the only person I ever met with a southern accent. Wouldn't know one if I heard one, if it weren't for Amos and Andy and the talkies and whatnot."

"Think hard. Old farmin couple called the Claytons, with southern accents."

"Nope. Sorry. I'm sure I'd remember. Definitely no farm called the Clayton farm." She shook her head and looked up at the ceiling. "Maybe they haven't been there that long." Then Betty's eyes widened and she impulsively grabbed Jud's wrist. "Or maybe ... maybe they don't own the place but just stay there. Farmers around here, sometimes they're charitable to old people down on their luck."

"Suppose to have been there since twenty-three, twenty-four, thereabouts. Heard they inherited the place, so they the owners."

Unconsciously Jud glanced at Betty's hand on his wrist and Betty withdrew it.

"Well," she said, "the farm might still be known by the name of whoever they inherited from. But if it's been that long, I doubt it. And I would have heard about an old southern couple, I'm sure. That would be something people talk about."

Jud had struck out. If a southern couple would get talked about and Betty had never heard of them, it wouldn't do much good to canvas barbers and grocers in Grafton. They wouldn't know about the Claytons either. Clutching at straws, he said: "Well, maybe their kin been through here on a visit, maybe folk without no accent." He found Suthrin's photograph and held it out toward her. "Seen anybody look like kin to this fella?"

"Is that ..." Betty said, staring in Jud's eyes before she dared look at the picture. "Is that the victim?"

Jud nearly grinned and laughed at Betty's sense of melodrama, but he caught himself and returned her stare with solemnity. "Yes, ma'am. It is. That ... that the victim."

Betty gently removed the photo from Jud's hand, as if it were a fragile, haunted relic. Thrilled, after one glance she exclaimed, "I recognize this guy." She seemed about ready to jump up and down.

"His picture been in the paper ..." Jud began.

"No, he's been in here. Never says a word. He's with the Guardalabenes and their crowd."

"Guardalabenes?" Jud asked.

Betty furrowed her brow and grew serious. "You don't want to mess with those guys. People say they'll kill you just for looking cross-eyed at them." Glancing at the drunk, she leaned in and cupped her hand by Jud's ear. "They're partners with Al Capone, people say."

Jud had never heard of anyone named Guardalabene. The Italians were all in the third ward, which in Jud's experience may as well have been further than Italy itself. But in the unlikely event some Grafton farmboys were "partners" with Al Capone, Jud doubted Suthrin had anything to do with it. Everybody knew eyewitnesses were unreliable when they were as eager to please as Betty, and all she had to go on was a fairly generic face in a black and white picture. A lineup, say, would be another thing. But even then, the story was just too unlikely. What would Suthrin be doing up north of Grafton with gangsters?

"Al warned me, first time they showed up, not to chitchat with those guys," Betty said, leaning back again and resuming a normal tone. "So I never have, even though they brought me a doll last time they were here."

"Brung you a doll, huh," Jud said. About to wrap it up, he turned to look at the shelf of dolls and politely asked, "Which one?" On inspection, he realized the shelves were packed three or four deep. Many of the dolls were no bigger than kewpies.

"It's not there," Betty said. "Those guys think they're such bigshots they had to bring me a real fancy one. Didn't fit in at all. People around here don't give away fancy things, and the whole point is all those dolls come from customers." She sped over to Jud's right and, crouching before the counter beneath the drunk's head, rooted around in a cabinet. "Here it is," she said, bringing the doll back to Jud. "I told them I would put it on my mantel at home, case they look for it next time, but I'm just going to give it to charity. Don't want anything from men like that."

Expressionless, Jud stared at the doll. "These Capone guys," he said. "The Guardalabenes. You sure they was the ones brung you this doll?"

"Course I'm sure. It was just last week. They said there was a shipment of these dolls and this one fell off a truck, whatever that means. A likely story, if you ask me. I wasn't born yesterday."

"Why they passin through here?"

"They were meeting another car by the pumps, after they ate. And that fella, the one whose picture you showed me, was with them. Don't ask me what they were up to, though. I wouldn't tell you even if I knew. The less I have to do with those people, the better."

Trying to keep calm, Jud dug through his pockets and found the pictures of the two Odenwald boys who had run away from the cop at the dance marathon. "Either of these two look familiar?"

Eagerly, Betty studied the pictures, but then frowned and handed them back. "Sorry. Never seen them before in my life."

Jud took the big ungainly doll from the counter and examined it. "Miz Betty," he said, "you wouldn't happen to know where these fellas come from when they drive through these parts, would you?"

Again Betty leaned in and whispered. "You kidding? Everybody knows. They got a 600-gallon still over on that farm. Biggest in the county."

At Jud's request Betty drew him a map after putting away the doll, which was identical to the one Flint had picked up from behind the bar at Mother's speakeasy. The one Mother's youngest boy said he'd never seen before, after being assured that, yes, Suthrin really was dead, and would not get up again.

31.

WHILE TECHNICALLY NORTH OF GRAFTON by perhaps half a mile, the farm of Jacob and Theresa Medinger was almost due east of the town, two miles south of Port Washington off Highway 141. Before turning onto the fledgling county road that led to the house and defined the farmland's southern border, Jud drove slowly up 141 to survey the land from the west. With his squad car casting a long north-eastern shadow across the snow from the setting sun, Jud spotted a granary, a log cabin syrup house, a spring-fed bathhouse, a milk house, a tanning shed, and another log cabin probably used as a blacksmith shop. All were spaced well apart to lessen the chance of spreading fire.

Still or no still, this was a legitimate farm dependent on backbreaking work, from which the winter no doubt came as a welcome respite.

Although Wisconsin had a few Italian farmers, were it not for Betty's unwanted doll Jud would have driven away, certain that no one named Guardalabene could possibly have anything to do with the place. But the doll meant Suthrin, and Suthrin, according to Betty, meant Guardalabene and the Medinger farm.

Jud turned onto the county road, pointing toward Lake Michigan from about a mile west. He could see a few other farms scattered haphazardly in the distance, and was unable to tell if the placement of telephone poles along the curb had conformed to the road or if the road had been forged for the poles.

Shortly he arrived at the Medinger's mailbox, set next to a handpainted sign reading ELK MEAT FIREWOOD STRAW + HAY, and pulled into the driveway toward a large open garage holding vehicles and farm machinery. He was careful to park the Pierce Arrow far enough back to be visible from the house. He took off his overcoat so his uniform would announce itself as quickly as his color and, leaving his cap on his head, walked to the door.

A healthy and congenial freckle-faced boy of about ten answered the bell, while a girl roughly the same age hovered half-hidden under the staircase behind him. The boy's eyes widened. Slapping his palm over his mouth, he turned around and looked at his sister to see whether she was seeing the same thing. She stared back and dramatically opened her mouth into the largest O she could manage, pantomiming great surprise.

Jud thought he'd better have the first word. "Afternoon, son. My name Detective Minor. I'm a policeman. Is your daddy at home?"

After thoughtfully freezing in position, the boy lowered his hand and extended it, as though playing at being a character in the pictures. "Elmer," he said. "Elmer Medinger. I'm ten. That's my sister, Elsie. She's nine."

Jud nodded at the girl, who pulled back into the staircase's shadow. He could smell dinner cooking. A pot roast. Also the smoke from a fireplace. For some reason the aromas made Jud feel lonesome. It would be nice to live someplace like this. "Please to make your quaintance Elsie, Elmer." He shook the boy's hand. "Where your daddy at?"

"He's fixing a beam in the tanning shed. I have a police badge. Wanna see it?"

An elderly woman in old-world dress made her way down the stairs and said with a German accent, "Who's at the door, Elmer?" Her hair was jet black and she looked a lot more French than German to Jud, who knew about such things.

The boy waited for his grandmother to see for herself, but Elsie's voice sounded from her hiding place: "It's a colored detective, gramma."

"Vell, let him in, boy," the woman said. "You'll catch your death from leavink the door vide open."

Having been identified as a cop, after he stepped in Jud removed his cap and respectfully bowed his head. "Detective Jud Minor, ma'am. Milwaukee Police Department."

"Mrs. Deppiesse," the woman said. "I see you haff met two of my grandchildren." Upstairs, a baby's wail erupted. "Und now, you haff heard three," she added with a slight smile. "Elsa, take care of little Harvey."

"Yes, gramma," Elsa or Elsie said before disappearing, again, but this time up rather than under the stairs.

The woman seemed friendly enough. Jud tried a little trick to enhance their rapport. "Alsace," he asked, "or Lorraine?"

"Such a detectiff," she complimented him. "Elmer, ve haff received a visit from Sherlock Holmes himself." She patted her hands together a couple of times to signify applause.

"Is Sherlock Holmes colored?" Elmer asked.

"Lorraine," his grandmother answered, ignoring him. "At the Moselle border mit Luxembourg. Vas it the accent?"

"Couldn't of told by just that," Jud admitted. "But add in your last name and the color of your hair. Good chance it Alsace-Lorraine."

"My hair is dyed," she said. "Und it vas my husband's name." Jud could tell she was being droll, so he smiled. "You know they put me in the government rolls last year, the man hears my accent und says I vas born in Germany. I said I vas born 1868. It vasn't Germany till 1871. I say now it's 1930. Hasn't been Germany since 1919. But he pays no attention to an old lady und there it is, in black und vite. Mrs. Deppiesse, born in Germany. A spy, maybe?"

Jud sensed the woman was bored here at the farm and glad to have someone outside the family to talk to. "I figure Miz Medinger's your daughter?"

She nodded sadly. "The one cryink upstairs is her fourth. Poor Theresa needs her rest. She got the baby blues. I'm lettink her nap in the den. I put in the roast. For her, I peel the potatoes." She stared expectantly at Jud, then turned to her grandson. "Elmer, go get your father und little La Verne."

"I wanna help the detective," Elmer protested.

"Schnell." After the boy ran out the door, Mrs. Deppiesse grew serious. "Let us haff a seat in the parlor," she said, and led Jud into a small homey room dominated by a Christmas tree beneath which sat a dozen immaculate new toys. She settled at one end of a couch and motioned for Jud to sit at the other. Across from them, the fireplace crackled without much visible smoke. "Is this about Jacob's ... uh, Jacob's tenants?"

Jud registered the word with interest. It changed the thrust of his inquiry. "Can't be goin into that, ma'am," he said apologetically. "That between me and the man of the house."

Mrs. Deppiesse nodded. "Jacob is a gut man. Franciscan." Jud wasn't sure what that meant, other than religious, so he kept his mouth shut. "Ya, he run into some trouble a vile back, und now there's the tenants. But Jacob, he does no harm. He provides for my poor daughter, still cryink her eyes out every day from the baby blues. That vill pass, as it always does. But please, detectiff, don't give her somethink real to cry about."

Without reassuring her, Jud produced Suthrin's photo. "You ever seen this man?" he asked, holding it at arm's length.

She scanned the picture without reaching for it. "Never see anybody here, except the little ones comink to play mit Elmer und Elsie. You vant some coffee, maybe? Sorry to say, all ve haff is chicory."

Jud's response was drowned out by the sound of Elmer bursting through the door in the other room and screaming, "Gramma, I found dad and La Verne. Told ya they was in the tanning shed."

Mrs. Deppiesse rose and returned to the front hall. "Jack," Jud heard her say, "there is a police detectiff here to speak mit you about a photograph."

"Like I says, Dad," Jud heard Elmer say, "he's colored."

"Run on, Elmer." The man's voice was hoarse but gentle. "Thank you, mutti."

"There is nothing to fear, Jack ... he is most intelligent and civilized," Mrs. Deppiesse said as Jack Medinger came around the corner holding a sleepy girl of three or four in one arm. He wore a wool stocking cap and had not removed his winter coat. As Jud stood he noted the haggardness of the farmer's deeply lined, almost brown face, and the circles under his eyes. He appeared to be in his early forties.

"Thank you, mutti," he repeated. Mrs. Deppiesse remained unseen in the hall, deferring to the presence of the two men about to talk business in another room. "Please take Elmer with you to the kitchen."

Jud caught a glimpse of the woman and the child passing toward the kitchen, Elmer complaining with every step.

"Detective Jud Minor, sir. You must be Mr. Medinger."

Jack Medinger laid his daughter down on the couch and, after shaking Jud's hand and pointing to an adjacent chair, took a place at the little girl's feet and removed his stocking cap. He started untying the girl's shoes. "No use in her wearing them in the house," he said with embarrassment. "Just wear out faster."

"Bet she grow out of em pretty quick," Jud said.

"Bought a size too big and put two pairs of socks on her. She didn't never wear shoes all summer till October." The girl observed the scene through one open eye, then put her thumb in her mouth and dozed off once her father was done.

"Mr. Medinger," Jud said, leaning forward with his cap in his hands between his opened knees, "I ain't here to cause you no trouble. Your bidness is your bidness. I'm here investigatin the personal connections of this man." For the fourth time that afternoon Jud revealed Suthrin's picture.

The farmer made a show of carefully examining Suthrin's face, then returned the photo. "I'm sorry, officer. Fraid I can't help." Then he responded the same way when Jud showed him the photos of the two Odenwald boys.

"This man," Jud said, indicating Suthrin, "he sometime with an Italian gentleman. Fella named Guardalabene."

"Well, I wouldn't know about that." Medinger's big Adam's apple bobbed up and down his long skinny throat as he swallowed. He was in need of a shave. Jud felt bad to have to trouble him like this. He was glad the man had sent away his son, and that little La Verne, had she been awake, was too young to understand.

Jud got to the point. "Mr. Medinger, do you have tenants on this farm?"

Medinger, prepared for the question, tried to rally. "Don't see how that's the business of the Milwaukee Police Department." Clearly, it went against his nature to be contentious, and he was unable to scrub the friendliness and civility from his tone. He was like a bad actor reading lines. "If I ain't under arrest, and you got no warrant to search my property, don't see how I got to answer that question. And even if I did have, uh ... as you say, tenants, that ain't against no zoning law I ever heard about in this county." He cleared the phlegm now audible in his throat. "It's a farm. Ain't no neighbors. No one to complain about it."

As the man spoke, Jud found himself reading an egg-shaped purple plaque on the wall, its edges decorated with flowery frills. Beneath the words HOME BLESSINGS, curved over a small golden crown, it quoted at length from the Book of Joshua, concluding, "AS FOR ME AND MY HOUSE WE WILL SERVE THE LORD." He wished he could leave.

"Even without no dry laws, Mr. Medinger," Jud said, "operatin a still is a public nuisance, no matter you got neighbors or not."

"You ain't no dry agent," Medinger said. "And I know enough lawmen to be sure you ain't interested in some still. I told you I never seen that fella in the picture. You said he was what you're investigating, so I think that's that." He got up and put a log on the fire, probably just to have something to do.

Jud sat back in the chair and sighed, frowning at Medinger's glances without a sense of intimidation, as one might react to a botched play by the home team or some other neutral irritant.

"Okay," Jud said, "I'm gonna try one more time. No offense or nothin, but way I got it figured, if you really square, no reason you be gettin so defensive." Jud waited till the business of arranging the firelog was done. "I think you got tenants on this farm and I think you scared of em. Well, no need to be scared of the man in the picture. He gettin cremated next week."

Jud let that sink in, then continued, again leaning forward.

"And you right. I ain't interested in no still. I'm jus tryin to make some connections. So, tell you what. I won't go back and get no warrant. I'll leave you alone the rest of your life and not mention you to nobody, not even my lieutenant or captain, and treat all this as stricly confidential, one man to another, you and me."

Medinger returned to the couch after nervously adjusting the angle of an ornament on the Christmas tree. He seemed to have prepared his response long before Jud had finished speaking. "Way the judges are in this county, take you a month to get a warrant. Maybe forever, if you got no case."

"I know. That one reason I don't wanna try. The other reason is, tell you frankly ..." Jud paused. "Don't wanna scare your poor wife."

Medinger absently smoothed a blonde lock out of his daughter's face. Jud felt him surrender. Finally the farmer said: "Think he's a driver, is all."

"A driver," Jud repeated. "What about the two boys."

"Don't know them." Again he cleared his throat. A visit from the law was frightening. "Look, officer. A few years back, I made some mistakes. Ended up owing more money than I could pay, and not to any bank." Medinger held one hand to his face and Jud feared he might start sobbing, but he just rubbed his eyes. "Foreclosure ain't the remedy we're talking about. Know what I mean? So the deal was, I let them use the old smithing cabin. OK, so, they get so much surplus from that still, sometimes they hide the product in the Lion's Den Gorge a mile from here. That fellow," he nodded toward the picture in Jud's hand, "has loaded the truck and driven over there, to the gorge. I heard them talking about it once. That's all I know."

"He with Guardalabene?"

"Guardalabene, Vallone, Tusa, Aiello, Dominick. Those are the names I've heard over the years. You'd get me killed, you know, if they ever found out I told you." He laughed bitterly. "I'd welcome a fed raid, since I would get rounded up, too, charged with landlord liability. And then I'd be done with the problem. Just say to the judge I had no idea what my tenants were up to. Get off with a slap on the wrist, and those Italians wouldn't blame me."

With some relief Jud knew he was done invading this family's privacy. He'd gotten the point. Done his job. Finished his work here. Either Suthrin was a special agent who had infiltrated a criminal gang, or he was the gang's mole in the police department. Jud wouldn't have to put much thought into deciding which scenario was more likely.

32.

MAKING HIS MOONLIT WAY down the paved diagonal corridor from Reservoir Avenue, with the brick wall of Reinhard Jansky's abandoned sheet metal shop to his right, and the tall chain-metal fence protecting against the steep bluff to his left, Bobby Bowen, already drunk, anticipated a good crowd of curiosity seekers at Mother's that night, what with the murder and all. He hoped to see some new faces. He had pretty much covered all the regulars. Still, there was always something to report, and lately in his travels even familiar characters, usually unworthy of comment, were giving voice to gradually more radical thoughts and inclinations.

Mother's had the typical crew of any neighborhood speakeasy, present in various permutations when Bobby casually dropped in every month or two. The businessman, the bodybuilder, the former flapper, the grizzled old man, the rich widow, the intellectual, the recent immigrant, the Great War vet, the red, the proto-fascist, the Hoover man, the Roosevelt man, the more upscale call girl, the less upscale call girl, the Theosophist, the lady astrologer, the occasional colored guys or couples, the regular colored poet seeking inspiration, in this case, beyond the nearby border of Bronzeville ...

Less than a decade ago the colored poet would have been the main object of Bobby Bowen's attention, pointing him toward other colored writers in the area, perhaps bringing some of them to Mother's at Bobby's suggestion, letting Bobby read their work and that of their acquaintances so he could earn the automatic bonus whenever he sent in a book report to Edgar Hoover. How obsessed Hoover and his peers had been with colored writers. Bobby had probably read more plays, poems, short stories, and novels by colored writers than anybody in Harlem, with its rinky-dink so-called renaissance.

But in mid-decade Calvin Coolidge had quietly declared the red scare over as far as the Bureau of Investigation was concerned, unaware that Brigadier General Moseley in the Army's Military Intelligence Division was picking up the slack, along with the United States Secret Service and the so-called "red squads" of most big city police departments. Bobby had worked for them all, in fact was one of their favorites, combining the literacy of his English degree with the ambulatory cover of his interstate trucking business. The spymasters even made a point of getting him contracts with sympathetic businesses in the midwest so he could continue traveling from place to place with his ears wide open and his typewriter waiting at the motel. Indeed, after the crash he would not have been able to remain an independent trucking contractor absent these job networks supporting his work as an intelligence stringer, haunting town after town to root out potential enemies of the state so the full-time professionals would have a shortlist to consult in identifying those who deserved special focus.

Over the years he'd learned to find places like Mother's, in working-class areas near a city's colored quarter, where rents and mortgages were lower. The downtown speakeasies had far less of a neighborhood feeling and were far more subject to raids than the hundreds of converted corner saloons, familiar for decades to the locals. Over time, places like Mother's offered a conveniently representative cross-section of a city's working class and its environs, where radicalism invariably had its roots. They were also the only "integrated" hangouts in town, since reputation was not much of an issue for an illegal business and colored folks' money was no less valuable. And like all metropolitan speakeasies they also hosted their share of the idealistic young women who were prime bait for jaded rabble-rousers recruiting fresh blood from among the easily gulled and brainwashed. There was no one easier in the world to manipulate than a middle-class twenty-year-old girl who recently had learned for the first time that poverty and injustice not only existed but were built in, literally integral, to the system. When Bobby sometimes wondered why colleges were not a top priority for investigation, after a moment he would come to his senses and realize that they almost certainly were. He just hadn't been told about it.

The copious blood he'd read about in the papers had been cleared from the snow at the end of Jansky's old driveway, where the pavement angled into the unpaved alley running alongside the nondescript wall at the back of the penny restaurant, meaning the front of the speakeasy. The metal fence continued at the new angle to his left, parallel to Hubbard Street on the other side of the building, even though the bluff now was at least ten yards distant. But with drunks stumbling around, it made sense not to take any chances, lest a customer tumble down the embankment to Commerce Street and get run over by a car or, say, by Bobby's tractor-trailer.

He knocked at the door. Randomly. Nobody, in any town he knew, used codes or passwords any more. There would be way too many to remember. Milwaukee alone must have sported five hundred saloons. The socialist city also had the peculiar distinction of leading the nation in the number of federal dry agents arrested by local police. Quite a point in its favor. Despite those he worked for, or rather in common with them, Bobby hated the dry agents as much as the next guy. Edgar Hoover, he knew, didn't give a damn about illegal liquor, being obsessed with reds and only reds, but had got into the gangster-busting business only for the incredible publicity it offered, as he'd learned from all the print devoted to dry agent Eliot Ness. And Brigadier General Moseley wouldn't dream of having a social event for his men and their wives without a well-stocked cabinet. As for the police and their secretive red squads, forget about it. Prohibition existed for those street-brawling thugs only insofar as it kindled the wound wrought by federal interlopers.

After the peephole briefly darkened to provide some lead time at any suggestion of a raid, the door opened outward, pushed by the hand of a drunken girl barely out of her teens. A humid burst of warm air blew past Bobby, who had to shove his way in. The place was packed, wall-to-wall with college kids on Christmas break who had apparently flooded into Brewers Hill after reading about the murder. Bobby didn't recognize anyone, at least among those relegated to standing room. He couldn't see the dozen stools or their occupants in front of the bar, and too many bodies blocked his view and the light was too dim to discern the faces of those customers packed six apiece in the booths. He struggled toward the bar, his hands held up and open beside his head so he would not inadvertently molest any of the college girls, or for that matter boys.

Something scurried past him from behind. At his feet a small brown hand plucked a cigar butt off the floor, then grabbed an empty Coke bottle perhaps brought along by Joe College to lower the cost on mixers. Crouching, the figure made its way among the legs of the standing-room crowd, cleaning up. It was Spook, the colored girl. While the college boys talked of murder, the girls were infatuated with this child.

"Oh, she's adorable," one girl said. "What's your name?"

Spook as always said nothing.

"She's so shy," another girl slurred through her evident drunkenness.

Bobby decided to flirt. What the hell. The conversational opportunity was too great to pass up. If he spoke loud enough, half a dozen of these janes would prick up their ears and ask him questions about the child. Bobby liked those odds.

"She isn't shy," he all but hollered. "She can't talk. She's dumb."

Sure enough, a third girl turned to him as Spook disappeared with her hands full on her way back to the bar, seeking the wastebasket. "Does she really work here?"

"Not only that," Bobby replied, admiring the co-ed's scarlet hair. "She lives here."

Like clockwork a fourth girl, the prettiest so far, joined the conversation. "There's a colored family here? I thought the guy behind the bar was one of the family, and he's white."

On tiptoe Bobby scanned above the bar. Delbert, Mother's third or fourth eldest at perhaps fifteen, stood serving drinks alongside an unfamiliar college kid who seemed to be boisterously volunteering as a second barkeep. "That's Mother's boy, all right. I don't know who the other one is."

"John Carson," the prettiest girl laughed. "From Marquette. What a character."

Bobby nodded, dismissing the interruption. "But the colored girl is in the family, too. Mother adopted her."

"And put her to work?" the redhead asked incredulously.

"She's so cute," the very drunk girl said.

Bobby affected the wisdom of age. He turned his attention to the drunkest girl. She would be his mark. "Before the crash a lot of the families around here could afford live-in help. That girl's parents…."

"What's her name?" the drunkest girl asked, then repeated: "She's so cute."

"Not half as cute as you are," Bobby said with a wink. "My name's Bobby. Own my own trucking company. As for the girl, her name is…." He started to say Spook, but then thought it might work against him. "Charlotte. Her parents were the live-in help, after Mother's husband died."

"Or escaped," a familiar boy said, noting the four-to-one gender ratio of the conversation and cutting it in half. "I've been coming here since I was a frosh. If you saw Mother, you'd wonder how she had any kids that weren't adopted. A bug-eyed Betty if I ever saw one. Meanest little thing you ever met, too. Mrs. Grundy all the way."

Annoyed at the competition, Bobby moved in close on the drunkest girl's ear, his nose brushing her bobbed hair, but spoke loudly enough for the other three girls to hear him. "It's a sad story. Charlotte's parents saved up for a lousy used car, a real flivver. Drove on an icy narrow road one night and the brakes went out. Dead on arrival."

"That's horrible," the prettiest one gasped.

Bobby leaned away from the drunkest girl and tried to assume an expression of world-weary cynicism. "Mother didn't think so, once it turned into a windfall for her." His mind worked quickly as to whether he should say more. He would be divulging a secret he'd learned only through his own research, unknown to the other regulars at the bar. At the time, he'd figured that adopting a colored child could mean secret pinko tendencies. It was his duty to investigate. After all, everyone knew interracial marriages were a dead giveaway, that the spouses were invariably card-carrying reds. The analogy was obvious. But in this case, Bobby discovered, the color-mixing had a healthy capitalist basis.

Fortunately the local boy, the only regular in the conversation, had been diverted by one of his fraternity brothers, who appeared to be about to vomit. The two made their way back toward the door. Regarding the girls, Bobby was certain none of them would ever return to this obscure blind pig after tonight's faddish gathering.

"Charlotte had an uncle," he said eventually. "Fixed refrigeration units for the army in the war. Once refrigerators started selling like hotcakes in the twenties, he came up with some improvements. Got three or four patents. Licensed parts in every refrigerator sold for the next five years. Made a million. But he was a playboy, didn't want to adopt the girl, so he set up a trust. Mother gets ten grand a year to look after her."

"Ten grand," marveled the prettiest girl, wide-eyed.

"And that's pre-deflation dollars," Bobby added. "Worth almost half again now as when the deal was set up."

He felt a cool rush of air and unconsciously turned toward the door, blocked from view. It seemed the two frat boys had made it to the alley without incident. At the same time, apparently, someone else came in, tall enough to be seen. Bobby knew that the guy must have just entered. He was sure of this because, still programmed by old instincts, he otherwise would have zeroed in on a thirty- or forty-year-old colored man. Although he wouldn't be able to get much done with the regulars till the college kids thinned out, Bobby thought, at least he could investigate this guy in the meantime.

33

"**H**OW ABOUT YOU AND ME claw our way to the bar and I'll buy you a drink," Bobby said to the drunkest girl after a few more minutes. He was glad he'd already tied one on at the motel, where he had a connection.

She clutched his forearm and followed him as he elbowed past the crowd. "How come you know so much about that little colored girl?" she asked.

He wanted her to leave the subject alone once they were within earshot of any regulars, none of whom knew of Spook's wealthy uncle or the man's arrangement with Mother. Everyone just presumed Spook had no family and so had been taken in by the Odenwalds, who had several adopted members providing Mother with free labor. There was no reason for the truck driver Bobby Bowen, of all people, to be the only one who knew Mother's secret. If word got around, he would be exposed as a snoop. No one would open up to him any more.

"I drop in when I get a contract in town," he said, trying to change the subject. "Railroads are so damn regulated these days, once people realize the ICC, uh, the Interstate Commerce Commission doesn't mess with trucks, you'd be surprised how many jobs I get all over the midwest with companies sick of red tape."

Obviously, the girl was far more interested in free drinks than in trucking, but she asked a token question anyway. Something about what sort of stuff he trucked around. Bobby rattled off a dull list of numerous products, relieved to put the subject of Spook to rest. It had done its job and provided an introduction to an intoxicated co-ed. Also, now that the girl knew he was someone familiar to the regulars, she would be less inhibited about hanging on the arm of a stranger twice her age.

The colored guy was leaning against the dead center of the faux mahogany bar, squeezed between two stools and surveying those who surrounded him, like he was looking for somebody. Bobby approached the two seated patrons to the man's right, a couple of college boys with their backs to the bar as they chatted with each other and scanned the girls in the room.

"I'll pay a dollar each for those two stools," he said to them, waving two bills in the air.

One of the kids was game. "Make it two each."

Bobby laughed, like a sport. "How about three total, and you can divide it."

The two kids looked at each other like they'd pulled off a successful con. Bobby handed them three dollars as the drunk girl looked on, no doubt impressed to see him throwing so much money around before he'd even gotten a drink. He sat down next to the colored guy and she scooted in beside him on his right.

"Hey, Delbert," Bobby said.

"Hey, Bobby. Long time no see. Boilermaker?"

Bobby confirmed his usual and got a rum and Coke for the girl without consulting her. He was wondering how to include the colored guy in his conversation with the girl when, to his surprise, the guy spoke first.

"You a regular, I see."

Bobby pretended he had barely noticed the man to his left. "Nothing regular about this gang tonight." He held out his hand. "Bobby."

"Judson. Please to meet you, Bobby." He released Bobby's hand and reached toward the girl, who nearly fell off her stool when she leaned toward him.

"Lil," she said, shaking his hand while steadying herself. "But not dirty Lil." She laughed stupidly at what must have been her standard joke.

"Why so many you kids here tonight, Lil?" Judson asked.

"It's a big lollapalooza ... everybody said it would be just the berries," Lil explained. "Don't ask me why. It was just one of those spontaneous things, people phoning each other and such. Everybody in college within two hundred miles got the word to check it out."

"Check it out?" Judson said.

"The scene of the murder, silly."

"Like swallowing goldfish and flagpole sitting," Bobby suggested.

"You a regular," Judson repeated. Bobby nodded then drained his shot. "Know much about the fella that done got killt?"

"Southern guy," Bobby said, happy that the topic would at least be of interest to the girl beside him, already halfway through her rum and Coke. He ordered another and secretly winked at Judson, one old horndog to another. "In fact, people called him Suthrin."

"Lots of yankee enemies?" Judson asked with a smile.

"He seemed to fit in well enough," Bobby said. "If by fitting in you mean lounging around with a scowl on his face and acting like he owned the joint." Bobby tried to figure out how to steer the conversation in a fruitful direction. He lowered his voice, confiding in Judson. "But aren't all cops the enemy of the workingman? Tell you for sure, he'd think you were the enemy. Thought colored people should be kept in their place. Typical pawn of the fascist corporate police state. Ask me, nothing more important to America's future than race relations. Once white workers accept colored workers as their brothers instead of competition for their labor, you'll see things change in this country mighty fast. Better believe it."

Judson didn't take the bait, at least not yet. "So he have trouble with colored folk comin here? Fightin with em, an such?"

"Well, not in so many words," Bobby continued at normal volume, while in fact having nothing of interest he was at liberty to say about Suthrin. He'd seen the guy half a dozen times over the years, found out he was a cop, and lost interest. Cops were never reds, though some of them were pushing for overtime wages and the eight-hour day.

"Wonder why he out back of a speak everybody know was closed," Judson said. "Think he doin bidness with one of the regulars here? Some kinda shakedown, maybe?"

Bobby improvised. "Shakedown? Well, it always did seem like he had something on Mother."

"Really?" Lil said, intrigued. "Do you think Mother did it? This is so exciting."

Bobby was relieved she hadn't lost interest. "Wouldn't put it past that old coot. She been in here tonight?"

"No," Lil said. "It's really disappointing. Everybody wanted to get a look at her." Lil drained her second glass and Bobby put his hand up for another. "Say," she drawled, narrowing her heavily made-up eyes. "Maybe she's on the lam."

Bobby led her on. "You know, now you mention it, it's the first time I've been in this place and Mother's not here." This was more of an exaggeration than a lie.

"What make you think Suthrin got somethin on Mother?" Judson said.

"Well, okay, maybe he was just being your typical bastard cop. Always getting his drinks free, that sort of thing. Cops like nothing more than sticking it to people making an honest living. Of course, they're working men, too. But you know what that's called?" He swiveled his neck toward the girl to gauge her response. "False consciousness. Identifying with your oppressors instead of your own class. Any of your professors ever talk about that, honey?"

"Consciousness?" she said. "What, like in psychology?" Delbert brought her another drink.

"Even if he troublin Mother," Judson said, "don't need to do that at midnight. Got to think he was up to no good with some other regular here.

Got some kinda deal goin. Both knew the place closed Christmas Eve, arrange to meet in the alley where bound to be no one else around."

"Only deal I ever saw him working on," Bobby said, "was what he'd get from the bar girls in exchange for not busting them."

"Givin trouble to the local talent," Judson said. "That can't make a man too popular."

"Bar girls?" Lil said. "You mean, like, prostitutes? Are they here now? I'd love to see one. That would be just the berries."

Bobby decided he'd better get Lil back to his motel before she got too pickled. Judson hadn't taken the bait, didn't even hint at anything subversive. Bobby could go have some fun with the girl, let her pass out in the room afterwards, and leave her there while he came back to Mother's in the wee hours.

"Tell you what, Lil," Bobby said. "Sounds like you're eager to see the real world. I know half a dozen gin palaces downtown that'll knock your socks off."

"Really?" Lil said. "That would be the berries. This is only the second time I've been to the city since I started college. There's nothing happening in Appleton."

"Just have to stop by my motel room first." Bobby turned to Judson and winked again. "Going to head on out. Tell you one thing, though. I for one won't miss that son of a bitch when I visit this place. Just a gloomy Gus, if you ask me."

"And an enemy of the workingman," Judson said.

"You got it, brother," Bobby said, encouraged. Now he would have something to report. He lowered his voice. "Think you'll close this joint tonight? I might find my way back. Might like to chat some more. Listen to all the scuttlebutt about Suthrin while the subject's still fresh."

"Well," Judson said, "if I don't see you again, just let me ask you about the guy, straight out. What you really think? Why you spose somebody wanna kill him?"

Before Bobby could answer, Spook trotted behind the bar with her hands full of trash and dumped it in the can under the sink.

"She's so cute," Lil said. She leaned over and grabbed Judson's arm. Flirtatiously? Bobby thought not. She could barely see straight. "Did you know," Lil said to Judson, "that that little girl has a millionaire uncle who gives ten grand a year to these people just because they adopted her?"

Shit, thought Bobby.

34.

No, Jud did not know that. So how, he wondered, was it possible the drunk girl did? She said she'd only been to the city twice. Maybe it was a stupid rumor making the rounds among the college kids at the speakeasy that evening.

Suddenly Bobby started singing: "Dirty Lil, dirty Lil, lives on top of a garbage hill, never washes, never will…." Jud had the distinct impression he was trying to step on Lil's comment about Charlotte. Why? Was he the source?

Lil stifled Bobby's singing by laughing much too hard, like she was being mercilessly tickled. "Stop it, Bobby. You slay me. I told you I'm not her."

"Where you hear that?" Jud asked. "About the ten grand."

Bobby slapped some money on the bar and all but pulled Lil off her stool. "Let's go, honey."

"I got to powder my nose," Lil said, struggling to her feet.

"They use the restaurant's johns, down the hall behind that door," Bobby said, pointing at the door behind the bar. "Here, let me show you."

"I'm a big girl," she said, breaking away from him.

When she was gone, Jud said: "Get the sense you don't want that girl talkin about Charlotte."

Bobby started to reply but stopped himself and finished his beer instead.

"Rich uncle," Jud said. "Ten grand a year. Ain't never heard none of that before."

"Look, buddy," Bobby said, putting his hand on Jud's shoulder. "Mother told me that in confidence. I was talking big to that girl, figured she'd never be in here again. You'd be doing me a big favor to keep it to yourself."

"So it true," Jud said. He recognized he'd gained an edge. Bobby had shown vulnerability, but naturally presumed Jud would not take advantage of it. The guy would never have said anything about a "big favor" had he known Jud was a cop.

"And, y'know, it's none of my business," Bobby went on. "I don't want to get Mother in trouble. If she doesn't keep the girl, in this nice big family of hers, who will? Girl would end up in an orphanage."

"Why Mother ever get in trouble for keepin her?" Jud asked. When Bobby shrugged, Jud leaned in and said: "Maybe I do tell the regulars about all that. Or maybe I keep it to myself, if you tell me what else you got to say." Somehow Jud was sure the threat would work. After almost a decade grilling lowlifes on his beat, he could sense it. He went in for the kill. "So, why Mother get in trouble just for keepin that little girl?"

Bobby sighed, and Jud knew at once he had succeeded. It always surprised him how easily certain types surrendered at the smallest threat. But this was the first time he'd experienced it out of uniform. "The girl's uncle," Bobby said, "is the one who adopted her on paper. She's supposed to be living with him. City and state bureaucrats got no idea the girl's here. That's why she's never in school."

"Don't say."

"And, you promise to keep it to yourself, I'll tell you something else." A bit too drunk, Bobby looked at Jud, who nodded, amazed at the man's stupidity. But then, of course, Bobby thought Jud was just some random colored guy. "I said Suthrin had something on Mother. Well, that was it. He gets ... got ... a piece of that ten grand, every year, for not informing the probate court, the truancy officers, and so on."

As Jud took this in, he noticed Del Odenwald, behind the bar to his right, suddenly becoming agitated. With a horrified expression Del started trying to signal someone across the room without being too obvious about it. At first Jud thought irrationally that Del had overheard Bobby, but that wasn't possible. He was fifteen feet away and the room was too loud.

Jud followed Del's eyes and turned around to look. Then he pulled his handcuffs from his pants pocket, having kept them with him when he'd gone home to eat dinner and change out of his uniform. He ducked low to avoid being seen and bulldozed through the crowd too quickly for the college kids to respond as he collided with them. He grabbed Ernst Odenwald's arm and cuffed his wrist, then did the same to Jacob with the other handcuff.

Clearly, the two had been attempting to slip into their home while camouflaged by the mob of their contemporaries in the bar. Knowing Jud was there, and surprised at the sight of his big brothers, Del had attempted to warn them away the moment he saw them arrive.

Amid cries and grunts of protest from those immediately surrounding him, Jud clutched the chain between the brothers' cuffs and dragged them back toward the bar. "You two under arrest for obstruction of justice," he said at the top of his lungs.

Startled, and increasingly thrilled, the college kids cleared a path for Jud, while also closing off any easy escape route for the Odenwalds. When Jud reached the bar, he said to Bobby: "Grab that one while I hold on to this one."

Bobby did as asked. "Holy shit," he said. "You're a cop?"

"Yeah," Jud said. He winked, mocking Bobby's previous gesture. "Don't work for no red squad, though."

In the dim light, Bobby's face itself turned red.

When Jud was satisfied the two arrestees were under control, he shouted at them, "Sit your butts down on the ground." They stared at him in incomprehension but did not move. After a glance at Bobby, Jud said: "Okay, we do it for you." The two older men pulled the brothers to the floor.

Removing the key from his pocket, Jud briefly uncuffed Ernst, slipped the chain around the iron footrail running the length of the bar, and reattached the cuff. He doubted the two young men, even combining their strength, would be able to pull the footrail off its bolts.

"Thanks," Jud said to Bobby after returning to his feet.

"Sure thing, officer," Bobby said. "Guess you probably know not to take any of the stuff seriously that I said about cops."

"I'll tell you straight," Jud said. "You really gots to work on your line." He shook his head and looked at the floor, expressing embarrassment on Bobby's behalf. "Too obvious, man."

Lil returned from the restaurant's ladies' room and could not but have noticed that everyone in the bar, now twice as loud, was staring at the spot where she and Bobby had been sitting. A semicircle of space had been formed by people getting out of the way or just retreating to get a better look at the tableau.

"Anybody back there in the restaurant?" Jud yelled over to Lil when she was still at the far left end of the bar, trying to push through that arc of the semicircle. He knew that the ladies' room entrance was perpendicular to the hallway's door to the restaurant. The door's window was directly in front of anyone walking all the way down the hall.

Puzzled, she loudly responded: "I saw the other bartender using the payphone." Pushing her way through, after a moment she stood before the cross-legged Odenwald boys. "Hey," she scolded them angrily, "that's our spot."

"They're under arrest," Bobby said.

Now she noticed the handcuffs. Her pencil-thin eyebrows shot up. "Are they the murderers?" she asked gleefully, echoing everyone else in the room.

"Who the other bartender?" Jud meanwhile demanded of Del, who was frozen in shock behind the bar and no longer concerned with doing business.

"Just some guy," Del said. "Uh, said his name was John Carson. Volunteered to help out behind the bar. Said it would be a hoot. Didn't even have a drink. I guess he needed to make a call and saw the key to the restaurant back here."

"Well, go get him out of there, and don't lock it back up," Jud ordered. "I need that room."

Lil was most amused by Jud's demeanor. "Somebody elect you the boss while I was gone?"

"Turns out Judson here is a cop," Bobby explained.

"You were investigating the murder?" Lil said, her voice briefly an octave higher. "Wow. And I was right there while you were doing it. I feel like I'm in the pictures. This would never happen in Appleton."

"Let's get out of here, babe," Bobby said. "Let the officer do his job."

"I want to stay," Lil whined. "It's like Sam Spade."

Del returned with John Carson. Immediately, Jud said to Bobby: "Give me a hand with these two. Wanna take em back into the restaurant. Have a little talk with em." Crouching as he unlocked the cuffs, Jud said: "Once they're gone, the show will be over and you can take Miz Lil to one of them gin palaces downtown." Then he and Bobby steered the two elder Odenwalds to the door behind the bar.

"I'll be back in a jiffy, babe," Bobby called out to Lil over the din. "Don't take any wooden nickels while I'm gone."

"I want to go back there too," Lil shouted. "It's like being in the pictures. I'm Thelma Todd."

"Stay there, Miz Lil," said Jud. "Bobby be back in a minute. Teach you all about ... what was it?" He laughed. "False consciousness?"

Milwaukee Tribune

SPECIAL EDITION

2 ARRESTED IN MURDER OF POLICEMAN

Faked Alibi In Look-Alike Dance Marathon Performance

Sons Of Owner Of Building Where Body Found

The bloody Christmas Eve slaying of Milwaukee Police Department patrolman Landis Humphreys may be one step closer to being solved following the arrest Saturday night of Jacob Odenwald, 23, and Ernst Odenwald, 21, both of 1866 N. Hubbard st., after an all day police manhunt for the two.

The two Odenwalds are the eldest sons of Mrs. Lothar C. (Herta) Odenwald, proprietress of Mother's Hubbard Penny Restaurant, located at the same address. Humphreys was found stabbed to death in the storage room at the back of the building, its door left open to the short section of Reservoir ave. providing truck access for the restaurant's supplies.

Elaborate Alibi Scheme Foiled.

Following a lead developed by acting Det. Judson W. Minor, negro, who is the lead investigator on the case and the officer who first discovered the heinous

(Turn To Page 2, Column 1)

(Continued From Page 1, Column 2)

crime, Patrolman Victor B. Horstmann, 23, tracked the Odenwalds down Sunday morning at the notorious dance marathon lately located on the city's far north-west side, in the area known as Pigsville.

After Det. Minor assigned Horstmann to investigate, the patrolman spotted the Odenwalds behind the dance hall—and the pair broke and ran. Horstmann was seriously injured in the pursuit, and is expected to receive a commendation for his heroic efforts.

A spokesman for Mayor Hoan stated:

"The ability of two murder suspects to hide out at one of these dance marathons where so many gamblers, confidence men, and other nefarious types gather, exemplifies why our state supreme court was dead wrong to prevent Mayor Hoan from shutting down, once and for all, these dangerous threats to the moral decency of Milwaukee's women."

Hid Among Students
Visiting Crime Scene.

On a stake-out after an exhaustive and productive day brilliantly chasing down leads, Det. Minor later apprehended the Odenwalds as they tried to "blend in" with a crowd of college students engaged in merry-making at the scene of the crime.

Det. Minor reported:

"Several dozen college students had gathered on a lark in the alley behind the restaurant. They poured into the storage room when someone in the house opened the back door. In the resulting confusion, lasting several minutes, the Odenwalds saw their opportunity. Apparently, they were hiding nearby, and joined the crowd in an attempt to enter their home without being noticed. They must have known we would have the building under watch. Fortunately, I made out their faces and arrested them as soon as they made their move."

Already being hailed as a master detective, Minor, a 10-year veteran and the first negro hired to the city's Police Department, is still developing evidence in the case. In the meantime, the Odenwalds will be arraigned next week on charges including obstruction of justice.

—by Walter R. Meinecke (with assistance from John Carson)

35.

JUD HAD BEEN DISCOURAGED by the mob of college kids in Mother's. Even had they not chased away every regular, the noise would have made it impossible to hold a casual free-for-all conversation with those seated at the bar or pausing there to get a drink. He'd intended to hang out at the bar for a couple of hours and let the subject of Suthrin emerge naturally, on and off, so no one would clam up as they would in an interrogation. Obviously, his plan wasn't going to work.

But he'd gotten lucky. If he hadn't noticed Del serving a boilermaker without being asked, he would not have known Bobby was a regular. He probably would have left, none the wiser about Charlotte and before Jacob and Ernst Odenwald made their surprise appearance.

Now the two young men were connected by the pair of handcuffs looped through one leg of a heavy buffet counter, the chain blocked from floor level by the median girder connecting each leg to the next. They were able to stand and lean their backsides against the counter without much discomfort.

Once Bobby was gone from the restaurant, having again implored Jud to keep their shared secret to himself, Jud used the restaurant's payphone to call the station for backup. He emphasized that there was no hurry. He had the situation under control. Then, standing in front of the Odenwalds, he said: "You Ernst, right?" Staring wide-eyed at Jud as if at a madman, Ernst, the one with buck teeth and glasses, nodded. The other nodded with similar confusion when Jud said, "That make you Jacob." Jud was putting them on, parodying their ruse at the marathon.

"You know who we are," Ernst said stupidly. Jacob, however, had quickly gotten the joke, and kept his mouth shut.

They looked a little older, more filled out, than they did in their mugshots, taken after their arrest for joyriding two or three years earlier. It hadn't been much of a crime. The undamaged car was never intended by them to be stolen as opposed to borrowed without permission. They got off with a fine and no probation.

"So, which of you want to tell me why yall run away from a uniformed officer ain't even said nothin to you."

Jacob, Mother's eldest, said: "You've known us since we was in high school, Minor." This was not disrespectful. It was the custom for men to call the neighborhood cop by his last name, as every other familiar man was styled. "We ain't no murderers."

"Didn't say nothin about no murder."

"Well, that's what this is about, ain't it?"

"I asked yall a question. Why you run."

"We wasn't gambling," Ernst said. "Swear we wasn't." Jacob gave his brother's shoe an unsubtle sideways kick.

Jud affected surprise. "Why I care if you gamblin?"

Ernst ignored his brother's kick. "Well, figure if it ain't Suthrin, it's the dance marathon scam. Why else a cop trail us?"

"Ain't heard nothin about no marathon scam," Jud lied. "But if you involved in fixin one of them things, and gamblin on it, that bunco. Fraud."

"We ain't never gambled," Jacob said. "We was just paid to do a job."

"And," Ernst added, "Mr. Buer told us, it ain't fraud. Mr. Buer said anybody gambling got unclean hands."

"Unclean hands," Jud repeated.

"It's a lawyer word," Ernst explained helpfully. "Mr. Buer, he said it means nobody's got a right to sue you for their own wrongdoing. Ain't no crime to cheat a cheater."

Jud laughed without smiling. "Oh, so now you two a coupla lawyers. Guess you ain't heard, there two kind of law. There the kind where a fella sue somebody. And then there criminal law. Hear me? Criminal law. So you right, them gamblers can't sue you." He laughed again. "Unclean hands. That a good one."

"Cheating gamblers ain't no crime," Jacob rallied uncertainly.

Jud let them stew. Having been standing close, in their faces, he went to the nearest table and took a seat facing them across it with his back to the street entrance. He stared at them a while, like an inquisitor trying to choose the best instrument of torture.

Finally, he said: "Okay, so I guess you got it all worked out. It either Suthrin or the marathon. Can't be the marathon, since what you did there, whatever it was, ain't no crime. I mean, unclean hands and all." Again he was silent.

Jacob was clearly the more disciplined of the two. Ernst managed a minute or so of Jud's silence without volunteering anything further, but then couldn't take it any more. "We was at the dance or in Mr. Buer's basement the whole time," he said at last. "Cripes, everybody seen us."

"Everybody seen the one at the dance," Jud corrected him. "And if your little lookalike act help the other one to kill Suthrin, that accessory after the fact for the one that ain't done it, and maybe conspiracy. Conspiracy to murder, as you two fine upstandin lawyers must know, gets the same sentence as murder."

"I thought you said you didn't know nothing about the marathon scam," Jacob said, pleased with himself.

"I lied," said Jud.

"We ain't no murderers," Jacob repeated.

"You've known us since we was in high school, Minor," Ernst quoted his brother.

"Why would we kill Suthrin?" Jacob said. "What's he ever done to us?"

"Why you run?"

"We didn't even know nothing about Suthrin," said Ernst. "Jeez Louise. Just saw a cop and thought it was something to do with the marathon."

"Maybe one of you didn't know nothin about Suthrin," said Jud. "Maybe the other one did. So. Which of you two want to tell me how much the other one hate Suthrin."

The brothers looked at each other, perhaps thinking for the first time that one of them was guilty.

"Wasn't no blood or nothin on Jake's clothes," Ernst said, adding quickly: "Or mine."

"We both thought Suthrin was a jerk," Jacob admitted, "but that's how he was to everybody. Come on, Minor. Cripes. You know we ain't got no reason to kill the guy."

"Maybe he got somethin on you," said Jud. "Maybe he got somethin on Mother."

"Got something?" Jacob said. "Like what? We let him drink for free. He was in all the time. Plenty of people would say so. He can't close us down."

"Not about the speak," Jud said. "About Charlotte."

The only light in the restaurant came from the window of the door to the hallway, but Jud could see the brothers well enough to conclude Charlotte was the furthest thing from their minds. Again they looked at each other in confusion, each trying to divine if the other had any idea what Jud was talking about.

"What about Charlotte?" Jacob said.

"About your deal with her uncle," said Jud.

"Her uncle?" Ernst said. "There wasn't no deal. The guy didn't want her, is all we ever heard. So Ma adopted her."

"Did she?" Jud asked.

"Course she did," said Jacob.

"Seen the paperwork?"

"Why would we? It was six years ago."

"How come Charlotte never in school?"

Jacob answered with confidence: "She's home-schooled. No school for dumb kids in Milwaukee accepts coloreds. She'd have to go all the way out to Madison."

Jud laughed again, this time to suggest how gullible he thought the brothers were. "That ain't true," he said.

"No, it is true," Ernst insisted. "Ma looked into it. Got special permission from the state to home-school her."

"And you believe that? Twelfth biggest city in the country ain't got no school for a dumb colored girl?"

Briefly the two were speechless. Jacob cleared his throat. "Aw, for the love of Pete. What's this got to do with Suthrin?"

"I think you both know," Jud said. "Suthrin was blackmailin your family about the ten grand a year you get from that little girl's uncle. Suthrin knew Mother ain't never adopted Charlotte. Worth a lot of money to you, to get rid of him. And too much of a risk to keep him around."

"I couldn't agree more," said someone behind Jud at the front of the restaurant. Jud was startled at the intrusion. He turned and saw a tall heavyset man bundled up in layers of winter gear. "Still haven't fixed this thing, I see," the man said, examining the hinges Jud had broken on the door two days earlier.

"Excuse me, sir," Jud said. "Restaurant closed."

"Walter Meinecke," the man introduced himself. "You must be acting detective Judson W. Minor. I only caught the last part. About Suthrin blackmailing Mother. A very impressive theory."

Jud was nonplussed. "So you know this is police bidness and you interferin with it. Get on outta here."

"I work with the young fellow volunteering tonight behind the bar," Meinecke said, ignoring Jud.

Curious as to what the man was doing at the restaurant, and how he'd identified Jud not only by name but by his brand-new rank, Jud heard him out.

"Boy called John Carson," Meinecke said. "Had him come in tonight, keep an eye out for any, shall we say, breaking developments in this dramatic story. Grabbed a taxi two minutes after I got his call. Working late, you see, at the news desk of the Milwaukee *Tribune*."

"That so?" said Jud. Even in the dim light he could make out the man's black eye.

"You done with us yet?" Jacob said to Jud.

"We don't know nothin about no ten grand a year," said Ernst. "And I got to pee."

"Told you," said Jud. "You under arrest."

"For running away from a cop," Meinecke laughed, "who hadn't even spoken to them."

"What the hell?" Ernst said. "Was that in the papers?"

"It will be," Meinecke said, to Jud rather than the Odenwalds. "I trust you've told these boys their rights," he added.

"He ain't told us nothing," Ernst said. "Pretended like he don't even know us."

"Crew cut, buck teeth, big black frames," Meinecke enumerated, for the first time peering closely at Jud's prisoners. "You must be Ernst."

"What the hell?" Ernst repeated.

"Of course, you've both got crew cuts now," said Meinecke, reaching into his pocket for a flask. He offered it to Jud, who frowned and watched him take a swig before putting the flask away, then came over and sat at the table.

"Walter Meinecke," said Jud, finally registering the name. "I read your piece. Didn't like you makin up stuff I never said."

"Well," Meinecke replied, "you had the right to remain silent, unlike these boys. And I had the first amendment. If you'd prefer, I'll publish a retraction. I'll say I read my notes wrong, quoted the wrong guy. Plenty of eager sources to choose from." He laughed. "We can give your quote to Officer Flint."

"You get on outta here," said Jud, "or I'll have you up on a B and E."

"Wherefore he broke the close," said Meinecke, intoning this strange phrase in an oratorical voice. "But I didn't. The door was unlocked." He addressed the Odenwalds. "So, you boys want me to call you a lawyer? First consultation is on me."

"All right, then," said Jud. "Make it trespassin."

"I simply wandered in by mistake," Meinecke responded blandly. "Saw two terrified boys, handcuffed and vulnerable while being intimidated by a colored man in street clothes. My civic duty obliged me to remain long enough to investigate. Good Samaritan kind of situation. And, y'know, I still haven't seen a badge."

The hallway door opened and Flint entered, dressed in full uniform. "You have now," Jud said to Meinecke.

"Hey, Minor. Jeez, what a crowd in there. Ain't nobody old enough to vote, neither." Flint walked over to the Odenwalds and looked them up and down. "Cripes, you really think you need back-up to bring these knuckleheads in?"

"Ain't got but one pair of cuffs," Jud said. He dug out the key and tossed it to Flint. "Not gonna drag them two out of the place and another two blocks from there to where my car at. And I still got other things to do before goin back to the station."

Flint uncuffed Ernst, used his own cuffs to secure Ernst's hands behind his back, and did the same to Jacob with Jud's cuffs, one of them still attached.

"Minor acted like he don't even know us," Ernst complained.

"Someone really ought to explain to those boys," Meinecke said, "that they have the right to remain silent."

"Who the fuck are you?" Flint said.

"This is Walter," said Jud, avoiding Meinecke's last name in case Flint might identify it with the previous day's front-page story. "He with me."

Flint turned back to the Odenwalds. "Either of you two been coerced?" he asked comically.

"No, Flint," Ernst said. "I mean, I don't think so."

"Officer Minor give you the third degree?"

"Uh-uh."

"He force you to answer his questions?"

Ernst shook his head, then said as an afterthought: "But I do gotta pee."

"You both got high school educations?"

They nodded.

Flint turned triumphantly to Meinecke. "You must of got us city cops confused with the feds. We don't gotta tell nobody nothin about their rights. Sheesh."

"Just thought it might be polite," said Meinecke.

"What we booking them for?" Flint asked Jud.

"Obstruction," said Jud.

"Cry-yi," said Flint. "Won't get past the arraignment."

"We be able to hold em long enough to find out whatever they know, leastways."

"You ask me, I say, why not start em off at murder?" Flint gave the evil eye to the Odenwalds. "Quit fucking around and just get to the point. I mean, why not?"

"Ain't got no evidence," said Jud. "For one thing."

"Why you taking us in, then?" Ernst asked uselessly.

Flint changed the subject. "Love to see Horstmann get a crack at these two. Don't think they'd remain silent too long in a room alone with that guy. You should see his face." Flint laughed at the memory. "Half of it looks like hamburger."

"We didn't have nothin to do with his face," Jacob said nervously, "whatever happened to it."

"Heard his knee messed up pretty bad, too," said Jud.

"Joke going around the station is he's not gonna be walking his beat, he's gonna be limping it." Flint laughed again.

"And Suthrin," said Meinecke, "shall be flying his, with angel's wings."

Flint didn't think that was funny.

Milwaukee Tribune

SPECIAL EDITION

SUNDAY, DECEMBER 27, 1931.

NEGRO DET. NAMED LEAD BY MAYOR, CHIEF

10-Year Vet Was City's 1st Negro Officer

The performance of acting Det. Judson W. Minor in investigating the crime scene after he discovered the body of slain Milwaukee Patrolman Landis Humphreys earned the immediate attention of Chief Laubenheimer.

As the Chief recalled:

"I spoke with Mayor Hoan by telephone as soon as I received the first reliable reports from those at Hubbard Street, about an hour after the crime was discovered. We were discussing the initial information when, just like that, the Mayor and I had the same idea at the same time. Officer Minor, we realized, was the ideal man for the job of acting detective on this high profile case."

Det. Minor, a 10-year veteran who was the first Negro to join the city's police force, accepted his appointment graciously.

A spokesman for the Mayor noted: "There was no attitude or anything like that on the part of acting Detective Minor. If any have wondered whether

Acting Detective Judson W. Minor

a Negro can be given a position in the public eye of such grave responsibility, I can assure them that such concerns may be put to rest. It is a testament to the tolerance and open-minded beliefs of the people of Milwaukee that their representatives have entrusted this extremely important case to Detective Minor."

Previously, Minor had served as acting detective on several cases, but always in low-profile crimes involving only those of his own race. The investigation into the brutal murder of officer Humphreys is easily the most important of the brilliant Negro officer's career.

—by Walter R. Meinecke (with assistance from John Carson)

36.

ALBY TUSA HAD BEEN WRONG about one thing. He hadn't loosened any of Meinecke's teeth. In fact, he'd done his job so skillfully that the newsman sported only a black eye, not counting the hidden bruises on his ribs. Even his upper lip, fattened on the same side as the black eye, wasn't all that conspicuous.

Meinecke had taken the day off. He planned to work from his typewriter at home on Sunday and have a delivery boy take the pages to his editor. Even that much weekend work was overtime, but he would restrict his labors to the Minor investigation. If his third district contacts got him Minor's initial report early enough, he could perhaps write the first stories this evening, Saturday, maybe after midnight but still in time for a special morning edition. By the time he reappeared at the press room on Monday his eye would look no worse than if he'd intercepted a drunken swing meant for the guy next to him at a bar Friday night, the story he intended to tell. He knew he would be believed. Meinecke was a highly effective liar. He had to be. It was his job.

Minor had not revealed his game plan for the day to anyone at the station, except presumably Kraemer. But Meinecke's contacts on this story were lower-level than the Detective Lieutenant. At least to begin with. He would be relying on those patrolmen who were easily bribed to provide copies of Minor's teletyped reports and thus insulate Kraemer and Laubenheimer from suspicion of the leak, even though Laubenheimer had surely been instructed by Hoan to promote Minor, and told of Meinecke's plan to sensationalize every false lead.

So Meinecke had spent a frustrating day waiting for the cop to return to the station and file his report. But Minor just kept going. Obviously, the speakeasy would be on the itinerary for his investigation's first day. The cop had not delegated even a single task to the other patrolmen at the third district, or so Meinecke's contacts assured him, so Minor himself was bound to show up at Mother's sooner or later that evening.

Pleased with his bogus bylines the day before, John Carson eagerly agreed when Meinecke phoned and asked for his services as a lookout. The handsome young wise-ass had gone above and beyond, actually tending bar, and then waited after Minor arrived to see whether anything of interest would happen before making his phone call. The appearance of the two Odenwald clods had been a godsend for the first day's coverage of the supposedly brilliant investigation. Rather than wait for Minor's report of the arrest, Meinecke sped to the scene from home in his own car, not from work in a cab as he'd claimed. Then after briefly conferring with Carson, he circled the building and dramatically entered the front door.

Meinecke imagined the colored cop might be dumb enough to think the Odenwalds, or one of them, had killed Suthrin at a prearranged meeting and then used the marathon dance scam to cover it up. Absurd. Besides the fact that your typical saloon owner's son, a few years past the terminus of his education in public high school, would never be able to dream up so clever and elaborate a scheme, the kids had run away from a cop at the dance. That was exactly the opposite of what a brilliant schemer would have done. Sure, the cop had seen both of them at the same time, but their lookalike scam was already scheduled, literally, to be revealed within the week.

Having worked this out, Meinecke was hoping the cop would go whole-hog on the Odenwald-did-it theory and provide plenty of misleading copy while wasting time that could have been devoted to better leads. Misdirection like that, at the very beginning of the case, would have made Meinecke's plan seem like genius to both Mayor Hoan and Alby Tusa's beloved padrone, Piddu.

But Meinecke never imagined that Minor would discover so quickly, or at all, Suthrin's shakedown of Mother. And he wasn't sure whether the discovery was a good or a bad thing. He knew immediately, however, that the information would never find its way into print.

"Let's stay out of the cold a few more minutes," Meinecke suggested to Minor, as Flint and the Odenwalds departed. "Thought we might have a word together."

The Odenwalds were escorted by Flint out the front of the restaurant to a patrol car, driven by another cop who had dropped off Flint at the diagonal alley in back and then brought the car around to Hubbard Street. Flint explained he hadn't known the door was still broken, and so had made his way in from the speakeasy after getting the hallway key. Both he and Minor expressed surprise that Mother had not been the one tending bar.

Still seated next to Meinecke, Minor turned his mouth down at the corners and regarded him with disdain. "Ain't got nothin to say to you. Why don't you just go ahead and make up whatever you want to print, and we be square."

"Those boys are going to be in tomorrow's paper," Meinecke reminded him, "whether or not we talk. Wouldn't you prefer to give me your angle?"

To Meinecke's surprise, the cop responded: "Them boys ain't had nothin to do with Suthrin."

"Surely," Meinecke said, not hiding his surprise, "they are your leading suspects."

"You bound to know this already, I reckon, but even if you don't, you probly will soon. There weren't a speck of blood in that basement where they was stayin, and no knife, neither."

"But what about the blackmail?"

"What you know about that?" Minor asked.

"Only what you were saying when I walked in," Meinecke lied. "Girl's name is Charlotte, Carson tells me."

"Why he mention that?"

He hadn't. Meinecke recovered quickly. "Journalist's eye for detail, needless to say."

With no experience of the third ward, Minor was unlikely to understand the implication of what he'd discovered. Whether in the third ward or otherwise, and certainly in places much further away than the sixth, Joey Vallone considered any independent shakedown to be an unlicensed use of his blackmail franchise. Years ago, the story went, Suthrin had drunkenly bragged of the arrangement to some hooker in a riverfront motel, who of course was employed by one of Vallone's capos and presently did her duty by passing the information along. And even if Suthrin hadn't admitted to it, someone connected to the Vallone gang would have found out eventually. It was small potatoes for Joey, but what mattered was protecting his trademark. Unlicensed franchises, no matter how small, could not be permitted.

And yet Suthrin got away with it. Which meant Suthrin was a Vallone associate. QED. But the sixth ward cop wouldn't know it.

"I can float the shakedown theory in the paper."

Meinecke said this now to Minor knowing he must never do so. It would create too many potential complications. No way would it lead to Vallone, but his gang wouldn't be happy about seeing it in print regardless.

"Don't you print a word of that," the cop warned him vehemently. "Just a rumor goin round the college kids in the saloon tonight."

Meinecke was curious what else Minor would have to say about the subject. "Have you never heard of unconfirmed sources?"

"You want to wreck that little girl's life over a rumor?" Minor spat out. This concern was unexpected. Perhaps the colored cop felt a special duty to protect his own people. "That somethin for me to investigate. If I find out it true, let the authorities handle it. Don't need no paper stirrin up all them readers who don't know nothin about it."

Meinecke would not be held responsible by Vallone if, without a word about it in the *Tribune*, the state took Charlotte away as a byproduct of the investigation, unwittingly ending the shakedown and any chance for

Vallone to inherit its spoils. That outcome had become possible as soon as Suthrin was murdered at Mother's, with or without Minor's promotion. So Meinecke would be in the clear.

At the same time, the little colored girl offered an excellent diversion, on top of the Odenwald boys' arrest. Vallone's capos would realize that no dangerous information about Suthrin could come to light as a result of the shakedown being investigated. The QED, however obvious in retrospect to those on the street, was above the heads of not only the public but also the courts, at least so far as probable cause was concerned. In a weird way, the fact that Suthrin was such a loose cannon served to make his association with the gang that much less imaginable. Of course, the truth about Suthrin was so unbelievable as to be the stuff law enforcement careers were made of, but Minor had no inkling of the real story. How could he? No matter how impressive Minor's skills might prove to be, he was not clairvoyant. No lead could conceivably lead him anywhere near Suthrin's actual origin. Someone would have to talk. And the only ones who knew, other than Meinecke, were the top men in the gang.

He made a mental note to encourage Minor to investigate the colored girl's background. Indeed, once the shakedown became public knowledge, as was certain to happen eventually, Meinecke could encourage his readers to believe an outraged relative of Charlotte's had committed the murder. It was a brilliant idea. Nothing could derail the investigation as thoroughly as trying to chase down the irrelevant girl's irrelevant family.

He changed the subject. "So. What else have you been up to today?"

Minor answered the question with another question: "Who told you I been named acting detective on the case?"

Meinecke smiled condescendingly. "Oh my. Has it really not occurred to you that everyone knows about that, not only at the third district but also the first?"

Minor looked away.

"But," Meinecke continued, "in the spirit of cooperation, I'll let you in on something."

"You got somethin to say about Suthrin, I'm all ears."

"Not about Suthrin. About you."

"You got nothin to say about me."

"Or rather about your assignment to this case." Meinecke paused dramatically. "I was the one who suggested it. If not for me, Rhodes would still be in charge."

"Okay," Minor said, getting up abruptly and heading for the door. "We done. Heard enough bullshit for one day."

"Your people need a hero," Meinecke said. "I argued that I could turn you into one, if you were promoted to cover this sensational case. And I will."

"Argued? Argued to who?" Jud said, standing by the door. "Kraemer? You think he gonna put his career on the line because of somethin some reporter got to say?"

"Not Kraemer. He's much too far down the totem pole."

Minor was at sea. "Who then?"

"Ask me no questions, I'll tell you no lies," Meinecke lied.

SUNDAY, DECEMBER 27, 1931.

NEGRO DETECTIVE CHASING LEADS

Clews Sought Far, Wide In 1st Days Of Hunt For Killer

3d district police head Det. Lieut. Adolph Kraemer had nothing but praise for the first 48 hours of acting Det. Judson Minor's search for the killer of city Patrolman Landis Humphreys, found stabbed to death in a storage room off an alley on Christmas eve.

Detective Lieut. Kraemer exulted: "The man is a force of nature. Almost single-handedly, Det. Minor has taken this investigation into areas we never imagined."

Within hours of discovering Humphreys' body, Det. Minor began utilizing his connections among his own people in the 6th ward. With the help of a colorful local street vendor known only as "Willie," Minor learned that leading suspects Jacob and Ernst Odenwald had been spotted

(Turn To Page 8, Column 4)

(Continued From Page 1, Column 2)

in line for the first day of the dance marathon at Avalon Hall. "Willie" was familiar with the Odenwalds due to their employment at the Hubbard Penny Restaurant, a charitable establishment that the colorful street character patronized during hard times.

The marathon was hounded out of its 6th ward location and two others by local authorities, finally taking root at a hall in the area of Milwaukee known as Pigsville, where last week's state supreme court decision has allowed it to remain over the protests of Mayor Hoan.

One might think that arresting the suspects was enough for one day. But the tireless and resourceful detective continued, next paying a visit to the Wisconsin Chair Company in Port Washington. It is speculated that Humphreys, known for his independent sleuthing beyond his post in the 1st district, was looking for a connection between a recent fire at the company and suspected arson in Milwaukee's industrial zone.

Det. Minor's next stop was a diner on Highway 57, where he interviewed relatives of Humphreys.

Finally, perhaps acting on a lead provided by those at the diner, Det. Minor visited a 6th ward street known for its houses of ill repute. Some have suggested that Humphreys had been investigating a 1st district white slavery ring whose tentacles reached to the city's Negro "ghetto."

A source at the 1st district station, preferring not to be named lest it seem the 1st district was trying to "steal the thunder" of the 3d, said: "Everybody here at the station is grateful for the efforts of this talented Negro detective to solve the murder of officer Humphreys. That boy is doing a mighty fine job."

—by Walter R. Meinecke (with assistance from John Carson)

37.

Jud PROBABLY KNEW Dolores, Carlotta, Peaches, Lizzie, and Becky, but not necessarily by the names Willie had provided the day before. Willie might have known their real names and Jud their street names, or vice versa. Or perhaps each knew different street names. Jud was vaguely familiar with a girl called Peaches, but she was young and so did not fit the profile Willie described.

He had considered cruising the streets near the cheapest movie theater, the most dilapidated dance hall, the incongruous chop suey restaurant, the train depot, all the various streetwalker magnets, but then got an inspiration. Willie said Suthrin patronized the older girls not for their age but because they were no longer run by anybody who might give him grief. For better or worse, they were independent. And that meant the girls, or some of them, had crossed paths with Junie.

When Jud reached Bronzeville's flophouse row he idled the throttle on his Model T halfway between the cross-streets to get the best view toward both ends of the block. He couldn't remember which place was Junie's and preferred to jog his memory rather than walk up and down the cold sidewalks that straddled the road.

Junie's building was two floors, not one or three. It had a fairly large window revealing the first floor parlor, whose drapes would be undrawn this time of night allowing shadows to be cast across the sidewalk from the moderately bright light within. It was not on any of the four corners near the streetlamps. And, like half the buildings on the block, it appeared not to be a place designed for short-term tenants but rather a somewhat run-down version of the middle-class residence it once had been.

Three of the block's flophouses matched his memory, so far as it went. He put the car in gear and drove midway between the two nearest to each other, then switched off the motor, set the brake, and jumped down. He found that neither of the places was Junie's, so he set off walking to the other end of the block to inspect the third.

Sure enough, behind the front window ten feet from the road Junie tilted forward and back in her rocking chair, smoking a pipe and wearing a kimono showing no evidence of corsets beneath. She saw Jud before he saw her, and waved when their eyes met. He knew she would not have done this unless she'd recognized him by the light projected from the window, and even then would not have done so for most of those whom she recognized. But Jud was a cop, not a caller, and moreover a cop who had never caused her any trouble, much less insisted upon bribes to allow her to stay in business. Jud imagined that had it been Suthrin passing by, even if Junie knew him she would have remained impassive.

She opened the door before he reached the bell.

"Still keepin up that girlish figure, I see," Jud greeted her.

Junie was about forty-five and not quite girlish, but she smiled and laughed at the compliment and, holding the lighted pipe, gave Jud a brief formal hug. "Sight for sore eyes," she said. "Not you, Jud. Me."

Jud returned her laugh. "My eyes just fine."

"Ain't never seen you out of uniform," Junie said, looking him up and down. "That a new overcoat?"

"Borrowed," Jud said.

"Hang it up for you?"

"Ain't gonna be here that long, Junie," Jud said. "Just lookin for some information."

"This time of night," Junie said, "if a friend want to visit, I have them sit there." She gestured toward a recliner near the wall by the foyer, some distance from her rocking chair and so not visible from the street. Jud declined her offer of a drink.

Junie was no longer a sporting girl, and far from a madam. She rented the house from an absentee WASP landlord who abandoned all responsibility in exchange for a hands-off attitude and regular rent payments at inflated rates. Junie's section of the former family dwelling, dating from the 1890s, had been converted into a reasonably spacious apartment for herself. The other seven rooms stood behind locked doors with numbers on them, as in a motel, and were accessible from a locked hallway or staircase leading from Junie's kitchen. Junie catered only to independent girls, like those favored, for different reasons, by Suthrin. If a girl picked up a trick within a couple of blocks she would bring him to Junie's and rent a room for one dollar. All the other flophouses on the street were for affiliated girls, and had arrangements with their pimps. Junie wanted nothing to do with the pimps, who wanted nothing to do with washed-up girls in their thirties or forties. Although her clientele was severely limited as a result, at a dollar per room per hour Junie did well for herself, and by reserving the right to turn away any girl whose date was too seedy she kept maintenance costs and labor to a minimum.

"So," she said, after settling back in her rocking chair and resuming her nightwatch, "without no uniform, guess you wasn't just passin by on a call. To what do I owe the pleasure?"

"Pleasure all mine," Jud said. He was about to continue when he heard the heavy door in the kitchen open and slam shut loudly on its springs. A middle-aged white man furtively crossed in front of Jud and walked out to the street, still buttoning his coat.

"Now that girl gonna use my bathtub," Junie said.

"Charge extra for that?"

"Didn't use to allow it at all," Junie said. "But with the hard times and all, guess old age turnin me soft. These girls ain't even got the poorest little cribs no more." Jud noted she hadn't answered his question, too proud of her hard business sense to admit being charitable. "So why you ain't in uniform?"

"Workin as a detective today. And even in uniform I don't walk a beat much nowadays."

"After the first couple of years," Junie remembered, "you cut this block off your beat. Stopped seein you, less there was a call brung you by the neighborhood."

"Figured all them pimps got the street pretty well under control."

Junie smiled affectionately. "That ain't why," she said. "You just didn't want to cause the girls no trouble. Always liked that about you. See no evil. All the cops use to be like that toward sportin girls, fore the do-gooders done took over. Girls use to at least have nice cribs, and the ones lucky enough to be in houses was a lot better off than they was bein domestics. Now there ain't even no domestic work no more."

Junie liked to talk about the old days, when she was working for Miss Jack Hunter's all-colored house on River Street, before the socialists shut respectable houses down. But Jud was tired so he moved things along.

"You know some older girls," he asked, "independents, called Dolores, Carlotta, Lizzie, Peaches, or Becky?"

"Know a couple or three called Dolores, Becky, and Lizzie, and at least one Carlotta. But there ain't no older girl called Peaches. Only girl called Peaches is a crazy little thing, can't be much more than twenty. Everybody talk about her. You right, though, she ain't bein run by nobody. Too much trouble. Poor thing is tetched. One day she Jesus, the next she got a demon inside her and she tell you its name. Then she calm down and work and save her money for a while, and fore you know it, she Jesus again, or an Egyptian queen. She was President Hoover's daughter there for a while."

Jud was impressed that Junie described Peaches in grim tones, without making a joke of it. Most people thought there was nothing funnier than the delusions of crazy people. Of course, Junie didn't know anything about Sally, so this wasn't just good manners.

"Think I seen her once or twice," Jud said. "Know where I can find her?"

"Mercy. That girl been foolin round in the third ward. Got it in her head she gonna be Mrs. Al Capone. Only reason they let her walk the streets without bein run by nobody, I hear, is she don't try to take over nobody's territory, go to a different place every night, and she always come back up here after a month or two. But right now, what I hear is she back down in the third again. Some folks say the gangsters get a laugh out of her, let her stick around, like that simple-minded fella the ballclub used to let stand by the field in uniform and pretend he part of the team. A mascot."

"A mascot," Jud said. "Don't sound like no gangsters I ever heard of."

"Just sayin what I been told," Junie concluded, tapping out her pipe. "You know, I started out down there, on River Street."

"Miss Jack Hunter's," Jud contributed politely, on cue.

"Whites-only place with all colored girls. Weren't but a few hundred colored folk in the whole city back then. Folks like you, they only come up during the war, or right after. Italians didn't run all the girls yet, neither. Or even most of em. Italians wasn't much yet. Half the restaurants had at least one waitress who a sportin girl. Mayor Rose, he just leave things be. Folks never complained about the houses, so cops never cause no trouble. Why would they? Ain't no complaints. Then the do-gooders come in, shut everything down in nineteen-twelve. Sent what they call a commission around, talkin to the girls. Come and talk to me. I say I make more in a day than I could in two weeks as a domestic. Guess they more concerned for my eternal soul than for my belly. Funny, now they let me vote, I give it to Mayor Hoan, even though things better for me when Mayor Rose still around and ain't no do-gooder socialists."

"Can't go home again," said Jud, trying to control his impatience.

Junie burst out laughing. "I know what that mean," she said. "It mean I ain't no girl no more. Even if Mayor Rose still in the city hall and nobody close down Miss Jack Hunter's, they wouldn't have me now." She laughed till she coughed, which went on for a while.

Embarrassed, Jud realized she'd described exactly what he meant. "So," he said, "you do know some other girls by them names I mention? Hope to track em down, ask em for some help with an investigation."

"Well, I know you ain't gonna cause em no harm, but I gots to ask." She refilled her pipe, perhaps to avoid looking at him. "If I find em for you, what this all about?" She lighted the pipe with a safety match. "Why you askin after them girls, anyhow?"

Yet again, Jud produced Suthrin's photo. He had withheld it to simplify his initial questions about the five girls, preferring Junie have no context for her answer. He stood up and, keeping his back to the window out of respect, quickly approached Junie before returning to his seat.

"He been in here with Dolores," Junie said, holding the photo at arm's length to focus her vision. Then, without another word, Junie propelled herself off her rocking chair and went to the kitchen. He heard her unlock the hallway door and swing it open.

"Enid," she hollered. "Finish up your bath and get on down here. You ain't in no trouble, baby, but I need your help with somethin."

"Yes, Miz Junie," Jud heard Enid say, her voice muffled by the ceiling.

"Hurry up, now," Junie added before gently closing the door. She came back and returned Suthrin's picture. "That girl thick as thieves with Dolores. Ain't known which Dolores you wanted till I saw that fella's face."

"Much oblige, Junie. Got anything you can tell me about them other girls?"

Junie sighed. "Me, I don't take much to gossip no more," she said. "Try to be all bidness. Nowadays, girls comin here keep they private life to theyself. But I might know where you can find em, if you stick with it long enough."

Enid appeared from the kitchen in three big towels and a pair of slippers. Like Junie, she had closed the heavy door quietly behind her. And like Jud, she avoided being seen through the parlor window. "What you need, Miz June?" She peered at Jud, her eyes an inch beneath the pink towel wrapped around her head.

"He ain't here for that," Junie said. "This my friend Jud. Want to know about a fella who go round with Dolores."

"Why ain't he ask Dolores, then?" Enid replied suspiciously. "Think I look like Dolores?"

"Dolores ain't here, and you is," said Junie.

Jud didn't recognize her, and knew it was mutual. "Miz Enid ..." he began.

"I ain't Dolores's keeper," Enid interrupted.

"No, but you is her lover," Junie said. "You two all lovey dovey. Tell each other everything. She done told me so."

"Miz Enid ..." said Jud.

"That crazy," Enid said. "You shouldn't believe nothin that girl say."

"You wanna keep usin my tub, you be nice and talk to this man. I can vouch for him. He lookin for a fella ..."

"Ain't lookin for him ..." Jud tried to clarify.

"…and don't want nothin else to do with you and your ladyfriend," Junie concluded. "Jud, you go ahead."

Jud waited to see whether Enid would object, but instead she leaned against the wall and stared at him resentfully.

"Miz Enid," Jud said, showing her the picture, "this a fella go by Suthrin. He passed the other day. I'm tryin to find out a thing or two so maybe we can track down his kin."

"You must know he a cop, then," Enid said.

"So you recognize him."

"Can't say I mind that he pass, neither," said Enid. "But Dolores didn't tell me nothin that would help find his kin."

"What she tell you?" Jud said.

"Nothin any use to you," said Enid.

"Answer the man," Junie said sharply.

To Jud's surprise, Enid laughed. She was done resisting. "Well, seem it ain't good enough for him just bein a cop. He like playin pretend-cop, too."

"Don't follow you," Jud said.

"He come around on duty, in his uniform and drivin his patrol car. Dolores say he play this game, pull up when he seen a girl and say he make a date round the corner. Pay the girl right there, but just half, tell her there more where that come from if she go round the corner and pretend she not a sportin girl, just walkin down the street like a nice girl, and then play like he arrestin her." Enid laughed again. "Well, Dolores, she heard about this fella from Carlotta. He done the same with her. So Dolores, she take him up."

"You know Carlotta?" Jud asked, beginning to want to ask more.

Enid ignored him and continued with the story, speaking more to Junie than to Jud and plainly enjoying herself. "So she go round the corner and walk down the street, like she ain't lookin for a date or nothin, and bye and bye he drive up in his patrol car and stop and get out and say, You under arrest." Enid mocked these last words in a booming voice. "Then he don't wanna do nothin else but say he searchin her for weapons. That all he wanna do. Search for weapons."

Jud briefly choked on his own spit going down the wrong pipe. He cleared his throat harshly without any effect on Enid's enthusiastic narrative.

"So he go ahead and do his search, and he search everywhere. And I do mean everywhere. And then after a while he pay the other half like he say he goin to, and go back in his car. That all he wanna do. Search em up, all over. But sometime, he make a date for later that night, come back in his own car off-duty but still wearin his uniform."

"He always wearin his uniform?" Jud asked slowly, looking at the floor. "Whether he on duty or not?"

"That what Dolores say, and she say Carlotta say so too. So he come back all liquored up and pretend he arrestin her again, and search her like before, but then he say she under arrest and they go get a room." Dolores glanced at Junie for confirmation. "That when I seen him, when they lookin for a room."

"That when I seen him, too," Junie said, "but he wearin a big coat so I didn't notice no uniform. Musta been carryin his cap so I don't see it."

Jud took a dollar from his wallet and handed it to Enid. She behaved as if nothing had happened and crumpled the bill in her palm.

"She say what happen," Jud asked, "when they get a room?"

"Like I say, he all liquored up. Usually call hisself Humphreys, Dolores say. Or Suthrin, like he from the south. But when he drunk enough, he tell Dolores she gotta call him Deputy Johnson." Enid laughed hard, at the thought of Dolores telling the story. "Dolores, she crack up when she get to that part especially. Fella payin her to call him Deputy Johnson."

Jud barely noted how much longer he remained before driving back to the station, where he wrote his report of the day's activity with, as Kraemer had ordered, excessive detail. But he left out H.C. Speir's story about Jackson, Mississippi, and Enid's specific reference to the name Deputy Johnson. And of course the story about Charlotte.

It was well past midnight when he entered the back door of his home as quietly as possible and went to sleep on the couch in the basement. He had too much on his mind to deal with Sally. And she wouldn't notice anyway.

PART FOUR

December 27, 1931 to December 31, 1931

38.

AFTER SEVERAL VERY LONG DAYS Jud had let himself sleep in and take his time in the shower. As head of his own investigation he didn't need to get permission. Still, he'd put on half his uniform before remembering that he was now, for a while, a plainclothes man. He changed into a sport coat and tie as Sally slept.

He nevertheless felt a little guilty and furtive when he arrived toward noon, telling himself he could say he'd gone to church if anyone made a point of it. Who could call him out for that? None of his colleagues knew anybody else who went to a colored church, so the lie was secure. He would be disbelieved only if he claimed to have been praying for Suthrin's immortal soul.

So he thought his leisurely arrival accounted for the strange looks he got from the others at the station, none of whom said anything beyond greeting him. They may as well have been framed and on the wall like silent Chief Laubenheimer. It was a quiet, understaffed Sunday morning during the chilly holiday season, with plenty of desk space to choose from. After signing in with the desk sergeant, he selected a spot in a far corner, hoping for isolation. Along the way he noted that the spittoons had not been emptied all weekend.

He'd decided while showering to begin the day with a look at the scrapbook of criminals Kraemer had handed him the morning before. He searched for anyone named Guardalabene and found none. Ditto for Vallone, Tusa, and the other names mentioned by Jack Medinger. The rap sheets included known associates, so he began looking for anybody from the third ward, to see if Guardalabene or the others would turn up under another crook's name. Impossibly, the only third ward characters in the scrapbook were low-level amateurs, often not even Italian, whose crimes hardly suggested membership in an organization. And the small number of these was inversely disproportionate to the third ward's relative population. Why would the third actually have fewer crooks per capita than other wards? Kraemer had mentioned removing those who'd been cleared during the initial manhunt, but Jud knew without doubt that the explanation wasn't enough. Someone, perhaps even Kraemer himself, had gone through the scrapbook and systematically removed gangsters before allowing Jud access. They must have presumed Jud would be too ignorant to notice. Perhaps he might have been, if not for Medinger's story. Jud reached for a blank piece of paper to jot down some notes, but then thought better of it. If something was being deliberately hidden from him, he didn't want to create a paper trail at the station revealing he'd recognized it.

"Minor," someone called out across the room. Jud turned and saw officer Warren carrying a half-eaten sandwich, wrapped as done at the deli down the block, and a newspaper. He must have just come in from lunch.

"Hey, Warren," Jud greeted him. "Thanks again for the overcoat. Mine finally dry out from the wash. Got yours in the car."

"Little did I know," Warren said as he approached, "that I'd lent my coat to such a bona fide hero." He waved the paper, apparently thinking Jud had seen it.

"What you talkin about?"

"Don't tell me you haven't read it," Warren laughed, dropping the paper on top of Kraemer's scrapbook. "You're on pages one, two, and eight." Warren leaned over and turned to page two. Several square-inches of column space were covered by a photo of Jud taken at a colored elementary school where he'd once given a talk.

"Damn," Jud said, grasping immediately that those who disliked him, or were on the fence, now had a new reason for their resentment. He also understood the peculiar reception he'd gotten when he'd entered the station.

"How could you not know about that?" Warren asked.

"Ain't come in till just a while back," Jud said, "and ain't talked to nobody." He began skimming the front page article. It didn't take long before he was furious. All three stories, he noted without surprise, were by Meinecke.

"You really think the Odenwald boys did it?" Warren asked.

"Hell, no. Look here." Jud pointed at the long quote attributed to himself on page two. "I ain't never said none of that."

"But you set Horstmann on them, huh."

"No. Ain't none of this true."

Warren kept talking but Jud ignored him and read all three stories as quickly as possible. Only minutes after concluding that Kraemer's mugshot book had been censored to exclude the third ward, he now recognized exactly the same dynamic at work in Meinecke's prose. There was not a word about Suthrin's gang connection, about anything Jud had learned from Betty Falkner and Jack Medinger, even though Meinecke obviously had access to Jud's complete report and so, for example, correctly named Willie and placed the diner on Highway 57 while mysteriously moving Wisconsin Chair from Grafton to Port Washington. Also, Suthrin's whoring, and his peculiar frisking fetish, went completely unmentioned.

"…can't expect them to report it's a speakeasy," Warren was saying.

"What's that?" Jud said, having stopped listening as he read the articles.

"We've been turning a blind eye to that blind pig," Warren said. "The reporters always play ball when cops send a clear signal like that."

Incredibly, Warren presumed the central fabrication in Meinecke's work was the part about the college kids flooding into a "storage room."

"No, no," Jud said. "That ain't it. Why I care about that? None of this true. Ain't no arson investigation. Ain't no white slavery ring. Only person I spoke to at the diner was the lady runnin it. Couldn't track down Suthrin's kin."

Warren's expression suggested Jud was nuts, or perhaps putting him on. "Who cares?" he said. "You're a hero. Jesus, man, they quote the mayor's office."

"You know where the phone book at?" Jud said, still not listening as he glanced around the station house.

"Allow me, O hero of the third district." Warren gave a comical bow and went to find the directory.

A moment later Jud was speaking to the news desk at the Milwaukee *Tribune*. Told Meinecke was out for the day, he gave his name and demanded angrily the reporter's home address and phone number. After replying No to the question whether Meinecke was suspected of criminal activity, Jud was told that Meinecke's contact information could perhaps be subpoenaed. Then the man at the *Tribune* hung up.

"We got this fool's personal information?" Jud asked Warren, who had observed with amusement Jud's half of the phone call. Before Warren could respond, somebody hollered, "Minor. Kraemer wants to see you."

"If Kraemer's here on Sunday just to see you," Warren said, "then you know you must really be something."

Jud grimaced and handed Warren the car keys. "Go get your coat," he said, unable to keep the irritation from his voice.

39.

Adolph Kraemer had himself just come in. The moment services ended at church that morning, when he and his family were barely out of the pew, a blue-haired bespectacled old secretary made her way down the aisle and told him his captain had phoned the church office. Knowing Kraemer would be unreachable once he set off in search of a novel venue for his family's brunch, the captain had asked that Kraemer, who out of political ambition rarely missed a service despite his undeclared German atheism, return the call as soon as God's work was done.

"Terrific job," Kraemer now said to Jud Minor through clenched teeth. He couldn't remember having ever before been obliged not only to conceal his anger at the behavior of one of his men, but instead pretend to be delighted by it.

Having just read Minor's report, Kraemer had not yet seen the newspaper stories. But his captain had adequately described them on the phone. The captain had also expressed bewilderment at Minor's uncanny discovery of Suthrin's connection to the Vallone gang, "which is in his report, not the paper," he'd explained. "Thank God Minor's report says he has no idea who the farmer ... the unnamed farmer ... was talking about. But they're all Italians, and the girl at the diner mentioned Capone. That might get him asking questions."

Capone, of course, was no longer at large, and his interaction with the Guardalabenes and Vallone had been limited to receiving his regular imperial cut of their profits.

But, as the captain had said: "Given the lead, Minor is bound to learn sooner or later that Vallone has his own local gang. I don't know if—or how—he could find out they recruited Suthrin, but he might. Fortunately, for some reason Meinecke didn't mention the gang connection in the paper, so at least it's not public yet."

Hearing the captain explain this, Kraemer wondered if Meinecke knew about the wiretaps. Unlikely. So the captain, or the chief, must have censored Minor's report before it was passed along to the reporter, and then pretended Meinecke himself had left out the gang connection.

The captain was not concerned about Minor's reports of Suthrin's whoring, though Meinecke, he said, had shown good judgment by withholding those details for the time being. "After a couple of months go by," he'd said, "it could be useful for such irrelevant diversions to become known. But for now Suthrin must remain a martyred hero. It just wouldn't look right for a police investigation to tear down the reputation of a murdered cop so soon after his death."

Between the lines of the entire phone call, Kraemer sensed that he was somehow being blamed for the wholly unexpected success of Minor's investigation. The captain implied that Minor could not have done the work without help, and reminded Kraemer that he'd been ordered to forbid Minor from involving anyone else in researching Suthrin's background.

The captain concluded by providing a false lead that he demanded Minor pursue. The lead had been suggested by Meinecke, but was to be described as an anonymous tip.

"I haven't read the newspaper stories yet," Kraemer said now in his office, "but I got a call from the captain himself. You've done a tremendous job."

"Thank you, sir." Minor was sitting alertly in the chair across from Kraemer's desk. "But I gots to say...."

"And collaring both Odenwalds after they got away from Horstmann. Very impressive."

"Yes, sir, but y'know, Horstmann found them on his own. Ain't true that I assigned him to the marathon."

Kraemer had no idea what this meant. He chose to ignore it. "But the captain is concerned you may be giving too much credence to some of your witnesses." He remembered he was speaking to the only colored man on the force, and toned it down: "Out of inexperience, of course. It doesn't reflect badly on you."

"I wasn't investigatin no arson," Minor said. "And don't know nothin about no white slavery ring."

Again Kraemer was unable to work out Minor's meaning. He found himself glancing repeatedly at his pipe-stand. Should he? No. It wouldn't make sense. "Tell you the truth," he said, "I'm not sure what you're referring to. Like I said, I haven't read the newspaper stories, and I've only had time to skim your report. But the captain took a look at it off the teletype after reading about you in the paper. I understand that the reporter omitted certain details."

"More than that, sir," Minor said, with an edge to his voice that Kraemer hadn't previously encountered. "That reporter, he flat-out make stuff up. Put words in my mouth."

Kraemer tried to be avuncular. "Well," he laughed, "that's something you've got to get used to in this business. We are on very good terms with the press, so there's a sort of gentlemen's agreement that they can invent our quotes so long as it sounds reasonably like something we might have said. If it's anything especially serious, we give a real interview, but usually it's just a waste of time. The newsmen understand our need for good public relations, and, uh ... take care of it for us."

Minor rolled his eyes around a little, glancing about the office as though trying to comprehend something he'd never before considered. He seemed at a loss for words.

"The captain was thrilled with the publicity," Kraemer continued after a moment. "He said, quite specifically, that we were to give full deference to Meinecke. Provide him with what they call an exclusive." Unconsciously, Kraemer removed a pipe from the stand and examined it. "The captain was, in fact, pleased that Meinecke did not mention what some of your witnesses told you."

"How Meinecke even know what they tell me?" Minor said with a scowl, again betraying more attitude than was proper.

"Well," Kraemer improvised uncertainly, "I suppose from when he met you at the penny restaurant." Still holding the pipe, he picked up Minor's report and flipped through it, pretending to look for the right page.

"No, sir," Minor said emphatically. "Somehow, he got ahold of my report. I filed it after midnight last night, and now there it is in the paper. But he change it all around."

Kraemer stuck to the subject. "Whatever his source, Meinecke left out the part involving the ... uh, the Italians. That's what I was getting at before." He cleared his throat, buying time without allowing Minor to say anything. "Okay, so a couple of your witnesses put Suthrin together with those Italians. But if you go flashing Suthrin's picture to everyone you meet, particularly after he's on the front page, there's bound to be some ... what the scientists call, false positives." Citing this term, Kraemer was pleased to show off the breadth of his knowledge. "What that means is...."

To Kraemer's great displeasure, the colored patrolman interrupted him. "Miz Betty say she seen him a number of times. And the farmer, whose name I gots to keep to myself, he so sure about the I.D. that at first he try to lie about it. That don't sound like no false positive. Last thing that farmer want to do is admit he seen Suthrin."

Kraemer willed his slight smile to abruptly disappear. "The captain doubts your witnesses, and so do I." He jammed the pipe back in the stand, knocking it over. Four pipes scattered across his desk. Minor leaned forward to set things right but Kraemer waved him away. "Nothing in this case suggests gang activity."

Minor wouldn't take the hint. "Sir, at this point it don't matter so much who killt Suthrin." He paused.

"Come again?"

"Question is, who was Suthrin?"

Minor seemed to search Kraemer's face for some acknowledgment. The lieutenant was determined he find none. "Who was Suthrin?" he repeated, with no enthusiasm.

"Somethin else goin on here," Minor said emphatically, "bigger than just some murder. I got leads I ain't even mentioned yet...."

"Like what?" Kraemer said. "You're supposed to put it all in your report."

Minor smirked, annoying Kraemer. "Now that I know Meinecke readin every word, glad I didn't. But that streetwalker I done talk to, the one called Enid...."

"Oh, that," Kraemer said dismissively. "You did a fine job looking into Suthrin's ... shall we say, nocturnal hobbies. When we talked yesterday, I thought we both agreed that it was probably some hooker or her pimp that killed him."

"Actually, sir, what I said yesterday was..."

"But those colored girls in the sixth ward have nothing to do with gangsters. And the pimps don't either, as long as they stay away from the insurance policy racket, and don't let the girls go beyond their territory."

"But that girl Enid say ..."

"And let me emphasize," Kraemer interrupted yet again, "the captain and I certainly do want you to pursue that angle. However, even if it leads to a quick collar, we want to spike the story about Suthrin's connection to the girls till there's been a funeral and some proper veneration and grief for a murdered cop." At last, anger cooled, his hands were steady enough to put the pipes back in their stand. "Eventually, we'll let the public know that Suthrin played around. Who cares? It's not like he was married or anything. He was just a good old boy having some fun with some colored southern girls, up here in the north. Probably just homesick. And he even paid them, your sources say," Kraemer paged through the report looking for the name Enid, "so there was no abuse of his authority."

"Enid say he pay them, but Willie, he say ..."

"So, yes, by all means investigate the, uh, prostitute connection, though we'll keep it out of the papers for a few months."

"I didn't want none of the investigation in the damn papers to begin with. Sir."

Kraemer pulled out his wallet and found the scrap of paper with the notes from his call to the captain. "And, as I've mentioned, the captain is thrilled with the publicity," he said, fully aware that he was responding to the opposite of what Minor had complained about. "But we have received an anonymous tip which the captain wants you to devote your full attention to, beginning immediately. This will be your top priority."

"Anonymous tip, sir?" Minor asked. "About Suthrin's murder?"

Kraemer tore off the bottom of his note and handed it to Minor. "That is an address. As you are probably aware from your long experience walking a beat in the vicinity of that Hubbard Street speakeasy, the owner has adopted several children, one of whom is a colored girl. We believe it is possible that the girl's relatives, out-of-town relatives of her deceased parents, were planning to kidnap the girl, to place her with blood relatives who would then bring her up. Somehow, Suthrin caught wind of the scheme and, according to our tip, he cleverly pretended to be willing to assist in the kidnapping in exchange for a fee. He met the kidnappers in the speakeasy ... supposedly about to gain access to the house and grab the girl, but actually to arrest the perpetrators in the act, as soon as they paid him off. But something went wrong and there was a struggle, ending in his death."

To Kraemer's surprise, as he was speaking he realized Meinecke's invention wasn't half-bad. With a few gaps filled in, like the strange detail of Suthrin not mentioning the scheme to anyone at the first district, the kidnapping story would actually provide a plausible theory of the case. For example, maybe Suthrin had done the whole thing off the books, intending to take the money while threatening to expose the scheme. Or maybe he was himself involved in the kidnapping plot. After all, he was already a dirty cop, being paid by gangsters. But the captain had described the plot as a red herring, meant to waste Minor's time and throw him off the scent. Kraemer began to wonder whether some other motivation were involved. Perhaps this was a way to investigate Suthrin without getting the first district involved. Perhaps the murder had been solved, but the captain had to play politics.

Minor, too, seemed impressed by the internal coherence of the so-called anonymous tip. After a moment he said: "That would explain the doll, I reckon. I mean, if Suthrin brung it along, like he plan on givin it to the little girl once they done grabbed her. But, sir, like I say in my report, it all but certain that Suthrin got that doll from them gangsters at the farm, since Miz Betty say...."

"For the last time," Kraemer barked, no longer making any attempt to disguise his irritation, "I want to hear nothing more about gangsters. Frankly, Minor, your attitude today surprises me. But I put it down to exhaustion. I'm sure that the next time we speak, if you're better rested, you will remember your place."

Minor maintained eye contact with Kraemer, silently. Not so much as a Yes Sir.

"So," Kraemer continued, "I want you to take the rest of the day off. Get some rest. You've been putting in very long hours. First thing tomorrow, you are to drive to that address."

Although having already read the scrap in his hand, Minor looked at it again, in disbelief. "To Chicago, sir?"

"Yes, Chicago. That is the permanent address of Lydia Boone, the colored girl's aunt. She's one of your people. The captain believes it will be best if you interrogate her in person. We have arranged accommodations for you at the same hotel. It's a legitimate place, not a flophouse. We booked four nights, should it be necessary to canvas others in Chicago, and will reimburse you."

Minor had probably never imagined such luxury. "This girl live in a hotel, sir? A legitimate hotel? And she live there every day of the year?"

"Apparently," Kraemer explained, "she's rich."

40.

IT WAS TOO EARLY IN THE AFTERNOON for serious drinking or a serial on the radio, too cold to sit in the park or take a walk, the wrong season for broadcast baseball and wrong week for the Rose Bowl, and too soon after his divorce to be in any mood to ask an eligible lady to a matinee. He'd already built a decent fire and eaten a big lunch. And he had never believed in God, much less the consolation of prayer. Meinecke could think of no activity to assuage his sense of panic, now mild but prone to become acute if he let it. He had barely slept since he'd read the words "Guardalabene, Vallone, Tusa, Aiello, and Dominick" in Minor's report, and he still could not quite believe it. His luck could not possibly be that bad. He paced around the room staring into the fireplace. He focused on reassuring himself. Certainly no one else would.

Go through the list again, he thought.

First, the gangsters would never see Minor's original teletyped report. As of now, their sole source of information was the newspaper's so-called exclusive. Unless and until the cop started snooping around in Vallone's territory, no word of his freakish hunch about Suthrin would reach the Italians.

Second, when Meinecke had gotten Laubenheimer on the phone a couple hours after putting the stories to bed, the chief seemed weirdly receptive to the supposed rationale for leaving the Italian connection out. Meinecke had sold the idea by bundling it with the streetwalker revelations, which, it went without saying, could not see print so soon after Suthrin's death, if ever. Astoundingly, Laubenheimer had agreed at once that there should be no intimation Suthrin was dirty, whether as a pervert or a cop.

Third, the chief had bought the kidnapping theory, and had not pressed the issue when Meinecke attributed it to an unnamed source who must remain anonymous. Indeed, Laubenheimer said he would have his men track down contact information for the colored girl's family, starting with her parents' death certificates and taking it from there.

It was almost as if the chief were as eager for Minor to go on a wild goose chase as Meinecke was. He would have to think about that.

So he had congratulated himself for putting out this unexpected fire so well and so quickly. But the congratulations were at best temporary. After Minor was through with the kidnapping theory, he was bound to look into Suthrin's connection to the gangsters. Would it be possible somehow to warn them? To advise them not to take Minor seriously?

There was no way around the problem. Meinecke owned it. He was the one responsible for getting Minor assigned to the case, a fact he'd so stupidly mentioned to Alby Tusa.

But suppose another detective beat Minor to it. Meinecke knew the first district was jealous of the third's jurisdiction in hunting for the murderer of a downtown cop. What concerned Vallone was not that Suthrin was on the take, but that he was on the inside. And far more important, how he'd gotten there. Vallone wanted the flexibility to try a similar scheme again, to replace Suthrin in the same manner that he'd placed him there to begin with. Lots of cops took bribes to look the other way. But only Suthrin was on the gang's payroll, full-time, to pass along everything he could find. And, of course, that implicated Meinecke, too. But if someone at the first district could discover a watered-down version of the story, and if Meinecke could limit it in print to simple bribery, the whole thing would blow over. Then Minor's investigation of the third ward would be prompted, apparently, only by the first district's supposed discovery, and not by Minor's own research and skills. The gang could hardly blame Meinecke for that.

He'd sat down to think this over in an easy chair before the front window, staring at his postage stamp lawn, chain-smoking tailormades and sipping bad scotch, when an old Model T pulled into the drive. None of his middle-class colleagues at the paper still drove such a thing. Paranoid, he wondered if it were a throwaway car used by one of Tusa's soldiers sent out on a hit. But, again, they would have seen only the newspaper, not the teletype. His time wasn't up quite yet.

He was hardly consoled to see Jud Minor park and jump out, wearing the plainclothes Meinecke had draped him in by way of the promotion to acting detective.

Prior to the evening before, prior to that final halcyon evening when the murder inquiry seemed limited to the likes of the Odenwalds and a minor scandal involving the little colored girl, Meinecke had never met Jud Minor, there being no reason to do so. He always got all he needed from sergeants and lieutenants, from teletype reports and boilerplate quotes, with the occasional pilgrimage to a captain or the chief himself. The crime beat was strictly color by numbers. Except for routine purchase of information, only rarely did he bother with patrolmen, and then only those at the first district to camouflage his role as go-between in relaying Suthrin's intelligence to the Vallone gang. He would frequent the downtown headquarters like one of the boys, bringing donuts and coffee and trading ribald stories with whatever polack was coming in from his beat, all to make his intermittent contacts with Suthrin seem random. Usually the two of them didn't pass the time of day, having made eye contact that conveyed the lack of news. But if something was up, they would find a way to bump into each other beyond earshot of the others. Then, amid booming banalities, Suthrin would lean forward and provide the information in whispered bursts. It was a system that had gone without a hitch for five years, almost from Suthrin's first month on the job.

For a while Suthrin masked his natural sadism. But as he became more arrogant over time, he began to enjoy insulting and baiting Meinecke during the audible portions of their banter. Just to be a bastard. Soon enough Meinecke hated the guy.

His opinion of Minor, after one meeting, wasn't much better. The colored cop struck him as a sour self-righteous prude, unwilling to play ball due to that surfeit of playacted integrity so many negro men assumed in a vain attempt to hide their natural lack of intelligence. Meinecke had read plenty about eugenics and concluded that the sole hope for Minor's race in America was selective breeding. It always had been. But in the modern era it would be for intelligence, rather than the slavery skills artificially bred during the previous two centuries.

Such breeding had also produced size and strength, and Meinecke felt a wave of fear at the sight of the big black cop approaching the door. Minor's expression was stern and, with its animalistic features, somewhat brutal. Undoubtedly the invented quotes and jumbled truth and lies in the paper had angered him, rather than having made him thrilled to be lionized as would be any sensible white man, or even Jew or Italian.

Meinecke went to the fireplace and grabbed a poker. "Come in," he called when the bell rang. His back to the room's entryway leading to the front hall, he pretended to be fiddling around with the logs when Minor came through the unlocked front door.

"Hello?" Minor said.

Meinecke waited, holding the poker, for Minor to look into the room and repeat the word Hello. Then he turned around and pretended to be surprised.

"Detective," he said. "What an unexpected pleasure." Immediately he noted that Minor had changed his expression in the moments since he'd walked up from the driveway. Now the cop appeared almost friendly. But only almost. Meinecke could tell it took some effort.

Minor removed his hat and held it in both hands, his long arms relaxed and extended down to his thighs, like an animal assuming a posture of submission. "Got the rest of the day off," he said. "Thinkin maybe you and me could have a little talk. Reckon we got off on the wrong foot last night. Figure I was too tired to be sociable."

"All I've got at the moment is scotch," Meinecke said, "or something colored to look like it." He felt self-conscious as soon as he said the word colored. He hoped he wouldn't blush.

"Don't mind if I do," Minor said. "But to pour it, you gonna have to put down that poker."

It took a moment before Meinecke realized he was being teased. Expressionless, he placed the poker in its stand and went to get another glass.

When he returned, Minor was sitting on the broad windowsill. To be visible from outside? "Much oblige," Minor said, and drained the glass in one gulp. Meinecke hadn't even sat down. He refilled Minor's glass and the cop examined it in his right hand with his hat in the left. "Color matches the taste," he noted, now restricting himself to an additional sip.

"Who knows," Meinecke said, taking his seat. "Maybe it really is scotch. Stranger things have happened."

"Maybe you can write an article about it," Minor said. "Say it barrel-aged thirty years and come straight from Scotland."

Again, teasing. This wasn't at all what Meinecke had expected. Minor was trying, with some success, to charm him. Most likely, he'd been told by Kraemer to make nice. Regardless, his bad attitude the night before had not been prompted by fatigue. And Meinecke had been around too long to flatter himself by imagining Minor had so soon undergone a change of heart.

"I take it you've seen today's paper," Meinecke said. "I'm sure you realize that I can't jeopardize my relationship with the city police by reporting your premature suspicions about Suthrin."

"Got no quarrel with what you wrote," Minor said. "Fact, just as well not go off all half-cocked, pay too much attention to what them witnesses say."

"All in good time," Meinecke agreed. "There's still no way to account for the whereabouts of whichever Odenwald was at large at midnight on Christmas Eve."

"Sho you right. But somethin else done come up. Concernin that little girl, Charlotte. Figured if I let you in on it, you be discreet."

"I didn't mention her in the paper."

"And I didn't mention her in my report," Minor countered, briefly allowing his mask to slip. But then he laughed. "Never spected you to get your hands on that teletype."

"I've been on the crime beat a long time." Meinecke sipped his scotch, acting like an old pro. "You don't stick around in this business without sources. And, Minor, without any way of knowing what's happened between you and the higher-ups since the paper came out, I'd give odds you haven't heard any complaints about my use of your report."

Minor set the glass down beside him. "You got that right. Kraemer say the chief happy with the publicity."

"How did I guess?"

"But, like I say, he also brung up somethin else. It the thing you gots to keep to yourself for a coupla days." He stared levelly into Meinecke's eyes. "We got a tip. Some talk that the little girl's got kin that ain't happy Mother adopted her. Had a long talk about it with Kraemer this morning. Tip say they was gonna kidnap the girl, and somehow Suthrin caught wind of it and got killt Christmas Eve when they go to snatch her. Maybe he pretend like he in on it with em, try to set em up but it gone wrong." He picked up his glass and swirled its contents, then put it back down without drinking. "Point is, it don't matter if Suthrin did some whorin and rum-runnin with gangsters and whatnot if this tip be true. Charlotte's kin wouldn't have nothin to do with that, so why bother with it?"

Meinecke had a sense of irreality, hearing his own invention repeated back to him in all seriousness and only a few hours after he'd dreamt it up. "The whoring I believe," he said, trying to appear coldly analytical. "The rum-running I don't. That was a rookie mistake you made, buying into random I.D.'s of Suthrin's picture the day after he was on the front page of the state's biggest paper. You were bound to find somebody who thought they'd seen him. Witnesses like that are so unreliable, experienced detectives ignore them altogether. I think you just made too much of the coincidence about the girl's doll. Must be a million like it." If nothing else, Meinecke really did believe the last part. Then he returned to lying: "And, anyway, Laubenheimer's squad is too clean for a cop to be any more involved with gangsters than accepting the occasional bribe, which everybody understands is business as usual since you patrolman would starve otherwise, and prohibition is a joke."

"I don't take no bribes," Minor said.

"The exception that proves the rule," Meinecke said. "But now you've got that bee out of your bonnet, I take it you are abandoning the ridiculous gangster angle and pursuing the tip you got. The, uh, kidnapping theory."

"Kraemer set me straight about them eyewitnesses. Called it a false positive. So, yeah. I'm headin out tomorrow to investigate Charlotte's aunt in Chicago."

So the chief, Meinecke thought, had located one of the girl's relatives. In Chicago. Too bad it wasn't New York. Or Australia. But at least it would get Minor out of town, which would look good to Alby Tusa.

"Gonna be gone maybe three, four days," Minor continued. "Maybe a week. That why I'm here. I'm askin you to take pity on that little girl and not say none of this in the paper. Don't mention Charlotte, and I'll cooperate with you as the story go on."

Meinecke finished his scotch, now very pleasantly drunk not only from the moonshine but also from relief. He'd dodged a bullet again. Twice in one day. Minor was going to leave Vallone and company out of it. "Well," he said, about to pour another drink before noting that Minor was no longer interested in his own, "I suppose if I can protect a dead man from reports of his whoring, I can censor myself about an orphan girl."

"Thank you," Minor said, standing up and putting on his hat. "Thing is, you ain't just helpin Charlotte. We don't want to alert the kidnappers that we on to them. I'm gonna talk to the lady in Chicago like I'm investigatin the Odenwald boys. Pretend maybe she heard somethin about the family Charlotte live with. But it really to size her up, find out about her other kin, check out their rap sheets and such."

This was too good to be true. With luck, the girl's extended family would take weeks to fully investigate. In the meantime, maybe some sixth ward pimp would get caught with the knife that killed Suthrin.

Maybe, in fact, that could be arranged.

"What am I to write about till you get back?" Meinecke asked, uninterested in the answer.

"Do what you always do," Minor said. "Make it up." He extended his hand and they shook. "Okay, then, Meinecke," Minor said.

"Okay, Minor." And half a minute later Meinecke watched the dumb colored cop crank the handle on his piece of crap car and drive away.

<h1 style="text-align:center">41.</h1>

As JUD DROVE HOME from Meinecke's house, which surprisingly was just a few blocks down Juneau Avenue from his own, he was relieved he'd kept the Deputy Johnson information to himself. No one knew Jud had discovered it. And now that he realized Suthrin's murder was not meant to be solved and that, indeed, his own investigation from the outset was meant to be a sham, he was determined to solve the greater mystery of Suthrin's identity.

All he needed was a little help from Charlotte's wealthy aunt. And he was pretty sure he knew how to get it.

Outside his house Jud peered into the bedroom window. Sally wasn't there. He went inside and she came out of the kitchen holding a dishcloth. Doing chores was a good sign. She'd been keeping normal hours after the all-night radio vigil Christmas Eve. In their little time together since, she was again grounded in something like reality, or at least knew the difference between minutes passing and hours.

"I didn't even hear you leave this morning."

"You were asleep."

"No. I woke up when you were in the shower. I wanted you to come in and kiss me goodbye."

He put his arms around her. "I'll kiss you hello instead."

"Hello," she said after they kissed.

"And goodbye," he said. "I'm going in to take a nap. Thought I'd caught up with my sleep but I didn't." Drinking Meinecke's rotgut on top of oversleeping that morning had made him groggy. He waited for Sally to tell him that Eddie Cantor was on at suppertime. Ordinarily, in her recent state, that would have been foremost on her mind.

But she didn't. Instead, still with his hands on her hips, she played with his tie and said: "Didn't you go to the station?"

"Yes, I did, but the lieutenant told me to get some rest."

She gave him a coy smile. "Come on," she said, "what have you been up to? Buying me more presents?"

Due to his schedule they had exchanged gifts in the late afternoon before he left for Halvorson's beat on Christmas Eve. It seemed like years ago. "You want more?" he asked. "Your birthday isn't coming up anytime soon. Maybe something for New Year's."

"I know a present you could give me," she said, brushing her knuckles against the front of his pants. "But first you've got to tell me where you were."

"I was at the station, like I said."

"So why aren't you in uniform?"

Jud realized he hadn't had a chance to explain his new assignment. "They've got me working plainclothes for a while. You remember the other times I was acting detective." He smiled and took hold of her hand, stilling it. "That's why I'm so tired. Now I'm going to kiss you goodbye, to make up for this morning, and go take a nap so I won't doze off when Eddie Cantor comes on tonight."

"Oh, that's right ... tonight's the show," she said. It was surprising she'd forgotten. "It's Sunday, isn't it. You don't usually go to work on Sunday. Are you sure you weren't out buying me a present?"

Now was as good a time as any to tell her. "No, but I'll buy you something at one of those fancy stores in Chicago. I've got to go down there for a few days. That's one reason the lieutenant is letting me rest. I'm leaving first thing tomorrow."

Tears came to Sally's eyes and she backed away from him. Any other husband would have been concerned by this over-reaction, but Jud was very pleased. It had been weeks, if not months since Sally had displayed any affect at all. During her bad times anything she said about her state of mind was no more than a guess as to what might be expected. If she said she was happy it meant she thought most people in the same circumstance would probably be happy. Or sad, or anything else. But now there were tears, not just words.

She turned her gaze to the floor and went to the couch, to keep Jud from seeing her cry. "How long will you be gone?" she asked, her tone constrained by the need to sniffle.

"It's okay if you cry," Jud said. "I'll miss you, too. But it will just be a few days. At most a week."

She lost the battle and sniffled. "Are you leaving me?" She wiped her eyes and added: "I won't have anyone to talk to."

"I'm not leaving you, Sally." He wanted to sit down and comfort her, but thought it would be better to let her emotions play out for a while. It hurt to be so cold, but there was no cruelty in it. For Sally, a spasm of fear and sadness, after so many weeks in the void, could be an emotional breakthrough. Jud wanted to give the mood all the room it could tolerate. He felt like a doctor refusing treatment until a fever broke.

"You didn't go to the station, did you," she said, draping her arm over the back of the couch and placing her forehead upon it, like a doomed heroine in the pictures. "You've got someone else. Is she from Chicago?"

Now Jud wasn't so sure he should be pleased. Paranoia was not the affect he'd hoped for. He sat down beside her and took her free hand.

"Missus, I'll only say it once more. I was named acting detective on a big case. That's why I'm not in uniform, that's why I went to the station on a Sunday, and that's why I'm going to Chicago tomorrow morning."

"Let me come with you."

"I can't, Sally. You know that's not how it works. Now, it's good that both of us get so sad about being apart. I know you're sad, because I'm sad too. And everyone is afraid of being alone. So it's okay to feel sad and a little scared. But ... but you can't go thinking I'd lie to you. That is not okay, Sally." He listened to her quiet weeping and then remembered something he'd planned earlier to say. "I'll go talk to old Mrs. Wloszczynski next door and have her come in and see you every day. You can go out to lunch together, or to the pictures. You'll have the car. After I go in tomorrow, I'm taking a patrol the rest of the week, so I'll have somebody bring our car back here." She didn't respond. Jud got an inspiration. "If I was leaving you...." He deliberately laughed, with affection. "If I was leaving you, would I do it in one of the third district's squad cars?"

And miraculously, Sally also laughed at the thought. Jud could not remember the last time she had been possessed by enough individuality and spirit to laugh.

After a while, when his wife was sufficiently reassured, Jud stripped and got into bed. He was relieved that nothing had come of Sally's brief flirtation earlier. If they had made love he would have spent the whole time evaluating her responsiveness, weighing the recent deadness within her against the new life.

She woke him a few hours later by crawling under the covers, still in her yellow house dress, and spooning against him.

Presently she asked: "Were you dreaming?"

"I don't remember." He rolled over onto his back and threw one arm behind his head. It was already dark outside.

She let him stare at the ceiling for a few minutes, then said: "What are you thinking about?"

Ordinarily during one of Sally's bad phases he might have censored the answer, but this time it wasn't necessary.

"Something a Frenchman said to me right after the war."

"You don't talk much about the war. You never have."

"I don't intend to. There's nothing I want to say about it. But this was in a cafe, after all the fighting."

"In a cafe?" Sally said. "He was a colored Frenchman?"

"No, that isn't how it works over there. They let colored folks sit right down next to whites. But this Frenchman, he was interested in the fact that I was colored, a colored American. Said he was real interested in American history."

The Frenchman had brought up Abraham Lincoln, whom he thought must be a hero to Jud as his liberator. Having been kept away from all white American soldiers during his service, allegedly at the express command of President Wilson, Jud did not feel very liberated. But he'd listened politely and, over time, something the Frenchman said had stuck with him.

"That's what you were thinking about?" Sally said. "A Frenchman said he knew about American history?"

"No, no ... more than that," Jud said. "Because I'm colored, he started talking about Abraham Lincoln. About how Lincoln was the smartest guy around. Said he was a genius. But all the old politicians in Washington thought he was just a country bumpkin." Jud laughed. "I can still remember his funny accent when he said country bumpkin, like he was proud he knew English so well."

"I don't believe that, about Lincoln," Sally said. "He was the president. He couldn't have been so stupid."

"Right," Jud agreed. "But Lincoln was a westerner, from the boondocks, and for thirty years, this Frenchman said, most of the presidents hadn't been all that bright. So the easterners thought Lincoln was the dumbest of them all. And, so ... this is the part I was thinking about. Lincoln was so smart, the Frenchman said, he took advantage of what they thought about him. He went to Washington and let everybody who didn't know him think he was stupid. That way, when he was doing business with them, he had the advantage. He could size them up, and they'd tell him everything they were thinking like they were explaining it to some schoolboy. But he kept his own thoughts to himself, so they wouldn't know he had any thoughts at all. Then he'd get the jump on them and make his move. Some of them wised up after a while. But the rest still figured somebody else was calling the shots behind the scenes, because they couldn't believe Lincoln was smart enough to do anything. So for years he got to hide behind the idea that he was just, as the Frenchman said, a country bumpkin. And the thing is, the Frenchman said, that's another example of how he was really the smartest guy around."

Sally waited to see if there was more of the story before saying: "That Frenchman sure must have made an impression on you, to have you thinking about him so many years later."

"I just always remember the thing about it being smart to let people think you're dumb, if they're dumb enough to believe it."

"I like that story," Sally said.

But Jud couldn't tell her the real reason it had come to mind. For the first time, he was now able to put the Frenchman's story to practical use. He'd rarely been in a position where it mattered one way or another how most people evaluated him, except in the sense of keeping his job or trying to avoid trouble. Around more volatile or threatening types he was able to dumb down, so long as nothing important was at stake. But that wasn't a function of intelligence. It was behavior he would never need to explain to any colored man or woman, or even boy or girl past a certain age. It was a necessary condition of survival.

The current situation with Kraemer and Meinecke, however, was something different. Particularly this afternoon with Meinecke, Jud found himself acting as the Frenchman said Lincoln had, and not out of the usual race-related caution, but for strategic reasons in unusual circumstances. And much to his surprise, with almost no effort or thought, he had made it work.

This, he understood, was not due to his own skill as a con man but rather to Meinecke's inability to imagine such a con. Had it been a poker game with both white and colored players, Meinecke would have been alert to bluffs and tells and so forth, regardless of race. But in the context of everyday life, the reporter was so blinded by his own presumption of superiority he bought Jud's act without a second thought.

The same was true of Kraemer, but that was more understandable. In Kraemer's eyes, after some token resistance Jud, the subordinate man, had accepted the instructions of his professional superiors. Still, like Meinecke, Kraemer too quickly assumed Jud believed what he'd been told. And also like Meinecke, he did so because he couldn't conceive of Jud conning him. Like a parent telling a child about Santa Claus, Kraemer took for granted that Jud would take seriously, or at least entertain, the asinine kidnapping story. That it was beyond Jud's primitive mind to work out what was really going on, or to avoid saying so if he did.

Kraemer himself said that Charlotte's aunt was rich. Rich relatives would not resort to kidnapping, at least not without failing in court first. But even if the kidnapping story were plausible, it did not justify ignoring Medinger's reluctant identification of Suthrin. Along with the removal of third ward gangsters from the mugshot book, this refusal to investigate Suthrin's gang connection could mean only that the connection was real. And, more important, that the higher-ups wished to bury it. Such a potential lead on Suthrin's murderer would not be abandoned otherwise.

Kraemer and his own superiors, it appeared, literally did not care whether the case was solved or not. And now they were sending Jud to Chicago.

He was certain Meinecke was the source of the anonymous tip. He wondered if Kraemer realized the reporter had made it up. Surely Laubenheimer must.

"Come on," Jud said in the dark bedroom to Sally. "Let's go listen to Eddie Cantor." And a few minutes later Eddie Cantor told a couple of jokes and then the Russian man played the violin and then there were some vaudeville routines and then Eddie Cantor said goodnight. It was the same thing every week.

42.

J UD VEERED THE SQUAD CAR off U.S. 41 to Michigan Avenue, no longer hugging the lakeshore with its alternating moonlike desolation and ugly industrial wastelands. A decade ago the windows in the Illinois Central colored car had revealed an already impressive cityscape, but now it may as well have been the next century. As he crawled through the snowbound traffic on the Magnificent Mile he didn't need to crane his neck toward the driver's side to marvel at the view. The windshield sufficed, as ahead of him for block after block the boulevard was straddled by buildings three or four times as tall as any in Milwaukee, or any he had seen since migrating through Chicago in the packed colored car.

Crowds of pedestrians spilled off the sidewalks onto the street, and each intersection was like a war between the innumerable people and the clustered cars, trading waved fists and blasted horns. With the windows up it was nonetheless the loudest place Jud had ever been. And there were more colored folks along the way than he'd seen, cumulatively, in all his years walking the Bronzeville beat. Even the freezing uncovered tiers of the double-decker busses were crammed with enough of them to fill every rooming house in the sixth ward.

It was slow going. For the tenth time since leaving home that morning he reviewed his checklist for the trip. He had bribed old Mrs. Wloszczynski to look in on Sally twice a day and bring groceries and have a friendly chat over coffee, the goodhearted white widow's senility a match for Sally's non sequiturs. He had sent two rookies to leave the Model T on the street in front of his house. He had telegraphed the Hinds County Sheriff's Office under Warren's name at the station, so that any return telegraph could be intercepted by his new friend before it reached Kraemer. He had brought along four empty gasoline cans to be filled at the last gas station south known to accept colored customers, an Esso in Memphis. And he had packed his own gun, having never been issued one by the third district.

Finally past the sprawling traffic jam beneath the five or six endless blocks of skyscrapers, Jud crossed Roosevelt Road and gradually realized that not only were there still more colored folks than he'd seen since leaving Georgia, but with each block south there was a higher and higher percentage of them. As their proportions grew, the quality of buildings and cars diminished and the number of tiny churches increased. Storefronts evacuated by the depression were scarred by broken and boarded windows and, often, wide open doors within which Jud could see legions of squatters, many of them children young enough to still suck their thumbs. In the twenties Chicago's South Side had been mentioned in the same breath as Harlem, the scene of a renaissance, but the hard times seemed to have aborted any rebirth. Twenty blocks to go before reaching his destination, he began to doubt Kraemer's description of the hotel as "a legitimate place," or to believe that anyone living there, full-time or not, could possibly be rich.

But then Michigan Avenue began to improve again, and the pedestrians, on the whole, to seem better off. It was as though he had sojourned through a buffer zone, one meant to warn people north and south not to pass unless they had definite business on the other side.

When he reached Pershing Street, just shy of the hotel, colored boys of all ages were swarming around an attractively painted and well-kept building on the corner which proudly styled itself the South Side Boys' Club. Not, Jud noted, Colored Boys' Club, but just Boys' Club, as though it had manifested on the spot from some utopian future. The sight would have struck fear in most Milwaukeeans, but the kids appeared cheerful and carefree, and, although some were in their late teens and early twenties, there was no sign of dice or bullying or booze or weapons. A few of the older ones eyed Jud's squad car with animosity, but the children, about a third of whom were visibly underfed, saw a colored man driving and waved and smiled, and Jud waved and smiled back.

Next door to the Boys' Club on the broad boulevard was the Hotel Brookmont, 3953 South Michigan Avenue, but Jud was too preoccupied looking for a parking space to examine it. Just past the next corner the tracks of the Chicago Junction Railroad disrupted traffic, something made worse by a perpendicular intersection, a block west, of two elevated rail lines. Jud sensed, without thinking about it, that this combination of tracks had once marked the southern boundary of Chicago's colored section, as it would still in most cities, but that the massive postwar migration away from lynching and peonage had forced the border much further down. Because of the triple railway obstructions he spent fifteen minutes driving around south of the tracks, searching for a space while finding it hard in the tangle of streets to get back to where he had started.

At last he parked but had to walk for another fifteen minutes before again spotting the hotel, whose four floors took up half a square block. The entrances sported roman columns in the middle of a half-floor of faux marble circling the building. The rest was the color of a new penny, with separately lettered signage on the roof of the long side reading HOTEL BROOKMONT. Four times on each side the walls bulged forth into castles on the second through fourth floors at the corners and, notably, in the middle, where indentations allowed for extra windows and thus views for rooms otherwise landlocked. Before the war, Jud could tell, this place had catered to well-off white folks, and in fact an elderly white couple emerged from the main entrance onto Michigan Avenue and were met by a touring car, whose spiffy colored chauffeur stepped out after idling the engine and held the back door open, the elegant white lady unoffended by his hand on her elbow as he helped her step in.

But when Jud reached the lobby he realized the old couple was an exception. Amid statuary and divans and a dozen tall tropical potted plants, or perhaps trees, their artificial green fronds drooping like giant handheld fans, the staff and guests alike were all colored.

He'd been in hotel lobbies before, but this was the first time he'd walked into such a place, the size of a ballroom and furnished exquisitely amidst dark marble columns, and felt as if he had any business being there, unless of course it was police business. Even on those occasions, however, he'd known his stay must be brief. But here he would be invited to lounge in overstuffed chairs beside gold lamps and silver cuspidors, to ask one of the half-dozen porters to bring him a drink, to listen to the early afternoon piano music drifting in from the velvet-covered lounge, to patronize the haberdasher or florist beneath the gilded ceiling, to peruse at his leisure any of the dozen different newspapers folded neatly on the marmoreal end tables. Obviously, in the context of such costly luxury, whatever room had been reserved for him would be the cheapest in the building.

Jud went to the front desk to check in, ignoring the legion of bellboys with their pillbox caps and brass-buttoned maroon uniforms. While he waited for the clerk to finish a phone call, he examined the rows of pigeon-holed postboxes in front of him, noting that there were a great many rooms numbered in the two- and three-hundreds, far fewer in the one-hundreds, and only four on the fourth floor. Each of those on the top, he concluded, took up a full quarter of the half square-block. And Lydia Boone's was one of them.

He received his key after paying two dollars up front for the first day, which as expected was the lowest rate available. Although he wanted to cultivate the staff if necessary, he waved away the bellboy who jumped off the hop-bench and offered to carry his single suitcase, finding the notion ridiculous. Not expecting to be reimbursed by the station for tips, he nevertheless handed the polite young man a quarter, just for being there.

His room was in the corner furthest from both the Michigan Street and 40th Street entrances, next to a door marked Cooper Studios which led into a small mirrored gymnasium visible behind plate glass where a Victrola was playing and a man and a woman dancing, the latter apparently taking lessons. Inside his tiny room he could hear their laughter and the Victrola through the wall. He set his grip down on the bed and divested himself of his winter clothes, then, leaving his hat on, selected a modest coat and tie from the suitcase. The bathroom held a toilet and sink, but no shower. For two dollars a day, to fully bathe he would have to use the first floor's shared facilities.

Jud found his way to the gated elevator and told the dignified elderly man within that he wanted the fourth floor. The elevator attendant expertly assessed Jud's clothes and said, "Are you sure you have business there, sir? Perhaps you mean the third floor."

Jud felt in his pocket for a dime but then reconsidered and presented the man a quarter. This trip, he thought, was getting expensive. "I am on official business," he said, deliberately emphasizing the adjective and repeating the attendant's noun, "for the city of Milwaukee. I need to speak with Miss Lydia Boone regarding her niece, Charlotte, a resident of Milwaukee." That sounded about right, but to Jud's chagrin the attendant ignored the proffered quarter and Jud sheepishly returned it to his pocket.

"I don't believe she is at home, sir."

"Rather see for myself," Jud said.

With a blank expression the attendant announced "Fourth floor," as though he were a trolley driver, and the gate closed only to open again one floor up.

"Good afternoon, Mr. Cooper, Mrs. Cooper," the attendant smoothly greeted a middle-aged couple.

"Fourth floor, please, Ray," Mr. Cooper said. He was compactly built, like a lightweight boxer, but otherwise an owlish man, with round rimless glasses and a head nearly bald. Both he and his wife were dressed well enough for church. Surprisingly, he shook hands with Jud and said, "Jack L. Cooper. This is my better half, Billie."

"Jud Minor. Please to meet you." Jud thought for a moment, then to make conversation added: "Are you the owner of the Cooper Studio on the first floor?"

"I don't answer such inquiries from strangers without my lawyer present," Cooper said.

Seeing the look on Jud's face, Mrs. Cooper laughed charmingly and said: "Don't mind him. He's just annoyed you asked about the studio instead of the All-Colored Hour." She glanced at her husband with affection. "Ever since he got on the radio he thinks he's a celebrity."

"All-Colored Hour," Jud said. "That ring a bell. I think my wife listen to it when there ain't too much static. We up in Milwaukee. Can't receive but half the Chicago shows, and sometime hardly none at all."

The gate opened on the fourth floor, redundantly announced by the attendant, and they stepped into the hall.

"WSBC," Mrs. Cooper said. "Believe me, they wouldn't allow an 'all-colored' anything on the stations that have strong signals."

"Can't control the atmosphere," her husband said benignly. "Wouldn't want to inadvertently offend our friends in the southern states, now would we dear?" Watching Jud examine the number on the first door they passed, Cooper asked: "Who are you looking for?"

"Miss Lydia Boone."

"Well, Jud," Cooper said, "it's your lucky day. We're heading there ourselves, and if you don't know the door, I imagine you'll need an introduction." They turned the corner into a new hallway, half again as long as the last.

Jud was displeased at the prospect of company. "That good of you, sir ..."

"Call me Jack."

"... but, tell the truth, Jack, me and Miz Boone need to discuss a private matter."

"Won't stay private for long in the Brookmont," Mrs. Cooper said with amusement. Halfway down the hall and past two unmarked doors, she knocked on the first that bore a number. After waiting a while for someone to answer, she made small talk: "I take it this is your first visit to the Brookmont."

"Yes, ma'am," Jud said.

"Ma'am is my mother," she replied. "I'm Billie." Having kept his eyes averted from another man's wife in close quarters, Jud looked at her directly for the first time and realized that her formal clothes belied her age. She was younger than he was.

"They got lots of fine places for colored folk in Chicago like this one?" Jud asked.

"This one's mixed, because of the older tenants," Billie said, "but it's only allowed blacks since twenty-six. Before the war they never imagined that one in ten people in town would be black, much less that Pershing and Michigan would be smack in the middle of the black belt. But Garfield Day hired Mr. Webb to look after the place and keep it stylish, and they've both done a good job. Every black entertainer in America stays here when they get an engagement in the city."

"You didn't answer the man's question, dear," Jack said, then pounded on the door much more loudly than his wife's demure knock. "And the answer is no. The Grand is the only other one, and if it weren't for showbiz, neither the Grand nor the Brookmont would have remained such decent places to stay."

"That why you visiting?" Jud asked. "Somebody on your radio show this week from out of town?"

"We live here," Billie said. "Two connecting rooms on the second floor, but...."

The door opened and a ruggedly handsome young man with wet hair appeared, wearing a bathrobe and holding a thick sheaf of typewritten pages. It occurred to Jud for the first time that he had no idea how old Lydia Boone was.

"Jud," Billie said, laughing, "this is Frank. As you can see, he has excellent hygiene."

"I was laying up in the bath," the man said, irritated. "Forgot you were coming over. Didn't want to slosh water on this manuscript I was reading, so it took a minute." He shook Jud's hand. "Frank Davis. Are you one of Jack's crooners?"

Jack stepped past him into the apartment. "We don't broadcast crooners, only singers," he said. "Where's the whiskey?" Billie followed with a giggle.

"I'm here to see Miss Lydia Boone," Jud said. He had taken off his hat but not yet stepped past the doorway. The view before him was like something out of the pictures. Lydia Boone was indeed rich. But, unlike in the pictures, all of the tables and even some of the chairs and a couch, plus most of the floor along the walls, were covered with books and papers. Just inside the door was a long shiny table where rested a telephone on a doily beside a typewriter. With a glance Jud counted two more typewriters in the spacious parlor, each beneath its own stand-up lamp. Whatever Lydia Boone might be in the context of Jud's investigation, she was not what he expected.

"I'm afraid she already has more manuscripts than she can handle," Frank responded strangely, "especially given the fact that the journal does not yet exist." His thumb marked his spot in the pages he'd been reading, whose typewritten title page read INFANTS OF THE SPRING. "On the other hand, if they're all as bad as this one, no number of submissions would be too many. But I should be more optimistic. These are only the first ten chapters, none suitable for an excerpt. But it's always possible we can get someone else to write the next few, to show the hapless author how it should be done."

"I just lookin for Miz Boone," Jud said, shaking his head modestly. "I ain't know nothin bout no manuscript."

Frank leaned in and said in a near-whisper, "You can drop the shuck and jive talk. I'd think the presence of Jack Cooper would have forewarned you that Lydia is not interested in vernacular fiction, though she is open to realism. Listen to how Jack talks on the radio if you really don't know how to speak proper English."

Somehow, Jud knew this was not meant as insult but rather friendly advice. "Mr. Davis," he said evenly, "would you please let Miss Boone know that I am here to ..."

"Oh," Frank interrupted at normal volume, "another thing. If you're a poet, go easy on the rhymes. I'm lobbying for an emphasis on free verse."

Jack Cooper had found the whiskey and now returned to the door holding a half-filled glass. "Let the man in, Frank."

"I am not stopping him, Jack."

"Gentlemen," Jud said, "is Miss Boone at home or not?"

"If she were," Jack said, "you'd hear her and Billie gabbing away." He studied his young wife briefly and added: "Not sure how long I'll be able to maintain patience with that woman."

"They're newlyweds," Frank explained to Jud. "Jack lost his first wife earlier this year."

"I'm sorry to hear that," Jud said.

"We were getting divorced," Jack said. "People warned me not to pick one up on the rebound. Met her at the station. Piano player for some of the shows."

Behind Frank and Jack, Billie was relaxing on one of the couches with her feet up on a glasstop table, some papers in one hand and a drink in the other, and surrounded on all sides by additional manuscripts. She had just put a record on the Victrola evidently called "Be On Your Merry Way," and was playing it so loud she had to shout: "My goodness. Is everything here written by black writers?"

"Is this truly the first time she's noticed?" Jack Cooper said, rolling his eyes to get a laugh out of Frank.

Since these were friends of Lydia, whose help Jud needed, he tried to indulge their conversation and speak as little as possible, lest he unwittingly give offense.

"Billie," Frank said loudly, "it wouldn't make much sense to call it *Race Digest* otherwise."

"*Race Digest*?" Billie hollered. "What kind of a name is that? Why not *Negro Digest*?"

"Robert Abbott at the Chicago *Defender* doesn't like that word," Frank explained over the music. "Insists on everything being race this and race that."

"What do you care what he thinks?"

"Because," Jack said, returning to her so he wouldn't have to shout, "he will never mention the new journal on the front page if he has to use the word negro. It'll get buried on page six."

"Mr. Davis," Jud at last interjected, "do you know where I might find Miss Boone?"

"I can't keep up with her schedule," Frank said. "Since you aren't coming in," he swung his arm listlessly toward the gorgeous room, "let me suggest that on your way out of the hotel you speak with the girl at the cigarettes and candy stand in the lobby. Her name is Page Ringgold. Lydia often checks in with her to get the latest gossip."

"I still like *Negro Digest* better," Billie shouted.

Jud said goodbye but they were no longer paying any attention to him. After he entered the caged elevator he could hear their voices echoing off the walls of the corridor, along with "Be On Your Merry Way," all the way down to the second floor, where the businesslike hubbub of the lobby below finally drowned them out.

43.

T HE ELEVATOR ATTENDANT pointed Jud in the direction of the cigarettes and candy stand, and across the vast lobby Jud saw a skinny woman of about fifty sitting behind the counter. By the time he'd walked there, his shoes squeaking on the marble floor, he realized she was not sitting but standing. She wasn't more than four foot ten. Around a wide snub nose the skin of her face was damaged, freckled, and blotchy. Jud imagined she'd been swindled by the snake oil salesmen who peddled so-called skin whiteners from mail-order ads in colored newspapers. She was frowning as Jud tipped his hat.

"Page Ringgold?" Jud said.

"The only names that matter here," she said with a snarl, "are Washington for the dollars, and Lincoln for the pennies and fives."

Jud wondered at the strange little woman, working in a fine hotel's lobby while unconcerned with being polite to the guests. Her expression, in fact, suggested more than lack of concern. She seemed to have instantly taken a profound dislike toward Jud.

"Miss Ringgold," he tried again, "my name Jud Minor. Mr. Frank Davis done told me you might know where I could find ..."

"Frank Davis?" she spat out. "I wouldn't give that communist the time of day. I have half a mind to get the police on you just for mentioning his name."

"Yes, ma'am," said Jud, "but I'm looking for Lydia Boone."

"Then look no further," she said.

Jud blinked. "You Lydia Boone?" he said, wide-eyed.

Another woman approached, much younger than the one behind the counter.

"I'm whoever you want me to be," said the first, who looked at the younger woman and, just like that, burst into hysterics.

"My big sister thinks she's a real comedian," the younger one said, taking her place behind the counter.

"I am a real comedian," she laughed. "Or a real comedienne."

"Muriel, you're going to get me fired."

"Oh, just look at this fella," she said, now eyeing Jud with good humor. "He wouldn't hurt a fly."

"My name Jud Minor," Jud said to the younger one. "I'm lookin for Page Ringgold."

"Then look no further," Muriel repeated, again beside herself. "You shoulda seen your face. 'I'm Lydia Boone,' I tell him, and he think the devil got a new name." After she calmed down she asked, "You any relation to Coleman Minor?"

"Not that I know of, ma'am," Jud replied.

"Use to work with him in revues before the war. Fact, played with him once or twice at the New Monogram here in Chicago. That man could act, I'll tell you right now. You do kind of favor him, you know. Maybe a long-lost cousin."

"I'm Page Ringgold," the younger one said. "This is my sister Muriel. Visiting from Harlem. She likes to stand behind the counter and make trouble when I'm on a break."

Jud put the names together. "You Muriel Ringgold?" he said with an unforced grin.

"The same," Muriel said, giving a girlish shrug of her shoulders and pretending to pose.

"Used to read about you every week in high school," Jud said. "The library took the Atlanta *Independent*. The colored paper? They used to call you the funniest woman on Broadway."

"Still am," she said. "Just got too old for people to care. Got a little slower on the pickaninny dance, too. Now I'm lucky to be in the colored papers twice a year. Since the war I been working mostly with Ernie Watts, mostly under the cork."

"Under the cork?" Jud said.

"Blackface," Page explained.

Jud suddenly remembered having heard of the song Billie Cooper had played on the Victrola. Sally owned a copy and he'd read the label. It was from Paramount Records and the singer was Issie Ringgold. "I just heard your sister Issie on the Victrola," he said with wonder.

"It's Izzy, not Issie. They spelled it wrong on the label. She ain't made but one record, but it got around, I guess." Muriel reached up comically to pat Page on the head. "Little sister here tried to take up the family mantle, but it didn't work out."

"You in show bidness, too?" Jud said to Page.

"I was on Broadway four years ago in something called 'Hey Hey,'" Page said. "Written by Mrs. Marcus Garvey, if you can believe it."

"Too bad Marcus couldn't take a break from politics," Muriel said, "and think up a better name for his wife's show."

"Muriel, Izzy, and Page," Jud said. "Quite a family." Now he would have something to tell Sally about. He'd already decided not to mention Jack L. Cooper, whose radio presence might trigger thoughts of Eddie

Cantor, but the Ringgolds would mean little to Sally beyond their novelty as part of the story of his trip to Chicago.

"And here I am running a candy stand," Page said. "What can I do for you, and why did Muriel say she was Lydia?"

"I'm lookin for Miz Boone, and Mr. Frank Davis told me you might know where she at."

Page regarded Jud with mild suspicion. "If you want to get printed in her journal," she frowned, shaking her head, "it isn't going to do you any good to chase her through the hotel."

"It about her niece," Jud said.

Page laughed. "That's very creative. I guess you must write stories, or maybe novels. But if Lydia has a niece, she's never mentioned it to me."

"A girl named Charlotte?" Jud said. Page shook her head again and Jud produced his badge, something he'd wanted to do as infrequently as possible while in Chicago, and preferably never. "I'm here to help her."

"Frank Davis was talking to a cop?" Muriel gasped in mock horror.

"I ain't mentioned I was a cop," Jud said, in case he had unwittingly marred Davis's reputation.

After a little more back and forth between them, Page was satisfied with Jud's credentials and pointed in the direction of his room. "She's taking dancing lessons in the Cooper Studio. It's over by the ..."

"I know where it is," Jud said, hiding his surprise. "Thank you very much for your help, Miz Page. And it a real pleasure meetin you, Miz Muriel." He shook their hands in turn and, exaggerating, added: "My wife gonna be thrilled when I tell her I done met you."

Muriel instantly dropped his hand. Appearing to be dead serious, she furrowed her brow ominously and said: "You didn't mention no wife."

Jud laughed and headed back toward his room, struck by the fact that he'd seen Lydia Boone and heard her laughter before he'd even turned his key. So much for detective work.

Through the plate glass window he watched Lydia and her teacher doing some sort of energetic modern jazz step. Jud hadn't danced since his wedding and knew nothing about the trends beyond what he saw in the pictures, which wasn't much. In the twenties he kept hearing about something called the Charleston and he wondered if that was what he was witnessing now.

When the record ended Lydia and her teacher picked up towels and mopped their faces. She was a pretty girl in her early twenties and, at perhaps five foot six, taller than her lithe and well-sculpted teacher. She wore a thigh-length red wool skirt over black tights, pink ballerina slippers, and a black stretch top which hugged her breasts. Although sweating from the dance she had not removed her tan cloche hat, from which several curls had escaped.

Jud knocked and walked in, prompting them both to turn to him with eager curiosity, as though watching a guest arrive at a party.

"Hello, handsome," the instructor said.

"Only my wife allowed to call me that," Jud replied, trying to be good-natured.

"Then make it gorgeous," the instructor said, an octave lower. "I didn't see you on my client list for today."

"I'm here to speak with Miz Boone." Jud stepped up to them and introduced himself. The instructor said his name was Billy Sibley.

"If this is about the journal ..." Lydia said.

"No, ma'am. I'm not a writer. Maybe we oughta speak in private."

"I know when I'm not wanted," Billy said with a pout. "And we'd gotten off to such a wonderful start."

Jud focused on Lydia. "It about your niece, ma'am," he said. "Charlotte. Up in Milwaukee?" He didn't want to mention he was a cop until it was absolutely necessary, and not around Billy. Or anyone, for that matter, but Lydia. He was disappointed he'd had to show his badge to Page Ringgold, but at least the subject hadn't come up with the trio on the fourth floor.

There was a tap on Jud's shoulder and he started. The tall white man behind him must have already been in the studio and silently approached. Jud was facing away from the mirrored wall or else he would have noticed him.

"I take care of Miss Boone's business," the man said, with more than a hint of violence.

"He looks nice to me, George," said Billy, who turned full-profile to Lydia and added, sotto voce: "Very nice."

"George loves to sneak up on people," said Lydia. She smiled shyly at Jud, then lowered her gaze.

Jud extended his hand but George ignored it while staring coldly into Jud's eyes, like a negative reflection of himself. The two men were the same height, identically built, and about the same age. They were even wearing the same style of hat.

"What is it that you want?" George said, with no trace of indulgence.

In other circumstances Jud would have returned the tough-guy talk to show he wasn't intimidated, but he had to be careful about the impression he made on Lydia. "It's private," he repeated. "Don't want no trouble, if that what you mean."

George took Jud by the forearm, his grip not tight but insistent. "Over here," he said, and steered Jud toward a corner of the studio as the other two looked on.

Jud noted that Lydia did not object to this treatment, which must have been standard procedure, so he went along until they reached a small alcove in the corner which held a water cooler and some cubbyholes for personal items. Sensing that he had little choice, he surreptitiously showed George his badge.

"I don't want to alarm her friend," Jud whispered, angling his head toward Billy.

George registered the badge without a word or nod or change of expression.

Jud put it together. Lydia was rich. Lydia was vulnerable. George was her bodyguard. And it made no difference to George whether or not he was talking to a cop. Being white, he didn't have to defer.

Jud started to explain. "Miz Boone got a niece called Charlotte in Milwaukee, where I'm on the force. A coupla days ago ..."

A new record, at much higher volume, sounded from the Victrola. It was classical music. A waltz. Jud glanced over and Lydia was looking at her feet as Billy swiveled her around the floor. Apparently the louder music was meant to ensure that Jud's conversation with George would not be overheard. Lydia left it to her middleman, it seemed, and until George conveyed the information to her she wanted no part of it. She was insulated.

Jud quickly summarized: A murdered cop in back of the house where Lydia's niece lived with her adoptive family. Jud leading the investigation. The bogus kidnapping rumor. The lieutenant's order to investigate Lydia and her relatives. Jud's need for Lydia's help in covering for him as he investigated the mystery of the murder victim's identity.

George silently observed Jud's face, demeanor, body language, but scarcely moved a muscle otherwise. When the waltz ended, he said, "Stay here." Billy saw him coming and discreetly stepped aside.

Lydia turned her eyes once or twice toward Jud as she and George, their heads together, conferred in a whisper. By the end of George's report she was staring at Jud and not looking away.

"I'll help you, Detective Minor," she called across the studio to Jud. "But only if you dance with me first."

44.

Sₕₑ HAD HEARD OF IT, of course, but never felt it. The thunderbolt. But he was half again her age and wearing a wedding ring.

Like Billy, she was most impressed with his looks, not to mention his build. Nothing new there. She had minor crushes all the time, though almost always, these days, on artists and intellectuals, and Jud was clearly neither. But he had a similar quality. The sense of woundedness. While he was talking to George and she was dancing with Billy she imagined telling a girlfriend about it, in the distant future when she and Detective Jud Minor were an old married couple. Or, better, writing a short story in the first person, when she finally found the courage and inspiration to begin composing something more ambitious than bad poetry: "The very first time I saw him I wanted to burst out in tears. I get vibrations, you know. Always have. They say people have auras you can't see. But sometimes you do see them and don't know it, like camouflage. Something about him made him seem like the saddest man on earth. I wanted to cradle his head and dry his tears. 'Baby, baby, it's okay, it's going to be okay.' And I'll tell you the most important thing. He didn't even realize how much he was hurting."

She imagined saying or writing this only in the future because she would never dare express it now. Her carefully styled persona was quirky and humorous and light, like the rich white girls in the pictures. In fact, the pictures were central to it. In breathing her air, other people, she hoped, would directly experience the same sort of glamour, the thrill, that they vicariously felt while watching the larger than life black and white creatures on the screen. Also, she was too young for her deeper qualities to be taken seriously by the others in her crowd, always older than she was and usually devoted for years or decades to the exploration of self in words, paint, music, dance.

Dance ... that was it. Insisting he dance with her would fit her persona beautifully. It would make a great story to tell people. It would also surprise and disarm Jud, and give them both a chance to talk more informally without waiting for the ice to be broken, if it ever could be in a police investigation.

"We'll make it a waltz," she said, after he protested that he didn't know how to dance. She took his hand and added: "They're the easiest." She angled her feet, with her left foot between his. "Put your feet at forty-five degrees, like mine."

Very tickled by her spontaneity, Billy hastened to the Victrola and played the Wayne King Orchestra record again.

The swirling, almost beatless opening strains of the *Blue Danube* provided time to get their bodies into position. Lydia took his left hand and Jud placed his right on the small of her back. "No, no," she said. "Up here, behind my shoulder."

"I done stranger things," Jud said awkwardly, "to get someone to cooperate on the job." He didn't smile or, in fact, appear to be at all pleased, much less amused. He was just going along with the whims of a crazy girl whose help he needed.

The melody began and Jud went through the motions as Lydia pretended they were actually waltzing. "Forward and back," she said. "Move your left forward and I go back, then your right forward and I go back, and then we reverse."

"I'll just follow you," Jud said, without much enthusiasm.

"You told George you needed my help," Lydia said while looking up at him, she imagined, coquettishly. "Why should I give it to you?"

"To protect your niece, that why. The newspapers are fixin to invent a whole lot of nonsense about that phony kidnapping plot. Your bodyguard told you all I said, didn't he?"

"He's officially my butler," Lydia said, trying to give the conversation some room to breathe. "He used to work for an ancient white woman on my floor, and always treated me with respect. When she died, I offered him a job."

"Don't your man Frank look after you?"

Lydia laughed. "Frank works for a paper in Atlanta. Left Chicago almost a year ago. He's just visiting for the holidays and helping me to read manuscripts." She deliberately stepped on Jud's toe and added: "I don't have a man."

Jud ignored her gesture. "I think I can get closer to the real story about the dead cop and, that way, make sure your niece stay out of it."

"Okay, now," Lydia said, "side to side. Move the left out, meet it with the right, then reverse."

"But," Jud continued, mindlessly following her instructions, "I'm under orders to be here in Chicago, and the press is watchin every move I make. Don't know why, but this newsman I mentioned, Meinecke, he get every report I file. He'll lay off Charlotte for a while, he tell me, but he bound to sensationalize it sooner or later. Then, that little girl's life gonna be tore apart." As Jud said this, Lydia felt strongly the righteousness of the man, and was sure her intuition about him had been correct. At the same time, she began to realize the investigation was more of a personal matter than she'd expected. It wasn't just about some cop in Milwaukee who happened to get killed near her niece's home. Jud was here because he genuinely cared about the little girl. "Right now," Jud said, "folks barely know she exist. But once she in the paper the state will sniff around. Then they'll find out about the deal your brother done made, and Charlotte gonna get taken away. Truth is, she oughta be out of that house ... but the kinda places she get put, they ain't gonna be no better."

"What deal?" Lydia said, confused.

"You tell me," Jud said. "Your brother got rich off them refrigerator parts. How come nobody in your family done took Charlotte in when her folks passed?"

"There wasn't anyone but Henry—my brother—and me, and I was only fourteen." She called out to George: "The record's nearly done ... could you start it over?" George did as asked then disappeared again. "Okay," Lydia said while waiting a second time for the song's introduction to end, "now the box step. Combine back and forth with side to side and make a box shape around the floor." Once Jud found the rhythm she repeated: "But what deal?"

"Your brother give ten thousand dollars a year to the family that took Charlotte in. The Odenwalds. They ain't even adopted her. Don't send her to school. Just make her work. And the girl never speak a word."

"What do you mean? Speak a word about what?"

"About anything. She dumb. Ain't never heard her say nothin. Meantime, that family treat her somethin awful." He frowned with disgust. "Treat her like a slave."

Lydia's eyes teared up. "Henry says the police check up on her. She's doing wonderfully, they always say. He gets reports. Every three months."

"That ain't true," Jud said, after a moment to think it over. "The reports musta been faked by Suthrin, the cop that got killed. He was blackmailing the family. Took a piece every year of the money your brother give em, from some trust they got set up."

"Please believe me," Lydia said, staring at her feet out of shame, "we had no idea." Without thinking, she continued the box step for almost all of the three-minute recording, but no longer felt very lighthearted doing so. "We're not bad people. My mama died in the flu epidemic and my daddy's heart went out a few years later. I was the baby of the family, by about a mile. Henry brought me up. Our sister Doris ... that's Charlotte's mother ... cut herself off when she got married. Seventh-Day Adventist, her husband was, and she converted. Didn't want anything to do with us, especially Henry, because ... well, Henry's like Billy, though he doesn't let on." She waited for a response to this information. There was none. "Doris found out about Henry and said he was going to hell. That was before he finished getting his patents. Took five years to get them, after the war. A whole team of lawyers. Then we went from rags to riches, as they say. Henry wanted to see me through high school and then to set me up on my own so he could go to Paris. That's where he is now. When we heard Doris had passed, Charlotte was only three, and neither Henry nor I have ever laid eyes on her. He found out Charlotte was already living with a big family. Doris and her husband were the live-in help. So he just figured she was better off with them than she could ever be with us. That was six years ago. I knew he gave them some ... uh, some assistance, but I never heard about any ten thousand a year, or any deal he made."

"Them lawyers who got him the patents," Jud said. "I expect Henry made em a lot of money."

"Right," Lydia confirmed absently, now watching the two of them dance in the mirror, and feeling somehow that she'd already seen the image before, as if in a half-remembered dream. "That's enough of the box step for now," she said, trying to get a grip on herself. "Go back to the first move." Jud obeyed and she answered his question: "Anyway, it was all done by the lawyers on what they call contingency. They had to wait for the money, just like we did. But why bring them up?"

"I figure they arrange to have your brother adopt the girl, on paper, as part of the deal with the Odenwalds. Keep the authorities out of it. Far as the state know, Charlotte don't even live in Wisconsin. And Suthrin probly help to keep a lid on it."

The song ended but Lydia didn't let Jud go. The record still spun and the needle scratched and popped at the end of its groove.

"I wasn't expecting our conversation to be ... to be like this," she said, uncertain how to end her statement. "George explained that it had to do with the house where Charlotte lives, but I never imagined all of that terrible information about her. We've got to get her out of there."

"Let me finish workin on the murder case, first," Jud said. She felt his palm sweat against her own. "That'll wrap it up for the papers, and you can move quietly once it over and done with. But you do anything right now and that newsman I mention, Meinecke, he gonna try to make it part of the story."

Lydia dropped her arms to her side and stepped back. "Why?"

"I don't know," Jud said. "But it clear somethin meant to be covered up. Meinecke made up that kidnapping story to point everything in the wrong direction, and my lieutenant and captain went right along with it. Ordered me not to look into any of the real leads I found. If you file papers to get Charlotte now, Meinecke bound to write stories tying you to the murder somehow. Say you try to kidnap her and it ain't worked out, or some fool thing like that."

"You still haven't explained how I can help," Lydia said. "George didn't know what you meant by saying I could give you cover."

During the waltz Billy had absented himself. Now he returned with three little girls in tow. "My next clients are here, Lydia," he said from the doorway. "You're free to stay and observe, with your splendid new friend, but I need the floor." He went to the Victrola and switched it off.

Jud looked over at George standing with his arms crossed against the wall by the alcove. "Is there somewhere we can talk?" he said.

"My penthouse," said Lydia.

"But you got company," Jud said.

Lydia allowed herself to laugh. "How do you know? And how did you know about Frank?"

"I been up there," Jud said. "Met three of em, including Frank."

"I want them there when you and I talk about what to do. I want their advice. I want you to tell them all about it. And then you can tell me how I can help."

45.

In the apartment Muriel Ringgold had joined the other three, making seven when Lydia, George, and Jud walked in. Lydia was pleased by the mix of types in her home, even the unsophisticated Billie Cooper, who at least evened out the balance of men and women if you ignored George. But why ignore George? What difference did it make that he was her employee? She was glad to see at least one white person there. She vowed to locate and bring in more as the years went by. Lydia dreamt of hosting a salon, like Gertrude Stein, whose *Three Lives* Lydia had tried and failed to read after being told it featured black characters.

A jazz instrumental, something by Louis Armstrong and His Savoy Ballroom 5, played on the Victrola. Muriel was saying: "Thought we was done with all you reds after the war." Lydia grasped at once that the old actress was teasing Frank. "But no. You was just waitin round for the crash. Then yall come back out of hiding."

"I'll join any party that stands for the only issue that matters," said Frank, "the eradication of white supremacy. I don't care if it's communist, socialist, progressive, liberal, democratic, or republican."

"I remember back when we was all Republicans," Muriel said.

"All the way back to last year, Muriel?" Jack Cooper joked.

Lydia joined in, taking a place on the floor with her back to the couch. "I'm still too young to vote, but I can't say I care for what Big Bill Thompson was up to."

Billie laughed. "Big Bill isn't so bad. Democrats in this town want to take all the fun out of everything."

"Except drinking," Jack said. "And I'll drink to that." He turned to Jud, still standing near the door, but addressed Lydia. "Get something for you and your, uh, friend, Lydia?"

"Join the party," Billie said to Jud. "You said you were looking for Lydia, but then you wouldn't come in. Well, now you found her." She pointed at George. "Or are you going to just stand there like the help?"

Jud took the chair closest to Lydia but left his hat on. "Don't mean to be rude," he said, "but ..."

"Just ginger ale and gin with a little ice," Lydia said to Jack. "Do you want anything, Jud?" He seemed so out of place, Lydia thought. She wondered what sort of social life he had in Milwaukee. Did his circle of friends include people like the ones here?

Jud shook his head and Billie exclaimed, "Nothing to drink ... he does act like the help." Lydia tried not to be annoyed by her.

"Maybe just a drop," Jud said. "What Miz Boone havin."

"It's Lydia," Lydia said. "And make it more than a drop, Jack."

Jack handed them their drinks and Jud repeated: "Don't mean to be rude, but ..."

"Play that one again," Muriel said when the record ended. At once, George tended to the Victrola. "What it called?"

"Beau Koo Jack," George dutifully read from the spinning label as the uptempo song began again.

"Well, then, this one for you, Jack ... since you be makin beaucoup jack from all them advertisers on the radio." Muriel stood up and began dancing. "Can't tap to Louis," she said, "but I done had it with rags, anyhow." She danced over to Jud and bent her tiny frame to put her face inches from his. "I hear you boys in blue got natural rhythm, so let's go." She grabbed his hand loosely and mimed tugging at him with all her might, leaning back and digging her heels into the floor. "This is one big cop you got here, Lydia. Hate to get in trouble on his beat."

"Cop?" Billie said.

"He's a cop," Muriel said, letting go of Jud's hand and pretending to rescue herself from a pratfall. "Showed me his badge." In one smooth motion from her near-pratfall she began to dance again.

"You didn't mention that," Frank said angrily to Jud. "Why'd you try to pass yourself off as a writer?"

"Never said nothin about bein no writer," Jud replied. "Keep tryin to tell yall ..."

"Yes, Jud is a policeman," Lydia said. She swallowed half her drink and added: "He doesn't know about the journal, Frank. I'm sure he wasn't trying to pass himself off as anything."

"I'm here to ask Miz Boone ..."

"Lydia," Lydia said.

"... to ask Lydia for some help on a case I'm workin."

"Is this some sort of a gag?" Jack said, grinning. "Muriel, did you bring in one of your actor friends to put us on?"

Lydia got up and turned off the music. Muriel froze in place like a warped statue in front of Jud and he couldn't help but laugh. She relaxed and said, "This fella been starstruck from the minute he saw me. He ain't no actor."

Lydia put her hands on her hips. "I'm not playing any more records till Jud has had his say. Frank, there's a short story here waiting to be written."

"Does he put us all in jail at the end of it?" Frank said, still upset. But the others stopped talking, all eyes turned toward Jud.

"Lydia got a little niece in Wisconsin she ain't never met," Jud said, "name of Charlotte. She an orphan, nine years old, and livin with a big old white family."

He waited for the group, everyone except George, to go the rounds on this startling information. When they were done, he continued:

"A cop got killed in back of the house where Charlotte live. I'm in charge of the case, but it clear nobody want me to solve it. So they send me here for a few days to talk to Charlotte's kin, just to keep me busy without nothin gettin done. But the place I really gots to go is Jackson."

"Jackson, Mississippi?" Frank said. Jud nodded. "Now I do know how the story ends. You get lynched for impersonating a police officer."

"Frank, shush," Lydia said. "I haven't heard all of this part yet."

"I got reason to believe," Jud said with authority, "that the dead cop ain't who he said he was. Called hisself Landis Humphreys, but I think he a fella name Johnson, use to work for the sheriff down in Jackson. Got hisself a new identity and moved north, joined the Milwaukee police. He also got connections to organized crime in town, maybe even an offshoot of the Capone gang."

"You're a cop, so you ought to know," said Frank. "That's what cops are: organized crime."

"The Capone gang?" Billie said, ignoring Frank. "Really? This is so exciting."

"Well, don't know about Capone ... Milwaukee gangsters, anyhow," Jud said. "But it obvious to me that no investigation of the murder make sense unless I find out who the victim really was. How else am I sposed to get a suspect list?"

"What has any of that got to do with Lydia?" Jack asked. He removed his glasses and rubbed them with a cloth from the breast pocket of his tailored three-piece suit.

Jud explained that he wanted to keep Charlotte out of the papers, and the best way to do that was break the story about the dead cop's dual identity and gang connections.

"You said no one wants you to solve the case," Frank said. "How will you get the papers to print it?"

"I got some ideas about that," Jud said. "But first things first."

"You still haven't explained why you're here or what you need from Lydia," Jack said, putting his owlish glasses back on.

"He was ordered to interrogate me," Lydia said, with some excitement.

"But he intends to break the order," Jack said, "so what does he want from you?"

"I was hopin Miz Lydia could give me cover when I go down south."

"Give you cover," Lydia said, pretending to be exasperated. "You keep saying that. But I told you I don't know what you mean."

Jud looked her in the eye and she hoped he would somehow, perhaps telepathically, pick up on her heat. "All you gotta do is teletype some pages from a Chicago post office every day," he said. "Just send em to my station and say they from me. I'll write up some fake reports in my room tonight, a few days' worth, for you to read to the teletype man. Say I'm travelin round meetin more of Charlotte's kin, that sort of thing."

"That's all you need me to do?" Lydia asked, disappointed. "Dictate teletypes?"

"Every day," Jud said. "My lieutenant will think I's just wastin time in Illinois, like he want me to, and the papers won't have nothin to print all week. Meantime, shouldn't take more than a day or two in Jackson to find out what I need." At last, Lydia noted, he took a sip from his drink. "Plus a day drivin down and a day drivin back, if I drive straight through."

"You can't be serious," Jack said incredulously.

"I'm sure Miz Lydia won't get in no trouble," Jud said, "even if ..."

"Not her," Jack said. "You. You'll never make it there and back alive. Where have you been the past fifteen years? Black men can't drive alone in their own automobiles for hundreds of miles through the delta. They just disappear."

"Jack right about that," Muriel said. "I left Alabama thirty-some years ago, but when Ernie Watts travel down there for a show, he bring along a chauffeur cap and coat and a picture of some white friend of his in whatever city he headin to, with a letter from the white guy that say Ernie deliverin the car. Otherwise, he be dead ten times over by now."

"But..." Jud said.

"We can't let you go," Frank said, standing up to make his point. "Little as I care about the safety of cops, I can't send a black man to his death."

"But I'll be in full uniform with a badge," Jud said, "and drivin a Milwaukee squad car."

"I was joking about you getting lynched," Frank said, "but that was before I understood you meant to drive down there alone. I figured when you said you were going to Jackson, you meant on a train and in the company of other cops, all of them white."

"I need a car while I'm down there," Jud explained. "This the only way."

Lydia found herself oddly thrilled to be in the middle of such a conversation. She remained silent, to take it all in. Also, she was sure anything she might say would betray her inexperience. Starting a literary journal was one thing, but what did she, at twenty, know about the dangers of the deep south? So she kept her mouth shut, thinking that this was the stuff of true romance. Big, strong, brave, handsome Jud Minor, venturing into the heart of darkness, risking his life to solve a murder and protect a little girl. And Lydia had a small but crucial role to play in it, like the third actress in a picture's credits. Moreover, her role also meant she held a trump card, should she wish to assert herself and have some say in whatever occurred. Daydreaming, Lydia realized she'd missed some of the exchange.

"…and what makes you think," Jack was saying, "the county sheriff would even cooperate with you?"

"Or even let you in the door?" added Frank, now standing only a few feet in front of Jud and waving his arms. "And I don't mean that metaphorically. I mean the actual door."

"I sent a telegram sayin detective Judson Minor of the Milwaukee police gonna be there within a coupla days."

"Did you mention you was colored?" Muriel asked.

"No," Jud said.

Muriel laughed, imagining the scene. "Well, that gonna be quite a surprise for the sheriff and his boys."

"Have you read about what's been going on down there?" Frank implored, almost shouting. "Since the war and the migration and the race riots? Mississippi is doing to blacks what Hitler wants to do with the Jews in Germany. It's imprisonment. It's the closest you can get to slave labor without it actually being slavery. People are killed just for trying to quit their plantation jobs and work somewhere else in the same county. When black families get a little property together, whites can steal it from them and claim it's in payment of debt, and what court will care? You can be beaten to death just for forgetting, just once, to say 'Sir' at the end of a sentence to a complete stranger. Black women are raped and there's nothing they or their families can do about it, because the criminal case doesn't get to square one ... not even a police report. And, you know, lynching isn't just beating and hanging ... they'll douse a man with gasoline and set him on fire, burn him alive. It's a cultural crusade.

Everyone's in on it. The postmasters in small towns read every piece of mail to or from anybody who's black, steal any money included, and destroy any letter that might give someone hope that they can get out. It's all but impossible for blacks to even leave the state without white patronage. The whites believe, literally believe, that the blacks are animals, an inferior species, which must be kept in its pen." He sat down in the nearest chair. "Of course, if you've been sheltered by the Milwaukee P.D., maybe none of this has come to your attention."

"Your plan won't work," Jack insisted quietly when Frank's monologue seemed to be done. "You can't get the information you want in Jackson without cooperation from your superiors in Milwaukee. You can't do it alone."

To Lydia's surprise, Billie spoke up. "But what about the thing Muriel said? About her friend pretending to be a white man's chauffeur?"

Lydia was intrigued. "What about it?" she said at once, to prevent the men in the room from ignoring Billie.

"Jud could go with George," Billie said, very pleased with her inspiration. "He's the help," she added impolitely. "He has to do what you say, Lydia."

Jack, who evidently didn't know his new wife very well, presumed she was joking. "That," he laughed, "at least solves the problem of driving there."

Frank took the idea more seriously. "You still won't get in the front door of the sheriff's office. You have no choice but to get a white cop from your station to do the investigation for you."

"But he will," Billie said. "He will have a white cop to do it. That's my point."

"What white cop?" Jud said.

"George," Billie said. "George can wear your cop uniform and you can put on his chauffeur outfit. Like the Prince and the Pauper." She laughed with delight. "George can ask all the questions. And you can tell him what you want him to ask, on the way down there."

"Why drive all that way at all?" Lydia said, tantalized by Billie's idea. "Just take the train."

"I need a car when I get there," Jud answered.

"Rent one," Lydia said. "Go to the DrivUrSelf."

"Figured they wouldn't rent to no colored man," Jud said, "even if he a cop."

"You need my help," Lydia said, playing her trump. "So I get the last word: You aren't driving. You and George will take the train to Jackson. George, wearing your uniform, will rent a car ... which you will drive as his chauffeur." She gazed at Jud with love. "And I'll pay for everything."

46.

WHEN THE ILLINOIS CENTRAL crossed the border into Tennessee in the dark predawn hours of Tuesday, December 29, 1931, the conductor came through to collect fares and directed Jud to move to the colored coach at the furthest end of the train. Jud would already have done so once the Tennessee crossing was announced but he'd fallen asleep in his seat next to George, who was also asleep.

Shortly after sunset in Chicago they had purchased their first-class fares for three cents per mile, with Jud's fare discounted to two cents for the miles through Tennessee and Mississippi because there was no first-class car for colored passengers, most of whom were already segregated by the less expensive lower-class fares through Illinois.

At the moment the conductor shook him, Jud was dreaming about a desperate search for a parking space. He woke with disoriented anxiety before recalling that he had fetched the squad car and moved it into the parking lot of WSBC, where Jack Cooper assured him it would be safe. Then he and George had taken a cab to the train station, Jud having hurriedly scribbled notes for Lydia Boone's several daily teletypes describing Jud's fictional trips around Illinois speaking to non-existent Boone relatives. In the comfortable parlor lounge car, a streamlined Art Deco compartment with smoking stands and upholstered chairs and staffed by several colored waiters and waitresses, he and George had spent two hours across a table from each other brainstorming George's role in Jackson, Jud receiving dirty looks only from those passengers with southern accents while the northerners ignored him as they obsessively discussed their business. When George was sufficiently prepared for almost any contingency, they returned together to their first-class seats without another word and managed to sleep.

Whereas the now-segregated car they'd occupied was heated and in excellent condition, with well-stocked restrooms offering hot and cold running water, wash basins, soap, and towels, the colored coach, partly used for carrying baggage, was cold, poorly ventilated, filthy, and stank horribly of odors from unemptied garbage bins and the men's toilet, which did not flush; and the closet that housed the toilet featured nothing but a low spigot producing ice cold water above a narrow drain in the floor. Because the other colored passengers present were still settling themselves as the train pulled away toward Memphis, Jud concluded that the coach was not normally used for passengers at all, except after crossing the Jim Crow lines at Tennessee or, on different routes, Arkansas.

After a while Jud moved from his claustrophobic seat and used the facilities, kneeling to urinate directly into the drain in the floor to avoid further filling the stopped-up toilet. He was glad he'd barely eaten since breakfast the day before, having pocketed the sandwich bought in the lounge car in exchange for his place there, and that he had moved his bowels both in his hotel bathroom and in the men's room of the first-class coach.

When he returned to his seat it was taken. Jud assumed a spot on the floor amidst the luggage, where somehow he slept long past daybreak.

The train pulled into Jackson shortly after noon. Lydia had telegraphed the largest DrivUrSelf in the city and made a car reservation for Officer Judson Minor of the Milwaukee Police Department. Along with the reservation, she also wired enough money to cover even the most expensive rental for a week.

George took a cab to pick up the rental car, fitting a trifle snugly into Jud's police uniform, while Jud waited in the colored section of the train station dressed as a chauffeur. There were few others present in that section, as the next train north was not due and colored folks from Jackson were not likely to be traveling in any other direction.

Now that he'd arrived he wondered at his good luck in avoiding the seven-hundred-mile drive. The girl in Chicago seemed the type inclined to sudden infatuations, focused for the nonce on Jud, and was spending what for most people would be a small fortune to enable the trip and keep Jud safe.

Bad as some of his experiences in Georgia had been, they were a long time ago and he never imagined that the notoriously more primitive delta states were still as dangerous as Lydia's friends had described. The fact was, for the past decade he hadn't paid much attention to anything other than his job and his wife, hearing only about the most publicized atrocities such as the fate of the Scottsboro boys. His contacts in Bronzeville rarely spoke of conditions anywhere else, though the more alert would occasionally relate some recent incident described in the colored newspapers. Certainly the mainstream papers had no interest in the treatment of blacks (as colored people were called by the folks he'd met in Chicago), whether in the delta or anywhere else. Every once in a while there might be an item about a lynching, but such news came and went, and Jud, safe in Milwaukee, didn't dwell on it. And the songs sung by the singers Sally liked, or for that matter by Walter Jacob in Grafton, never mentioned men being doused with gasoline and burned alive. He was embarrassed to have had his naiveté exposed by Frank, Jack, and Muriel.

George left the car running outside the colored section and got out to look for Jud, who'd seen him pull up and went to meet him. At first Jud was disconcerted when George turned around and got into the back seat, but then he remembered his role and climbed in front. The sunny afternoon was cloudless and a bank's electronic sign reported the temperature to be seventy-four. George was looking at a new map he'd just picked up. Within a few minutes they parked near the sheriff's office, an ordinary two-floor commercial building on a street populated by identical buildings but also, crucially, by the tall ugly county jail, a few doors down.

Careful to remain several steps behind George, Jud followed him inside and was amazed to find the premises abandoned. He wondered if the brass placard on the facade was out of date and the office had been moved elsewhere. But the walls of the main corridor held old paintings and newer photographs of former sheriffs and their staffs, the latter increasing in number as the decades went on and now numbering eight or ten.

"Where is everybody?" Jud whispered to George.

They saw an open door beside two office windows. A slot beneath the word SHERIFF held a slate reading TOM MOORE, as though the title were presumed to be temporary for any occupant. George entered the office a moment before Jud, and a weathered woman in her late fifties or sixties, visible as Jud passed the windows, took one look at the police uniform and said: "Anybody you lookin for gonna be over to the jailhouse, or maybe at lunch. Ain't nothin happenin here today ... least, so far." She wore black hornrimmed glasses on a skinny pickled-prune face that hadn't caught up with the increasing girth of her body.

"I'm Detective Judson Minor of the Milwaukee Police Department," George said. "My station telegraphed this office. I'm here to see Sheriff Moore."

Jud walked in. At first too shocked to be outraged, the woman yelped immediately, "Git on outta here," as she would to a stray dog.

"He's my boy," George said, using the word they'd agreed upon. "I came down all the way from Milwaukee and I need an assistant."

"Well," she said, "I can only imagine how yall do things in Milwaukee, a place I never hope to visit, but unless he got handcuffs on, he ain't got no business being in this building."

Jud said: "I can wait in the hall."

The woman stood up from behind the sheriff's desk and, having now located within herself the proper outrage, all but shouted: "Anybody talkin to you, boy?" She turned to George heatedly and said: "There's a case on the wall behind me got eight shotguns. You tell that boy if he looks me in the eye again, I'm gonna open that there case up and he ain't never gonna see it close." Then she added, to Jud: "And that's ma'am to you. 'I can wait in the hall, ma'am.' But you can't wait in the hall, neither. Either grab a mop or leave this building. Now."

Jud stepped into the hall. "This will only take a minute," George said. "I need him here due to a medical condition. I've got the falling sickness. He's been trained to respond to it. You don't want to be the only one here if I have a seizure, do you?"

She thought over the lie George had prepared and then resumed her seat. "Good thing for you they all down to the jailhouse. But anybody come in, that boy gotta leave ... and you can have your seizure."

Jud examined the office through the windows in the hall. A black rectangular safe, nearly the size of two men side by side, stood next to the gun case, and both were straddled by an American flag on the left and a bigger Mississippi state flag on the right. A huge map of the county and a calendar were on the wall opposite, beside a glass-fronted bookshelf incongruously boasting only a few tattered legal codes. The sheriff's desk held an inkwell on a blotter and a teletype machine and telephone, and there were three high stools along with the padded swivel chair where the angry woman sat. On the wall furthest from Jud hung a strange multi-leaved cabinet, like a book, opened to one of its middle leaves to reveal a five by five array of mugshots. Beside it and the inevitable rolltop desk, covered with doodads and paperwork, a tall chalkboard listed the number of jail occupants in each "tank," then broke them down by category, omitting the default categories of white and men: women, girls, boys, colored, felony, federal, holdover, miscellaneous, and, most ominously, "hole." There were currently six prisoners in the hole.

"I assume you received our telegram," George said.

Now that Jud was out of the room, the woman relaxed and said, "Fact, it was the first thing I saw, my first day on the job, Monday morning. I'm Martha." She and George shook hands and she added proudly: "I'll be workin for Warren ... uh, Sheriff Ferguson. He's my godson, bless'im."

George glanced reflexively at the name on the door. This variation had not been in the script, so he just repeated: "I'm looking for Sheriff Tom Moore."

"Tom done got himself voted out last month," she laughed. "Damn fool made his whole career off that father-in-law of his. Thought he'd married Mississippi royalty, what with his wife's grandfather being a famous old doctor and all ... best-known in three counties, they say. Confederate soldier, too, spent two years in a yankee prison, then come home and helped write the state constitution, served in the statehouse ...

and her father, Julius, he was Rankin County Chancery Recorder a while back."

"I see," said George, a northerner unprepared for her effusion.

"But if you was from around here, you'd know what a damn fool Tom is. Got himself knocked out cold in a fistfight over politics with Kenny Klinker in the county courthouse. That don't sound very sheriff-like to most folks. Then he extradited some old lady from Harrison County ... don't know if extradite's the right word, but, anyways, he lets on that she's really Belle Gunness." When George didn't respond to the name, Martha explained: "You know, Belle Gunness ... the gal what lured all them men to her farm twenty-some years ago and killed em all for their money. Everybody knows she got burnt up in a fire before the war, but folks always claimin they spotted her someplace or other, like Jesse James." She paused to laugh at the stupidity of other people. "So Tom, he hauls her in here, all the way from Gulfport. Seventy if she's a day. Gets them to hint in the papers that, lo and behold, Tom Moore is the sheriff gonna finally bring Belle Gunness to justice. Then nobody never hears nothin else about it, and the poor old woman gets to go home. Made Tom the laughingstock."

"I see," said George, expressionless.

Martha frowned at his lack of manners. "How come you yankees never want to pass the time of day?" she complained. "Always in such a goldang'd hurry."

"So," George said, "I take it Sheriff Moore is out of the office."

"He's out of office altogether, in three days," she laughed. "That's why there ain't no staff here yet, nobody but me, fixin to help Warren Ferguson take over. And like I said, the deputies are all ..."

"Down to the jailhouse," George finished for her. "You know where I can find Tom Moore?"

"Your telegram ain't said why."

"I'm trying to get information about one of his former deputies. Maybe you can help. Young guy named Johnson who was here in the mid-twenties."

"Before my time," Martha said. "And I don't know my way round all them record books yet. Fact, they reorganized the sheriff's office in twenty-eight. Some kinda big bureaucratic thing, like they startin all over again from scratch. Probly got everything before that in boxes somewhere, if the flood didn't get them first. Course, you yankees probly don't know nothin bout the twenty-seven flood, do you?"

Lacking diplomatic skills, and perhaps any ability at all to relate to plain dull folks like Martha, George sighed with obvious impatience. "So, again, since you can't help, where can I find Tom Moore?"

While listening to this exchange Jud had stiffened in fear at the sight of a big blonde dog loping into the hallway from around the corner. It ambled up to him and he was relieved to discern an ancient ragged collie, blind in one eye and long past any aggression. It paused to lick his hand and snuffle George's odor on the chauffeur uniform, then limped into the office in time to quell Martha's irritation at the rudeness of her visitor.

"Well, I never," she was saying. "Who do you think you ..." Then she brightened at the sight of the dog. "Mabel, you old mutt, you," she squealed, petting the collie as it curled into position at her feet and promptly fell asleep. "What mischief you been up to, you dirty old sheepdog?" She took her time scratching behind Mabel's ears and babbling inanities before deigning to regard George again. "Tom's probably with that damn horse of his," she said. "Calls it a racehorse, but it ain't no thoroughbred. Even with his wife's money, Tom can't afford no thoroughbred. Nothin but a trotter, not even fifteen hands high." Martha turned her attention to Mabel again and talked to her for a while, deliberately testing George's patience. He was at least perceptive enough to know when he was being provoked, so he refrained from speaking. Looking around in her purse for what turned out to be a dog biscuit shaped like a bone, Martha finally said: "Tom keeps that damn horse up at Julius Robinson's farm. That's his father-in-law. It's straightaway up highway 25 to Sandhill. Can't be much as thirty miles from here." She described the landmark at which George would find the intersecting farm road, just past the sign welcoming everybody to Sandhill, Mississippi. Then she fed the biscuit to Mabel, and George left.

"Go back in there and thank her, George," Jud whispered in dismay.

George grimaced, for the first time revealing any trace of unprofessional emotion in Jud's presence, and stepped back half-way into the office.

"Thank you for your help," he said, not tipping his cap.

"You're welcome, I'm sure," Martha replied coldly.

"And thank you for being so kind to that dog," George added. "It more than makes up for how you treated the man standing in your hallway." He shut the door on his way out, not caring to hear any response Martha might have to his bad manners.

47

"Now be polite to them two kids," Jud said to George, looking over his shoulder at his passenger from the driver's seat as they pulled up to a ten- or fifteen-acre pasture occupied by half a dozen horses. After an hour's drive they'd found the Robinson farm but elected to bypass the house and continue down the estate's bumpy dirt road in search of a pasture or stable. With luck Tom Moore, the soon to be erstwhile Sheriff of Hinds County, would be busy outside and George would not need to navigate the courtesies of a southern farmhouse's front door. But when they spotted the pasture no grown man was in sight, only a couple of adolescents, a boy and a girl, studying the horses from behind a perimeter fence. "Southerners expect you to talk a while before gettin to the point," Jud continued. "Can't just jump right in and ask your questions and leave. Let em jabber a bit. And try to jabber back."

George nodded and Jud parked the luxury rental on the grass, close enough to hear whatever might be said through the open driver's side window. The two kids turned their attention from the horses to the car and approached.

George leaned forward, preparing to hold the conversation through the open window. "Get on out, George," Jud whispered. "Get on out and talk to them about the horses or the weather or whatever they want. That way, you fit in, and don't cause so much suspicion."

The boy watched George emerge from the back seat. "You sure got a fancy car, mister," he said.

"It's rented," George said brusquely. He stepped past both of them to the fence. "Does one of those horses belong to Sheriff Tom Moore?"

Jud sighed.

"That don't look like a regular police uniform," the girl said, catching up with him. Jud took her to be about thirteen.

"I'm from the Milwaukee police," George said. "I need to speak to Tom Moore."

The boy ignored him and stayed by the car, examining every inch, having barely looked at George.

"He's my daddy," the girl said. "I'm Kate Moore and that," she giggled, pointing at the boy in overalls, "is my Uncle Woodrow. His middle name is Wilson. He was named for President Woodrow Wilson at the beginning of the Great War." She enjoyed reciting this information, clearly finding it somehow ridiculous.

"Your uncle?" George said skeptically.

"Well, step uncle, I guess," Kate said, unconsciously swaying with her hands behind her back so that her calf-length gingham dress swiveled about her legs. "Grampa Julius … that's my mama's daddy … was a widower with six kids, out of eight to begin with, when he up and got married to Woodrow's ma, Nannie Moore, daddy's second-cousin. Then he had six more with Nannie. Reckon he tryin to put her in the ground, too." She laughed at her family's standard joke and seemed disappointed when George did not.

The boy, Woodrow, thrust his head and one arm through the driver's side window, as though no one else were there, and began fiddling around with the dashboard. For a moment Jud was as frightened as he'd been upon first seeing the dog in the sheriff's office. He had no idea how to respond to the intrusion, unsure what he was and was not permitted to say. Satisfied, the boy withdrew without a word and Jud caught his breath.

"I was told that your father would be out here with his horse," George said, taking no interest in the girl's colorful family history.

"He's over at the track," she said. She gazed at the horses, all in various states of idleness as they foraged for grass in the winter mud and occasionally nuzzled each other. "Ain't they beautiful? I think it's a shame daddy's tryin to turn Robert T. into a trotter. Robert T. is daddy's horse. Works him to death just to run a bunch of silly races at county fairs. Daddy says Robert T. is an investment, though. Says Robert T. cost money and he's gonna win enough purses to earn it all back. But I can't stand to see the poor thing draggin along that horrible sulky, stuck there with a bit in his mouth. And when he's not trainin, sometimes daddy keeps him in that little box stall, not much more than twelve feet square, so he'll get used to the idea of not havin no pasture when he's travelin round to the county fairs."

Jud observed George impatiently shifting his weight from foot to foot, no doubt exerting great effort to obey Jud's request and let the girl jabber.

"Grampa Julius lets him rent space in the pasture with them other horses. They're owned by folks from all over the county. At least daddy doesn't keep Robert T. in one of them fancy jockey clubs and just visit for a ride every week or two, like they do with Thelma Benson's horse. Thelma is so stuck up just because she's twelve and has her own horse, but they don't even look after it themselves. Don't feed it no special diet, don't brush it down, just take it out once a week and forget about it." Squinting under the bright sunlight, she angled her head up to look at George. "That's no way to form a bond, do you think?"

Uncle Woodrow had lost interest in the car and now rudely stood at less than arm's length from George, perusing his uniform. "You from across the river?" he said to George.

"Don't you recognize his accent, dummy?" Kate said. "He's from up north."

"Don't much cotton to yankees," Woodrow said, trying the cliché on for size and then spitting for good measure. Jud doubted the boy had ever laid eyes on a yankee, or for that matter anyone from outside western Mississippi. "Thought yall stopped keepin darkies." Woodrow stuck his tongue out at Jud, finally acknowledging his existence.

"Where is your father?" George said to Kate, deliberately turning his back on her uncle.

"Told you," Kate said. "At the track, trainin Robert T."

"City racetrack?" George said, frustrated by the girl's imprecision. "County racetrack?"

Kate seemed to pity his ignorance. "Who said racetrack? It's grampa Julius's half-mile trainin track out yonder, past them trees other side of the pasture."

George surveyed the area and followed the private dirt road with his eyes. It continued more or less straight, at a ninety degree angle to the direction Kate had pointed across the field. "I didn't see a road branching off that way," he said.

"Oh, you can drive straight across the grass," Kate said.

"You'll get mud all over your fancy car," Woodrow warned, then cackled: "Your darkie gonna have to clean it off."

George turned on his heel and waved a fist at the boy. "You'll stop calling him that, if you know what's good for you."

"Well," Woodrow said, stepping back and glancing at his niece and cousin for support, "what you yankees call em?"

George strode irritably past the boy and opened the car door.

"Thank them, George," Jud whispered fearfully.

"Thank you, young lady," George said to Kate, then slammed the door after he'd taken his seat in the back.

Jud rolled up his window. "You gonna get us run out of town," he said to George, not bothering to control his anger.

"It's over there," George said, leaning forward so Jud would see where he was pointing.

"I heard," Jud said. He started the car and pulled further away from the dirt road to circle the pasture. "Listen here, George. The man what own this farm is the son of a confederate hero, a rich bigwig. They gonna have connections all over. You can't go shakin your fist at his fifteen-year-old son for callin me a darkie. We still gots to drive off his homestead, go twenty-five mile down a country highway, middle of nowhere, and maybe even stay the night in Jackson if there ain't no train by the time we get back and return the car, or if I don't get what I'm lookin for today and we stick around."

"So?" George said.

"So, that a lot of time for somebody to take a shot at us," Jud said, nearly yelling. He took a breath to calm himself. "Now, we about to talk to a long-time county sheriff. A Mississippi county sheriff. You gots to get ahold of yourself and treat that man like he a king. Talk to him about his horse like you give a damn. He want to call me a darkie, you ain't gonna say nothin. All right?"

In the rearview mirror Woodrow Wilson Robinson chucked a rock at the car, safely beyond his range. Jud and George drove in silence over the grass and mud.

48.

SHERIFF TOM MOORE, a tall gaunt man in his late thirties wearing a three-piece suit and a low-crown derby, concentrated fiercely on the American Standardbred pulling a sulky and a colored teenaged boy around Julius Robinson's private half-mile track. Jud knew that George wouldn't have the sense to leave Moore alone before the training paused, so as they walked from the car, now parked next to Moore's truck, he said: "Let's hold back. You just gonna irritate that man if you start askin questions while he don't want nothin on his mind but how his horse runnin."

"Check out that high starched collar," George said. "Guy looks like Connie Mack." It was his first purely conversational utterance since he and Jud met the day before. Jud nodded, unable to remember who Connie Mack was.

"Don't let him go into a break," Moore shouted at the jockey. He seemed displeased with the boy, who sat back at an angle holding the reins atop two huge wheels. "He's taking hold of the bit. Steady him, you fool."

Jud watched the horse, Robert T., and saw nothing at all worth commenting upon. But Moore continued to find fault in everything the young jockey did.

"Don't let him start single-footing," Moore shouted. "That's a bad habit, boy. He's scalping himself." The sheriff threw his hat on the ground and cursed. "You stupid darkie, don't let him jog or single-foot on the turns. Look ... he's brushing his hind pasterns with his front shoes. And that horse is shod just fine. It's all your fault, you idiot." Swiveling his head to watch Robert T. take the next turn, Moore spotted George, standing five paces ahead of Jud, but ignored him, despite the peculiarity of George's uniform. "You're scaring him," he yelled, now cupping his hands around his mouth. "Steady him. Take him back, before he commences to tangle, you damn coon." It went on like this, a torrent of complaints and insults, until the horse completed two more rounds and the jockey pulled up beside his owner.

George took this as his cue and cleared his throat to say something before Jud stopped him with a quick gesture. The sheriff was still too preoccupied, not to mention heated, to shift his attention elsewhere.

The colored boy extricated himself from the sulky and removed his cap, holding it in two hands while looking toward Moore's feet. "Look, suh," he said, tilting his head toward the horse but keeping his eyes where they were. "Robert T. ain't scalped hisself, and his hind pasterns is just fine."

Jud got the point. The boy was being chastised not for mistakes he'd made but for those Moore presumed he would make. Jud also sensed that Moore didn't know much about how to train racehorses but the boy did.

"You questioning my judgment, boy?"

"No, suh." Eyes to the ground, the boy tilted his head again, this time toward George. "Look like a policeman here to see you, suh."

Moore raised his right arm and backhanded the boy across the face, knocking him to his knees. "You tryin to tell me when I'm done talkin to you, boy?"

"No, suh," the boy said, rubbing his cheek.

"Get up," Moore said, "and give Robert T. some walking without the sulky." Then he was done with the boy and turned to shake hands with George, who had gone pale under the high sun. "Tom Moore," he said. "I can see from your uniform you ain't from around here, so what can I do for you?"

George let go of his hand after the most perfunctory shake. "I'm detective Judson Minor of the Milwaukee Police Department. We wired your office yesterday."

"Ain't my office no more, detective." He picked up his derby and put it back on. "You descended from William J. Minor?"

George took a moment to make sense of this sudden turn in the conversation. "No," he said. "I'm here to ..."

"Good," Moore said, "because if you was, we'd be done. In the days before the war of northern aggression"—pointedly, the sheriff studied the Milwaukee P.D. badge on George's uniform—"William J. Minor was the most highly regarded horseman on the southwestern Mississippi tracks. A great man. But then he hid himself on his estate, Ascension Parish, Louisiana, and turned traitor. Started paying his own slaves. Wouldn't support the secession. Gave aid and assistance to the yankees even before the war was lost." Moore looked George in the eye. "So be glad you ain't descended from him, detective."

"That's very ... uh ... interesting," George said, giving the conversation his best shot.

Moore stared at Jud. "Somethin wrong with your boy?"

George glanced back for a moment and shook his head. "No ... he's fine."

"Then why does he keep lookin at me like that?" Moore said. "Whatsa matter, boy? Think I'm gonna steal yall's fancy car?"

"No, sir," Jud said, baffled.

"Then take your eyes off me," Moore demanded. He turned back to George. "I'll let it slide this time, since you're a man of the law and we're all brothers in blue, even though of course a sheriff don't wear no uniform, but get your darkie in line or I ain't gonna stay in a good mood much longer."

Jud cast his eyes to the ground. George fidgeted with the buttons of his coat and finally managed to say, "Nice horse."

"Yep ... and he's somethin proper for your boy to be lookin at," Moore replied. "Don't he never smile? What is he, simple?"

Jud looked up at George long enough to see him clench his jaw. "I heard you call your horse Robert T.," George said through gritted teeth.

"Named for Robert T. Davies," Moore said with pride. "Best breeder in Canada before he passed on. Sold some studs to a fella in Kentucky who sold one of Robert T.'s line to a man in Natchez, and so on down to me. Cost me a pretty penny, even though his dam was only a Dutch trotter."

"Well," George said, "call it an investment."

"Not even four years old yet," Moore said. "But I know a tape line trotter when I seen one. Gonna run him in his first race, oh, must be about three weeks from now."

"Good luck," George said.

The jockey and the horse had walked through both turns and were now headed back. "Run on over here, boy," Moore called down the track. The boy hesitated, looking back and forth between the horse and Moore. "Just leave him be for a minute," Moore clarified. The boy broke into a sprint until he was close enough for Jud to see the new bruise on his high yellow face. "Do you like horses, boy?"

The boy broke into an exaggerated grin, and bowed oddly back and forth while gesturing with both arms, "Oh, yessuh, Mistuh Moore, suh, I sure do like them horses, suh." He laughed theatrically, stupidly, and slapped his thigh with his cap. "Them horses just about the finest creatures I ever done laid eyes on, and they couldn't be nicer to me, suh."

"See?" Moore said to George. "That's the proper attitude for a coon." He pulled an egg-sized cloth bag of chewing tobacco from his pocket and rummaged around in it. "Go on back, now," he ordered the boy while putting a plug in his cheek.

"Yessuh. Thank you, suh." The boy hightailed it back to the horse.

"Why don't you ask your boy," Moore said with a frown, "how he likes Robert T.?"

"I'm here to ask you about a case..." George said.

"Aw, hell," Moore said, working his jaw. "I'll ask him myself." He spit tobacco juice in Jud's direction. "You like that horse, boy?"

Jud carefully kept his eyes to the ground. "Seems like a fine horse, sir."

"Look at that," Moore said with disgust. "He don't even smile."

"We've had a long trip," George said. "Left at sunset yesterday. We're both very tired."

"Then my advice to you," Moore said, obviously accustomed to the deference of white men when he had advice to offer, "is get yourself a boy who don't tire so easy. If he ain't got enough pep just to behave like a proper coon, I don't see how useful he could ever be." Robert T. and the jockey passed in front of them and, after examining the horse's shoes, Moore leaned back on the fence with his arms slung along it. "But I reckon you got a job to do, officer, so let's get on with it."

Jud could only imagine George's relief.

"I'm looking for information about one of your former deputies," George said. "Man in his early twenties named Johnson ... used to patrol the roads on a motorcycle five or six years ago."

"Andy Johnson?" Moore said, straightening his tie. "I don't think he's likely to be of much help to you."

"Oh?" George said. "Why is that?"

"Because he blew his own head off in 1925," Moore said with a thin smile.

49.

As they drove back down Highway 25 Jud waited in vain for any response to the startling news about Andy Johnson, suicide. They were bound for the last known address of Johnson's grandmother, upon whom Sheriff Moore had paid the obligatory visit when her grandson's body, identifiable only by its badge and boots and scraps of clothing, had washed up on the banks of the Pearl River a month after the deputy went missing. His motorcycle and suicide-rigged shotgun were later found on a high bluff overlooking the river fifty miles northeast of town, where Johnson was believed to have shot himself in such a way as to propel his body over the cliff and into the waters below, guaranteeing that a non-fatal but crippling misfire be compensated by drowning. As for the motorcycle, Sheriff Moore credited it with Johnson's deputation. It was the best model available on the local market, and when in 1923 the 25-year-old Johnson applied for parttime patrols on the county roads Moore could not pass up acquiring, in the bargain, such a fine piece of machinery. Moore said there were rumors after Johnson's death that he had bought the bike with money earned in criminal activity on Jackson's notorious Gold Coast, leading to speculation that his suicide two years later was due to unpayable gambling debts that had accrued in the meantime. But Johnson was a loner and nobody really cared why he had done it.

"Ain't you even gonna ask," Jud said after they passed through Jackson again and headed southeast, "why you about to question the grandmother of a dead man?"

"You want information about him," George said, also speaking for the first time since they'd left Sandhill.

Jud had to laugh at George's consistency. "Yep," he said. "That why."

He waited until they were a few minutes from their destination before continuing: "But you also know I thought Johnson was Suthrin. If Johnson dead, though, he can't be."

George said nothing.

Jud tried a direct question. "What you fin to ask that old lady, then?"

"The same thing you would," George said. And left it at that.

"And what you think I wanna ask her?"

"About the suicide," George said. "You don't believe the body they found was Johnson's. You think Johnson faked his suicide, maybe with help, and assumed a new identity up north. You're wondering about the rumor that he had gambling debts, but you're not sure it's true, or that it explains everything if it is."

George was done talking. So was Jud.

They proceeded to a modest house in Florence, "Population 272," where the elderly man at the door informed them that Mrs. Johnson had moved. He provided a location, if not an address, where he had dropped off a few things she'd left behind.

When they found Grandma Johnson's two-room cabin, a pathetic dwelling well within a rural area lacking any evidence of electrification or even plumbing, Jud had an idea. "Let me put on my coat and badge and cap," he said. "Old lady livin like this ain't gonna care what color I am."

"And then what?" George said. "I just stay in the car?"

"No. Go on in and say you a plainclothes detective. Say I'm an officer assistin you. I'll hang back. But at least this way I can pipe in with some questions, too, when it seem like maybe I should."

The cabin was built of long wood planks beneath a pyramid roof missing, in discrete patches, a third of its shingles. A small outhouse only a few yards away was partly caved in and appeared on the verge of collapse. Jud wondered why the outhouse was so nearby, on flat land whose carpet of brown grass was too low to hide snakes, several acres from the closest of the other shacks scattered about the barren plain, and in a climate rarely threatening frostbite. No matter how old the woman was, if she could make it a few paces she could manage a few more. But then he remembered she had moved into the arrangement only recently, sometime in the past several years and probably after the crash. He also noted that the place was not without the occasional visitor, given the presence of a rusty bicycle with two large baskets perched in front of its handlebars.

George vaulted over the three steps up to what passed for a front porch, his right foot descending an inch as the board beneath it made an abortive launch against its nails. He had probably never encountered so ramshackle a residence before. Jud thought it best not to have the weight of two men on the flood-damaged planks and remained beside the bicycle.

The woman who answered George's knock was basically what Jud expected, seventy or eighty and heavyset with wire-rimmed glasses and white hair back in a bun, except for the unpleasant detail of a substantial goiter resting on the collar of her homemade dress. The goiter was decorated by a necklace terminating in a cylindrical glass phial holding grayish-black metal shavings.

After the introductions, in which Jud was described as "Officer George," the three of them gathered in the cabin's front room, the remaining quarter of the home hidden behind a closed door. Grandma Johnson had returned to her knitting, in an old store-bought rocking chair beside a woodstove and beneath a framed portrait of Jesus. Only the window in the east wall let in much light, the drapes being drawn against the sun on the south and west, while a single kerosene lamp stood ready for use after dark.

"Sorry I can't offer you nothin to drink," Grandma Johnson said. "Ran out of ice for the icebox. Usually got some lemonade in there, or maybe a Coke or Nehi. Don't think you'd care much for the well water."

"That's fine," George said, standing next to Jud at the door and holding his breath against the ambient stench of the outhouse.

"Why don't you fellas take a seat?" she said, gesturing toward two chairs that appeared to be the product of whittling and glue.

George, Jud knew, was about to decline and say they wouldn't be staying long, a response that would have struck the old woman as utterly foreign. "Don't mind if we do," Jud said. "Much oblige, Miz Johnson."

"Call me Hattie," she said as Jud and, reluctantly, George sat down. "So the yankees lettin colored boys on the police nowadays," she remarked without malice, making conversation. "Who said there ain't nothin new under the sun."

"The Lord did," Jud said, pointing at the Bible in her knitting basket. "Right in that book there."

She smiled. "I like a colored boy who got religion."

"But about your grandson," George said, returning to the subject he'd broached at the door.

Hattie ignored George and pursued her own subject, religion. "Bought this from a travelin preacherman," she said to Jud, taking hold of the glass phial. "Them shavings inside it is iodine. Man said if I wore it round my neck, the goiter would plum shrivel up and disappear." She leaned forward and whispered with a wink, "I got the mixed-up deema."

"Had an aunt with that," Jud lied. He was certain the glass cylinder contained nothing but ordinary metal filings dyed black.

"I don't think," George said, "iodine works unless ..."

"Preacherman said the iodine full of ready Asian," she explained. "Reckon a Chinese fella come up with it."

"Reckon you right, Hattie," Jud said, giving George a look.

George dropped the subject of iodine, along with every other subject but one. "We've had a long trip, Mrs. Johnson ... uh, Hattie. What can you tell us about your grandson."

"Ain't much to say, detective. Ran with the wrong crowd, over on the Gold Coast. Don't know what they done to scare him ... what with him bein deputized and all ... but it must of done the trick." She knitted in silence for a moment, thinking it over. "Weren't no probate. The sheriff up in Hinds County just handed over his motorbike and shotgun and some cash they found in his mattress and whatnot, and we sold everything to pay what we borrowed for the cremation. Couldn't afford no plot."

"How long that been since you seen him, Hattie?" Jud asked.

"He come by once and a while. His granddaddy and me still had our little house in Florence. By the Methodist Church. Then his granddaddy passed just when the hard times took hold, and before you know it the bank come and take the house away, and all the furniture still on credit, and I moved here." She waved vaguely at the cabin's walls. "This was just a huntin shack we kept, but weren't no mortgage on it. Since then I get by on the death pension from the phone company ... Mr. Johnson cleared timber for their lines ... plus sometimes I get some relief, if the county's satisfied the monthly pension done run out and I ain't got nothin else." She shook her head in disgust. "Relief don't give you a penny if they think you already got one. Don't matter if you're a hundred years old and worked every day of your life."

"But did you see the body?" George said.

"What body?"

Jud cleared his throat to shut George up. "Ma'am," he said, taking off his cap, "after Andy done passed, who identified his remains?"

"Well," she drawled, and then stopped to look at the ceiling, apparently having never considered the question before. "Reckon the sheriff did. Andy worked some for the sheriff, you know, on his motorbike."

Jud pulled the newspaper story about Suthrin from his pocket and unfolded it. "We tryin to find out," he said, getting up and handing the page to Hattie, who placed her knitting in her lap, "if maybe Andy's death have somethin to do with this man. That story was published a coupla days ago, in a paper up north."

If she could read the Bible, Jud reasoned, she could read a headline. If not, the photograph of Suthrin was a good one, taken shortly after he joined the force in 1926.

"Up north, you say?" Hattie squinted through her glasses and read the headlines aloud. When she was done, Jud saw her eyes move down the page to the photo. At first she stared absently, as one would at any unfamiliar picture. Then she let the page fall to the floor and began to scream.

When the screams turned to words, the words were: "My boy is gone. They took my boy. God have mercy. My boy is gone."

<h1 style="text-align:center">50.</h1>

For the first time Jud realized George was packing a gun, and perhaps the same was true for George in regard to Jud. They had pulled their pieces the moment they saw the hunting knife held by the man who burst in from the bedroom in his shorts, looking about the cabin wildly, still half-asleep and hollering, "Granny? Granny?"

"They took Andy, Roy," Hattie sobbed, blind to the scene with her head in her hands.

"Drop the knife," Jud shouted. The man could lunge the short distance separating them and they'd both be dead. But George was there, too, and seeing Jud's uniform and no sign Hattie was hurt, the man, Roy, raised his arms into a V and loosened his grip, with the knife handle between his thumb and palm. His ribs stuck out distinctly against the skin of his chest.

"Easy now," Roy said. "I'll just toss it back behind me."

"Lower that arm," George said, "let the knife slip to the floor, and kick it over by the knitting basket."

Roy did as told. "I just heard granny screaming," he said, staring at Jud. "Didn't spect to see no policeman."

George picked up the knife and slipped it in his boot. "Mrs. Johnson," he said, "who is this boy?" Jud noted that Roy's emaciation did make him appear to be a teenager, misleading George as to his age, but the man was probably in his early twenties.

Hattie had removed her glasses to wipe her eyes. She kept her palms against her face, her head bent as best she could against the goiter toward her lap, and said, "Roy, tell these men about your brother."

"That's what this is about?" Roy said, still holding his hands in the air.

Jud put away his gun and signaled to George, who did the same. "You got another chair in that room?" he asked. Roy nodded. "Bring it out here and sit down." Jud picked up the news story beside the feet of the quietly weeping Hattie, then handed it to Roy once the young man had settled himself in the crowded little room. Just in case, Jud loomed over him for a while longer. Soon he came to the obvious conclusion that Roy, naked but for his shorts, posed no threat. So as Roy mouthed with difficulty the words he was reading, Jud resumed his seat in the whittled chair and waited.

Apparently unaccustomed to looking at newspapers, it took a while before Roy had read enough of the story to comprehend that the accompanying photo illustrated it. His eyes widened but he said nothing.

"Recognize that man in the picture?" Jud said.

"Can I get my shirt?" Roy said.

"Tell them about your brother," Hattie repeated. She sat up straight and put on her glasses. Roy had placed his chair in the only practical spot remaining in the cabin room, behind his grandmother and to her right, and she turned to look at him. "Don't matter no more," she said, and then began to weep again.

"Reckon it don't," Roy said.

"Go ahead and get dressed, Roy," Jud said kindly, aware of George's irritation at the delay. "And while you doin that, you can put together what you need to say."

George got up and stood by the bedroom door, keeping an eye out for weapons.

"Some of this ain't fit for Granny to hear," said Roy, no longer in Jud's line of sight. "She only know but half of it."

"We can step outside," Jud said.

"Reckon you fellas must of drove here," Roy said. "Sure would preciate a lift into town, if you can fit my bike."

"Be glad to," Jud said.

"Usually, I just ride the bike on in and pick up some ice and groceries and this and that and head on back, unless I'm fixin to hitch to Jackson, look for work, and then I got a special place to hide it. That's where I gone yesterday but ain't nobody hiring, not even day labor." He emerged wearing faded overalls and a hickory shirt with patched elbows. "Couldn't get a ride back from Jackson all night. Musta walked ten miles. Fella finally picked me up around noon. Good sleepin weather, I figured, so yall caught me just snoozin away." He crouched behind the woodstove and pulled out a pair of shoes that had seen better days. After sitting on the floor to lace them up, he went to the sink and grabbed a metal breadbasket beside it.

"Easy there," George said, reaching toward his gun. "That better be bread."

"Got a false bottom for cash and that," Roy said. He removed the bottom and pulled out a letter-sized envelope, which he put in a deep front pocket of his overalls. "I'm takin the letter, Granny," he announced.

"You do what you think best, honey." Hattie had stopped weeping but what little color there'd been in her face was gone, and she stared hopelessly at the idle knitting in her hands.

Both Jud and George withheld their curiosity about the letter, letting Roy decide when to explain it. After thanking the sad old woman and offering their condolences, they went out to the car and resumed the uniforms they'd worn before pulling up to the cabin.

When Roy was finished attaching his bike with rope to the rear bumper, George held the back door open for him, then got in the other side.

"Thought you was a cop," Roy said to Jud as they drove away. "Now you a chauffeur?" He laughed. "Figured it weren't too likely, a colored fella bein a cop." He seemed pleased to get a lift, and didn't press the point.

"That's our business," George said. "But, yes, Officer George is a Milwaukee policeman, and I'm Detective Minor. That news item you saw is from the Milwaukee papers."

"So that where Andy end up," Roy said. "Milwaukee." He laughed again. "Couldn't find it on a map, myself." But then he went silent and after a moment Jud heard him sniff back tears.

"Your granny talk about Andy bein cremated, years ago," Jud said without glancing back. "Then she seen that picture in the paper and start screamin."

"Guy what got cremated was just some hobo," Roy said, still sniffling. "They blew his face off and put him in Andy's clothes with Andy's badge, and dump him in the river after soakin him somewheres private for a few weeks, I figure. I'm just guessin the last part, but otherwise it sure took a long time for him to wash up on the Pearl."

"Who?" George asked. "Who blew the hobo's face off?"

"Let the man talk, detective," Jud said. "Roy, you go ahead and tell the story your own way."

"Well," Roy said, "Granny told me I ought to tell yall, so reckon I should. Reckon you fellas just tryin to catch whoever stabbed Andy like that, and Granny want me to help."

"That right," Jud said. "That why we come all this way. More'n seven hundred mile." By now Jud had picked up the smell of moonshine in the close car and knew that Roy had been doing something more than just looking for work or hitching and biking when he'd shown up at the cabin and passed out in the early afternoon. George rolled down his window.

"Andy was my hero," Roy said. "I always looked up to him, hung on his every word. We got the same daddy, but different mamas, who neither of us never seen. Young girls who stuck around long enough for the midwife to do her job, then I guess they couldn't stand Daddy no more and took off. Heard my mama headed out to Hollywood, but don't know if nothin come of it. Daddy died of consumption when I was five and Andy was fifteen, and Granny took us in. She'd been raisin us half the time anyhow. Andy weren't around much after that, always up to some kind of mischief, but the tales he would tell, let me tell you, they were somethin. He knew I ate it up, so he told me pretty much everything. Well, one night, I was maybe sixteen and none too wise to the ways of the world, and he stop by our old place in Florence and, y'know, he's had a toot or two. He tells me he's out on patrol a few nights previous and spots a mixed couple walkin side by side in Jackson, just like they ain't got a care in the world. Well, Andy, that don't sit too well with him, white man with a colored girl at night, so he keep an eye on them. Sees them get into the fella's car, and he follows them out of town and onto a plantation road. Well, now, that's too much, white fella goin round with a plantation hand, but to make it worse, they pull off and Andy figures they about to engage in some hanky panky, it bein a pitch black night out, and he ain't havin that, so he pulls his bike up by the car and tells the fella to get on out, and the fella got an attitude about it, Andy tells me, so Andy works him over, him being a deputy and all. After gettin some from Andy the guy falls back and hits his head, knocks him out, right? So the colored girl is screamin by now and Andy, he wads up his motorbike gloves and puts em in her mouth, just to quiet her down, but she's strugglin and all that, so Andy, he gives her a wallop and gets her out of the car and cuffs her hands behind her back. Well, he figure any plantation spook out about town with a white fella, she already got somethin in mind for the evening and ain't too concerned about her virtue and all that, so Andy pushes her over the hood of the fella's car facedown and has his way with her. But after he pulls the gloves back out of her mouth, why, if she don't start talkin Italian. Can you believe it? Weren't no colored girl, but a darkskinned Italian, almost black after puttin up the crop, this bein the month of July. But don't really matter one way or another to Andy, he always said them Italians ain't much better than the coons. No offense, officer."

"None taken, Roy," said Jud, feeling like his head was about to explode. "You go on with your story like I ain't even here."

"Them Italians back then, this was twenty-five, they'd been comin in waves since the war," Roy said, "takin the plantation jobs left by them darkies movin up north, and this girl just off the boat. Andy don't mind the difference much, like I said, lots of folks around here figure them Italians just half a step above coons anyhow. So he takes her cuffs off and goes to check on the fella she with, and she says, 'Teacher, teacher, English, English,' like that, so she's pretendin like the fella was just gonna learn her to talk right, and he says, Andy does, 'Well I reckon you got your lesson tonight,' but he's checkin the guy, and damn if the guy ain't dead. You believe that? Fella cracked his skull open on the hood of the car when Andy give him one. So Andy, he points at the keys in the car and says, 'Drive? Drive?' like that, and lucky for the girl she must of learnt how back in Italy, and she gets in the driver's seat after she seen the other fella ain't gettin up, and Andy acts like he's zippin up his lips and then zippin up hers, and says 'Shush, shush,' and points to the dead fella and points to the girl and draws his hand cross her throat, like it a knife, so she gets the picture, and then she drives off. Next day Andy hears that some fella got killed by robbers on the plantation road, girl the dead man with reported it, he hears, and they haul some colored fella in and get him to confess, and that's the end of it, Andy figures. But a month go by and Andy disappears, and then another month till they find his body and one thing and another they find his bike and his gun, on a river bluff a mile east of Ofahoma."

"You said it wasn't his body," George interrupted.

"Well, I'm a-gettin to that," Roy said. "A coupla days after Andy goes missin, I get this letter at our old place in town."

"The letter you took from the breadbasket," Jud said.

"That's right."

"Hand it up here," Jud said.

"I was fixin to just read it to yall."

"Let me read it myself," Jud said. They had reached Florence and Jud pulled over. He took the letter from Roy and read it silently.

"Think maybe you could take me to Jackson?" Roy said when Jud looked up from the letter again. "I got unfinished business up there from last night."

"Sorry, Roy," Jud said. "Detective Minor and I have some things to discuss in private." He pocketed the letter and added, "Detective, give the man his knife back."

"I'll be wantin that letter, too," Roy said.

"I'm gonna need to hang on to it for now," Jud said. "Once the investigation is over in Milwaukee I'll mail it RFD to your granny."

Roy and George got out of the car and, as Jud watched in the rearview mirror, George took the knife from his boot and handed it over. Roy untied his bike and said through the open window, "Promise you'll get that letter back to me? There ain't much else of Andy's to remember him by."

"I'll do more than return it," Jud said. "I'll send you the newspaper we print it in."

51.

Jarius Anthony Josie, known to some as the Mayor of Bronzeville, stood facing away from the front door of his place of business when Jud entered the two-story converted house, the rays of the setting sun through the windows falling on the back of the well-dressed man to whom Josie was speaking. Between the two men Josie held up a newspaper opened to its middle and folded in quarters to frame a photograph of a grinning colored girl cradling the hollowed-out half of an enormous watermelon. Jud could read the caption above the picture, which like a cartoon purported to reveal the child's thoughts: "Lawdy, But Dat Am Melon." Beneath the picture were the words "THAT'S WHY DARKIES WERE BORN."

"Should negro businesses advertise," Josie was saying, "in a paper capable of such a humiliating act? Should not the proper response be resentment?"

"We only do so during the holiday season, brother Josie," the other man said. "A third of our yearly revenue is earned between Thanksgiving and Christmas. The rest of the year, our notices run exclusively in the *Blade*."

"This was printed just yesterday," Josie said. "Had it run but a week earlier, it might have appeared on the same page of the *Tribune* as your ad. How long would it have been before your customers could get that taste, which isn't of melon, out of their mouths?"

An attractive young woman entered from another room and after a brief glance at the photo, which Jud sensed she'd heard Josie discussing all day, sat at the front desk behind a nameplate reading BERNICE LINDSAY. "May I help you?" she said to Jud. Both men turned to look at him but before he could speak the woman said: "Why, you're the gentlemen they've been writing about in the *Tribune*. The detective on that murder case."

"Don't tell me you've been reading the competition, Bernice," Josie said, letting his hand fall to his side so that the offensive picture was no longer visible. He winked at Jud, producing a most congenial effect as the brow of his completely bald light-brown head crinkled and his smile revealed a large black gap between his two front teeth. Jud had heard that Josie was a militant, yet sensed nothing but good cheer from the man. But then it would be hard to publish Milwaukee's only colored newspaper, the Wisconsin *Enterprise-Blade*, and not be tagged militant after writing the mildest editorial or two.

"That right, ma'am," Jud said, politely addressing himself to Bernice since she'd asked the question, not Josey. "I'm Jud Minor. Not really a detective, though." He was taken aback at being recognized out of uniform. "Like the story in the paper said, I'm investigating the death of Landis Humphreys."

"Why didn't you bring the story to us, son?" said Josie, who was indeed old enough to be Jud's father.

"I'm bringin you one today," Jud said, and then immediately regretted it. He wanted to keep his story confidential, prevent anyone from knowing he'd been the source, and although Josie's secretary must necessarily be aware of it, the businessman standing beside Josie ought not to be. "Sir," he said at once to the man, "I'd be oblige if you keep that to yourself. Don't want nobody to know I was ever here, talkin to Mr. Josey."

"Sounds most intriguing," the man said. He turned to Josie with a conspiratorial look and mock-whispered: "Have you no cure for the window's son?" Both men burst out laughing at what Jud took to be a private joke.

"You can trust him," Josie said to Jud. "But you have to join our lodge first."

"In all seriousness, brother Josie," the man said, "I dropped in merely to pay for January's notices. I'll let you and your anonymous source discuss this non-existent story in private." He took out his wallet and handed some bills to Bernice. "Just apply the change to February if you would, Sister Lindsay." He and Josie exchanged a few more words and then he left, tipping his hat as he passed Jud.

"I'll be with you in a moment, officer," Josie said. He then dictated an editorial about the watermelon picture to Bernice, who took it down in a small stenographer pad. "Get that in type for tomorrow's edition," Josie instructed.

"Oh, that right," Jud said. "Your paper come out on Thursdays."

"Yes," Josie said, "and if you've really got something to give to me, we can have it in thousands of issues circulating throughout the city by noon tomorrow. Got a new printer, takes up the whole basement of this building. It cost more than I'd like to say, but at least I don't have to start the presses till first thing tomorrow morning. Then it is up to a small legion of enterprising boys to get it out to our subscribers and on the newsstands."

"That good, sir," Jud said. "The sooner the better."

"Well, due to the postal holiday, those few who take it by mail won't get it till the day after New Year's. But word quickly gets around our community if there's really anything newsworthy." They had begun walking to Josie's office, passing several other offices and half a dozen employees along the way. "Usually aren't many people here these days, other than me and Bernice. Wednesday's different, of course. Had to cut everybody down to half-time after the crash. If you can believe it, I bought the new printer in September of twenty-nine. Talk about badly timed capital expenditures. Fortunately, the good man in the White House tells us that the hard times can't last much longer. Let us hope he is re-elected." Having done his duty as a Republican booster, Josie shut the door behind Jud and offered him a seat, then perched informally on the edge of his desk.

"First off," Jud said, "you should know that my lieutenant think I'm in Chicago right now. I got off the train from Jackson, Mississippi, in Chicago this afternoon, and just now got back to Milwaukee in my car."

"Playing hooky, are we?" Josie laughed. "You know, when I saw you in the *Tribune* this week, I was struck by the fact we hadn't met. I've lived here since twenty-seven, two years after my paper in Madison merged with the colored paper here. Thought I'd met just about every negro man in town, at least those of any note."

"I ain't of much note, sir," Jud said. "I just do my job. Don't socialize much."

"You just do your job," Josie emphasized, "as the only negro on the city police force."

"Well, I try not to let that get in the way. But I spose that why I'm here to see you. I can't go to neither of them two other papers. The police and the newsmen, it like they all on the same team. And right now, nobody seem to want me to do the job the paper keep praisin me for."

"Yes," Josie said, "they're making you out to be something of a hero. I found it a little suspicious."

"You know how it is, sir," Jud said. "They all just take it for granted that I ain't got a mind of my own… or, if I do, it ain't much of one. So after I got assigned to this murder case, didn't take long fore I seen that they assigned me because they think I'm too stupid to run an investigation. Somethin been hushed up, and the papers is in on it. You my only option left to get things pointed in the right direction."

"But you say you wish to remain anonymous," Josie noted. "Wouldn't it be better if you were named? I could interview you."

"Like I said, right now they think I'm in Chicago. Got me chasin down phony leads, just to waste my time." Jud carefully avoided any reference to Lydia or Charlotte. "Instead, I went to Jackson. They'd fire me if they found out." He took Roy Johnson's envelope from his pocket and handed it over. "Read that. But don't be confused by …"

The telephone on the desk rang and Jud stopped talking. "Got a Jackson postmark, 1925," Josie noted as he picked up the phone. He took the letter out and held it along with the mouthpiece stand, extending his right arm far enough to read the letter but close enough to speak into the mouthpiece, and held the envelope in his left hand with the speaker to his ear. "Wisconsin *Enterprise-Blade*, J. Anthony Josie speaking," he said, listening to the response while reading the letter. Frustrated, Jud noted Josie was viewing the wrong side of the single page. "For a show New Year's Eve ... tomorrow night?" Josie said to the caller. "Certainly, though if you have a graphic you should bring it by here before the end of the day, so I can discuss any changes that might be necessary ... Oh, I see. Is that the new black and tan on Galena? Haven't had a chance to stop by yet, myself ... Yes, those are our rates, but for a new business you get half off the first ad ... All right, I'll see you then. Thank you, Mr. Garner." He hung up and said to Jud: "This is nothing but a letter complaining about a defective mail-order motorcycle part. I must say, I am ..."

"Look at the envelope," Jud said.

Josie put down the phone and examined the address. "The motorcycle shop's address has been crossed out and replaced by another."

"Now read the other side of the paper," Jud said. "The one in pencil, not ink."

Josie raised his eyebrows. "The man changed his mind about whom he wished to write. I can imagine using the same envelope once he's put the stamp on it, but are they really so poor in Jackson that he couldn't afford a fresh piece of paper?" He laughed and squinted to read the hurriedly scribbled, nearly illegible pencil marks of the letter, the one addressed to Roy Johnson in Florence.

"That was written by Landis Humphreys in 1925," Jud said. "The cop who got murdered last week."

"It's very vague," Josie said. "Doesn't say where he's going, except north. Doesn't name any names, except the strange reference to one Andy Johnson: 'Don't go looking for Andy Johnson. Ain't nobody you know named that no more.' And what's this about a hobo?"

"Mr. Josie, look at the return address on the envelope. And look at the signature on the letter about the motorcycle."

"He calls himself Andy Johnson," Josie said after a moment. "But you say it was written by Landis Humphreys."

"That the story I'm bringin you," Jud said. He went on to explain the cryptic letter, especially its reference to "the Italian girl" that omitted the detail of her rape.

"If only to play devil's advocate," said Josie, "I hesitate to accept your interpretation of this letter without more to support the astounding idea that the Milwaukee Police Department was ..."

"Look," Jud interrupted, a bit impatient after three days spent in trains and cars. "Andy Johnson got hired as a deputy in Jackson because he had the best motorbike on the market. Landis Humphreys was crazy about motorbikes. Fella I met up in Grafton said Humphreys was a dead ringer for a motorcycle cop he run into in Jackson, somebody with a common name like Smith, Jones, or Johnson, somebody who grab colored girls out of cars and put his hands all over em. Then two sportin girls here in town I.D.'d Humphreys as a john who played a game where he a cop who arrest the girls and mess around with their bodies. One of them girls said he'd get drunk and call hisself Deputy Johnson. Another man I tracked down rented a building to gangsters, and he seen Humphreys with at least four of em. I was directed to that man by a woman who seen Humphreys with Italian bootleggers, but the book of suspects my lieutenant give me ain't got nobody from the third ward. And here the clincher. Andy Johnson's brother and grandmother, down in Mississippi, positively identified the picture of Humphreys. They both knew that Johnson ain't shot hisself in 1925. His brother said that somebody blew some hobo's face off, soaked him in the river for a month, and put Johnson's deputy badge on the body. The death certificate must say Andy Johnson on it, but that don't mean a thing."

The phone rang again. Josie engaged with it only long enough to tell the caller he would be busy for the rest of the day, and to call back in the morning. He hung up and asked Jud: "Is there more?"

"Well, them newspaper stories about me," Jud said after a moment to think, "was written by somebody who must of known about it, since he made up a lie about Humphreys havin grandparents up on a farm past Grafton. Thing I can't figure is, the fake lead I was sposed to waste my time on in Chicago was probly given to my captain by the same reporter, and the captain just went along with it. Maybe they found out about being fooled by Andy Johnson … maybe when the coroner look at his body … and they don't want word to get out about it."

"Or maybe they've known for some time," Josie suggested, "and were using Humphreys as bait." He slipped down off his desk and sat in the chair behind it, reaching into a drawer for a notebook. "When you, uh ... translated the letter for me, you said the gangsters it refers to were in the third ward. But the letter itself mentions only two people, an Italian and a gangster, and says only that they are up north. I'm going to need some names."

"I'm sorry, sir," Jud said, "I don't know who the Italian girl's kin was, since Johnson's brother didn't know the girl's name. And I can't give you the names I got of the gangsters. Don't want to bring no harm to the man who give em to me." He also could not mention the doll at Betty's Diner, since it might put Charlotte into the story.

"Well, as a journalist," Josie said, "I can understand protecting your sources. But even the papers said Humphreys was originally from Jackson. Is it credible he would maintain that?"

"The forgers who made the new identity papers must of used old ones that already said Jackson on em, had Mississippi seals on em and whatnot ... and the forgers just took six or seven years off his age to help the trail go cold. Probly useful, too, to say he from Mississippi if anybody ever recognize his accent. To a southern ear, every one of them states down south got its own accent ... as you and me both know, since by now we both got each other pegged as Georgians."

Josie laughed heartily. "Once we're in the north, we're all too polite to say, aren't we? So, yes, that's a good point, and the forgers surely believed that by the time anybody might think Jackson was relevant, it would be too late anyway ... why would anyone make anything of his birth certificate if they hadn't already suspected he was not who he claimed to be?" He started scribbling down notes. "So, officer ... what exactly do you want the story to say? And more important, what should be left out?"

"You can publish the whole letter as it is," Jud said. "As for the rest, keep my name out of it."

And then, as Josie turned their conversation into prose, the two of them proceeded to collaborate upon the biggest scoop the *Enterprise-Blade* could ever hope to print.

The Wisconsin Enterprise-Blade

MURDERED COP WAS IMPOSTER

Humphreys Assumed New Identity On Gangster Payroll

City Police Had Traitor In Their Midst

In a shocking development revealed for the first time here, the *Enterprise-Blade* has learned that Landis Humphreys, the city patrolman stabbed to death on Christmas Eve, was an imposter who had infiltrated the Milwaukee Police Department in order to work on the "inside" as an agent for Third Ward gangsters.

Humphreys was actually a former Hinds County, Mississippi sheriff's deputy named Andy Johnson, who was falsely believed to have died by his own hand in 1925.

Even more astounding, Johnson's false identity as Humphreys was created by persons unknown among this city's gangster element, who gave Johnson the choice to either assume his new identity as a city policeman on the gangsters' payroll—or die.

Marked For Death After Ravishing Italian Girl

As partly described in a cryptic letter received by an unnamed recipient several days after Johnson's disappearance in 1925 (*see sidebar*),

Johnson had been targeted for death after local gangsters sought to avenge his ravishing of an Italian plantation girl in Jackson, Mississippi. Unable to seek retribution in the Nordic justice system of Mississippi, where at that time Italians and certain other dark-skinned immigrants ranked only above Negroes in the social order, the girl reached out to a relative in Milwaukee, who provided payment to Third Ward gangsters to have Johnson killed.

Instead, the gangsters shot gunned an indigent man in the face and planted his body, dressed in Johnson's clothes, in a local river. Owing his life to these criminals, Johnson agreed to their scheme and moved to Milwaukee, where he served the gangsters while working for the city police under the name of Landis Humphreys.

Blows Case Wide Open
Suspect List Greatly Expanded

These revelations open up the investigation of the Christmas Eve murder far beyond what had been assumed. Reports that "Humphreys" had relatives in Wisconsin must therefore be taken as completely false. For example, the statements published in another newspaper, which were attributed to his alleged grandparents who purportedly reside in Ozaukee County, were certainly fabricated.

Now that it is known that "Humphreys" had already been targeted once for death in 1925, there is no reason to focus upon such unlikely suspects as the two young men who happen to live in the building where the body was found. This newspaper never took seriously the idea that cheating in a dance marathon should expose anyone to a charge of murder.

Certain other details that have come to our knowledge cannot be revealed at this time, except to the police—to whom the original copy of Andy Johnson's 1925 letter (*see sidebar*) will be provided once this issue of the *Enterprise-Blade* hits the stands. Further details will be provided to our readers as the weeks go by, so be sure to watch for next week's number on Thursday, January 7.

TEXT OF 1925 LETTER FROM MURDERED COP UNDER FORMER IDENTITY

————————

At right is the exact text of a letter written in 1925 by Hinds County Sheriff's Deputy Andy Johnson, also known as Milwaukee City Police Officer Landis Humphreys. (For the sake of clarity, the spelling has been corrected.) The *Enterprise-Blade* has knowledge of the identities of both the recipient of the letter and the woman referred to in it as "G", but is withholding this information to protect these people from retribution. However, it should be emphasized that neither the recipient nor "G" is responsible for bringing this shocking revelation to our attention.

The "Italian girl" mentioned in the letter is a Mississippi plantation hand whom Johnson ravished in 1925. The "gangster" mentioned is a person unknown, believed to be from Milwaukee's Third Ward, who was hired by a relative of the Italian girl to murder Johnson. The "hobo" is an unknown man whose corpse was dressed to appear as Johnson and dumped in Mississippi's Pearl River. The "job in law enforcement" was with the Milwaukee Police Department. The phrase "I will be working for them" refers to Johnson's work, for gangsters believed to be from the Third Ward, as an agent within the city police under the name "Landis Humphreys".

I ain't gone missing. I'm writing so you and G don't worry. Tell her I am fine no matter what you all hear. When they say they found me don't believe it. It's just some hobo in my clothes and badge. Go along with it. You remember the Italian girl. She got kin up north and he paid a gangster for vengeance. He will believe he got his money's worth when they find the hobo. But they gave me a choice. It was me or the hobo. They said the hobo would get it if I went up north with them. I cannot tell you who or where. They propose to set me up with a job in law enforcement, but I will be working for them. But don't go looking for Andy Johnson. Ain't nobody you know named that no more. One day I will contact you again. Tell no one but G, so she don't worry. I would be in big trouble if they knew I was writing this, and I cannot risk it again. Now that you know I am fine and you should pay no mind when they find the hobo with my badge, I will not be writing again.

PS They didn't find this envelope and letter when they frisked me, and I am scribbling this with a pencil stub in the middle of the night on the back of a letter I was going to mail about my bike when they picked me up. I will slip it in a post box when they ain't looking.

————————

52.

Armin Weinberger walked into Max Maglio's.

"Here comes another Jew like you, Lou. Hey, that rhymes. Jew, like you, Lou."

Alby Tusa smiled. He was tired of being a tough guy. He liked it much better when the man in front of him was laughing, like Lou Simon right now, than when he was bleeding, like Meinecke a few days ago. When Alby was a kid, first in New York and then in Cicero and Chicago, people said if you couldn't be a boxer you'd better be a comedian. Too bad for Alby, he'd always been a boxer. Then he'd gotten married, like you were supposed to do, and the unhappy couple moved to Milwaukee, where he had to look to the third ward's padroni for a living. He'd longed for the days spent training in the gym with other boys and young men, so from loansharking enforcement for the Guardalabenes he moved into fight promotion, where he'd met bookmakers like Lou Simon. Lou, in turn, introduced him to the nightclub people like Armin. Armin booked acts into the Chateau Country Club, a gambling joint built from a farmhouse in the boondocks near Granville on the Cedarburg Road, eight miles north of the city. Then Alby's wife died and he was free to spend all his time with such men, of whom Lou was his favorite. Lou managed the Manchester Club in Milwaukee and the Chesterfield Club way up in Ozaukee County, meaning he managed the bets.

"Hey, Armin," Lou greeted the new arrival, a bright kid in his early twenties. "I was just telling Alby here about the great opportunities available in the horse wire services."

"You got to have some crowd stimulators," Armin said, "other than the lousy acts we book. Otherwise, what are you going to offer? Bingo?"

"Bingo might work," said Lou, "if it was the right kind of bingo ... and if you got the races on the wire in a private room. I've been talking to this kid Annenberg. Maybe you've heard of his old man, publishes a racing sheet. Anyway, this kid tells me he's trying to raise enough cash to corner the wire market, but says it'll probably take five years in this economy."

Lou had been talking about young Annenberg for a month or two, during which time Alby Tusa had developed a fantasy about going into business with Lou and running a bookmaking and loansharking operation under the cover of a supper club, with acts booked by Armin, who was clean but couldn't possibly be blind to how the Chateau Country Club actually made money. Alby had recently settled on the Tic Toc Club as his joint's name. In fact, Alby's fantasy had grown more and more ornate, and now involved him and Lou living in adjacent fancy apartment buildings on the lakeshore up in Whitefish Bay. That way they could see each other not only at work but every day at home, and not raise any eyebrows. Of course, for appearances Alby would eventually have to remarry.

"Want anything?" Chubassi Bellistrari, the chef, asked Armin. Lou and Alby had already eaten.

"I'll just pick something off the counter," Armin said, referring to the platters of meatballs, sausages, and pasta always available at Max Maglio's, a restaurant at Jefferson and Clybourn that had become the preferred meeting place for the third ward's padroni and affiliated gangsters.

"Suit yourself," said Chubassi, a cheerful portly man with a mustache and wearing a white apron barely stained on this slow afternoon, the day before New Year's. The chef returned to the game of briscola he was playing with three local retirees, mustache petes who still had business interests in common with Maglio's younger customers.

"Five years?" Armin said to Lou. "Don't Annenberg know how to raise money?"

"Lou says the guy's a chump," Alby explained. "Gonna rely on his old man's publishing profits and then go to the banks."

"He figures he'll have enough trouble bribing the antitrust regulators," Lou said, "without adding to that the loan sharks."

"But when it happens, Lou's gonna be in on it from the ground floor up," Alby said proudly. Lou Simon was just about the smartest guy in town, he figured. "Then maybe Lou can bankroll the Tic Toc Club."

"Tic Toc Club?" Armin said.

"I'm thinking of opening a place," Alby said. "High quality acts, chorus girls, spotlights out front like it's Broadway, right in the heart of downtown."

"So go to Vallone," Armin said. "Lou says you're one of his best men."

Alby was very pleased by the compliment, coming from Lou. He smiled affectionately at his friend and said to Armin, "Aw, you're just a kid. What you know about those kinda things?" Armin was a dozen years younger than Alby, but Alby appeared closer to forty-five than his actual thirty-five thanks to having a face with a quarter-century's worth of accumulated scars and being almost completely bald, though lately he'd taken to wearing a rug. Alby knew he was homely. Always had been. Lou, on the other hand, had fine features. Alby liked to joke that Lou should've gone into the movies, like George Raft.

"Armin is right, you know," Lou said. "Go to Vallone. It's New Year's. You always tell me you never ask him for anything. That's what friends ... your kind of friends ... are for."

Alby was hurt. "What you mean, my kind of friends?"

Lou reached across the small square table with its red and white checkerboard cloth and patted Alby's hand. "I mean business friends, buddy. Third ward friends, among your people, like I got business friends among mine." He squeezed Alby's forearm. "I don't mean real friends, like you and me."

Armin coughed and said he was going to get some sausage from the counter. "That ain't kosher," Lou joked.

"Well," Alby mused, "I suppose it wouldn't do much harm to pitch the idea to Piddu. What's the worst can happen?"

"It's New Year's," Lou repeated. "Do it today, like you're a man with plans for the future, and not just some schmuck running his mouth off on the thirty-second of never."

Alby thought this over. "Can I tell him about Annenberg?"

"Everybody already knows about Annenberg. Kid wants to go straight, but his father used to run with Capone."

"But, I mean, your connection with the guy."

"Sure, sure, Alby," Lou said, looking meaningfully into his friend's eyes as he withdrew his hand. "Any way I can help out, just say the word."

Armin returned, chewing on a sausage and carrying a plate with spaghetti and meatballs. "Think we can get a drink in this joint?"

Alby winked at the kid. "Chubby," he said to the chef, "is the basement unlocked?" A few minutes later he returned with a bottle, which he placed discreetly on the floor, and three glasses filled with ice cubes and whiskey. "Well, Happy New Year's, fellas," he said, unsure how Jews offered a toast.

They sat there talking until the bottle was gone and Alby had convinced himself Piddu would arrange financing for the Tic Toc Club. On the spot, he hired Lou as his bookmaker and Armin as his talent coordinator, sealing the deal with handshakes. Then he peeled off a five for Chubassi, picking up the table's tab including the kid's dinner, and left after asking the bemused chef whether he knew anybody who might like to cook for a swell downtown supper club with high-quality talent.

53.

ALBY COULD HANDLE HIS LIQUOR but didn't want to slur his words when he talked to Piddu, so he rolled down the windows of his car and let the cold air swirl around him on the drive over to Commission Row. Arriving at 424 North Broadway he noted that Piddu had bought a new delivery truck, already stenciled with the words Migliaccio & Vallone Grocers and Try San Giorgio Pure Olive Oil. An Italian flag blew about in the winter wind in front of the display windows, where cheese, produce, olive oil, and Sicilian specialty foods were displayed behind the gold-leaved store name. Pasquale Migliaccio ran the operation, which sold enough on the premises to provide cover for the furtive men in and out all day to see Joseph Vallone but which relied, for the legitimate end of its business, almost entirely on retail to neighborhood restaurants and speakeasies that were forbidden to buy from anyone else.

The boy behind the counter recognized Alby. "They're in the office," he said, "havin some kind of big discussion. Somethin real important. You might wanna wait till somebody comes out."

"How long you figure?" Alby said.

"Mr. Migliaccio's got a driver pickin him up at three."

By the self-winding Western Union clock, above the door marked PRIVATE, that meant twelve minutes. Alby went out into the brisk air to have a smoke and sober up a little more. The driver showed up at three but another ten minutes went by with no sign of Pasquale. Alby wondered what business could be so urgent on the last day of the year. Bored, he tried to identify Pasquale's driver through the tinted windows of the car. If it was somebody he knew, maybe they could have a chat to pass the time. Then he noticed the young colored woman in the back seat. It was the crazy hooker everybody laughed about. Peaches, he remembered. "What the fuck?" he muttered to himself, his breath making steam in the air.

His hands were cold so he went back inside. "What's the big deal back there?" he asked the kid. "Been here half an hour already."

"I dunno. Somethin they read in the paper."

Lou Simon had been late meeting him at Maglio's, so Alby had read the paper, or at least all of its headlines outside of the society section. "I ain't seen nothin in the paper," he said. "They ain't still writin about Joe Pessin, are they?" Joe Pessin was a recently convicted bootlegger who'd been on the lammister since his latest appeal was denied, a few weeks earlier, a matter that for no apparent reason had caught the attention of the local press. Alby and Joe had held up a couple of trucks together over the years, on orders from Piddu to screw the competition, so Joe's whereabouts were of some concern.

"No," the kid said. "And it ain't the regular papers. It's some other paper I ain't never heard of before. The Entertaining Blade, something like that."

"*Enterprise-Blade*?" Alby said. "The colored paper? What's Piddu give a damn about somethin in the colored paper?"

"Beats me," the kid said. Then he smiled. "I ain't even known there was no colored paper. Didn't know any of them people could read." He laughed at his little joke.

Alby started to follow up on his question, to see if there was some connection between the colored paper and the colored hooker outside in the car, but then realized it didn't make any sense and that it would be stupid to ask about it.

Fifteen minutes later Pasquale Migliaccio came out of the office looking seriously disturbed. Maybe Joe Pessin was causing trouble, threatening to turn state's evidence. The grocer, second only to Vallone in the gang's hierarchy, squinted at Alby and said, "Piddu knows why you're here." Then he brushed past and went out the door. Looking through the display window, Alby noted that the car did not drive away after Pasquale got in the back seat with the colored hooker.

How could Vallone know why Alby was there? Then he got it. One of the mustache petes at Maglio's must have overheard his conversation about the Tic Toc Club and called the boss to see if he could get a piece of the action.

The office door was closed and Pasquale's car still hadn't driven away, so it was possible the high-level conference wasn't over yet. Alby went ahead and knocked anyway. Inside the office a 1932 calendar was already on the wall. Probably, Piddu had left the day before without expecting to be called back on business. Skimping on fuel costs in the chilly room, the boss wore a magisterial overcoat partly obscuring an expensively tailored suit fit for attending the opera. He looked tired and had his feet up on the desk, his imported Italian slip-on shoes worn over white cashmere socks that probably cost more than Alby's whole outfit.

"Happy New Year, Piddu," Alby said. "You get your hair cut? Looks great." And he did look great, Alby thought, with his fine white hair circling around a strong and noble brow, his small clipped mustache beneath a classic Sicilian nose. No doubt about it, Piddu was a handsome man, rarely ruining his aura of power with a smile.

"What have you got to say for yourself?" Piddu asked neutrally, folding his manicured fingers together on his stomach. Had the positions been reversed, Alby would instantly have removed his feet from the desk and sat up straight, but for Piddu to do so would have been to suggest he owed deference to another man, something impossible except upon the visit of certain guys from Chicago.

"Well," Alby said, confused by the question, "I been thinking, Piddu. About my future. You know I ain't never asked for nothing. I just do my job like I'm told and don't make no waves."

Piddu cocked his head to one side and looked at Alby curiously, but said nothing.

"I been talkin to Lou Simon … you know, makes book at the Manchester … and he's workin on a deal with this Annenberg kid, tryin to corner the horse wire services." Alby realized he was babbling. Something about Piddu's demeanor made him very nervous. "Well, I figure maybe sometime in the new year I can start a club, get it going and make it look real legit. Then once Lou and this Annenberg kid work out the wire service angle, I'd be ready to go, the minute Lou got the deal done. He is a close personal friend of mine, and I am certain he'd cut me in from day one." Alby stopped talking and swallowed.

"You want," Piddu said, "to open a club?"

"That's the thing, Piddu," Alby said. "To get it off the ground and have it, uh, firmly established once Lou and Annenberg corner the wire services, I'd need some, uh … financial backing." His voice grew hoarse and he cleared his throat. "This being the new year, and all, y'know, best time for new beginnings."

"Yes," Piddu said, "it is the new year." The boss had a noticeable Sicilian accent but he spoke English perfectly. "It's the new year, as you can see by the calendar Jenny put up yesterday when we closed the office, we thought, for the rest of 1931. Yet here I am, today." He paused to look Alby up and down. "When you appeared at my door, I presumed you knew why."

Forgetting entirely the details of the colored paper and the colored hooker, his short-term memory scrambled by nerves, Alby said, "Is it Joe Pessin? Joe ain't willin to do his time or somethin? Says he's gonna talk?"

Piddu swung his feet off the desk and stood up, revealing the newspaper that his legs had hidden from Alby's view. He was several inches taller than Alby and, although two decades older and not as well built, carried in his bearing the constant reminder of his power, of the violence of other men under his control. Alby stepped back unconsciously but Piddu imposed himself, stopping only when the men were inches apart. "You're drunk," he said. "I can smell it on you."

"Well, hey, boss," Alby laughed hollowly, "it's New Year's, ain't it?"

"It is no holiday for you."

Now Alby was really at sea. Had Joe Pessin told the cops about the truck heists? Alby's mind raced, trying to think of anything he might have done to receive such peculiar treatment from Vallone. "Piddu, I ..."

"Not one week ago," Piddu interrupted, "you assured me that our friend from the press had made it impossible for the southerner's murder to create difficulties. You even rewarded our friend for his part in assigning a colored cop to the case."

Colored paper, colored hooker, and now colored cop. Alby couldn't put it together. Had Meinecke fucked up? There hadn't been anything by him in the newspaper that day. But then, Piddu wasn't looking at that paper. The one on his desk was the *Enterprise-Blade*. "Last story I read," Alby said, finding it difficult to get the words out, "put the colored cop in Chicago, chasing after a bunch of bullshit."

Vallone stared down at him. It was all Alby could do to avoid lowering his own gaze to the floor, to meet his boss's eyes like a man. "We have a friend who was doing business this week in the south, had to rent a car. He said there was a cop from Milwaukee in Mississippi a couple of days ago. A white cop returning a rented car in Jackson, accompanied by a colored chauffeur. He called to ask if we knew of any investigation down there. We said no ... and that was the end of it. Until today. We contacted our friend in Jackson again to have him check the records. The white cop's name, the name that he gave, was Judson Minor. Of course, the colored chauffeur didn't give any name."

"But the colored cop is Minor," Alby said. "How can a white cop be Minor, too?" As Vallone stared at him Alby put it together. "Oh ... you think the chauffeur was Minor? I get it. Snoopin around in Mississippi while the papers thought he was in Chicago."

"And the reason we called back today, after ignoring the report, was this." At last Vallone pulled away from Alby, turning to the desk to pick up the colored paper. "Read it," he said. "Then tell me how it fits into your plans for a club."

Alby had a hard time focusing on the words while Piddu was glowering at him, still standing but leaning over with his palms flat on the desk. He skimmed over the headlines, barely registering the phrase "On Gangster Payroll" until he'd mouthed its syllables twice. Then he felt the contents of his stomach liquefy and his sphincter loosen. He had to concentrate hard to avoid shitting himself. Although his eyes continued to move over the page, he was unable to read further. But he'd read enough.

54.

Alby's stomach began to settle once he realized there was plenty of blame to go around and his own role consisted only in approving Meinecke's strategy. That had been a big mistake, but it was only six days ago and by then Meinecke had already lit the fuse on this time bomb. Obviously, the colored cop was far more competent than the reporter had presumed, and had even bypassed Meinecke and his cooperative colleagues, who might have kept a lid on the story, and gone instead to the colored press. And ultimately, Alby reassured himself, the blame rested on Piddu, who as Guardalabene's underboss had argued for years in favor of extorting some unknown out-of-towner to get sheepdipped into the city police force. When the hit on Andy Johnson was ordered in 1925, it was Piddu who realized they could take the money for the job but kill some drifter instead, meanwhile retaining the southern bastard for their own purposes. Now, having become the padrone of the padroni, he could never admit to being responsible for anything that had ended up going so wrong. Fortunately, Alby thought, the guy who paid for the hit in twenty-five had moved back to the old country after the crash, and would likely never learn he'd been swindled.

"There is a room with a cot upstairs," Piddu said unexpectedly. "You will remain there, resting in the dark, until you have sobered up. We don't want to move until this evening."

"Move?" Alby said.

Joseph Vallone sat down again but did not offer his soldier a seat. "The story in the colored paper came to our attention three hours ago. This situation must be dealt with at once. We have spent the afternoon determining the most direct and efficient path we must embark upon to dispose of all aspects of this matter."

Alby knew, of course, that Meinecke would be killed to eliminate the link between Suthrin and Vallone, but he couldn't see any way to undo the revelation of Suthrin's identity. "All aspects of this matter," he repeated, as a question.

"It is not enough simply to deal with our friend in the press," Piddu said, reading Alby's mind. "We must end the investigation itself. The city police will be humiliated by the news in the colored paper. They, too, will wish to stop the bleeding. But they will be obliged to pursue the case vigorously as long as the southerner's murder remains unsolved. If the case itself were to be closed, however, they could go through the motions, internal reviews and the like, until the public loses interest in the source of their terrible humiliation."

Piddu never took his eyes off Alby as he spoke, and now fell silent and watched for signs of comprehension. In these few moments, Alby had moved from the obvious conclusion that Meinecke must be killed to the realization that he himself had been selected to kill him, and to do so that evening. But killing Meinecke would not end the police investigation into Suthrin's death. Only finding Suthrin's killer would do that. Alby was scared to say anything, so he kept his mouth shut and let Piddu watch him try to figure it out. When it was clear the boss would not speak again, Alby finally said: "This must have somethin to do with the hooker in the car outside, right? The crazy one?" Piddu refused to respond, even so much as raise an eyebrow, so Alby continued: "You think she done Suthrin? What's that got to do with me?" Piddu shook his head. "So," Alby interpreted, "you don't think she done Suthrin. You got some other kinda thing in mind for her. I mean, otherwise, what would she be doin here ... especially today of all days, with that story in the colored paper."

Pasquale came into the office without shutting the door behind him. He handed Piddu a notebook open to a page Alby could see was covered with large black letters scrawled in blotchy ink. Piddu examined the page and nodded at Pasquale, who left and closed the door without a word.

"You mentioned," Piddu said, "the Annenberg boy. You know, he was born in this town. I knew his father. And his father knows Robert McCormick, the Chicago *Tribune* publisher. And Annenberg's father and McCormick both knew Jake Lingle."

Alby waited but Piddu had stopped speaking. Nothing he'd said meant a damn thing, Alby thought. Jake Lingle was a deadbeat reporter in Chicago who'd gotten plugged by a guy named Leo. "Lots of guys probably knew Jake Lingle," Alby said, just to get Piddu talking again.

"Yes," Piddu said, "including Mayor Big Bill Thompson, Commissioner of Police William Russell, and Al Capone."

Again Alby put it together. "Like Meinecke," he said, "except in Chicago, not Milwaukee." Then he realized his error and corrected himself: "I mean, our friend in the press ... uh, also has lots of connections, up and down the line."

Piddu nodded, once. "When Lingle was killed, almost nobody knew anything. They made him out to be a martyr. The heroic reporter. But then the investigation into his murder revealed his connections, as you put it, not only as a reporter, although he could barely write, but also to the people in the city hall, police headquarters, and the Chicago branch of ... our thing."

"But they caught the guy," Alby said. "The guy who plugged him. Lingle played the ponies and couldn't pay up."

"They ... caught ... no one," Piddu said, sarcastically emphasizing both of the first two words. "Capone handed them a patsy. A two-bit nobody called Leo Brothers. 'Buster from St. Louis,' they called him. The court went along with it, being a Chicago court, but it was too late. Capone waited till more than six hundred men had been rounded up. Perhaps that led to the discovery of a certain ledger, subsequently provided to the IRS. And now he is imprisoned." Piddu raised a finger toward a chair across from his desk. Relieved, Alby sat down, still clenching his stomach but less desperately. "Even as a boy in Bagheria," Piddu continued, "I knew that the day to offer up a patsy ... preferably, the craziest person you can find ... is the day of the killing. And the way to offer up a patsy, on the day of the killing, is stone-cold ... within walking distance of the first corpse, and holding the murder weapon. With its next bullet through the patsy's brain."

Alby was too slow to connect Piddu's description of Sicilian strategy to its intended subject. "You mean," he said, "after somebody did Suthrin ... I mean, the southerner ... it was a mistake not to find a patsy right away?"

"Not him." Piddu frowned at his soldier's stupidity. "We read about him in the papers on Christmas Day, like everybody else did." Instead of waiting for dimwitted Alby to get the point, Piddu handed him the notebook brought in by Pasquale. "That girl is illiterate," he said. Alby didn't have to ask which girl. "But she can copy the letters of the alphabet if you point to them on a slate. We wrote this for her today, but it's her handwriting. And she now has matching ink on her hands."

The notebook page read:

> *I wuz seein Walt and Landis. But I loved Landis, to the Bottum of my Hart. Walt done got jellis and kilt Landis with his own Nife. I saw the bluddy nife he dun it with. I saw it last time I wuz at Walt's playce. Now thair aint no mor reezon for me to go on livin without Landis. And I mean to take Walt with me. I rold a john and took his Gun. Walt and me aint goin to see the New Year. Forgiv me mamma Love Peaches. PS Everbody always call me Crazy and I gess may be they are rite.*

Alby was glad he was sitting down. "She ain't gonna have no powder residue on her fingers," he pointed out.

"No one will care," Piddu reminded him.

"Do we really have his knife?"

"He flashed around an ordinary hunting knife," Piddu said, "like half the boys in the south own. But there was no knife at the scene of his murder. Then the cops searched his place. It wasn't there either. He must have been killed with it ... his own knife. Wasn't hard to find another one just like it and stain it with traces."

"And now the fake knife ends up," Alby said, "in the house where they find our friend from the press. Cops are gonna wonder why he didn't get rid of it."

Piddu opened a drawer and showed Alby the prepared knife. Then he took out a gun, a Mauser with a Maxim Silencer attached, which he slid across the desk. "That's not for you to think about. By the time they're asking any of these questions, you'll be in Canada. Stay a few months, maybe a year or so. Then we can talk about opening your club ... after the depression ends, of course." His eyes traveled from the gun to Alby to the door. The audience was over. Piddu kept the notebook. Alby took the knife and the gun and walked out.

To his surprise, he dozed off after about an hour lying on the cot in the dark room upstairs. Then someone shoved him awake. It was the driver he'd seen through the tinted windows of Pasquale's car. The driver turned on the light beside the bed and handed Alby a couple of cigarettes and a big cup of coffee. Then the driver, whom Alby had never seen before and who identified himself only as Jack, explained to him how the evening was supposed to go. He also provided Alby with an overcoat whose interior pockets were designed for secure transport of various weapons.

Peaches was listening to music on the radio in the room next door. She was also high on smack, courtesy of Vallone. Jack and Alby let her stew for an hour or so, drinking red dago, then they escorted her with some effort to the back seat of the car.

"Am I gonna see Mr. Capone now?" she said.

"We're driving over to his place," Jack said, "but you got to wait with me in the car till the arrangements are made."

Alby went back inside to call the lookout, who reported that Meinecke's car was in his driveway and asked to be relieved of duty. Alby, the only person remaining in the building, locked up and got in the front seat with Jack.

The traffic in town was slow, the roads slushy and the streetlights dimmed by moderate snow flurries. The nightlife through downtown, midway between Migliaccio & Vallone Grocers and Meinecke's house, made every intersection a challenge, with everybody already drunk though the midnight countdown was still several hours away. They reached Juneau Avenue heading west and Jack parked a block or two east of their destination. Alby hustled up the sidewalk until he saw Meinecke's car, then went to the unlocked front door and walked inside.

There was a fresh log burning in the fireplace but no sign of Meinecke. Alby cased the rooms on the first floor and the bathtub and the closets, checked the basement, then went to the second floor. After glancing toward the small bathroom, occupied only by a sink and a toilet, he continued to the bedroom and looked in the closet and under the bed, and did the same in a smaller guest bedroom. He was examining the ceiling in the hallway for any attic entrance when he passed the bathroom again and caught the smell of vomit. The toilet seat was stained with a quantity of matter that had missed its target. Along with the log in the fireplace, this confirmed Meinecke had been present very recently. The bathroom window, too small to crawl through, was open halfway, revealing the street and sidewalk below. Clearly, Meinecke had been sick and opened the window for fresh air, then had seen Alby approaching and got out of the house as fast as he could.

After tossing the prepared hunting knife under Meinecke's bed, Alby bolted down the stairs to the back door and opened it while switching on the outdoor light. There was a small wooden deck lightly covered with new snow, in which was definitely visible the imprint of bare feet. Meinecke hadn't even stopped to put his shoes on. Past the deck in the yard below, amorphous prints in older snow cover led west through the neighboring yards and, Alby soon discovered, all the way down the block. Since Meinecke could not possibly have gotten very far, Alby had no choice but to follow the trail immediately without retracing the two blocks of sidewalk to return to the car and notify Jack. He ran through the back yards and crossed two streets, correctly guessing that Meinecke would continue his hidden journey in back of the neighborhood's houses. At last the tracks headed south around the corner of a long brick building and disappeared in the street slush of Juneau. If Meinecke didn't stop for his shoes, he probably didn't have his wallet, either, so it was unlikely he'd be accepted, barefoot and panting and hysterical, by a cabbie who wasn't shown some money up front. He might have pounded on the door of a house or run a block east to All Saints Cathedral, but he probably had just kept heading west on Juneau.

Alby considered his options and elected to turn around and run the numerous blocks back to the car. He was in such good shape he barely registered the effort. When he reached Meinecke's house he darted just inside the door and grabbed a pair of shoes and a coat from the front closet.

"What took so long?" Jack said, startled a moment later by his partner's sudden appearance. "You didn't give the signal."

Alby had a torch in his pocket he was supposed to flash after shooting Meinecke. "Drive up Juneau," he said, tossing the shoes and coat on the floor as he got in. He rolled down his window and stuck his head out. "He's barefoot. He won't get very far. With luck, we'll see him while we're drivin around. Raises too many questions if he's found without his shoes, though, so I grabbed a pair to put on him when I'm done. You hang on to them for now."

"Mr. Capone is barefoot?" Peaches asked from the back seat.

Jack had been assigned as her handler. "Alphonse has a special exercise regimen," he explained, while attempting with little success to drive at elevated speed through the heavy traffic and drunken horde.

They got to within several blocks of the spot where Alby had turned around, and Alby glimpsed in the distance a tiny flash of bare feet slipping their way down an industrial metal ladder affixed to a building at the side of the road.

"There," he shouted. "He's comin down from the Pabst sign. I was right underneath him. Fuck." Apparently, as soon as Meinecke reached the street from the final back yard, he had climbed up the ladder to the defunct bridge, marked by the giant individual letters P A B S T, which before prohibition had connected the former granary on one side of Juneau to the former brewery on the other. Meinecke must have crouched behind one of the letters and watched Alby run back down the street, then waited on the bridge a while longer till he figured the coast was clear.

The car proceeded only half as fast through the slush and traffic as Meinecke did on his own bare feet, so while they kept him in sight they didn't gain on him. After a couple blocks their quarry suddenly darted off the road and up to a house on a corner, bursting through its front door without a moment's pause. He could not possibly know he was being followed.

"We got him," Alby said to Jack. He rolled up his window. "Park right up in front of the house next to the place where he went inside. If I flash the torch, you're gonna have to come inside to handle whoever's there. We'll have to do them, too ... no way they'll keep their mouths shut. But if there's no trouble, I'll just waive you in."

"Keep their mouths shut about what?" Peaches slurred.

"About you and Alphonse eloping tonight," Jack said. He passed the house on the northeast corner of Juneau and 12th Street and parked in front of the one next to it, then added to Peaches: "If I go inside, you just wait in the car like a good girl and we'll come and get you when it's time."

"You got a silencer?" Alby asked him, handing him the shoes and coat.

"What you think?" Jack said. They opened and closed their doors as quietly as possible. Jack stood waiting by the car in his bulky overcoat as Alby went inside.

55.

AFTER A NICE LONG BATH Meinecke judged that his hangover was almost gone. Having stayed home and slept late, he allowed himself the novel luxury of ignoring the phone when it rang as he worked through the stages of headache and nausea. He'd set the pattern when the phone woke him at two, refusing to extend his arm from the downstairs couch, where he'd passed out, to the end table from which the ringing erupted. Then every half hour or so the damn thing went off again, probably, he thought, to tip him to various New Year's Eve celebrations that he could locate well enough on his own. Even the doorbell had sounded, not once but twice in the course of an hour, when he'd been sequestered in the tub after sunset.

But now it was late enough in the evening, and also in the progress of his hangover, for human interaction, so while still in his bathrobe without his slippers he put the speaker to his ear and picked up the mouthpiece after the first ring. "Happy New Year," he said. "This is Walt."

"It's John Carson," said the voice on the line.

Meinecke was disappointed. He didn't need some college kid tagging along after him as he went from party to party looking for an easy lay. "I've got plans tonight, Carson," he said. "But thank you anyway."

"Where have you been?" Carson said, much too loudly. Maybe the hangover still had some life in it. "Everybody's trying to reach you."

"Yes. I am much in demand as a man about town. Could you please lower your voice?"

"Have you seen the colored paper? The *Enterprise-Blade*?"

"A wonderful source, I agree, for information about our city's more exotic nightlife ... but I am attending only private parties."

"Nightlife?" Carson said. "No ... the story about Suthrin. And the letter he wrote in twenty-five."

Meinecke was barely listening. "Suthrin wasn't even in town in twenty-five. What do I care?"

"Not Suthrin. Andy Johnson. Deputy Andy Johnson of the Hinds County Sheriff's Office in Jackson, Mississippi."

From that point on, Meinecke was unable to offer the conversation more than a word or two at a time. Carson read aloud the story in the *Blade*, then read the letter. "This is huge," he concluded. "They scooped us."

Meinecke's hands were shaking. He was already uncertain what exactly he'd just heard. "Could you repeat," he said, "the part about his grandparents?"

"'Reports that' quote 'Humphreys' unquote 'had relatives in Wisconsin,'" Carson again read aloud, "'must therefore be taken as completely false. For example …'"

"That's enough," Meinecke said. "Thank you, Carson."

He hung up and willed himself to remain calm. With deliberation he went upstairs to his bedroom and put on underwear and a shirt and a pair of pants, and was about to start packing a suitcase when he was overcome by nausea, a rush of saliva pouring from behind the back of his tongue and filling his mouth. He made it to the bathroom across the hall and kneeled before the bowl, then flushed the toilet and stood up to open the window for air.

Two blocks away, visible through the small opening, Alby Tusa approached on the sidewalk. From the east.

Meinecke's nervous system ordered his body to seek the west. Before he knew it he was downstairs, then outside closing the back door behind him and barely registering the cold that enveloped his body and, in particular, his bare feet. Not pausing for breath, he made his way through five, ten, twenty back yards, crossing the numbered streets between without deference to the cars. Finally he leaned up on the rear corner of a brick house midway through a block and panted heavily, filling his lungs with freezing air as he allowed himself for the first time to glance back. In the distance, just then, a figure became visible. Meinecke ducked around the house and stared wide-eyed and desperate at Juneau Avenue. It was the only direction he could go without being seen. Having not paid attention to his surroundings, he realized he stood beside not a house but a building. A ladder ran up the front of the building's middle to the familiar bridge, three floors above, marked PABST. His feet were numb and felt nothing as adrenaline drove his heavyset body up the ladder to the bridge. The five giant letters were bisected by the platform. Meinecke crouched behind the top of the B and, with greater focus than he'd ever known, studied the street below. A little while passed but he experienced it in the immediate duration of a nightmare, Alby appearing, it seemed, at once. The gangster looked up and down the street and then began jogging back in the opposite direction. Meinecke's eyes moved over every pedestrian Alby passed, but there were no greetings exchanged.

When his pursuer was no longer discernible, Meinecke wracked his mind for a place nearby to go. The answer came to him quickly, almost as if his brain too were made more agile by his sheer animal panic. He'd written the address several times in the past week and then re-read it in the proofs and in the newspaper itself.

Jud Minor lived only a couple more blocks west on Juneau. And Meinecke had to get out of the cold.

He waited a few more minutes then climbed down the ladder, for the first time fearing he might fall now that the more emphatically lethal fear of Alby had abated. There were fewer and fewer pedestrians as he advanced west, but still a lot of traffic, so he was held up only by the intersections. Finally, after crossing one last numbered street, he reached Minor's house on the corner and hurled himself through the door without knocking.

"It's Meinecke," he tried to shout, his throat constricted by cold. "Minor ... help! ... it's Meinecke. Please. I need help."

A few lights were on but nobody was around. Meinecke glanced in the kitchen and then through the open door of the bedroom, his panic subsiding as he repeated, "Hello? Hello?" With relief he entered the bathroom, grabbed some towels that were folded on a counter, and sat on the side of the tub to run the spigot over his frostbitten feet. Waiting for the water to heat up, he arranged the towels in layers over his shoulders and thighs and shivered himself warm.

"Jud?" he heard a woman say, somewhere below him. He heard footsteps on a creaky staircase and realized Minor's wife was coming up from the basement.

"Mrs. Minor?" he called out. "I'm a friend of your husband's ... don't worry. I'm in the bathroom. I was outside and my shoes got soaking wet, so I'm running water on my feet in the tub."

Minor's wife appeared at the bathroom door. "Did Eddie Cantor send you?" she said, with what appeared to be a sense of wonder.

Then Meinecke remembered. There were rumors that Minor's wife was nuts. "Yes," he said, looking over his shoulder at her. She was very pretty, he noted. "Uh ... that's right, Eddie Cantor. Is your husband at home?"

"I'm doing laundry downstairs," she said. "I need to go back down and finish, but I'll be done in a jiffy."

"And your husband?"

"He wanted to see if he could buy a bottle of champagne." She giggled. "It's against the law, you know."

"When do you expect him back?"

"I thought the champagne was for New Year's," Minor's wife said, "but Jud must have been planning to surprise me with your visit. Now the three of us can celebrate, and you can tell Eddie Cantor all about me."

The water had finally heated up and Meinecke adjusted the faucet knobs to prevent scalding. His feet itched and burned and felt like they'd swollen double. Minor's wife turned and left. "When do you expect your husband?" Meinecke repeated.

"He should be here any minute," he heard her say as she descended. "And I'll be right back up."

After a while his feet had recovered. Meinecke turned off the water, unstopped the drain, and started drying off with the towels. Just as he finished with one foot and began drying the other, he heard the bells tinkle on the front door as it opened and closed. He stood up from the side of the tub and went out to the hall, saying, "Minor? Minor? It's Meinecke." When he reached the parlor he saw Alby, who took a gun with a long barrel out of his overcoat and pointed it at Meinecke's forehead. Then for a microsecond Meinecke was asleep, and dreamt of his mother's face just as if he were gazing at it in childhood, prettier even than that of Jud Minor's wife.

56.

As far as Alby could tell, no one else was in the house. Meinecke had obviously come out to greet someone at the door, though Alby had been too preoccupied to catch the name.

He opened the front door wide enough to stick his left arm out and waive it around. Holding the shoes and coat, Jack got Peaches out of the car and followed her up the sidewalk and diagonally through the small yard, his tiptoed footprints filling hers.

Alby stopped looking outside and instead braced his back against the front wall, extending his arm full-length with the gun pointing about five and a half feet from the floor. "Go on in," he heard Jack say. Peaches opened the door and stepped inside, perhaps glimpsing for a moment the bleeding body in the room. Alby shoved the silencer against her temple and pulled the trigger.

Jack squeezed through the now-obstructed entryway and stepped over Peaches's body. "Anybody else here?" he whispered, taking the purported suicide note from his wallet.

"I don't think so," Alby said. "But I think Meinecke was expecting somebody, so let's make it quick."

Jack stuck the note into one of the dead woman's pockets, then went over to Meinecke's body after tossing the coat on the back of a chair.

"Shit," Alby yelped, attempting to unscrew the silencer. He vigorously waved the fingers of his left hand, fanning them. "Fuckin silencer is on fire." He pulled out a handkerchief.

Jack finished shoving the untied shoes onto Meinecke's bare feet, pulled the body into the room further from the hall, and started for the door now that his job was done.

Alby wrapped the handkerchief around his fingers and was about to try again to unscrew the silencer when a colored woman appeared from the hallway.

"Jud?" she said.

Alby lifted the gun and shot her through the forehead.

"Now it's going to be really hot," Jack said, his hand still resting on the doorknob. He located his own handkerchief and gave it to Alby, who wrapped it over the first and managed to unscrew the burning silencer. Jack took the handkerchiefs and the silencer from him and went out to the car. Alby knelt beside Peaches and placed the Mauser in her right hand.

When Alby was back in the car, Jack made a U-turn on Juneau then immediately turned left at the next street, intending to head for Bronzeville and then go east toward the river. On the way they passed a colored man driving an old Model T in the opposite direction.

Beneath the fleeting illumination of a streetlamp Alby caught a glimpse of the man, who appeared, however slightly, to be smiling.

MILWAUKEE SENTINEL

FRIDAY, JANUARY 1, 1932

HUMPHREYS' KILLER FOUND DEAD IN LOVE TRIANGLE

Negress Kills Self After Reporter Slain In Retribution

Innocent Bystander, Wife Of Detective, Also Dead At Gruesome Scene

Walter Meinecke, reporter for the Milwaukee *Tribune*, was shot to death New Year's Eve by a negress known only as "Peaches", who then turned the gun on herself after a stray bullet fatally wounded Sarah Minor, wife of city detective Judson Minor. The crimes took place at Minor's residence, 1202 W. Juneau av., where Meinecke apparently sought protection from the crazed woman, believed to have been his lover. Detective Minor discovered the bodies after returning home some time later.

A suicide note written by the murderess claimed that Meinecke was the killer of Landis Humphreys, who was stabbed to death Christmas Eve, and that Meinecke had been motivated by jealousy of Humphreys' relations with "Peaches". Several sources in the city's third ward have confirmed that Meinecke was frequently seen in the woman's company, while residents in the sixth ward had seen her equally as often with Humphreys. Unwilling to live without Humphreys, "Peaches" stalked Meinecke before finally killing him with a stolen gun

Weapon That Killed Humphreys Found In Reporter's Apartment.

According to reliable sources, the suicide note stated that Humphreys had been killed with his own knife. A search of Meinecke's home turned up a bloodstained knife, matching the description of a missing knife known to be owned by Humphreys.

In a bizarre twist, Meinecke was covering the story of Humphreys' murder for the Milwaukee *Tribune*. In this capacity, he had become acquainted with Minor, lead investigator on the case. When Meinecke sought refuge at Minor's home, the policeman was elsewhere. "Peaches" apparently stormed into the house shooting, her first bullet striking Minor's wife and the second killing Meinecke.

Authorities Doubt Validity Of Negro Paper's Claims.

The crimes took place only hours after the Wisconsin *Enterprise-Blade*, the state's only Negro newspaper, alleged that Humphreys was an imposter hired by unnamed gangsters to infiltrate the city police force. Every authoritative source denies the veracity of this claim. A letter said to have been written by Humphreys, admitting to the scheme, is uniformly believed to be a forgery. "They were just trying to sell papers with this crazy story," one source at the safety building commented. "The people in the sixth ward will believe anything."

DEPARTMENT OF POLICE

City of Milwaukee

WISCONSIN

January 7, 1932.

Dear Officer Minor:

I am writing you today as a courtesy. In light of the tragedy you have recently suffered, I thought you should be given the opportunity to prepare yourself for events that are now imminent.

At the end of your last shift during the week of January 11th to 17th, your desk sergeant will hand you an envelope containing a terse, two-sentence form letter signed by Chief Laubenheimer. The letter will inform you that your service with the Milwaukee Police Department is to be terminated as of February 1, 1932.

Ordinarily, I would not provide such warning, but, again, due to the tragic loss of your wife I felt it was the ethical choice. I ask that you regard this as personal correspondence to be kept between ourselves.

Your termination results from the fact that the mileage recorded by the patrol car you commissioned from December 28th through December 31st, inclusive, indicates that you drove only the round-trip between Milwaukee and Chicago. We have therefore concluded that the daily reports you teletyped, indicating several long car trips around Northern Illinois and back to your hotel each day, were mere inventions. Apparently, you did no more than take a vacation at a fine hotel for the better part of a week, all at taxpayer expense. Needless to say, this prevarication cannot be tolerated. Perhaps if you had simply sloughed off work, we could have suspended you without pay as a sanction, and then welcomed you back. But instead you fabricated official reports. No excuse for such behavior is conceivable. It is a terminating offense.

In light of this, we must doubt whether, indeed, you ever conducted your investigation of Landis Humphreys' murder in good faith. Even though you knew Walter Meinecke well enough for him to seek shelter in your home the night of his death, not once did you suggest that he might be a suspect. True, the name "Peaches" appears in the list of various women provided to you by denizens of the Sixth Ward, but you made no effort to investigate this woman. Instead, you wasted your time concocting fantastic theories that somehow the alleged "gangs" of the city's Third Ward were connected to Humphreys' murder, a notion shown to be ridiculous by the simple, sordid truth -- a story heard throughout history -- of a love triangle gone wrong.

This situation is especially unfortunate given that you are the only representative of your race, out of some 8,000 in the city, to serve our force. I hope it comes as some consolation that we are in the final stages of evaluating a fine young Negro man, Sidney Loveless, for employment as a patrolman in the coming year.

Again, my deepest sympathies upon the death of your wife. I wish you all possible success in your future endeavors.

Sincerely,

Adolph Kraemer
Det. Lieut.

Mr. Judson W. Minor, Jr.
1202 West Juneau Avenue
Milwaukee, Wisconsin

MILWAUKEE SENTINEL

Dedicated to Truth, Justice and Public Service

MONDAY, DECEMBER 31, 1951

Remember When ...

———

Today's "Remember When..." is guest-written by a veteran reporter on our crime beat, John Carson, who looks back with a personal connection to two of the most shocking crimes in the city's history. —*Ed.*

* * *

Twenty years ago, I was a Marquette University senior majoring in journalism and working as an intern for the Milwaukee *Tribune.* I was assigned to work with a man soon to become notorious, indeed infamous: reporter Walter Meinecke.

For our younger readers, allow me to recap.

Twenty years ago today, Walter Meinecke and two others were found shot to death in a private residence on Juneau Avenue. A week earlier, Meinecke had stabbed to death city policeman Landis Humphreys (though he was never suspected in the crime) during a confrontation over a Negro woman the two men shared, known only as "Peaches". This mysterious femme fatale, whose true identity remains unknown, divided her time between Meinecke in the city's third ward and Humphreys in the sixth. Meinecke confessed his crime to "Peaches", even showing her the murder weapon, Humphreys' hunting knife. Unfortunately, the unstable if highly attractive young woman preferred the much younger Humphreys.

Distraught over the death of her true love, "Peaches" arranged to meet Meinecke on New Year's Eve. She was carrying a gun, and apparently pursued her quarry through the crowds of pedestrians celebrating the holiday. Meinecke attempted to take refuge in the nearby home of Judson Minor, a policeman whom he had interviewed when "reporting" on the murder which he himself had committed. Tragically, Minor's wife was killed by a stray bullet when "Peaches" arrived, then Meinecke himself was shot before his lover took her own life.

The *Sentinel* has asked me for my thoughts on this matter, after two decades spent contemplating it.

First, I am struck by how run-of-the-mill the story is. Reduced to essentials, it is a simple love triangle turned violent—with the dramatic twist of Meinecke "covering" his own crime for the Milwaukee *Tribune.*

Second, it serves as a reminder of what can happen when a long-time veteran becomes complacent in his job. As a youth working with the man, I was shocked by Meinecke's habits. He fabricated quotes, wrote descriptions of scenes he had never visited, and spent much of every day in a state of inebriation—even though this was during Prohibition! Of course, in the two decades since, the standards of our profession have greatly improved, and it is unlikely that a reporter with Meinecke's habits could now enjoy so long a career.

Third, the story is a classic example of why philosophers advocate applying the principle of "Ockham's Razor". This principle mandates that one search for the simplest solution before concocting Rube Goldberg-like scenarios to explain a mystery. Judson Minor, the officer assigned to the case, theorized that a Dance Marathon scam run by two young men allowed one of them to ingeniously murder Humphreys while maintaining a perfect alibi. Indeed, I was present when Minor arrested them! Other far-fetched theories have been propagated by those seeking always to uncover "conspiracies". One area newspaper, little more than an advertising sheet and now defunct, went so far as to forge a letter claiming that Humphreys was an agent of what is now known as "organized crime", working for the Police Department under an assumed name. It is particularly remarkable that such a half-baked theory should be advanced here in Milwaukee. After two decades on the crime beat, I can state with assurance that there has never been an organized crime faction in our city. Even during the height of the Capone era, the worst we experienced were the occasional "beer wars" by small-time players. Never once has any area newspaper suggested that a resident of this city is in fact the "boss" of a local organized crime gang.

Contrary to such fanciful speculation, this story comes down to the closest possible "shave" by Ockham's Razor: that ancient motto, *cherchez la femme.*

Finally, one detail that has always intrigued me is the question of why Officer Minor was assigned to the case. True, he was the officer who actually discovered Humphreys' body (while walking his beat in the sixth ward), but he was no detective. In fact, within a month Minor was fired by Chief Laubenheimer for fabricating police reports while living it up in a Chicago hotel. Meinecke told me that he was certain Minor would never uncover so much as a decent lead, much less solve the crime. But according to at least one source (whose identity I am not at liberty to reveal), Meinecke claimed that he had been responsible for Minor's temporary promotion to acting detective, having advocated for it with his contacts on the police force. If so, his cunning is all the more remarkable, for he had arranged to have the least qualified man assigned to investigate his own heinous crime—a crime that might never have been solved but for the suicide note of a mysterious woman known only as "Peaches".

Jud kept that unopened bottle of champagne for the rest of his life, almost forty years, and was buried with it. He wasn't a religious man, but it comforted him to imagine that he and Sally would finally share their New Year's toast in the hereafter.

Aunt Lydia accepted that Jud would never get over Sally's death—or his guilt for setting in motion the chain of events leading to it, by publishing the story about Suthrin in the Blade. More indirectly, the chain began the night he killed Suthrin. I think he viewed the loss of Sally as fate's way of punishing him for never facing justice. Even if in self-defense, he had taken a man's life and ought, he believed, to answer for it.

During the months after he lost his job, he devoted himself to Aunt Lydia's campaign to adopt me. He assisted the Milwaukee lawyer she hired, and eventually gave testimony as to my mistreatment by Mother. The case was difficult because Uncle Henry, who could not be located (we later learned he was traveling in Asia), had set up the trust for my care, presumably favoring Mother over Aunt Lydia, and I had spent my whole life at the Hubbard Street residence surrounded by a family. My lack of schooling and the labor enforced upon me should have been dispositive, but the judge seemed more concerned about Uncle Henry's "intentions" and my "stability" than the obvious fact that I would be better off elsewhere. And surely more important to the judge, Aunt Lydia was unmarried and accused of being a "bohemian," as they used to say. She was also, demonstrably, black.

But then I startled everyone by speaking up in court. I was not on the stand, of course, and the other lawyer said I should be "disregarded," but the judge took me into his office and asked me questions, which I answered truthfully. When he asked why I had remained silent for so many years, I explained that when I was alone with my parents as a very little girl they had warned me never to speak in the presence of white people, that if I needed something I should rely only on family. After they passed away I was terrified, and observed their advice as though it were something God commanded in the Bible. Not even Jud knew I could speak.

That was why Suthrin thought he could get away with what he planned to do to me: I had no way to tell anyone about it.

I didn't know of his intentions when he said Santa Claus would bring me a present Christmas Eve, a tradition the Odenwalds did not observe. Mother had given him a key to the speakeasy, and he told me he would let Santa Claus in if I would come down after everyone else was asleep—but it would have to be our secret. I nodded my head and grinned. It was the most wonderful thing I'd ever heard.

Like every nine-year-old child I knew how to tell time, so I crept silently downstairs and through the hall to the speakeasy at 11:30 that night, carrying the key in my slipper. The door locked behind me after I switched on the lights from the hall; Suthrin was already there, in uniform but without a gun. His big overcoat was on the bar covering something. He said I was late; that Santa Claus had gone on to another house but had left me a present which I could see if I took off my nightie. Then, with me standing there in my underpants and slippers, he pushed his coat aside and showed me the present beneath it, the prettiest, fanciest doll you can imagine. He told me to sit up on the bar and look at the dolly, so I did. Then he sat on a stool in front of me and tried to take off my underpants. I wouldn't let him; so he took the doll and opened the door to the alley, threatening to throw her outside. I took my underpants off and he closed the door, but he was too focused on me to realize it hadn't closed all the way. He sat down again and put his face between my legs after tossing the doll on the floor, and I felt a jolt of fear and horror. That was when Jud walked in.

Jud saw what Suthrin was doing to me—saw the doll and got the whole picture—in the split second before Suthrin, probably thinking the wind had blown the door open, turned around to look. Then Suthrin knew he was caught. Perhaps he also thought that a black cop would not observe the code of silence, the so-called blue wall. In any case, he didn't even try to talk his way out of it. He just pulled the big knife out of his calf-length boot and lunged, meaning to kill Jud right then and there—and leaving for later the question of what to do next. But Suthrin slipped on the doll and Jud got the better of him in the sound-proofed room. Before I knew it, Jud was holding the knife and Suthrin's throat had been slashed.

Jud pulled Suthrin's bleeding body out the door and (he later told me) slashed his thigh deeply to make sure there would be plenty of blood in the snow before his heart stopped pumping. He didn't yet know that the key to the speakeasy was in Suthrin's coat pocket (not his fist, as he later claimed) and presumed I'd let him in, which would have made the story inside the bar much more problematic. He also wanted to limit the forensic investigation inside, to minimize evidence of his own presence there. He left Suthrin in the alley to bleed out and die while he cleaned up most, but not all, of the blood on the floor, using the inside of his own bloodstained coat. Then he dragged Suthrin back inside and clothed the corpse with his bloody overcoat, careful to tear out the name tag, after slashing shallowly at the hands and chest and belly to conform to the story he planned to tell. He posed Suthrin's body on the floor along with his cap a few feet away, then took Suthrin's clean coat off the bar and, again removing the tag, put it on over his own uniform. He conceived of this with such swift intensity of thought, it was as though he had forgotten I was there. Finally he told me to go back in the house, turn off the speakeasy's lights from the hallway, and pretend nothing had ever happened—or else he would be put in jail and probably put to death for protecting me. I didn't want that to happen, so I put on my nightie and underpants and did what he said. The last detail I remember is the doll on the floor, untouched by even a drop of Suthrin's blood. (Mother's youngest boy hid it in a bedroom closet; eventually Mother sold it.)

You know the rest. Jud circled back and pretended he was approaching the speakeasy door for the first time (after hiding the knife, of course), then deliberately fell over Suthrin's body to receive some bloodstains. He let his flashlight smash when he fell so that his supposedly initial examination of the body, illuminated only by a cigarette lighter, would be clumsy. Somehow he interfered with the phone lines—I forgot to ask about that detail—then, after breaking in the front door, he sent the boys out back, knowing they would disobey his orders and thoroughly disturb the crime scene inside and out.

His main concern was that Detective Rhodes would run out of suspects and realize that the first man on the scene deserved a closer look. Then when he replaced Rhodes, Jud knew that the crime could not be "solved"—a failure which would set back his hopes for promotion—so he looked around for something else to discover. Years later he told me he'd tried to imagine he knew nothing, to pursue the case as if he'd really come across a shocking crime scene; and his experience that night convinced him that Suthrin was a scab needing only to be scratched for the most vile pus to pour out. Meanwhile, of course, the more time that passed, the less anyone would imagine that Jud had been the culprit ... so he was protecting himself, too.

I never told anyone what I knew. When Aunt Lydia gave me my own trust, a dozen years later, I started hiring investigators to look into the people mentioned in the news stories and to take it from there. For two decades I gave these hard-bitten gumshoes carte blanche to offer bribes and promises, though I kept Jud out of it. To my surprise, and unknown to him, Jud's police reports led my men to the third ward gangsters and other lowlifes, and in particular the bookie, Lou Simon, who fulfilled Alby Tusa's dream by moving into the apartment house next door to his on Prospect Avenue, the street where the gangsters tended to congregate after Joey Vallone died in 1952. Alby told Lou Simon his most intimate secrets; and via my "investigators" I bailed Simon out of several potentially lethal financial problems in the fifties in exchange for everything he'd heard. For those people who didn't have to be bribed, I did the interviews myself, such as Mayor Hoan (who in 1961 told me about the wiretaps on Suthrin) and Betty Lubhan (née Falkner) and John Carson, that stupid man. Finally, when Jud was dying of cancer in the late sixties, I bought a reel-to-reel tape recorder and insisted he let me interview him about everything he remembered. Having kept his secret, something forever unknown even to Aunt Lydia, I said I was owed that much; and he agreed.

Needless to say, Jud knew that the whole "Peaches" story was a scam—that it wasn't Meinecke's "crazed lover" but rather some third ward soldier who had murdered Sally. But Sally was gone and nothing would bring her back. Jud let the story stand, knowing that it permanently insulated him from suspicion of his own crime.

But like I said, it weighed on him. It took three or four years after Aunt Lydia hired Jud (and moved him into the Brookmont Hotel) before he began to respond to her affection. They were never married— Aunt Lydia was too independent and vivacious for that—but he was the love of her life, and they stayed together till the end, bringing me up and then helping me through the psychological problems I suffered as a young (and not so young) adult. I also got to meet all the wonderful intellectuals and writers and artists who flocked around Aunt Lydia, such as Frank Davis, who later retired to Hawaii, where I visited him often and met his friends and their families. I hate to brag, but at eighty-six I am still in touch with some of those folks.

— C.B.

January 20, 2009

9 7 9 8 2 1 8 9 6 7 9 8 7